An Act of Love

Carol Drinkwater is a multi-award-winning actress, who is best known for her portrayal of Helen Herriot in the BBC Television series *All Creatures Great and Small*. She is also the author of over twenty books, both fiction and non-fiction. Her quartet of memoirs set on her olive farm in the South of France has sold more than a million copies worldwide, and her solo journey round the Mediterranean in search of the olive tree's mythical secrets inspired two books – *The Olive Route* and *The Olive Tree* – and a five-part documentary film series, *The Olive Route*. She is also the author of several novels including *The Forgotten Summer*, *The Lost Girl* and *The House on the Edge of the Cliff*.

Carol lives in the South of France where she is writing her next novel.

By the same author

An Act of Love

CAROL DRINKWATER

PENGUIN BOOKS

PENGUIN BOOKS

UK | USA | Canada | Ireland | Australia
India | New Zealand | South Africa

Penguin Books is part of the Penguin Random House group of companies
whose addresses can be found at global.penguinrandomhouse.com

First published 2021

001

Set in 12.5/14.75 pt Garamond MT Std
Typeset by Jouve (UK), Milton Keynes
Printed and bound in Italy by Grafica Veneta S.p.A.

The authorized representative in the EEA is Penguin Random House Ireland,
Morrison Chambers, 32 Nassau Street, Dublin D02 YH68

A CIP catalogue record for this book is available from the British Library

ISBN: 978–1–405–93336–0

www.greenpenguin.co.uk

MIX
Paper from
responsible sources
FSC   FSC® C018179
www.fsc.org

Penguin Random House is committed to a
sustainable future for our business, our readers
and our planet. This book is made from Forest
Stewardship Council® certified paper.

I encounter so many young girls in my travels whose stories are not so very different from my 'Sara's'.
I dedicate this book to them, for the courage it takes to face the world when the world does not accept you.

The great events of world history are at bottom profoundly unimportant. In the last analysis the essential thing is the life of the individual. That alone makes history, here alone do the great transformations take place, and the whole future, the whole history of the world ultimately spring as a gigantic summation from these hidden sources in individuals. In our most private and most subjective lives we are not only the passive witnesses of our age, but also its makers.

Carl G. Jung, *Collected Works*

A story has no beginning or end: arbitrarily one chooses that moment of experience from which to look back or from which to look ahead.

Graham Greene, *The End of the Affair*

Author's Note

In 1996 when I was travelling through many of the villages and places of interest in the Lower Alps, I came across one village in particular whose story seeded itself within me. This village, or small town, has become recognized as a beauty spot – the 'Switzerland of the Alpes-Maritimes' – with its elegant medieval houses, stunning scenery for walking and, in winter, modest ski resort. While wandering about its cobbled streets, I noticed it had a museum, about the size of a laundry shed. I poked my head inside and there I discovered an extraordinary true story that took place in 1943.

I touched upon that wartime summer in my young adult novel, *Nowhere to Run*. And I thought that was that. But this buried corner and its inhabitants, Italian and French, would not let me be and I felt the need to come back to their history.

An Act of Love is entirely a work of fiction. Its characters were born from my imagination. However, the incidents of 1943 that took place in that out-of-the-way corner of France have most certainly inspired me.

Carol Drinkwater, Le Cannet, 2020

PART ONE

I

Alpes-Maritimes, France
The Present

The temperature is falling. Evening settling beyond the window. Darkness soon, a darkness that will enshroud me. I start to shiver. Not cold, but fear. Fear for what is to come. And yet ready. So ready.

A tall figure rises from a chair, which creaks. He tucks the bedcovers tighter about me, encasing my useless legs. 'Calm, Maman.'

My breath rasps, sawing at my lungs, burning my bronchials. Let this be over soon. Please, let this be over.

'How is she?' I catch the words from across the room.

'A little restless. She mutters to herself constantly. I cannot make out any sense. A few words, nothing lucid, except Papa's name. She repeats it constantly. Calling, calling without voice to Papa.'

'Does she need anything?'

'What could she need now, at this stage?'

'A little water, perhaps. Dab her lips, Albert. Here, let me.'

Another figure moves to my side, leaning over me, leaning low, wetting my mouth with the feathery touch of a finger. I taste the salt of her flesh.

'Sara, Sara, can you hear me? It's Hanna. Is there anything you require, my dear, dear friend? Anyone you need to see?' She waits. I cannot respond. I have no strength. 'Is anything holding you back from your journey?'

I smile. Always thoughtful, always ready to lend me a hand ever since the beginning. I lift my fingers a few centimetres to caress her. The effort overwhelms me. My arm flops back to the mattress.

Forgiveness. For the many mistakes I've made. Clemency for the man I killed. Yes, I killed a man in cold blood. What would my sons think of their old dying mother if they knew that truth? In spite of the circumstances, I have never spoken of that occasion.

Never divulged it, that unerasable moment from my story of so long ago.

Alpes-Maritimes, France
The first week of March 1943

The hairpin bends were dizzying on roads as narrow as zips.

'We call this a balcony route,' yelled the driver, above the engine's growl. 'Take a look to your right – see for yourselves that scenic drop.'

Nobody cared to turn their heads, either clutching their purses or hands clasped in prayer. My parents, seated in the row in front of me, cleaved tight to one another.

The bus was rocking and rolling. A thousand metres we had climbed and the rattle-trap was showing its age, coughing and spluttering. The quality of petrol, when it was available during these days of wartime rationing, was dismal.

Down along the coast, spring was on its way – almond trees in pale pink blossom – but up here the temperature was steadily dropping. I was hunched into myself, muffled in my bedraggled navy coat, picking with my nail-bitten fingers at the loose strands on the cuffs. It was a recent habit triggered by anxiety. Here we were, embarking on yet another flight, facing yet another precarious future while our suitcases slid back and forth in the overhead racks.

Beyond the windows, I caught glimpses of snow on the higher caps of the mountain ranges. The bus swung a curve too sharply to the right, brakes screeching. The passengers, as one, let out a cry. Was this old coach about to spin us over the mountainside? Our driver pressed on, cowed by nothing.

Higher up, I spotted a village clinging to a rocky peak as though suspended by a safety-pin. One gust of wind and it would be blown off its perch, lost for ever, its population vanished into the universe. I was rather taken with that idea. It might be the safest place for us. Missing in outer space.

The driver lifted his right hand from the wheel. I squeezed one eye shut, dreading the result of such a reckless act. He pointed to the hanging community and called its name. It was not our destination. Still further to ascend, then.

The landscape was altering. Craggier, less undulating. Gone were the olive and lemon trees. The brightly baubled fruit groves had been replaced by larch and conifers. Trees with straight trunks and pointed tips, like sharpened pencils. Gone were the umbrella pines with their spreading canopies: the shade of Mediterranean summers.

Oh, how I would miss the Mediterranean, the glimmering sea with its warm, gentle breezes, the Riviera with its elegant hotels, its outmoded opulence . . . Not that we had ever indulged in such luxuries. We were refugees. Stateless.

I liked to dream, though . . .

I bit my lip. Through the scratched glass window, I gazed out on monolithic limestone rocks. How different this austere scenery was from our lives of the past eighteen months, holed up in a dark rented basement in the old town of Nice, venturing out for bracing walks along the seafront, with its famous Jetée, sipping freshly made lemonade at one of the street cafés along the Promenade des Anglais, ogling the waterfront world as it went by. Foolishly, I had allowed myself to believe that we were free spirits, that we belonged in that cosmopolitan city. I had felt connected.

That was before the Germans crossed the Demarcation Line.

Before documents had to be stamped with the word 'Jew'.

I glanced about the bus. Deadpan faces, grim expressions. My fellow passengers, exiles one and all, lost in their inner worlds, gearing up their weary souls for whatever was to befall us next.

Where, for heaven's sake, are we headed? How much further?

My silent questions were soon answered when, beyond a ridge and a winding descent, I spotted cultivated greenery, and before we knew it, we were whizzing towards a settlement. A lone stone house perched lopsidedly on a slope facing southwards. Byres, barns, mules and donkeys grazing in outlying fields patched with snow. Then one narrow street after another, twisting, turning, leading us – where? Into a pretty village square with a church, a bell tower. Here the bus shimmied to stillness.

'*On arrive!*'

This was it. Journey's end.

A shuffling of feet. A cough. Hats plonked onto heads, scarves knotted beneath chins. Fingers chilled from the cold.

No one made a move, all hanging back uncertainly.

Butterflies in my stomach.

'On you go, Sara.' My father, encouraging me.

Our driver in his beret, hand-knitted scarf drawn tight

7

against his throat, descended the coach, feet in wooden clogs slapping noisily against the metal steps. Positioned by the open door, he offered his hand as each of us disembarked hesitantly, clutching our possessions. I was first out and gladly accepted his outstretched arm. The strap of my bag, crammed with books, was cutting into my shoulder and my head was reeling from the ride. Oh, but the air was fresh, several degrees cooler than at the coast, and scented with resin.

I glanced about me and felt the pent-up tension in my muscles begin to release. We had been delivered into the main square of a medieval stone village. Backwards in time we had travelled. Tucked out of sight from the real world . . .

Nice, the Côte d'Azur, with its graceful estates and farmlands, had been one of the last bastions in Europe where fugitives could hide. Until last November, when overnight our situation had changed. The Allies had won North Africa and Hitler had marched his army into the Free Zone. But here? This was the world's end. No one would find us up here.

Stepping down from the bus in my rope-soled espadrilles, I was instantly hit by the sound of running water. It seemed to be everywhere, all about us. There was a sweet fragrance in the air, too, and the music, the rush of water, as if the mountains themselves had been unplugged and were emptying.

Above us, a wide open sky.

Several of my fellow passengers were troubled, confused by the cascades so close by.

'Has there been a flood?'

'Spring is on its way, *mesdames, messieurs*. Look up behind you to the peaks – the snows are beginning to melt. Feel the brush of the sun on your faces, see the sprays caught in the sunlight, inhale our fresh alpen air. Welcome to La Ville-Vésubie. I am Lieutenant Philippe Decroix and I am here to assist you in every way I can.' This from a man in glasses, enveloped in a buttoned-up overcoat and heavy boots, hugging a thick wad of paperwork.

I glanced about me, stamping my feet to keep warm.

Hunched tightly together on a quartet of stone benches, leaning against wooden canes, a congregation of old women dressed in black. They trained their rheumy eyes upon us. Were they waiting in their huddled groups to greet us or to protest at our arrival?

Lieutenant Decroix took another step forward. He called across to the driver, 'How many?'

Perched against his vehicle's bonnet, smoking a cigarette, the fellow answered, 'Thirty-four,' and picked a shred of tobacco off his tongue.

The lieutenant pouted, frowned, scribbled the figure into his notes.

'*Bonjour, mesdames et messieurs*. Do any of you speak French?'

My father prodded my shoulder with his fist, nudging me towards the administrator, who, it turned out, was a high-ranking member of the gendarmerie. I shuffled into his eyeline. He shook my hand. His fingers poked out from threadbare gloves.

'*Bonjour, Mademoiselle*. You speak French?'

I nodded politely, keen to give the best impression. The truth was I was bashful about expressing myself in front of strangers, especially such a high-ranking figure.

'Don't be shy, Sara. She's very adept at languages. Speak to the gentleman, please.' Papa patted my arm encouragingly.

'Lieutenant,' I cleared my throat, 'Monsieur, I've been handling most of the daily negotiations for my parents – with shopkeepers, our previous landlady translating for us during the eighteen months we've been resident in Nice.'

'You hear, sir, how eloquently she speaks.'

The official nodded.

I refrained from mentioning it now, but sometimes Father had asked me to eavesdrop on the discussions taking place around us. Only to reassure ourselves, as far as possible, that we were associating with allies, not enemies. Nice was a city with many eyes and not all looked favourably upon us. It was vital to be able to single out those who would risk themselves to assist us rather than those who would inform on us. It had certainly tested my skills in French and Italian.

On that first afternoon in Ville-Vésubie, my parents and I were three of thirty-four. It didn't seem so many to relocate, but we were learning now that others like ourselves had been settling into this village for months. The creaky old bus we had just stepped off had been making the arduous journey, coast to mountain village, once a day since the previous November when the Germans had crossed into the Free Zone.

'We offered to open our little town to immigrants, and we have been inundated. There are more than five hundred foreigners living among us now.' The gentleman in the glasses was apologizing to my father. 'The fact of the matter is that our resources are overstretched.' The man fell silent, embarrassed, juggling his pencils and glasses. 'I have already notified the agency that organized your transfer. Our modest town – little more than a grown-up village nestling in the Alps – is bursting at the seams.'

I saw the sunken expression on Father's face, the disappointment. 'Sir, are we to be left with nowhere to live?'

Monsieur Decroix shook his head. 'Rest assured, we will do the very best we can. For everyone.' In his early forties, not far off Papa's age, he patted Papa's shoulder and moved along the line, shaking the hand of each and every stranger. I liked him. His approach was caring.

'Welcome, *bienvenus, willkommen.*'

He returned to us: we were first in the queue. I stood tight to Papa's chest, ready to translate if he got his words muddled. He struggled when he was distressed.

'Now . . .' The man was poring over his papers, from one page to the next as though hunting for inspiration, while listening to my father.

'Monsieur, we will gratefully accept any accommodation. Please don't worry if it hasn't been cleaned. My wife can . . . We'll make the best of whatever you offer.'

Monsieur Decroix nodded, scratched his head. 'Most of the houses have already been rented. The hotels . . . Well, there's nothing to be had in any of them. The Italians, who have been here since November, have nabbed the best for themselves.'

While my father and the local representative were in discussion I glanced about. The village had been planted with some handsome trees. I spied two cafés, a bar, a few shops and the smart-looking Hôtel des Alpes, its walls clad with ivy. There were two shiny black Citroëns parked carelessly outside. I later learned they had been requisitioned by the Italian 4th Army.

Alongside the bar was a bakery. A small group was queuing to buy bread. My tummy growled.

'We have the required letter of invitation signed by General Lospino.' Papa was delving into his coat pocket, fumbling for the official note from the agency. I noticed a tremor in his hands.

The officer glanced at him, then along the straggly line of other homeless.

'Monsieur Decroix, sir, perhaps you haven't heard the news from Marseille.' My father again. 'Thousands arrested, some murdered, others packed into trains, deported . . .'

Monsieur Decroix shook his head. 'No one in this community looks kindly on such behaviour.'

'Please, don't send us back to the coast.' It was my mother, tears rising, begging in Polish.

My father squeezed her hand.

'Before the war, our tourism was taking off. Alas, no

longer. Fortunately, it means there are beds . . .' Monsieur Decroix raised his head and called to those waiting. His breath rose like smoke. 'Everybody will be allocated a place to sleep. Bear with me, please. Young lady, repeat to your travelling companions.'

Which I did. There was an audible sigh of relief, a shuffling of feet.

Papa wrapped his arm around Mamma's waist and drew her tightly to him. He had never been a man to display his innermost feelings in public, so to observe the heart-warming way in which he cared for her during these troubling days made me love him all the more.

'Monsieur, do you have money or valuables to pay your way?'

'We are not rich, Monsieur. Sara, please.'

'The people who led us out of Poland and into Germany demanded payment,' I tried not to recall the ghastly memories, the fear and the flight. 'Other expenses too. *Les passeurs* . . . the boat, our clandestine passage from Italy into France. It all cost dearly. Still, my father is confident we have sufficient funds for several months.'

'If I could secure some form of employment, a position in your hospital. In Nice, I managed to . . .'

Monsieur Decroix was running his index finger down his sheets of paper. I could see handwritten lists. More sheets of paper, more lists. 'You have visas, identity cards?'

Papa shook his head.

My breath caught in my throat. There was no certainty these people would welcome us without papers. There was no certainty about anything any more.

A small group of boys in ragged trousers cut to the calves, muddied feet slipped into wooden clogs, was congregating near the bakery, giggling, making a racket, like a flock of starlings at sunset. One waved at me. Embarrassed, I shifted my gaze elsewhere.

I spotted a band of Italian soldiers. They ambled from the hotel, passing between the badly parked cars, and made their way to one of the cafés. One lifted his arm and signalled to the waiter, who came running. He was a dark-haired lad of about my age.

'The Italians require paperwork. In return, they'll provide you with ration cards,' Monsieur Decroix was explaining. 'You will be obliged to check in with them on a daily basis. No need to fear them. They pay no regard to the rules and regulations brought into force by the Nazis. If you or your family want to ride bicycles or use one of the few telephones that exist in our modest burg – there's one over at Pascal's bar – there will be no problem with that. We don't segregate. And, by the way, we keep French time here. The Germans may have shifted the rest of France to their Berlin clock, one hour ahead of us, but we pay it no attention. We are rural people, farmers. We live by the light and the seasons.'

'When we first entered France, we were registered as asylum seekers and furnished with temporary visas, valid for six months. I have those. See here.' Papa was pulling open Mamma's handbag, rummaging for the identification. 'I attempted to renew them at the Nice prefecture. Unfortunately, my request was refused due to the "unpredictable circumstances of the war" so, we are, formally speaking, stateless.'

The lieutenant, without glancing from his paperwork, ticked a couple of boxes. He must have heard our story a dozen times a day. There were thousands of us without legal status all over France. We had always planned to return to Poland, but that was looking unlikely. If we couldn't return home, Papa had promised to buy us passage to Palestine, or even America, which was both thrilling and terrifying. It was so far away. We had no relatives or friends there. A few of our neighbours might have made it through. We had lost touch with everyone back home.

'Please remember to keep even outdated papers with you at all times. If you are stopped and are without them,' Monsieur Decroix pushed his glasses back up the bridge of his nose, 'it makes matters complicated. So, this young lady is your daughter?' He smiled at me. 'Such eyes. What's your name?'

'Sara Rosenbaum, sir.'

'And I am Samuel Rosenbaum. This is my wife, Marta.'

'Your profession?'

'General surgeon.'

'Excellent. I am constantly on the lookout for those with medical expertise. So many arrive here in a damaged state, both mentally and physically. Traumatized children, undernourished. People whose lives have been destabilized, emotionally broken. And then there are those among my own people . . . Yes, I can certainly make use of your skills.'

'I speak fluent German as well as Polish, if that helps, plus my inefficient French picked up throughout this . . . odyssey.' A modest smile broke across my father's face.

'Your wife?'

'Polish only. This is very difficult for her. However, as you see, Sara's French is first class and she learns fast. We will not be a burden on your community . . .'

Behind us I heard the engine of the bus turn over. I glanced back. The vehicle was reversing, readying for its return to Nice. Not a single passenger on board. It would be almost nightfall by the time it reached the coast, which would be tinged pink by the sunset. My heart called out for the sea. The good news was that the driver was leaving with an empty bus. This calmed me. Nobody would be turned away. Not today.

'Unfortunately we have no hospital. Several temporary surgeries have been set up. All need manning . . .' Monsieur Decroix's index finger was running the length of his crumpled sheets of paper. 'Ah, now, here's a property, a private residence. It's out of town, but should do the trick.' He scribbled hurried directions on a torn strip of paper and handed it to my father.

'Two bedrooms. Never previously let. The proprietors, Monsieur and Madame Allingham, are an English couple, employed in the film industry. They used to reside in Cannes and occupied this villa during the hottest of the summer months. Otherwise, it was left empty. Madame Allingham is never here now . . .' he paused '. . . due to the war. Her husband enlisted with the RAF.'

'Will we need transport?'

'No, a kilometre to walk, less. It's an elegant house with a lovely garden. The lower half is locked and shuttered. Madame Allingham moved their personal belongings to the ground floor. You should find it more than suitable. The charges are here at the bottom of your rental agreement. It's reasonably priced, but if you cannot meet the payments, there are several aid organizations I can put you in touch with. Welcome, Monsieur Rosenbaum, to Ville-Vésubie. We hope that you and your family will feel at home during your stay with us. There are no informers among us. The Wehrmacht and their war are a long way from here. We live peaceable lives. Long may it continue.'

4

Armed with our precious key and a map with the official's handwritten instructions, we made our way out of the main square. Our new residence was situated at the far end of a straight, flat lane, which dissected a wide-open prairie, east of the town centre. Yonder, an elevated amphitheatre of snow-capped mountains.

Judging by the villa's architecture, it was a recent addition to the town's habitations, possibly 1920s. Once upon a time, it must have been a thing of elegance and beauty. Powder white as the snow falling all about it during the long, locked-down months of the alpine winter. Nestled away, buried from sight, camouflaged by weather.

The ideal place for us to take shelter.

As we drew closer, it became evident that the exterior of the house had suffered neglect. The teal paintwork on the shutters was flaking. The snow-white walls were patched with clouds of brown, where the top layer of plaster had fallen away, eaten by damp from the banked-up snows in winter. The 'lovely' garden beyond the iron gate was a wilderness. Vernal-equinox flowers, weeds and muscular shrubs fought for the sunlight. Tangles of fragrant herbs, rods of twisted and spindly roses, strangled by growth.

The house stood alone at the far end of the lane, substantial, prepossessing. Beyond the rear of the building there was another plot of garden, equally gone to seed. At some point – I couldn't distinguish where – it mutated into never-ending nature, mountains, forests, valleys, rocks, fields, gushing water, all beneath a vast swathe of perpetual sky.

This was a property in splendid isolation. Its companions were trees, larch, indomitable hardwoods, gnarled and sweet-smelling bushes buzzing with life. Trees to offer shade in the blistering summer months and feed us exotic fruits, mulberries and chestnuts mostly. Trees with flowers and perfumes, with stories to tell of all they had borne witness to. This forsaken residence was located in what, in an earlier incarnation, must have been a paradisiacal setting. Once upon a time.

Before.

Before the war had broken out.

Who would abandon such a heavenly spot? Why would anyone choose to leave all of this to flee a war that was still hundreds of kilometres distant?

As each step drew us closer, an energy began to gather force within me. *Une vraie tristesse.* The place was deathly silent. Why had it never previously been rented? Had this house been party to tragedy? The sense of desolation it exuded was overwhelming.

Or was it a warning? A foreshadowing of tragedy yet to come? Ours? Was this a bad omen? I stopped in my tracks, feeling nauseous.

My parents were walking loosely alongside one another, several metres behind me. I used the excuse of hanging back, waiting for them, to give me time to catch my breath, regain a level head, get a grip.

The prescience dissipated as quickly as it had arisen. I linked my left arm through my mother's right, clinging to her. 'Our own house,' I managed, still shaken. 'Aren't we lucky, Mamma?'

I would not mind beginning all over again in a house that seemed a bit spooky, just as long as we were together, and safe.

No matter what we found, this hideaway was a new chapter and we'd make the very best of it.

We reached our upstairs apartment by an exterior concrete-and-iron staircase secured with rusted filigreed railings.

'Watch out for any cracks or loose footings,' called Papa, as I accelerated towards the steps, made slippery by a few errant weeds but perfectly safe. I waited outside our front door on the upper landing with growing impatience as he turned the key. He was making a great ceremony of the moment, winking and playing the fool, to sweeten our arrival, our admission into yet another temporary dwelling far from home. He pushed hard on the heavy door. It creaked and shuddered, then stuck obstinately.

'Come on, Sarina, shoulder against the wood and *puuuush* with all your might – that's my girl. Once again. And once more, or we'll never release the blasted thing. It's swollen with the damp and lack of activity.'

A door guarding its secrets.

But with one conclusive shove it surrendered, letting out a long, slow creak as it opened.

'Well done!' we cried out, all at the same time, stepping cautiously, one after another, into a musty passageway, with a red-tiled corridor and three generous-sized picture windows facing northwards towards the mountains. I leaned my elbows on one of the sills, pressing my face to the glass, peering outwards. Such a stupendous view. So remote. It was as though no other house existed, no village lay close by, as though we were the sole inhabitants of this mountain land.

Tears sprang, dampening my cheeks. My head swam with memories I longed to expunge. The distant ring of gunshots, tracker dogs, our clumsy feet pounding beds of pine needles; a crowded crossing in a boat that threatened to sink beneath the weight of too many; the round-ups, the raids of last summer, others bundled into trains . . . How far we had come. So many hardships we had survived.

I was choked, overwhelmed by this stroke of good fortune.

'Sarina?'

I turned my head. Papa was standing in front of me, hand outstretched. 'Coming, little one?'

I nodded, smiling, though I hated him calling me 'little one'. I was coming up to seventeen.

We stepped, my father first, me next, my mother grasping my shoulders, into the interior, showers of dust and desiccated insects, and a medley of peculiar smells, most of which I didn't recognize. We were assaulted by intricately latticed cobwebs that hung from the upper beams and tickled our faces, causing Mamma and me to shriek. Smells prickled my nostrils: mothballs, camphor, mildew, from a house that had been closed up, unloved for far too long.

My mother proceeded ahead, banging at the stubborn windows, thrusting them open in all the rooms, flinging wide the firmly closed doors. As if by magic, fresh air began to stream in. The stale air was mixed now with perfumes rafting through every open window, wave after wave of sweet and spicy fragrances, delivering a pleasant, auspicious atmosphere to the house.

I held back, observing my parents in our new home. They were all I had left in the world. My heart almost burst with love for them but what if something should befall them? What if I should lose them? Mamma, as she bustled to the kitchen to make a thorough inspection of her future domain? Or Papa, my gentle rock: what if he should be taken from me?

Quietly, his thoughts possibly not such a distance from my own, my father placed our worldly goods on the table in the dining room and sat down wearily, hand resting on his closed briefcase. This room was to become his domain, his office for letter-writing. Missives to save our lives.

Mamma was opening and closing cupboard doors, busily slapping aluminium pots and pans from one surface to another, creating a system that would satisfy her, her thoughts already on cooking. Mamma buried her pain, her yearning for her aged parents and younger sister left behind in Lodz, in cooking. No news of them. No news of anyone. Tomorrow she would bake a cake with whatever ingredients she could scramble together. And we would eat it together, as a family.

A family adrift, clutching each other tightly.

A lavatory flushed. A tap was running. My parents were settling themselves in.

I deposited my bag in the hall, relaxed my shoulders and padded from room to room, gazing out. Every window offered a different view: hidden paths, mountain passes, shaded forestland, all to be discovered. Then I closed my eyes. I prayed we could live here in peace, not lie awake frozen with terror, listening to the unrests of the night. The cries of neighbours being hauled away. Parents separated from their children. Please, let that never happen to us.

Monsieur Decroix had assured us that the war was a long, long way from us now. May it always be so.

In that instant, I promised myself I would be happy, satisfied with the gift we had been offered: shelter in this abdicated dwelling. Perhaps something wondrous lay ahead, yes, a blessed future, not a miserable, penny-pinched existence on the run. It was as though this white house, and its ghosts, were making a silent pact with me, embracing me, encouraging me to let go of the past, entomb for ever those harrowing memories. Our lives had been divided, split down the middle.

Two lives: Before and Since.

We had lived Before the war in Poland and now we were inhabiting Since. Since our escape.

Our existence had been grisly for the best part of the past three years, sometimes terrifying, always uncertain, but it couldn't always be so. Life had to get better. Didn't it?

It also began to dawn on me, on that first afternoon, as a milky late-winter sun poured its beams across the floors, that I would not stay with my parents for ever. I was finished with 'little Sarina'. Almost an adult, I had my own journey to carve out. One day, I would choose another direction. It would not be easy, but . . . Oh, how I wished this unspeakable war would end so that I could get on with my life.

We had so few possessions – a meagre assortment of kitchen accessories, my prized collection of seashells from the beaches in Nice, as well as a handful of second-hand French grammar books, and my modest library of well-thumbed novels – *Gone With the Wind*, *Jane Eyre*, *Little Women*, *Peter Pan*, *Wuthering Heights*, and two Polish favourites: *Street of Crocodiles* by Bruno Schulz and *Quo Vadis* by Henryk Sienkiewicz – all of which I had read and re-read. Our wardrobes consisted of the threadbare remains of the garments we had escaped in and a few other bits and bobs purchased at one of the markets in Nice. We could not afford to leave them behind or buy them again.

I flung off my shabby Polish coat. It was too small now, with frayed cuffs creeping up my arms, but it had served me well, had been my blanket as frequently as an outer garment. With so little to call our own, the exercise of moving in, unpacking, was accomplished within an hour.

In both bedrooms, sheets, pillows, pillowcases and bedspreads had been supplied and the beds had been neatly made – no need to shell out from our dwindling resources to buy more – except that every item was damp and fusty.

'Strip them, let them air,' commanded Mamma. I yearned for lavender sachets, like the delicate ones I had coveted in the Cours Saleya market, but they were a luxury well beyond our means. I threw open a linen cupboard. 'Plenty of towels,' I sang out. Along with dead flies and bumble bees, mini-hillocks of sawdust, which Papa said suggested mites or wood-eating beetles.

I came across two boxes in the old dresser in the dining room. One contained baby toys, rattles, a small wooden train with a wheel missing, the other, jigsaw puzzles and playing cards. 'Look here, Papa.'

He lifted his head, only half listening, muttering under his breath. He was studying one of my French grammar books.

'There must have been children living in this house before the war.'

23

Children horse-playing in that once glorious garden.

Mine was the smaller of the two bedrooms but it didn't feel cramped, mainly because it had a shelf for my books and an expansive window that looked south, with views that tumbled and rolled. Best view in the house. Today it was patched with snow, shoots of green in sodden fields, and wind-waving trees.

Hours I was to dally there over the coming months, forehead pressed against the window, dreaming, waiting, longing for someone's safekeeping, safe return. Praying on my knees for the salvation of those who had taken the onward path. The escape route.

But I'm getting ahead of myself . . . All of that came later.

5

Around five o'clock, after I had changed into more comfortable footwear, my sturdy, well-worn walking shoes, we made our way back into town to stock up on provisions. Disencumbered of our belongings, we strolled lighter of spirit. I realized then that I was famished: we hadn't eaten anything since a hurried stick of bread laced with olive oil in the old town of Nice before walking to the port to board the ancient bus. Already, it seemed a lifetime ago.

We were laughing now, looking about us, pointing out curiosities to one another. In Poland, our home had been close to the city, an industrialized environment. Neither my parents nor I had ever spent time in rural surroundings and this was rural and rugged to the extreme. So much was unfamiliar. Plants we had never set eyes on till now. The scents in the air, tangy, fragrant, herbal. This was a nicer part of 'Since'. One of the best bits so far. Even my mother appeared serene, her perpetual melancholy cast aside.

The light was beginning to fade. We soon discovered that night falls quickly in the Lower Alps. There were birds, flocks of them, diving and circling beneath the darkening blue of the immense sky, chattering in the not-yet-budding chestnut trees as we strode to town. The altitude made my head swim. The air was so pure, unalloyed. I breathed deeply. It was like inhaling shards of ice. Every gulp burned into my lungs, but I relished the agony. It was intoxicating.

As we approached the centre, we were greeted by the dulcet strains of dance music, punctuated by cries and laughter. When we entered the principal square, with its gushing fountains, an entirely different scene greeted us.

The *place* had been transformed. It was teeming with life. Groups of people were gathered together, conversing, smoking cigarettes, drinking shots of coffee. Older men in overcoats, some with trilby hats or berets, were tippling brandy on the outdoor terraces of the two *bars-tabacs*. We had not been expecting this. So many people. It might have been a scene from a theatre play or a party, a country jamboree. It *was* a party. Animated. Open. Convivial. No crouching in darkened corners, hiding in basements here, listening with an ear pressed against a wall or curtain, fearful of the sound of one's own digestion.

Huddles of refugees were seated around the periphery, dazed by their good fortune. Some were participating. I recognized two from the bus earlier. I gave a shy wave to a middle-aged woman with doleful eyes, sitting on her own with a shiny shawl wrapped about her shoulders. She nodded back, even managed a trace of a broken smile. I wondered why she was travelling alone. Had she lost all her loved ones along the way?

Children – upwards of three or four to eleven, twelve – were bulleting about, gleeful squeals from small girls, the boys in boisterous pursuit. These were the village infants, not the foreigners, the fugitives.

The offspring of the refugee families were present too, but they were paler-skinned, less robust. They lacked that beetroot-tinged mountain radiance in their cheeks. Mostly they clung to their parents' skirts and knees, monitoring the local children with envious eyes, sucking their thumbs, reining back with effort their itching to break free, to jump and whoop and howl like jackals. That licence was to come for them. It was to come for me too.

However, my bid for freedom was to take an altogether more life-threatening direction.

6

Mingling with the crowds were men in uniforms, Italian infantry from their 4th Army, and their police, the *carabinieri*. Mostly they strolled about in twos and threes. We had grown accustomed to their presence in Nice where, since their arrival as custodians of the South of France the previous November, they had patrolled the seaside streets, the waterfront promenade and the cafés, always one or two on perpetual guard in all of the city's public places, such as the old opera house. They were a dashing lot, with fancy feathers in their hats. The Cappello Alpino was the crowning and most distinctive feature in the Alpini troops' uniform and most of them wore it with an almost ridiculous pride. I can't say why, but I had not expected these foot-soldiers to be in residence so far inland, although I was fully aware that they ruled on behalf of Hitler's armies throughout this southern quarter of France, their regiments patrolling as far west as Marseille.

They paid no heed to us, expressed no interest in the Führer's ethnic-cleansing programmes. It was well known that these soldiers abhorred the whole business of singling out Jews, shaming and imprisoning them. As long as the Italians remained the overseers of the Alpes-Maritimes, we were safe.

According to Monsieur Decroix, they had requisitioned the Hôtel des Alpes – the poshest hotel in town – with its lively restaurant, where violin music was playing now in the dining room as it did at every mealtime.

On this our first evening, I couldn't help but notice the Italians and their antics: laughing loudly in groups at the café tables, legs outstretched, leather-booted feet crossed at the ankles. In Nice, they had behaved in a more formal fashion, less casual in their manners. Here they were whistling at and flirting with the promenading girls. Not at me. I was invisible as I walked directly by them in my worn boots, drab skirt and navy-blue coat, chaperoned by my parents. Secretly, I would have been flattered to receive a wolf whistle or two, a wink or a smile. I yearned to be a young lady, one who was admired. I was tired of hiding.

We spotted a sign that directed us to an *épicerie*. Turning off the central square onto a narrow street, we found it easily. Barely bigger than a family grocery store, it was still open and well stocked, surprisingly so, given rationing. Along its exterior wall, beside the open door, half a dozen wooden crates tempted the passer-by with appetizing merchandise. There were kilos of swedes of course. They were available everywhere. Everybody was sick to death of them.

'Look, they have a few fresh vegetables, Marta. Oranges, too, and the remainder of last season's almonds.'

As we stepped inside, a bell above the door clanged. A dry, pungent smell greeted us: milk, both condensed and fresh, and a huge wheel of goats' cheese, locally produced. Its tart odour – we were still getting used to it – wrapped itself around the shelves and counter. Pale in colour, almost white, but creamy and delicious.

I hadn't seen such spreads of food in more than a year. Choices more varied than anywhere we'd shopped over the past few months. Table olives, olive oil at eleven francs a litre, which was a vast improvement on the sixteen to eighteen francs Mamma had been paying in Nice.

The store was presided over by a petite, silver-haired lady, who nodded as we entered. 'Welcome,' she said.

In front of her, three fifty-litre barrels of local wine with a tap at the base. The choice was a light red, dry white or rosé, so stated a handpainted sign, which was illustrated with a bunch of black grapes and a hatted man with a basket on his shoulder.

I glanced at the old lady. Was this her artwork?

She gave me a puckish wink. 'Next time you're in, bring an empty jug and I'll serve you a litre,' she told me. 'These wines are produced in the vineyards of Bellet in the hills behind Nice. All excellent and available.'

Even with a jug to hand, we wouldn't have bought any My parents never drank alcohol, though I fancied trying some. Elsewhere on the shelves were clusters of fresh and dried dates. I had never seen fresh dates before we settled in Nice.

'The prices are a little high,' Mamma remarked, under her breath in Polish, so the shopkeeper wouldn't understand her.

I was still admiring the signs that accompanied the various produce. Each was decorated with a miniature watercolour. They were charming and cheery.

'Look at the great swags of herbs.'

Velvety bunches of sage tied with string. Sheaves of bay leaves thick as brushes. Slender shoots of rosemary with delicate purple flowers. Bunches of deliciously scented narcissi to embellish a table. Sprays of parsley, tufts of chives. It was too early for tomatoes and fresh garden salads but there were a few leeks on offer. Then Mamma discovered, in a darkened corner, a wooden crate packed with straw, cushioning a batch of potatoes still coated in dark clods of earth.

'These *pommes de terre* are ideal for baking, and the oven in that house is working. I tested it before we came out,' cried Mamma.

At the counter, where I was hovering because I was keen to get into conversation with the old lady – something about her ignited my curiosity – dried sausages lay in metal dishes alongside slices of salami that looked freshly cut, but we didn't buy any of the pig meat.

The shopkeeper stood by the scales in fur-lined boots with zips, following my parents' movements as they toured her stocked shelves, of which she looked exceedingly proud.

'I have a few grams of sugar to spare if you are partial to a *petit* cupful,' she whispered to me conspiratorially.

'Sugar, Papa?' My father was the one with the sweet tooth.

'No coupons.'

I apologized, declined.

She lifted a finger to her lips, engaging me in confidence, then proffered the small bag of sweetness as though coupons were not something to worry our heads about. Surprised, I accepted it gratefully.

Father handed me the notes to settle our bill. I was counting – *dix, quinze, dix-huit* – as I stepped forward, negotiating my path between milk churns and sacks of cereal.

'*Merci,*' I muttered. I was eager to tell the little old lady my name and to confide how relieved we were to be here. She smiled, nodded as though she could read my thoughts, then craned her scarved head towards her green metal money box and handed me my change. Her fingers, bent out of shape and swollen at the joints, trembled as the coins clinked into my palm. Dark brown eyes, she had, like overripe winter berries.

7

As we wound our way back, our shopping bag bulging with mouth-watering foodstuffs, the main square was still gyrating with life. Lights were popping on in the windows above the shops, which were closing until the morrow. Lights also illuminated the four side-streets that fanned out from the central square.

Someone was playing an accordion. Gypsy music. People were breaking into dance, a foot extended, an arm offered. Others were clapping, or stamping booted feet against the cobbles, beating time.

I yearned to join in, turn in circles, rap my hands.

I caught the occasional word . . . could it be . . . ? Yes, it was . . . A group at a table chatting openly in Polish, others conversing in Yiddish. In a public square, without fear or shame. What a miracle of a hiding place we had fallen upon.

The accordion player wrapped up his song with a flourish and his audience cheered. Next, the sweet, stricken notes of a violin slid into a waltz. The mood was hushed. My parents, engrossed in conversation, meandered slowly onwards hand in hand.

Evening had settled on the stone-strewn landscape and with it came something beguiling: a gathering of many strangers by streetlight in this village of cascading waters and medieval masonry. I glanced about at the wealth of faces, each one, eyes glistening, transfixed by the Hungarian music. Were the refugees heartsick, homesick, for the occupied cities of their birth? Transported to their forfeited lands, to their yesteryears? Or were they content to be in this high plateau place, which seemed so joyous, liberated?

Here, where all and sundry mingled, where the war was a distant fret in our minds.

A woman, tall and slender, with hair all a-flourish, auburn and wavy, drew my attention. One arm extended high above her head, she was swinging her hips from side to side. One of the soldiers — he was the Italian captain — lifted his cigar from between his lips and applauded her energetically. He jumped to his feet and crooked his arm: an invitation to her to promenade with him to the centre of the square. She slipped her arm proudly into his and the crowds, silenced, shuffled sideways as the pair began to waltz. Her gown was various shades of green. It glittered like the scales of a fish as they twisted and turned. Falling in folds about her ankles, it might have been tailored for attendance at a ball.

I gazed, open-mouthed. I had never witnessed anything like this before.

Two, then three of the uniformed Italians followed their leader, jumping to their feet and shaking out the creases in their trousers. With charm and insouciance they insinuated themselves into the company of a huddle of peasant girls not much older than me, but less skinny than I was, full-bosomed country lasses. Two girls were wearing pinafores beneath their coats. They were giggling coyly, lashes a-flutter. They nudged their hands up against one another, conspiratorially, encouragingly, when one of the Italians bowed, like a courtier. Suddenly, from out of the crowd, a ravishing girl with golden hair pushed herself forward. Elbowing the other young women aside, she accepted the request to dance. The black-haired Latin, eyes agog at his catch, swept her into his arms and spun her away from her friends towards the centre of the square, where his commanding officer and the lady in the green dress were rotating gracefully.

While the townsfolk looked on, the soldiers were wooing the local females.

My parents had paused, taken aback. The Italians might have shown themselves to be less ruthless than the Germans but, even so, they were the enemy, the overlords.

Such familiarity was shocking to some. 'If she were my daughter . . .' muttered a gruff voice.

The blonde threw back her head in a gesture of abandon as the young Italian spun her in giddying circles. The expressions on the faces of the onlookers were mixed. Some were disapproving, while others were beating time to the rhythm of the traditional music, which was in one moment haunting and mournful, and in the next, hopeful and sweetly lyrical. Then, without any warning, the pace of the music speeded up. It became really fast, from waltz to polka. People leaped to their feet, joined in, swept along. They jigged about, whirling in circles, while children jumped and skipped and screeched with delight.

I was so awestruck by the crowd's exuberance, transfixed by the blonde girl, that I didn't at first notice Monsieur Decroix. He was negotiating his way through the crowds towards my parents. He was introducing Papa to a young man who was wearing a beret. Papa turned, perplexed, looking about him.

'Papa,' I called. He couldn't hear me.

Had something happened? Did he need me to translate? I hurried over, but in my haste tripped over a paving stone. Our six precious potatoes, two anticipated baked dinners, tumbled one after the other to the ground, rolling away from me, hopping and wheeling along the cobbles, like the fast-paced musical notes. I bent to gather up our food as nimbly, rapidly, as I could but I was too slow. When I stood up, the men had disappeared, lost within the throng, and my parents were on their own again making their way casually towards the plateau, beyond the town.

No emergency, then.

I was about to catch up with them when, from somewhere across the square beneath trees not yet in leaf, a man in a shabby brown suit stepped up onto a bench. Standing at the centre of his makeshift stage, he lifted a harmonica to his lips and let slide a chord, a stream of chords. The sound that drifted into the night captivated me, drew me back. I closed my eyes to listen. The tune triggered a flood of memories that fractured my heart. 'Czerwone Jabłuszko' was a celebrated Polish folk song. Others around me had paused to listen. Still puffing from their exertions, they were entranced by the man in his creased clothes, their hands clasped in wonder.

'Remember this, my love? *C'est une merveille*,' a voice close by me purred.

Even as I turned from the town, the music streamed in all directions. The urge to run back, take part, dance taunted me until the melody grew too faint, disappeared. The sweet tantalizing strains were swallowed by soundlessness, by the ebbs and flows of the universe. I had caught up with my parents. Now our footsteps dominated the deep-sky night. The shadows of nature commanded the scene. Father stopped, eyes Heavenwards.

'Who was that with Monsieur Decroix, Papa?'

'Look at those stars, Sarina.'

I drew to a standstill and spun on my heels, still diligently clutching our precious potatoes, gazing about and above me. The sky was so clear, polished, unpolluted. The stars hung so close, I felt I could reach up and ping my fingers against them, flick them on and off, one after another. It was in every sense celestial. I let out a soft cry. The sound of my voice disturbed some nocturnal creature, squatting among the laneside grasses. Someone in hiding? No, a rabbit, or possibly a hare. It took off at such a lick, leaping and bounding, until it was out of sight, invisible within the wild alpine meadowlands.

Concealed from danger, as were we.

A few hundred yards in front of us, a silhouette glowed almost eerily in the darkness. The white house, *our house*, waiting patiently for us to step inside, switch a light on, throw our coats onto the moth-eaten sofa, sigh with relief and prepare our dinner.

The white house. Our fate, my destiny, our interval of respite.

I already knew I loved this place. And something deeper was awakening, a warming in my heart. For the first time in more than two years – since Before – I felt a sense of ease begin to embrace me. A long-forgotten sensation. Gently optimistic. A slender thread of happiness was creeping into the void within me. *Espoir*. Hope. I was excited to go on living, not on the run but engaged, to take charge of my life, make friends. I wanted to dance, like the girls with the soldiers, to be swung in circles in the arms of an alluring stranger, but most of all I wanted to find a way out of the political hell we were all inhabiting.

8

Early the following morning, I was woken abruptly by a sharp knocking at the front door. The intrusion sent a bolt of terror through me. I tumbled from the unfamiliar bed losing my balance, feet tangled in the sheet, and then I remembered that we were no longer in Nice, our lives no longer threatened.

But footsteps along the passageway. Father's? The creak of the front door. Voices, then the door drawn closed. An ominous silence. I slipped from my room. Mamma was rattling about in the kitchen.

'Where's Papa gone?' I begged.

In a sharp tone, she bade me get washed and dressed and not to start with the questions.

While Mamma boiled tea and sliced our loaf, I scrambled onto a chair by my window craning to see who had come calling. I cocked my head and caught sight of Papa disappearing with long strides down a hilly pathway on our side of the village. He was in the company of Monsieur Decroix and another man, who was leading the way and whose face I couldn't see. Father was carrying his small medical bag in his left hand. Called to a patient, then.

When the trio was out of sight, I turned my attention to a cluster of boys perched on a cart rocking down the hill to the wheatfields. Before they were too distant, I leaned tighter to the window, one hand flat against the glass, which was cold and frosty. I was sure that at least two of the boys, slapping one another and laughing, losing balance with the clop of the mule against the ice-hard runnels of earth on the path, had been among the crowd in the square when we'd descended the bus.

But where had Papa hurried off to? If to a patient, why was Mamma so bad-tempered?

9

The landscape was fabulous, magical.

After breakfast, after Papa had returned from his patient without a word of explanation, we walked to town as a threesome and joined the queue to register ourselves with the Italians.

It was the only commitment required of us. To present ourselves along with our expired papers, each morning or evening, in front of the main door of the Hôtel des Alpes. A trestle table had been rigged up, around which half a dozen of the Italian soldiers presided, checking our out-of-date *cartes*, ticking our names off lists.

On that first morning, Papa was handed three ration cards.

'Keep them with you at all times,' the young soldier instructed. He then directed us to a shed at the back of the hotel. There, we queued again to be allocated five kilos of pasta and a small sack of dried vegetables.

Inside the kitchens, I spotted the fair-haired girl who'd been dancing the evening before. She was ticking off a scullery maid, who was sobbing while washing and slicing a mound of potatoes, a barrel of murky water at her wooden-clogged feet. When her superior noticed me peering in, she crossed to the open door.

'Hello.' She smiled, stepping outside. Close up, she was quite striking, with her hive of straw-blonde locks. Leaning with one foot against the stone wall, she pulled a packet of cigarettes out of her pocket. 'You one of the new lot off yesterday's bus?'

'We've moved up from Nice,' I confirmed, delighted to make the acquaintance of someone my own generation.

'I'm Sylvie. Fancy a ciggie?'

I shook my head. 'No, thanks.'

Sylvie lit hers, pulled hard and let out a long, slow exhalation. She was fiddling with the hem of her rather pretty skirt and sniffing at her painted fingernails. 'Phew, these kitchens stink.'

'Is this where you work, Sylvie?'

'Are you kidding? My mum drags me in to lend a hand. She's the hotel manageress. So many mouths to feed, these days. Been queuing for your rations?'

I nodded. My parents had disappeared, I noticed. 'I'd better catch them up.'

'See you later, then,' she trilled, crushing the stub of her red-smudged cigarette into the cobbles with her low-heeled shoe and pulling out a lipstick from another pocket. As I was scooting off, Sylvie called after me, 'What's your name?'

I was glad she'd asked.

'If you fancy some company, Sara, come and find me.'

10

During those first days, all our energies were centred on the business of settling in, finding our feet within this community of farmers and asylum seekers from all the way across Europe and further. We were free to do as we pleased. No one bothered us. No municipal restrictions or regulations were laid upon us, and no obligation to sew one of those foul yellow stars on our coats.

I tried not to perceive the daily queuing as a humiliation, but to see the encounter as an opportunity to practise my Italian, to meet people and be a part of the village activities.

'*Buon giorno*, I'm Sara,' I'd say.

Every morning the same greeting. 'Papers?'

I'd make sure that I'd combed my hair. Was this to be the day the soldier would raise his head and, recognizing me from my previous appearances, beam at me? Was it today he'd see me for the first time, even though he had seen me every day? Was it today that his handsome face would break into a grin as he said, '*Buon giorno, bella Sara. Bellissima.*'

'Surname, Sara, please.'

'Rosenbaum.'

'Thank you.' Tick. 'Next.'

Not this morning, then.

No, not this morning. Not a glance at Sara in her humdrum hand-me-down attire.

After the formalities, I chose to hang around the town

while my parents returned to our white house. The hours spent in our apartment might have been used to reconstruct a family life, to inhabit a modicum of normality, domesticity, too long snatched from us, yet neither of my parents seemed to choose to do that. My father's mind was turned to the future. He was determined to build us a new life in Palestine or America. He was looking forward, as was I, while my mother's mind was resolutely set in the past.

And so began their disputes. This was something new and rather shocking given that we had only each other. It tore at my heart listening to them. I don't mean physical violence, but incessant disagreements about nothing, or every little thing. Hen-pecking, bickering. It seemed an irony to me that Fate, Luck, had afforded us this lacuna, a parenthesis of peace, and my parents were wasting time nagging at one other. Why? What was at the root of it? Father's absences, which were growing more frequent? Strangers at the door? At odd hours too, before dawn once: two young men in berets, rifles on their shoulders, assisting a third, who appeared to have been injured. Father signalled them to the kitchen. As he passed, I caught a flash of the unsightly burn on the young man's cheek and forehead. I was hanging by my barely opened door, one eye trained along the corridor. I excused my snooping because Papa might need me, but he did not call for me. He boiled a kettle of water himself, not even Mamma present to lend a hand. I would have helped. The men exchanged barely a word.

Once he was gone all night.

Unable to sleep, I sat by the window in my room watching a sliver of moon rise, like crystallized lemon, above the valleys and distant wheatfields, waiting for his return.

I recalled the woman in the green dress, spinning to the music with the Italian captain. Had Papa met someone else who was kinder to him than Mamma? Were we losing him? Who were the unknowns calling for his skills?

He kept his counsel.

Was it Mamma's endless reminiscing? The way she gilded our Polish history with flawless images? For Mamma, our lives in Poland had been idyllic. In actual fact, most of the memories had been airbrushed in her imagination. They bore little resemblance to our past.

'Marta, stop talking about yesterday!'

And so they squabbled and I stayed out of the house, drew into myself. Rarely did they notice my absences, my restlessness, or that I was turning my attention to the world beyond our family.

After I had registered with the Italians, I'd take one of my novels and make myself comfortable on a bench in the main square, idly reading the texts I almost knew by heart, or studying my advanced French grammar books. In reality I wasn't being studious, I was observing the comings and goings, making myself familiar with the faces, the routines.

Almost every morning, I sighted the lady with the auburn hair who'd danced in the sea-green dress. She ran a laundry business and rode a tricycle with a trailer attached to its rear mudguard. In the trailer, she transported stacks of neatly pressed linen. Other times, I saw her bustling to and fro, accompanied by a boy of about my age. They were weighed down with baskets piled high with soiled sheets from the hotel where the Italians resided. He was the boy who'd waved to me on our first afternoon.

His name was Albert. I knew this because I eaves-dropped on the gossiping biddies, the old crones in black, glued to their stone benches in the central square. They tittle-tattled about Albert's mother 'larking with the Italian *capitano*'.

'More than larking, deary me.'

'*Les amants*,' they concurred. 'Lovers. And she a married French woman.'

Heads shook in condemnation.

But they were kind to me, those old widows, stout as stuffed hens. They did not frequent the bars. Instead, they congregated beneath the shade of the elegant plane trees, greening now with leaves. Every day, after Mass, they gathered like a clattering of jackdaws, hunched in a circle, peeling almonds or peas with pink arthritic fingers that resembled lobsters' claws. Or sometimes with crochet in their laps, but always remarking every person's transit, rasping and cackling till their throats ran dry. Occasion-ally, one would beckon me over.

'New here, eh? Where you from, *jeune fille*?'

I replied good-naturedly, no matter how many times the question was put to me.

'Not French, then?'

'*Non, Madame.*'

'Speak it well, though, don't you?'

Their wart-studded faces glared at me, appraisingly.

'Pretty little thing you are. The doctor's daughter, isn't that so?'

Nothing missed their attention. What did they know?

'Good-looking, ain't she? Eyes as black as jet.'

'Yes, good-looking. Shame what's happening to them.'

I'd nod my thanks and wend my way.

Most mornings I wandered round to the kitchens

where the big wide door at the rear of the hotel was always open. I popped my head in and enquired after Sylvie. The two scullery maids, frazzled and perspiring, shook their heads.

'Any idea where I could find her?'

They shrugged their shoulders and continued with their vegetable preparations. Mounds of turnips and potatoes surrounded them.

I was hoping to make friends. A chance encounter.

There was Le Petit Café de Pascal, one of several bars in the town. It was the most popular, always bustling with customers or people queuing to use its telephone. Popular French and Provençal music emanated from a wireless high on a shelf behind the bar. The news, too, came booming down the airwaves.

Pascal's was the hub for the village elders, for their daily exchange of gossip and philosophizing about the current state of the world. Pascal had a teenage son who waited at tables. Soon after the crack of dawn, when the sky was lilac and gold, Pascal rolled up the shutters and his lad was out sweeping the stone terrace with his straw broom, tidying and rearranging the round iron tables and chairs.

It was never more than five minutes before the first of the residents shuffled to their habitual seats to sip cloudy glasses of pastis and smoke themselves into a fog.

One morning, before I waited to present myself to the Italian soldiers, I decided on the spur of the moment to introduce myself to Pascal, and enquire after temporary employment, but when I stepped inside, all went deathly quiet. It was as though my act was brazen, an infraction. I glanced from face to face, lost my nerve and, without thinking, ordered a lemonade, then didn't have sufficient centimes to pay for it. It was mortifying. Pascal sent me to sit outside. 'Thomas'll bring the lemonade to the terrace.'

His son served me a brimming glass. 'No charge,' he said. 'What's your name?'

'Sara,' I replied. Too humiliated to stay and chat, to enjoy the drink, I jumped to my feet and hurried off to join the refugee queue, which by then was snaking in length. I would happily have swept that terrace, lent Thomas a hand, welcomed in the locals of a morning and earned a few francs to help Papa pay our passage to onward lands.

11

Whenever I returned home with our bags of shopping from the *épicerie*, Mamma would be cleaning for all she was worth. When she'd worn herself out with housework, she'd install herself at the kitchen table buffing with the sleeve of her blouse her collection of photographs, a wad held tight with frayed string, polishing the ghosts from her past, while silently the tears rolled down her sunken cheeks. I couldn't bear to watch her. I longed for her to find peace of mind, for acceptance of our present situation, which was not so bad after all.

I had few words to console her and felt incapable of lifting her out of her suffering, unable to light her a torch to the here and now.

The past was forbidden territory. This was my mantra to sanity.

I tried to engage Mamma's interest in the jigsaws I'd found. 'Shall we do one of them together?' I coaxed, but she gave them hardly a glance. 'Then how about I teach you some French, Mamma, and we can go shopping together?'

She shook her head disconsolately.

Father ignored Mamma's mood swings, her deteriorating state of mind. When he was home, which was less and less frequently these days, he occupied himself by writing letters, page after page of handwritten missives requesting applications for exit visas for the dreamed-of onward journey. Tax documents from Poland, police certificates, birth certificates, copies of this or that and Heaven knew what else – all to secure the unattainable, the now almost unaffordable sea passage and entry into a free land. Our funds were diminishing, so on top of everything else we would require sponsors. Papa fired off requests to dozens of rescue agencies, charitable organizations. I had lost count. From the Federation of Jewish Organizations to the JDC, a joint overseas-aid corporation, whose goal was to help fleeing families primarily from Crimea.

'Crimea? But that's not us, Papa.'

'We must try every avenue. Do everything we can, Sara.'

I sensed the weight of his frustration and concern.

Even when we didn't meet the criteria, he would put forward our case. There were several bodies in Nice, including the Dubouchage synagogue, all working against Nazi intelligence services, which just might guarantee our good names and offer financial assistance. We knew no one, had no contacts outside Europe. The challenge he had set himself on our behalf was exhausting.

If only I could earn my own passage.

Some days, I would spot Papa seated on the terrace of one or other of the cafés, usually Pascal's, flanked by a group of other men, elders, patres familias. Occasionally, the young rabbi would hurry along and settle himself at Papa's side. They were a gentlemen's coven deep in dialogue. Monsieur Decroix seemed to preside over the gatherings, listening, jotting down notes when others spoke. On many occasions, the Catholic priest would also join the gathering. He'd drink a glass of wine with them, accept a stack of letters and secrete them in his robes or the small satchel he carried about with him.

I gathered from my father's words over our bowl of evening soup that plans were being hatched.

'Samuel, please, let's not discuss this in front of –'

'What sort of plans, Papa?'

'Plans for our escape, Sarina. We have formed a small organization . . .'

At the mention of this Mamma rose from the table, accidentally dropping her spoon to the floor as she carried her dish to the sink. She was shaking her head.

'Marta . . .'

'Why must you link yourself to these secret clubs, these illegal activities? We are safe here, Samuel, after a fashion, and now you are putting all our lives at risk. Best to mind our own business, keep our heads down, until we are free to go home.'

Papa let out a sigh. His eyes were puckered with pain. He watched without a word as Mamma strode from the room.

It burned me up to observe them. 'Tell me, Papa,' I begged, when Mamma had gone, 'who are these people?'

He confided that he, with others of standing in the village, had formed an organization of their own, and the inhabitants of Ville-Vésubie did not oppose it. 'In fact, many are supporting it, Sarina. These are broad-minded folk, courageous too, the majority of them.'

Father talked to me in almost hushed tones of a very distinguished gentleman, one Angelo Donati, an ex-soldier, a Jewish Italian banker living in Nice, who was working hard to organize the escape of as many immigrants from southern France as possible, either via Switzerland or Spain. Others were smuggled into Italy, and onwards by boat to north Africa.

It was estimated that there were fifty thousand Jews in Nice or hiding in the Alpes-Maritimes.

'But how will he find us all?' My heart beat fast at the

prospect of it. I remembered our desperate journey to get here, after we had fled Poland. Were we to endure those dangers all over again?

'The local priest, Father Scaramoni – have you met him yet?'

I shook my head.

'He's at liberty to travel wherever he pleases. Each time he takes the bus to the coast, his satchel is crammed with letters. These contain requests on behalf of many of us newcomers here.' Letters pleading for the means that would aid us to be gone before the Nazis reached this corner of France.

'But the Nazis are far from here, aren't they? They are not coming here.'

'For the moment we are not at risk, Sarina. Still, our safest option is to flee Europe altogether.'

'The only valid papers we have are our ration cards!'

At that stage, I was ignorant of the underground organizations operating in the vicinity of La Ville-Vésubie, providing the necessary paperwork, and sometimes funds, to assist refugees to escape. Every now and then, a family disappeared. They had been furnished with false identity cards, exit visas and boat tickets to locations outside Europe.

Counterfeit documents could be purchased, offering safe passage to Palestine: an immense and fertile state between the Jordan river and the Mediterranean Sea, where date palms grew, where there was desert, oases, seaside towns of affluence, with endless sunshine, mandated by the British.

An exotic, mythical land.

But I was oblivious to all of this until one night, when a commotion in our kitchen – a scraping of a chair, hushed but charged voices – disturbed my sleep. It was two nights after my conversation with Papa. I opened my eyes to a full moon casting a nacreous light across the room. A barn owl was calling from somewhere in the back garden, but that hadn't been the cause of my waking.

Clandestine visitors – wounded men seeking medical care? No, it was my parents arguing again. At this hour. Papa had been absent when I went to bed. I hovered by my table and chair, deliberating whether or not to go to them, when my door opened a fraction. It was Papa.

'You're awake, Sarina? We disturbed you.'

I shook my head. I was trembling, scared, but couldn't explain the root of my fear.

'May I come in?'

Mamma, behind him, bullied at his elbow. 'This is wrong, Samuel. She's just a girl. I don't hold with this. I don't approve.'

Without turning his head, Papa spoke sharply. 'Woman, for pity's sake . . . stop interfering . . .' He rubbed at his face, regretting his outburst. 'Marta, please, go back to bed, get some sleep. Sara, I need your help. Dress yourself, quick as you can, and accompany me.'

The brightness of the sky belied the pre-dawn chill. I was walking fast, trying to keep up with my father, who was moving at an urgent pace along a rocky track. We were aiming for somewhere above the village dwellings, beyond the most northerly of the habitations, a zone where I hadn't ventured. On high, a coliseum of limestone mountains gilded by the moon's irradiation.

'We must avoid the Italian night patrol,' explained Papa. We were taking a circuitous route, not cutting through the town. 'Prepare yourself, Sara. A man has been hurt. He speaks only Polish, a few words of French. What he has to tell us needs to be translated with accuracy.'

I nodded. Little else was said while we proceeded. I was puzzling over 'us'.

We ascended the curved lane that abutted the village school to a building all the way to its rear. It was a semi-hidden barn, used for storing agricultural equipment, set within an enclosed farmyard. Father pulled a torch from his overcoat pocket. He flashed it several times, pointing it towards the ground. A young man appeared, wearing a beret, a scarf wrapped tight around his face, like a bank robber. He nodded and we followed him. I shivered with uncertainty.

Within the semi-open barn, pressed into a distant corner, were two adults. A man stretched out on the ground, cocooned in blankets, a woman crouched at his side. She was anxious, I could read that in the way she wrung a handkerchief between her fingers, using it every now and then to dab the forehead of the prostrate man. It was dark and difficult to make out the faces and expressions unless one of the torches was focused on someone's features. I was reasonably sure, though, that I had seen the injured man before – in the main square on our first evening, a ghost of a fellow in a shabby brown suit, playing his harmonica while standing on a bench. Polish melodies to tear your heart open.

Papa wrapped both arms round my shoulders and bent low to me. 'Try not to be distressed, Sarina. This man has been badly injured and his life is in danger. I need you to listen very carefully, concentrate and translate precisely what our sick friend conveys to you to my young colleague here.'

I was quaking as I approached the couple. The woman,

possibly in her fifties, had been crying. Her face powder showed a snail trail where the tears had fallen. I crouched down alongside her. The man displayed a grotesque gash, a laceration between the base of his neck and his right shoulder. Blood encrusted his thinning dark hair and what remained of his brown jacket.

'I'm listening,' I said in Polish, for want of other more compassionate words. I was at a loss, out of my depth.

'Henryk can't speak,' began the woman, swallowing back more tears. 'He's losing consciousness.'

'Can you share any details with us?' the young Frenchman butted in from behind me.

'We were attacked.'

Furnished with their counterfeit papers, the couple had left the village a little in advance of the appointed hour, descending southwards on foot by narrow lanes and passes cut through the jagged rocks. The arrangement had been to leave all belongings behind. Their necessities in one small bag had been collected in advance by one of the team organizing their escape. They had been instructed to wait by a stone cross.

'It was a surprisingly long way south of the village.'

'Yes, that's one of our regular pick-up points.'

Someone with transport – neither she nor her husband had been given any further identifying details – was to collect them from a sloped field, used for summer grazing, to the left of the cross. From there, they were to be transported to the coast where a boat was waiting.

'We hurried down the sloping track in the moonlight, cautious not to be pulled up by an Italian patrol, and eventually came upon the cross. We were far too early, but waited there as instructed. Henryk lit a cigarette. He couldn't keep still, jumping with agitation. From out of nowhere two men appeared. We took them for our drivers, but they had no vehicle.'

'Were they Italian?' asked the Frenchman in the beret.

Henryk's wife considered the question, then shook her head. 'No, I don't think so. They weren't in uniform. There was no place, no time, to hide ourselves. The men demanded to know what we were doing out at such a late hour. Their manner was unpleasant, aggressive, and we were afraid. There was no sign of our convoy. We were stranded. Henryk was nervous. He panicked, tried to tackle the taller of the two who was yelling, shouting 'filthy Jew' at him. He and the man were struggling – it all happened so fast. The fellow drew a knife. They fought, he stabbed . . . Henryk staggered backwards, fell, hit his head against a stone.' She dropped her face into her hands, sobbing.

No one spoke, each considering the scene.

'What happened to the aggressors?'

Henryk's wife shrugged. 'They must have run off. They grabbed my bag, my jewellery within it, all we had to pay our way. I was on my knees . . . at my husband's side . . .'

'Would you be able to describe them for us? Anything that might locate . . . It was a clear night,' urged the Frenchman. His expression was solemn, almost desperate.

I repeated the descriptions the lady was giving me, but there was little detail. As I listened to her story my eyes were fixed on her husband. I could hear his music playing again. He seemed to be slipping from this world. Blood had begun to ooze from the corner of his mouth. I was fighting a desire to vomit.

'Papa,' I mewled. He coaxed me to my feet and ordered me to stand back. The young Frenchman took my arm and led me to the far side of the barn where a horse and two donkeys were tethered. I hadn't been aware of their presence before.

'Sara, any detail at all that you haven't yet translated, I need it. If someone knew, somebody possibly intercepted our plans . . . Lives depend on identifying those two men. If they are traitors, *mouchards* . . .'

'*Mouchards*?'

'Informers.'

I closed my eyes and faithfully recounted the events one more time, precisely as they had been narrated to me. There were few clues to the thieves' identity. While I went over the facts once more, the man laid out on his back behind me lost his life.

12

The following morning I slept late and missed our daily appointment with the Italian soldiers. It wasn't a catastrophe. I could join the afternoon queue. My parents had already been to town and, after escorting Mamma home because she wouldn't venture outside on her own any more, Papa had gone to one of the medical centres to lend a hand. It was raining, not heavily, a spring mizzle. I grabbed a cup of coffee and one of my dog-eared novels and descended the steps outside to the lower level of the white house, taking shelter by the front door. I needed air on my skin, to be outside, to be cleansed of the shadowy images in my head.

Those two faceless robbers, where had they come from? Who were they?

The garden was a jungle of dripping leaves and briars so I pressed myself tight to the villa's front door. It was the first time I had stood so close to it. I asked myself about the identity of the property's owners. I hadn't really given them any thought until now. Why had they locked their home and gone away?

I settled cross-legged on the tiled floor at the side of the house with a veranda. I didn't read, couldn't concentrate, but stared instead at the steady stream of rain on the heavy-leaved plants, listening to its thrumming. I couldn't get the image out of my head of the man, Henryk, who had died. Of his gift with music, his ability to transport us to somewhere beautiful. I had never exchanged a word with him. Yet he and we, along with so many others, were in the same hopeless mess. Perhaps Mamma's advice was the wisest. Perhaps we should just keep our heads down, minding our own business until the war was over and it was safe to leave: if Papa was arrested what would become of us?

The fear we had been nursing for so long, that had haunted us, travelled with us, that at any moment a stranger would step out of a crowd and arrest us, had all but melted away since we had been welcomed into this mountain community. But now I wasn't so sure. I didn't know whom we could trust. Was Papa putting us in danger? And if we weren't safe here, where else was there left for us to hide?

By the time Papa came home, I was upstairs in my room, doodling at my small table and gazing out of the window, counting the mule- or horse-drawn carts returning from their day's work in the lower fields. The drizzle had ceased. A weak late-afternoon sun was peeping through the clouds. Father knocked gently and came straight in. 'How are you, Sara?'

I shrugged. Where to begin?

He crossed the carpet, placed his hands on my shoulders and caressed my neck. 'Thank you for your help,' he began. 'It was a difficult night.'

'What will happen now?'

'Henryk's widow will remain for a short while in a neighbouring village. She doesn't want to return here. A passage will be found for her on another ship. Her husband will be given a decent burial here in the local cemetery. The priest will see to it.' Father let out a deep sigh.

I nodded, taking this in, feeling sad and angry for Henryk's wife, who had lost everything. 'What about the robbers?'

'Philippe Decroix came to see me at the surgery. He'll be leading the investigation, the search for the two men. He believes, given his lifelong acquaintance with all local residents, that they are not from here. Robbers, bandits, traitors, whoever they are, they will be found and punished.'

'And what about us? It's too dangerous to leave, Papa.'

'This was a very unfortunate incident.'

'I think we should remain here. None of this would have happened if they had stayed put.'

'As long as the Italians continue to protect us, we are secure in this little town. However, we cannot allow ourselves to forget, Sarina, that the Nazis will not rest until they have rounded up every one of us. And they are fast losing confidence in the Italians. Our safest option is to get out of France before the Germans reach this eastern corner. But for that we need documents.'

As I lay in bed I could hear my parents quarrelling in whispered tones in their room next to mine. Mamma was complaining that she was always alone, that I was rarely at home.

'Let her be, Marta. We cannot be too strict. Who can say how many summers are left to her, to any of us?'

Papa's words unnerved me. His allegiances unnerved me. Within the shadows of these great mountains, another landscape was unfolding. Beneath the sweet chords of music, the distant sounds of war were drawing closer. I felt frightened. Yet another sea change. A tear slipped down my cheek beneath the blankets. How I wished I could swap my life for that of one of the village girls, Sylvie, or the laundry lady who danced with the *capitano* of the Alpini. All I wished for was to be carefree, to dance, fall in love, to live my life like every other ordinary young woman.

13

A day or so after the incident in the barn, Monsieur Decroix came to see us.

'Samuel, *bonjour*. Ah, Madame Rosenbaum, good to see you. I hope you have everything you need?'

My mother affirmed that we were managing quite well but I observed the coldness in her response. I judged her ill-mannered, especially since this man was one of the town's most important public servants, who always went out of his way to help others.

'Good, good. Then, with your permission, I would like to have a few moments with young Sara, if I may?'

I froze.

'Has there been a complaint, sir?'

'Nothing of the kind, Madame. *Au contraire.*'

He had employment for me: babysitting duties.

'They are a young couple, Sara, very decent people, who arrived here a few weeks before you. They have two small children and the mother, Ilse, is pregnant again. If you are happy to accept, they'd be grateful if you could begin without delay.'

This was just what I needed.

'That sounds splendid, eh, Sara? Come in, Philippe.' My father showed the lieutenant through to the kitchen where my mother offered him refreshment – a chicory mix that passed for coffee. Over coffee, even Mamma agreed that the work would be beneficial for me.

'What do you say, Sara?'

I glanced at Papa. 'I'd be glad to help, sir,' I replied.

'Good, then what are we waiting for?'

I collected my cardigan from my room, changed from my slippers into my espadrilles and walked back into town to meet my potential employers. I was excited at the prospect of a job and I was bursting to ask Monsieur Decroix whether he had caught the robbers, but sense warned me against saying a word. He might not be aware that I'd been present on the night of Henryk's death.

As we approached the main square, he directed us to a residential district where there were no shops or bars, only private houses and one doctor's surgery. In its window, I saw *Temporary Medical Centre, north*. Father helped there sometimes. We strode by a sign that read *Polish Chess Club, All Welcome*. There were plenty such signs posted about the village for clubs founded mostly by refugees. It was a pleasurable method of engaging with French citizens and getting acquainted with other refugees who shared similar interests.

The neighbourhood was neat, extremely clean and echoingly silent, save for our footsteps. A ginger and white cat dozed on a doorstep. An older man in a beret appeared from a side lane. We heard him before we saw him. He was whistling 'Parlez-moi d'amour' and wheeled a bicycle that was hung with onions. As he passed us, he nodded to Monsieur Decroix who, without breaking his step, slapped the fellow on the shoulder and said, 'Well done, Clément. *Merci.*'

Once we had climbed a few hundred metres from the centre, we turned left onto a narrow street lined on both sides with slender terraced houses. From many of the windows, sheets hung to dry in the fresh air near boxes of red and pink geraniums. The brightly coloured flowers were a cheerful sight. Outside number ten, Monsieur Decroix came to a stop and knocked. The door opened almost immediately.

'Herr Lindemann, let me present Sara.'

A man in his thirties with thinning hair nodded and led us into a ground-floor flat, which reeked of cooking odours. It was dark and confined. There, Frau Lindemann stood anxiously waiting for us. They were from Germany, a district west of Berlin, the husband said. A Jewish couple with two small children.

'Come and see Daniel. He's in the bedroom at the back.' Frau Lindemann took my hand in hers. Her fingers were freezing. 'Thank you for coming,' she said earnestly. 'I was getting desperate.' She was speaking in German. I was unable to follow precisely what she was telling me as she led me the few paces along a hallway, stepping over boxes into the bedroom. It was cluttered with clothes and ornaments, a silver cutlery set, a worn suitcase open on the floor. Their housing was so cramped that I felt a twinge of guilt about the space we had been assigned at our white house.

'He's only eighteen months,' she spoke now in broken French, 'but hearty and very good-natured.' The blond baby boy in his makeshift cot gurgled and burped and dribbled, gazing intently at me with warm grey-blue eyes as round and bright as bottle tops. He smelt of milk, a bit rancid. I felt hesitant but I shuffled up close, laid a finger-tip on his forehead and grinned into his dancing eyes as he kicked his feet, clearly delighted by the arrival of company.

'*Bonjour, Daniel,*' I whispered. The unfamiliarity of such a fragile being was a little overwhelming, but his face was so open, soft-skinned and trusting that he made me feel comfortable. The newness of his life, its innocence, was heartening.

The other child was Hanna, an intelligent-looking, serious girl of five with dark ringlets that hung to her shoulders and an olive complexion. She was so unlike her sibling, it was hard to believe they were brother and sister.

Ilse Lindemann was blonde, fair-skinned, with grey-blue eyes, like her son's, but she was also extremely pale and seemed sickly. She spoke softly to Monsieur Decroix in faltering French interspersed with long incomprehensible sentences in German spattered with a few words of Yiddish. The gist was that she needed help because she was suffering from incessant bouts of nausea and insomnia. Their journey of escape, which had eventually led them to this far-flung upland, had taken its toll and her pregnancy was proving more difficult than the previous two.

I nodded politely, conscious of my cheeks flushing as Monsieur Decroix translated as best he could the details I hadn't grasped.

Herr and Frau Lindemann were offering to pay me a very modest sum to spend my mornings babysitting for them. This would entail preparing the children's breakfast, feeding them, then washing the dishes and cleaning the apartment. I sneaked glances about me. There was a stack of dirty crockery in the sink, a heap of soiled garments on the unswept floor.

Afterwards, I must keep the infants entertained till midday. My assistance would offer Frau Lindemann an opportunity to sleep for a few extra hours, to recover her strength.

'What do you say, Sara?' Monsieur Decroix's arm was resting on my shoulders.

I had zero experience with small children, having no siblings of my own, although before the war I had often dreamed of a younger brother.

I nodded my acceptance, grateful for the employment and the distraction.

My decision seemed to please Monsieur Decroix no end. 'Well, that's settled, then.' He clapped his hands together. 'Well done, young Sara.'

And so it was agreed that I would return the following morning. I would begin.

14

Those first few days with the children were exhausting, fun but arduous. Hanna never stopped asking questions, most of which I couldn't understand. We settled on Yiddish as our stilted means of conversation, but I longed to communicate with her in more depth. It spurred me to begin to learn German and to teach my young charge basic French. While Daniel dozed in his pushchair in the main square, Hanna and I would attempt one of the jigsaw puzzles I had brought from home. By lunchtime, I was ready to hand the children back to their mother and the chaos of their lives in their rented digs, grateful for my free time.

My expeditions were confined to the afternoons now. I grew bolder as the days lengthened. Humming, craving wide-open spaces, I would stop to buy myself a cold drink at Pascal's, with my earned centimes, then head for the hills or, as the warmer weather approached, the river.

One afternoon, I chanced upon a winding goat track, transformed into a path with the stones beaten flat into the pale earth from centuries of service, the turn of carts, packhorses, the booted feet of men. It plunged to a swirling stretch of river with a vast shingled bank. The noise of rushing water as I approached was stupendous, like a train steaming over me. I vaulted from the grass ridge down onto the bank, slipped off my well-worn espadrilles, tiptoed to the water's edge and dipped in my toe. It was Arctic, but so clear, like liquefied crystal shot with a pale green tinge. I bent low to see every detail on the riverbed.

Deep water grasses drawn by the current. Pebbles of red and black and white. Silvery fish darting between the round, smooth stones. Hot from my trek, I would have liked to immerse myself in the fast-moving currents, spin in the whirlpools, but I couldn't swim.

Sometimes, in my darker moments, I had wondered if it wouldn't be better to drown myself, give in, to lie in silence at the bottom of the cold stony riverbed, clothes billowing, sucked deep to death. I would be liberated from the loneliness, the estrangement from our previous lives, my parents' squabbling, and the torment of what lay ahead, but then I'd picture the Polish émigré in the barn, Henryk, who had lost his life trying to find freedom. I didn't want that. I didn't want to die. I liked it among this cathedral of mountains. Very much. All I wished was for our lives to be normal.

'Hello! Hello!'

A voice. My heart almost skipped a beat. Was I trespassing? Was I in trouble?

'Hey, you there.'

I swung about, as though I had been caught in some subversive act. Standing behind me was a boy, a teenager with dark red hair. It stood erect yet leaned sideways as though he had been caught in a fierce wind. I recognized his face at once – one of the lads from the main square on the day of our arrival. I'd passed by him on many occasions since but we'd never exchanged a word. He was Albert, the son of the fancy lady who owned the laundry business. He helped her carry her loads, his back charged with great swinging sacks of dirty sheets and tablecloths. I'd watched them doing the rounds together, mother and son, from one establishment to the next.

'You're one of the new arrivals, aren't you?' His voice

was raised, almost hoarse, to be heard above the din of water.

I nodded.

'What's your name?'

I felt so awkward, my hands screwing themselves into tight fists. I didn't know what to say to him, yet I was thrilled to see him there. My disobedient hair was flying in the wind, as if sending out smoke signals. What a sight I must look.

'Hey, miss, you speak French, don't you? *Parlez-vous français?* I'm Albert,' he called, when I hadn't answered him.

Still I said nothing, tongue-tied. Images came hurtling back, of nights on the run, my parents ahead of me encouraging me onwards, my mother on her knees drained from exhaustion, my father silently imploring her to get up. The man in the barn. His folk music. His weeping wife.

'Hey, sorry if I spooked you. I just wanted to say hello. I've seen you walking about all over the place, always on your own. I'll leave you. Didn't mean to scare you.'

'No, Albert, please wait.'

Albert had already taken a step and was now paused in profile.

'I'm S . . . You didn't frighten me. It's just . . .' *I've been waiting so long to make friends with someone my own age.*

'You want half an apple? Look, I've an apple and a knife to divide it. Hungry?'

I was, I now realized. And thirsty. Nothing since weak tea with the Lindemann children, then a swiftly downed lemonade at Pascal's.

'I'd love half an apple.'

He swung back towards me and hopped down from the grassy ledge onto the riverbank. He was digging in his trouser pocket, pulling out a folding knife, and with his right hand, from his jacket, a shiny red apple. 'Are you going to tell me your name?'

'Sara.' I was delighted to make Albert's acquaintance. I could feel the smile break across my face. He didn't seem boisterous and cocky, like some of the other lads. His eyes always looked so unhappy. I wondered whether he knew that everyone was gossiping about his mother, mocking his absent father while she entertained herself with the *capitano* of the Alpini, Cuneense division, Italian infantry.

Albert settled on a large smooth boulder, polished the apple vigorously against his ragged sleeve, then sliced the lustrous fruit into two.

'*Merci*. That's very kind.' I took one step but no more. I needed to calm my nerves. I was silently kicking myself. I never used to be so awkward, ungainly in the presence of strangers.

He paid my timidity no attention, instead proffered the bisected *pomme* and I closed in towards him to accept my portion.

As he chewed, spray flew from between his lips. He had a broken front tooth and the very palest line of ginger hairs over his upper lip. 'You speak French?' he quizzed, through a full, munching mouth. 'I mean more than a few words?' He wasn't looking at me, was sideways to me, one leg crossed over the other knee, staring along the riverbank into the distance. Then he turned his attention to me and grinned. His eyes were dancing and bright now, tawny-green, like a young frog in the river. His smile was wide, appealing. He resembled his mother. I warmed to him immediately and knew instinctively that we'd be friends, that I'd met someone I could be at ease with.

'I speak it pretty well.'

His face creased into a frown. 'I never see you talk to anybody. Always on your own, tramping about.' He was sucking the juice off his fingers now that he had demolished the fruit.

'We're . . . quite new here, and . . .'

'No Jews your own age to hang about with?'

I shook my head.

'Why not come hiking with me and my mates tomorrow afternoon? I can introduce you to some of them. We're planning to walk down to a few of the lower villages. We'll be delivering milk and cheese to a couple of families and bringing provisions back up with us.'

I was elated by his offer. 'I'll ask my parents, but I'm sure it won't be a problem.'

They'd be sleeping, or Mamma would be 'resting', Papa at his paperwork or assisting at one of the health centres. They would barely notice my absence, since I was missing most of the time during daylight. They accepted that I was restless and couldn't stay cooped up, even though I loved our apartment in the white house.

'Good.' He jumped to his feet, wiped his hands on the sides of his short trousers and pulled down his fraying jumper. 'Tell you what, one of us'll be waiting outside the church in the market square at a quarter to two. Usually, we meet at my friend Sylvie's, but you might not find her place. It's a bit tucked away.'

My heart soared at the prospect of seeing Sylvie again. 'Oh, I've met Sylvie! She's lovely.'

'One of us will be at the church. See you there.' And with that he set off, great strides along the riverbank, soles of his clogs crunching stones, and then an easy ascent onto the grassy bank before he progressed to the village, whistling to himself.

15

It was Sylvie who'd been given the commission to wait for me beneath the church's bell tower. Hands in the pockets of her trousers – I'd never owned a pair of trousers – kicking a stone lazily to and fro with the toe of her boot, she gave a brief wave as I approached.

'I'm Sara, remember me?' I called. I was cock-a-hoop to see her again and pleased it was she Albert had appointed to wait for me. 'I came looking for you,' I said. 'At the hotel.'

She pouted, confused. 'Oh, right. I remember you. I stopped helping there.' She kissed me on both cheeks. 'We should get going if we want to be back before the sun sets.'

We fell into step as she guided me down one of the lanes that plunged towards the fringes of the small stone town. The narrow streets echoed with our footfall. Bougainvillaea, just coming into blossom, climbed the stone walls.

'Thanks for meeting me,' I said, for want of anything better.

'We've been told to be kind, to welcome the Jews who are new here. You've had a hard time of it, isn't that so?'

I was stung by this. I had hoped that Albert had invited me because he found me interesting, attractive even, not in obedience to some collective edict. A sense of duty. For a moment I considered turning on my heels and bolting, but what better recreation had I for my afternoon? And I craved friendship.

I had to begin somewhere.

'Come on,' Sylvie encouraged, gaining pace. 'Let's have some fun.'

A bunch of boys was waiting outside Sylvie's house when we reached it, each loaded with bulging burlap sacks or woven baskets stuffed with triangles of cheese, bricks of butter. Handkerchiefs had been wrapped around eggs, their shells pasted with feathers. A bounty of locally produced delights – another reason to be seduced into believing the war had disregarded this corner of France.

Albert nodded and introduced me to the others. We were six altogether. Albert, Sylvie, Thomas, Pascal's son from the bar, whom I'd embarrassed myself in front of, and two boys I'd never set eyes on before. They were brothers, Sébastien and Antoine, from a village on the lower slopes.

Heads acknowledged my arrival. Each in turn stepped forward and pecked me on both cheeks, as was the custom, and we began to walk.

Conversation was limited to the occasional comment between one or other of my new friends, drowned mostly by the river. One of the boys was whistling. There was little else to be heard except the clumping of our feet, clogs against cobbles, the incessant torrents of water and the slop-slop of milk swirling within the cans Albert was carrying. The metal containers hung from a bar that straddled his shoulders and cut into his freckled flesh.

I offered to share the load but he shook his head. 'It's too heavy for a girl like you,' he answered.

Like me. I was puzzled by what he meant. Was his

remark intended to be derogatory? Did he perceive me as a weakling?

We took the course that led us to the River Vésubie and from there we turned off, choosing a sharply sloping footpath to the right. This route was new to me. The track was pebbly, then sandy and not too wide. A curling descent, it wound for what felt like kilometres in a semicircle, like the head of a scythe, all the while leading us south. We hopped over rocky ridgeways, clambered over boulders that had cut loose from the mountain, driven by the force of the water flow, and blocked our path. So difficult were they to negotiate that on two occasions I almost lost my footing.

'Give me your hand,' offered Sylvie, clutching mine tightly. 'It's easy when you get used to it. Don't look down if you're afraid of heights.'

We walked, holding on to one another, arms swinging. Then the vista opened wide, as though curtains had been drawn back, and we plunged beyond forests and hills towards a series of wide green terraced valleys. I walked slower than the others because I was admiring all these new sights and, to be honest, I found their pace a bit taxing. It was hellishly steep, and occasionally the pathway stones slipped from under my feet, almost sending me skidding onto my bottom. My companions moved with the agility of goats. They leaped and hopped and swung from foot to foot, skipping from one conversation to another, while I was occasionally forced to stop, steady myself and catch my breath. Sylvie, with her long blonde hair, held back to keep rhythm with me. She'd smile as I caught up, puffing, her face as radiant as the sun.

Further south, the trees thinned. Forests no more, there were velvety plateaux of flat green fields with small shoots pushing through the red-brown earth. My eye was caught by an imposing stone cross taller than a man, set back from the track. I paused, heart in my mouth, recalling the barn and the night with the Polish refugees. I glanced about me, to the field across the pathway. I moved over to get a better view. There was nothing to see, no traces of blood, no signs of a skirmish.

'What are you looking at?' Sylvie had retraced her steps to find me.

I shook my head. In its own way the sight of that relic, the reality of its presence, was like another ambush.

'There are dozens of these old crosses in the hills and valleys around here. They're ancient religious things. This one's a local meeting point.'

I nodded and hurried on from the site with its chilling associations.

Hereabouts the crop was wheat. The vineyards were further south. Smallholdings, villages, isolated farmhouses dotted the setting. Elsewhere, within what looked like temporary enclosures, sheep were grazing. A few goats mingled among them. Occasionally we'd encounter a sheep dog and a herder, with a long wooden pipe, who waved a friendly greeting as we passed by while the dog released a series of frenzied barks. Sometimes we made a stop and one of the boys would pass a packet from his sack to a shepherd, who nodded his thanks, handed over a coin and returned to his work.

'So many sheep,' I murmured breathlessly. I was amazed by the sheer numbers of woolly white-rumped animals amid the undulating green fields.

'It's the *transhumance*,' said Sylvie, who was waving in a rather provocative fashion at a young shepherd with jet-black hair and a nut-brown face. 'Every year in the spring, usually around the second week of April, the animals are herded up from the lower meadows where it is milder for them to winter. The ascent takes about a week and they stay here for the whole summer until mid-September when they return south.' She was still giving the eye to the young peasant boy. 'The grass in this sector of our commune is one of the purest in the whole region for grazing, irrigated by all the mountain streams. Our parish is famous for it. The shepherds – there are about a dozen of them up here now – sleep out under the stars with their flocks, keeping watch.'

The concept of *transhumance*, of driving beasts from one grazing spot to another, was completely new to me.

'We bring the men cheese from one of the *vacheries*. Sometimes a flask of wine.'

All the while I listened to her, I also tuned in to the bleating of the sheep. Hundreds and hundreds of bleating sheep. It lifted my spirits to listen to them, to stand beneath this wide open sky in the company of new friends. Running water and bleating sheep. Baa, baa. They made me laugh out loud.

'What are you laughing at?' frowned Sylvie.

'Nothing. I'm having a good time, that's all. Happy to have been invited along.'

She drew her attention back to me and her lovely ice-blue eyes roamed over my face. 'Poor you, it must be difficult,' she remarked.

'What?'

'Being so far from your real life and your friends. Stuck in this out-of-the-way backwater.'

I shrugged. 'I like it here.'

'Do you? Jesus, I can't wait to get out. Move to Nice or, I don't know, some place really far away. Like Marseille, with clubs and bars and rich blokes. A big city, where the whole world doesn't know your business. How old are you, Sara?'

'Nearly seventeen.'

'Got a boyfriend?'

I shook my head. Sylvie laughed. 'Still a virgin?'

I felt the heat travel up from my neck, the blush a rising tide to my hairline. Of course I was. Those were the words on the tip of my tongue, but I didn't voice them for fear she'd make fun of me.

'Isn't he gorgeous, that shepherd? Sometimes, if they're really lucky, a couple of the local girls slip down to keep them company for a few hours.'

'Hey, get a move on, you two.' The boys, pressed tight up against one another, were watching us, kicking stones, impatient to be on their way. Antoine was smoking, Sébastien singing loudly. His voice rose and bounced off the ranges, echoing like a choir in full throttle.

'You're right, he is.' I was talking about the shepherd, who was, indeed, irresistibly handsome, but he had eyes only for my companion.

'Want me to introduce you? You're certainly pretty enough for him.'

I shook my head. 'Maybe next time. Let's go.'

Sylvie was nineteen, her long blonde hair flecked with gold. It hung down her back, swung and bounced, like ripe corn in the sunlight, her fringe cut sharp across her forehead. She was daring, outspoken, and I admired almost everything about her.

I watched her, silently appraising her, as she sashayed forth, swinging her hips, catching up with our companions, no longer flirting, bored with the attention she had compelled. I waved goodbye to the young peasant, who

combed a hand through his black hair, dejected, abandoned, with only his beasts for company.

'Do you think he has Italian blood?'

'Who? The shepherd? Everyone here has Italian blood.'
She laughed. 'It's why the soldiers are so at home in our
neighbourhood. This corner of France was under Italian
rule until 1860.' Sylvie paused to refresh her lipstick,
dabbed the back of her hand against her flushed cheeks.
'So, having the Italians as the ruling force makes little difference to us. Except, of course, France is occupied and
that's a fact. And we need to fight for our freedom. All of
us, Sara. You understand, don't you?'

I nodded, considering my father's activities, the stranger who had died in the barn and those who had conspired
to help him and his wife.

'Anyway, enough about the wretched war. Has someone told you about tomorrow?'

I shook my head.

Sylvie mentioned that there was to be a ball the following evening at the Hôtel des Alpes. There would be a
band and wine and refreshments. Most weekends dances
were held at one or other of the hotels. 'It's how I got to
know my friend. He's staying at the hotel my mum runs.'

Her voice hummed when she mouthed the words, *my
friend*. Was her friend the soldier she had danced with
when I'd first set eyes on her?

'The social events are an ideal way for the Italians to
meet women,' she confided. 'They enjoy our company.
Some of the lasses from outlying farms come in the hope
of being given extra textile coupons in return for favours.'

'Favours?'

'I'm not bothered about the coupons. I just enjoy the
dancing and the sex.'

I think my eyes popped out of my head. Albert was waving to us to get a move on. The milk on his shoulders was weighing him down, making him impatient to deliver it. I skipped after him, trying not to be shocked by Sylvie's explicitness.

'You should come to the ball, Sara,' she called. 'Have some fun. Who knows what hell lies ahead? And who wants to die a virgin?'

16. Mid-April

Six weeks resident in the white house. Spring with its blithesome florescent mornings was upon us. I woke early in good spirits. I was casting aside my demons, enjoying my little job, mastering the peculiarity of being in the company of children I could barely converse with. But my German was improving in leaps and bounds. Madame Decroix, the local schoolmistress, had passed by in my absence and left me a French–German dictionary.

It was not long after that first excursion with Sylvie, Albert and the others, on one of those kicking-my-heels sort of afternoons, that Sylvie intercepted me in the main square, waving and hallooing my name loudly from outside the Hôtel des Alpes, causing all the old biddies to turn on their benches and stare. I was queuing outside Louis's bakery for a baguette, intending to enjoy a sandwich somewhere in the fresh air before returning home to help Mamma.

'I'm going to the river. Want to come along?' she called, as she sprinted towards me.

I was delighted by her offer.

'Let's go.'

The sky was cloudless, the temperature benign, as we strode out of the town. Every day was warmer now. Dandelion seeds and pollen drifted through the pure mountain early afternoon.

Sylvie sprinted on ahead. Her long locks were knotted in two plaits, like intricate embroidery, over the top of her head. Her trousers were cut short above her ankles. She wore trousers almost all the time – I rarely saw her in a skirt.

She barely threw me a backwards glance, as she jogged onwards until, when we were well out of earshot and range of the town, she braked, drawing to a sudden stop. Bending forward from the waist, hands on her knees, she was panting. A rabbit hopped into view. From the rear pocket of her slacks she pulled a stub-nosed gun, rose to her full height and fired it, killing the grazing rabbit.

'Bullseye!' she yelled.

I was shocked.

'Why don't you run and get it, Sara?'

I remained stockstill. Her target was still twitching. I hadn't been expecting this. 'Why did – Whose gun is that?'

'I nicked it.'

'*What?*' My attention was glued to the now motionless brown furry creature, a wine-dark blemish seeping into its coat. I pictured Henryk and the blood at the corner of his mouth. I thought I was going to throw up. 'Who from?'

'One of the Italians. My special friend, while he was washing.'

My eyes were wide with disbelief. Was she making this up? 'What will he say when he finds out?'

She shrugged. 'I'll slip it underneath his bed at the hotel later. He'll never know the difference. Anyway, I don't care what he says. Everyone has a gun here. We are a community of hunters.'

'Yes, but not one of those.' Even I knew the difference between a hunting rifle and a firearm used for military purposes. And this one had been fired. The soldier would smell it. Sylvie marched into the *maquis* and snatched up the limp, warm animal. She pushed it at me, shoving it towards my chest. I skipped backwards, fearing the stain on my clothes.

'Dinner,' she snapped. 'Take it.'

I dithered, but didn't accept it.

'Your mother will appreciate it.' She strode on ahead of me. Her catch was swinging at her side, dribbles of blood falling to the earth. 'Someone has to hunt them. I shot it for you.'

'No, you didn't.'

Her crazy mood, the gun, the entire incident had unnerved and saddened me. We climbed back towards the town without having reached the river, me dragging my feet, tongue-tied. I didn't know what to say. I didn't know how to placate her, or clear the atmosphere between us. She was my friend and I didn't want to lose her. 'Sylvie, Sylvie, I'm sorry . . . I – I'll take the rabbit, if you like. Mamma can cook it.'

I intended to bury it beneath one of the boulders at the side of the lane on the plateau on my way home.

She swung back to face me, glaring angrily into my eyes. 'You know, Sara, you should be more grateful.'

'Grateful?'

She flung the creature at my feet and flounced off. I stared at it, its red-speckled flank, and tears streamed down my face.

17

Glorious spring days stretching out, unfolding one into the next, soft and warm and radiant. I was still shaken by the incident with Sylvie, which I hadn't got to grips with – the irrationality of her mood swing, the unkindness – so I was keeping my own company, preferring not to be led astray or get involved in any further confrontation. Albert had promised to take me fishing but he'd been swept up by his mother, and buried under kilos of laundry. I'd delivered Hanna and Daniel back to Frau Lindemann, had shopped for them and Mamma, washed up after our lunch – we'd eaten a plate of onions and dumplings together – and now I was in limbo, contemplating how to fritter away the rest of my afternoon. My parents were indoors.

I was outside, where sunlight was breaking through the tall trees, bleaching out the shadows along the white house walls and dappling the pathway that led to the gate. I was leaning against the rail of the upper step of the concrete staircase, monitoring a pair of birds with yellow flecks under their wings and on their throats, warblers, flitting back and forth, energetically gathering twigs for a nest at the back of the house. I guessed that it was in one of the larches, but I wasn't sure.

Deciding to investigate, I jogged down the steps and shouldered my way through the thorny growth to penetrate the depths of the garden. It was a larger space than I had originally estimated, with all kinds of hidden nooks and recesses. I almost walked into an impressive antique iron table. Oval, once green but the paint had flaked, leaving it to rust. It had been pushed tight up against the thick trunk of an elephantine fig tree. I'd seen plenty of them down at the coast. I threw my head backwards and scanned its branches, in search of the nesting birds. Through the boughs I glimpsed patches of sky so blue, a sparkling sapphire, almost indecent in its extravagance, in tune with so much else here: Sylvie and her escapades; life lived to the extreme, as though there was not a moment to waste. I recalled Papa's words to Mamma: *We don't know how many summers she has left to her.*

My stomach churned. I had lost sight of the birds.

I counted ten toppled-over chairs, rusting in the undergrowth, a match with the table. I pictured a scene in which the seated diners had been caught off guard, risen suddenly, knocking chairs to the grass in their haste to be gone.

Bad news?

About my feet, dark green shards of glass were embedded in the earth, remnants of broken champagne bottles. Parties? Friends gathered together for laughter and happiness? Sunday lunches? An interrupted meal? The outbreak of war?

I remembered the toys I'd found upstairs in our dining room. A family with children. How many? A large family? Who had slept in my room? Each item was a trace, a testimony to the lives of the true occupants of this house, savouring their summer days in the alpine heights, entertaining family and friends before they had been obliged to pack and leave.

Rather like us, although not like us at all.

I tried to imagine what they looked like. How their existences had been. I longed to see their faces, to give life to the phantoms. I was suddenly curious to know everything about the house we were living in and the family who owned it.

Deep within the tangled scrub I stumbled across a narrow pathway, concealed from the light, paved with big slabs of stone, green and slippery with moss. I pushed my way through the brambles to see where it led. It divided off in several directions. One path took me to a water-sodden hut, sinking beneath the weight of dereliction. When I touched it, its planks fell loose.

Later we put those planks to good use.

Another trail led me back to the house, to a rear entrance I hadn't been aware of. The door was locked, held fast by an immense padlock. The two panes of glass in the upper half were so grimy I couldn't see through them. Suddenly I longed to get inside, yes, to trespass, to make myself acquainted with the family in whose home we were residing. Did they know we were here? Did the rent Papa paid each month arrive in their bank account in Cannes or England with never a thought given to the identity of the sender? Were they aware that their tenants were immigrants?

I had a million questions. I made my way around the exterior of the house with some difficulty due to the sheer tenacity of the vegetation, scanning for a point of entry.

My parents, barely more than a few feet above, would be beside themselves with rage if they could see me. But I couldn't resist the temptation.

There was a cherry tree to the right of the house: the side less visible from the lane, which was useful. It grew in front of a small window where one of the two panes was cracked, the other broken. The window was high, a good arm's stretch beyond my reach: even on tiptoe, I couldn't see in. I made several attempts to scale the cherry tree, but it was hopeless, dangerous. I slipped and almost twisted my ankle.

I retraced my steps to the rear garden, to the table and the fallen chairs. They were solid iron. I staggered back with one and wedged it between the tree and the broken window.

The aperture, once I had carefully knocked in the broken glass, was a tight squeeze to pass through. I tore my shirt and grazed the underside of my left arm. It stung and drew a few drops of blood, but nothing to fuss about. Once through the window, I jumped to the tomette-tiled floor, now spangled with glass shards, and found myself in a compact, high-ceilinged cloakroom. The door was closed. I panicked, praying it had not been locked on the far side, or I would have foolishly trapped myself inside. I had not thought this through, for if the window was my only exit I had no means of climbing back up to reach it. The lavatory was positioned too far from the window for me to catapult myself from its seat. So, too, the washbasin.

The tap in the basin resisted my turning until it eventually squeaked and released a trickle of rusty water, which I used to sluice the blood from my arm. A mouldy old towel was on hand to act as a dressing.

I turned the handle of the door and it opened. Relief. I stepped out of the cloakroom into a bowl of darkness that reeked of mildew. A house shuttered and locked with no light entering except through the small space I had breached. I needed a candle, a match, a discreet form of lighting. A beam that would not betray my presence. My heart was pounding. Common sense told me to turn back, to get out of the house before I caused an accident or chanced upon something ghastly – who knew what? Decomposing rodents, or worse? But before I left I wanted to provide myself with a means of entering and exiting this ground-floor level with ease. Then I could come back if I wanted to. If I had the courage to steal back in.

There had to be a key secreted somewhere safe. A spare set. Didn't all households have one? In Poland, we had kept the extra bunch in a dresser in the kitchen.

My sight was adjusting to the gloom. Objects were taking shape. I was trying to work out the geography of the lower floor, taking as a plan the layout upstairs and the angle from which I had entered the house. I was in a corridor that led from front to back. There were doors in the wall opposite and one at the far end to my right. If my sense of direction was accurate, the far door was the back of the house and therefore, possibly, the kitchen lay beyond it. There, I might find matches. And, with luck, a key. There was a light switch to the right of the doorway where I was still standing halfway out of the cloakroom. I hesitated and decided against flicking it. I didn't know the condition of the electricity or the intensity of the light it might give off.

I crept along the corridor towards the room I believed to be the kitchen, pushed the door. It was indeed the kitchen.

Expansive, protected by shutters closed across a huge window, with slender stripes of light coming through the slats. They reached in, like elongated piano keys, across a massive wooden table. I took a step. The room smelt foul, of something rotten. Decaying food? The dreaded rats? I retreated, leaving the door open to circulate air.

Each of the other doors, six in total, revealed spacious rooms. A dining room with a long table, candelabra, three, placed along its centre. A free-standing fan on one of two carvers. I glanced about for a cupboard, sideboard, drawers. If there were candelabra there must be candles and matches or a lighter. A tall armoire against one wall displayed serving dishes, soup tureens, elegant crystal glasses, plates facing outwards, like an assembly of full moons. As I stepped, something crunched underfoot. I let out a cry. The darkness was too spooky. I decided to return the following day with my own candles and matches. I could explore when I had light.

I found my way to the front door, unhooked an inner chain and turned the lock. It opened. I could get out but how to find my way back in? A coat stand pushed tight into a corner was heavy with hanging coats and jackets. I pressed my hand against pockets, searching. Two umbrellas were hooked over one of the stand's wooden branches. Burberry raincoats, walking shoes. Leather boots. Tall black wellingtons. Empty pockets save for leather gloves, woollen scarves. A printed silk scarf that exuded faint draughts of an expensive scent. A favourite of the lady of the house? There was a drawer. I pulled at it. It rattled. Keys. A set of keys. Jackpot! I jingled them through my fingers, slipped one into the front door. It slid in comfortably and turned. I had my key.

18

I decided that it would be imprudent to borrow matches from our kitchen. Mamma would notice. She might be depressed but she didn't miss a trick. So, next day, after another radiant sunny morning spent in the square with Hanna and Daniel, I requested two boxes and another of candles at the provision store off the main square. The old woman with the berry eyes, whose name was Marie, nodded a warm greeting as I entered. Ahead of me was a whiskered fellow in beret and blue labourer's jacket. Maurice I'd seen him about often enough. He was delivering garlands of onions and several large jugs of honey. His face was scored with lines and a salt-and-pepper moustache. I waited while he counted aloud the centimes needed to purchase a bottle of pastis. He said to Marie, 'News in yet?'

She nodded.

'Give us it, then, while you're at it.' He threw a half-glance over his shoulder to where I was waiting beside a crate of unripe tomatoes. 'Just a girl,' he muttered under his breath. Clear enough, though, for my sharp hearing to catch the exchange.

Marie handed him a copy of *Le Figaro*. So sleight of hand was she, I almost missed her slip something inside the folded newspaper as she passed it to him.

The old codger coughed his thanks and left, newspaper under his arm, bottle of spirit and burning fag clutched between his fingers.

86

'Problems with the electricity in that house?' Marie quizzed me. Her voice was high-pitched, a little reedy, as though it was slowly wearing out. I shook my head guiltily. 'No, not at all. I . . . I like to read in bed far too late,' I lied, 'and I don't want to disturb my parents.'

Did I imagine how she looked at me? Disbelieving me? Why would she doubt me? It was my guilt playing tricks on me.

'I'll take a copy of today's newspaper too.'

She studied me with her brown probing eyes, then peeled the newspaper from the pile and handed it across to me. 'Anything else, young missy?'

I hesitated, dying to ask the question, then shook my head.

Everyone in this town seemed eager to acquaint themselves with the business of us foreigners. Yet they were guarding secrets of their own, or it was certainly looking that way.

As I crossed the main square, two Italian police officers were nailing pamphlets to the trunks of several of the plane trees. Notice of the next weekend's dance? A small crowd was gathering. I paused to see what the fuss was about.

16 April 1943
An edict from Nice

1. *A curfew is to be imposed. Each night from eleven p.m. until four the following morning.*
2. *No travel allowed without current identity papers. Anyone found beyond their declared place of residence without up-to-date papers – stamped 1943 – will be arrested.*

Today was the twenty-first, so the notice had taken several days to reach our secluded hamlet. A handful of villagers were gathering either side of me, vociferous in their cursing of these new developments, including several of the old crows, whose rasping voices were raised in outrage. They were beckoning others to come and read for themselves and calling the news across to neighbours supping away the afternoon outside Pascal's bar. One old-timer, his glass of *violet* – pastis and lavender syrup – still in his hand, had risen to his feet and was haranguing a young Italian, spitting fire at him as he was packing his hammer and nails into a small tin box. The Italian ignored the tirade.

I was not clear why the Vésubais folk were so up in arms. They all possessed valid papers. The first paragraph would not affect Mamma and me greatly. We were indoors from early evening, never venturing out after dark, but what about Papa and his clandestine visits to the sick? Or those who came knocking in the dead of night, seeking his help? But what was of even greater concern was the second paragraph. No movement permitted without identity cards and the cards needed to be stamped with this year's date, 1943. Without them, there could be no travel.

No attempted escapes.

We lacked them.

The daily prattle from the old girls provided me with useful titbits, most of which I kept tight to my chest, fearing to unsettle my family further.

Barbed-wire fences were being constructed around a huge swathe of the *maralpin* zone, in the areas up behind Nice. Were we being walled in? Was this the decision of the Italian 4th Army? Or Nazi Germany? A vast open-air prison?

Other new laws had been passed. Only local inhabitants were allowed to swim in the sea. Was that because the Italians or, worse, the Germans feared we'd reach the coast and escape from the beaches? Swim to Africa or from the shore to clandestine vessels? I remembered Henryk's wife and hoped she had managed to board a boat for her new life.

No photography in sensitive areas. Albert told me that a young Frenchman, not from this village, had been sentenced to twelve days in prison for photographing his sister at a railway station.

Our chances of getting out of here, of moving on, were rapidly fading. Our liberties were being squeezed tighter, millimetre by millimetre, one day at a time. Papa's hopes would be dashed. Without valid documents, we were little better than prisoners. We could not voyage anywhere beyond this village.

The noose was tightening. It was madness to try to get away.

19

The sky was blue and gold. It was Sunday. I was up early, gazing out of the window. Before leaving the house, I laid the table for my parents, scribbled them a note and then I set off, running all the way to town. The church bells were chiming – on and on they pealed. I pretended it was in my honour: 9 May. Today was my seventeenth birthday. It felt important, a milestone. I was a young woman and still alive. I could marry, bear children. It was a long, long way since 1926, the year I had been born in our first-floor apartment in Lodz.

'I am grown up now, almost an adult, and yet . . .'

I spent my morning with the Lindemann two, preparing their breakfast. Soft-boiled eggs, one each. They slurped warm milk and ate Louis's freshly baked bread – the village still had supplies of wheat, which were diminishing but the warehouses were not bare – while their mother slept. Or, rather, she tossed and turned. I could hear her sighs, her restlessness through the walls of the cramped apartment. Her husband confided that she was suffering from bad nightmares, which prevented her from sleeping soundly.

'She never stops fearing for our future.' He sighed, out of earshot of the children. 'Doesn't want this one born in France.'

I dared not mention the new laws. In any case, he must have heard about them.

Even though it was Sunday, Herr Lindemann went off

to work soon after I arrived. Back in his Berlin life, he had been trained as some kind of technical engineer, Hanna had told me. I didn't know what work he was engaged in here. Factory employment, of some sort. Curious, though, that he was called in on a Sunday.

After Hanna and I had washed and stacked the dishes, I dressed the children, gathered up their outdoor jackets, a small rubber ball and a gourd made into a rattle, and we set off downhill into the centre. I had promised Herr Lindemann I'd return with ingredients for chicken soup, if we could find any. I'd make a broth for his sickly wife. Little Daniel was in his pushchair. His sister walked alongside me, erect, correct, holding the handlebar or clasping one of my hands in hers.

In the fresh morning light, she and I were identifying objects along the street. The passing flagstones, the cobbles, the shutters on the windows, their locks, the names of the shops, their trades, which were declared on hand-painted wooden signs: hosiery, wine merchant, horse butcher, pharmacy. I was pointing out each to Hanna while spelling out their French names. In turn, she gave it back to me in German. House, *la maison, das Haus*.

Horse, *le cheval, das Pferd*.

Slowly, brick by brick, we were building our methods of communication with one another and I was thoroughly enjoying it.

The sun was shining. Groups of the Italian soldiers were gathered outside the Hôtel des Alpes. Their trestle tables had been folded away, the column of refugees dispersed. They were kicking their heels as though waiting for some entertainment to buck up the day. It was at that moment that a cry of '*Attenzione*, let us pass, please!' drew the scrutiny of all in the square. A short squat man was being marched to the Hôtel des Alpes. He was escorted on either side by an Italian soldier. I gasped when I recognized him. He was the man I'd stood behind in Marie's shop. Everywhere fell silent, save for the calls of birds in the trees and glasses being plonked on tables. Pascal appeared at his café door, watching with a solemn expression.

Was Maurice under arrest? It certainly looked that way.

I caught sight of Sylvie passing among the clusters of soldiers, dallying, drawing attention to herself before she entered the lobby. Heads turned. Several men whistled at her. She stepped inside so speedily and without a glance in our direction. It bruised me that our friendship had soured. But what of Maurice, the old farmer? His head was bowed now. Was he being handcuffed? I couldn't see clearly. Too many passers-by.

Hanna caught me staring.

'Soldiers,' I said, '*les soldats, die Soldaten.*'

I would have liked to tell Sylvie that it was my birthday, a special one at that, to sing it to the bright blue day. I wondered where Albert might be. Perhaps, later, we could go for a walk together to the river. Thomas was serving in the bar: in and out with trays of drinks, non-stop, dodging by his father, who stood, like an obelisk, in the doorway taking stock of the goings-on. His establishment was doing a roaring trade – war was profitable – but all eyes were trained upon the neighbouring hotel.

Hanna, Daniel and I promenaded the square twice more – I was keen to get a clearer picture of the incident taking place. A senior officer had appeared, not the *capitano*. At the sight of him, Pascal slung his apron onto one of his tables and, full of purpose, advanced upon the proceedings. After several minutes of heated discussion and raised voices, Maurice was released. Pascal's arm across the older man's shoulders, they aimed for the bar where Maurice, eyes cast downwards, was served a strong shot of liquor.

His captors glanced about the square, then disappeared inside the hostelry.

We collapsed onto a bench near one of the fountains. Peasant women dressed in their Sunday outfits with small lacy bonnets, oblivious to the disruption that had just taken place, were passing through the oak door of the lovely baroque church, pausing to make conversation with their neighbours, waving to friends, clutching their prayer books and rosary beads. I envied them their sense of belonging.

'Sara? Sara?' Hanna was tugging at my arm, confused by my distraction.

'Birthday,' I blurted eventually, putting on a smile, not wishing to alarm her, *'l'anniversaire,'* pointing at myself. Hanna beat at her own chest and gave me the words, *'frische Kleidung.'*

'Was ist das? Yes, you have clean clothes. I was trying to tell you that it's my birthday.'

She nodded and stabbed at herself again.

'Yours too? No, I don't think so.'

We shrugged and giggled shyly, companionably. I tuned in to the flow of water gushing from the fountains as I rolled Daniel's pushchair back and forth, still puzzled by the incident I had just witnessed.

I was recalling the slip of paper Marie had furtively passed to Maurice.

From somewhere beyond the centre of town, beyond this market square, came the distant clop of horses, wooden wheels rolling. The carts were transporting farmers to the fields in the valleys below. Work didn't stop for their Sabbath. Neither, it seemed, did the hostilities.

Most of the local children, those over twelve years old at least, had been earmarked for land labour. A few were lending their strength to the family rural enterprises because their fathers and uncles were absent. Rather like Albert assisting his mother with the laundry. The men had gone to battle, had been taken prisoner, or were living underground in the *maquis*. It was a town devoid of virile young men, except for the Italians. Were those who remained behind fighting this war on their own terms? Breaking curfew, assisting escapees ... What offence could Maurice, a harmless beekeeper and vegetable grower, possibly have committed to warrant arrest?

I caught sight of Monsieur Decroix, who had turned up – I hadn't seen where from – on the café terrace. He was deep in conversation with Pascal, or was nodding, listening, placating Pascal as the bartender waved his arms, gesticulating furiously. After a final mollifying word to Maurice, the lieutenant hurried across the square to his wife, who was waiting outside the church in conversation with a group of other female parishioners. I had hardly ever exchanged a sentence with her, the headmistress at the local primary school, though I would have liked to. She was always on the go, haring to and fro, occupied: a small, wiry figure, rather muscular, with a head of dark chestnut hair. A glance in our direction, she caught my eye and waved to me. Then, after a brief nod to her husband, she bustled over to where we were sitting.

'Sara, yes?'

I confirmed it.

'Philippe tells me you speak excellent French. Can you

read it as well?' she called, as she approached, wasting not a second.

I assured her that I could.

'And you can also write in French?'

I nodded.

'That is very useful indeed. Come and see me tomorrow, will you, please? After you've finished with the tots. Philippe says you're doing wonders with them. Well done.'

I watched her as she strode back to her husband, lifting her hand acknowledging neighbours as she passed. What could she possibly want with me?

The following midday, alone with Madame Decroix in her school, she gave me a written test, which I passed, she claimed, with flying colours. 'Your grammar is almost perfect. Almost. We will work on the faults, but you need to expand your mind, challenge your literary experience, try to glean as much as you can of French manners and history. Our way of life, Sara. Take it all in.' She pressed upon me a stack of books. I carried them home, thrilled by the prospect of the universes she was tendering up to me.

She was a lovely lady, younger than Mamma, with her hair pinned neatly into curls, always elegant in brightly coloured cotton dresses that she proudly claimed she had 'run up' herself. Dresses with buttons all the way down the front. So many buttons! So much passionate energy.

And she loved children. She suggested that I teach Hanna to read simple French texts.

'In fact, why not bring the Lindemann twosome to school in the mornings? It will help you to integrate too, not be such a loner, Sara, help you become a part of our community. Play your role. Which are your favourite subjects? What would you like to do with your life when this war is over?'

I hadn't been drilled with so many questions, such important questions, for a long time, an eternity: since our lives in Poland. I had stopped asking them of myself. I shook my head, proffering no answers.

'How old are you, Sara?'

'Seventeen,' I proclaimed proudly. 'Yesterday.' I had told someone. At last.

'How would you fancy teaching with me, assisting me?' she encouraged. 'I am juggling two classes on my own right now and your contribution could be a huge asset.'

I stared at Madame Decroix in disbelief. I couldn't credit my good fortune. I had to fight with myself not to throw my arms into the air and hug her

20

After Madame Decroix's proposal I got into the habit of climbing out of bed before daybreak, and hurrying from the house well before the appointed hour. How I relished my early-morning walks. Being outside, eclipsed by the magnitude of the mountains, put our concerns on a different level, a more even keel. The natural world, vast and inexhaustible, which I had never taken much interest in before, calmed me. Insects, plants, water life: so much vitality thrumming all around me. I began to feel protected, less threatened.

Most importantly, I had been designated a purpose. Me, the assistant teacher. For that special hour, it was as though the world belonged to me. I felt invincible.

On many of those early mornings, I encountered groups of women and boys on their way to the wheatfields or the even longer descent to the vineyards in the lower valleys. Albert promised that if we were still here in the autumn, he'd take me grape-harvesting. I waved to the passers-by and they, in turn, heaved their arms high to acknowledge my greeting. I paused frequently to listen to the birds, attempting to distinguish between one species and another, their calls, their songs.

I was trying to learn the identities and properties of the various plants, too, many of which were coming into flower. Sometimes I'd pick a few blossoms, carry them to school to determine their names. There were wild fruit trees in our garden humming with bees, butterflies aplenty, lavender bushes, ferns, gentians. Everywhere, honey-sweet and wondrous. The light was astonishing as the sun rose from behind the mountain tops, breaking, like a spill of molten gold, all across the land. It was as though the earth was born anew every single morning, and I was a participant in this sacred pageant. It filled me with a sense of belonging even if I knew, deep inside myself, that my charmed existence couldn't last, but it was powerful while it did.

I strode into town, registered with the Italians – I was usually first in the queue. '*Buon giorno, Sara,*' was their greeting, these days. Then I dashed to the baker, queued again and bought two loaves from Louis for the Lindemanns, for which the father never failed to reimburse me. Once the children had eaten their breakfast and I had quickly tidied the flat, we made our way purposefully, excitedly, bristling with different-languages chatter, to the red-roofed brick school. I felt so elated by this opportunity that I determinedly banished all images of the first time I had walked up there with Papa in the dead of night.

The school had been constructed in the middle of a modest fenced-in yard with gravel and tufty grass where the children spent their mid-morning breaks in the fresh air. The grounds were furnished with plenty of swings and wooden benches. These faced south, looking out across the valleys towards a distant horizon.

Inside the classroom, Hanna was allocated a desk of her own. She was thrilled to be given a pencil and blank sheet of paper. Such basics were precious now. Daniel was settled in his pushchair. His sister, alongside him, watched over him, kept his fidgeting to a minimum or sat him on her lap and rocked him to sleep, while I was at the front, assistant to Madame Delphine Decroix, brimming with pride.

Before the surrender of France in June 1940 two teachers had been employed here, Madame Decroix explained during one of the class breaks. Her younger colleague was a Monsieur Joseph Laforet.

'Did he go to fight in the army?' I asked, when she was bemoaning the loss of him and the difficulties of running the place by herself.

'In a manner of speaking.'

I wondered if he had been killed in combat but I sensed by her comportment that it was better not to delve too deeply. She loved to introduce me to myriad new subjects and to help me learn. She respected and encouraged my curiosity. It is a positive quality, she assured me, but she closed like a clam when my questions became personal. During those early weeks, her behaviour frequently bewildered me.

'Due to my staffing difficulties, only one of the two classrooms is operational. I closed off the other,' Madame Decroix explained that first morning.

This meant that the mountain children – of all ages from five to twelve – along with a handful of the offspring of temporary citizens – were bunched together in the one room, which was light and airy with a huge window so it didn't feel quite the crush that it was. We were thirty-seven, excluding Madame Decroix, baby Daniel and me. So, forty souls in total.

'Together, we will be taking the first steps in the process of learning to read. We will all help others younger or less capable than ourselves. Mixing with one another and sharing. These are our goals. Sara here is my new and very capable assistant. You can count on her. Her French is almost as proficient as mine.'

I blushed the colour of a robin's breast.

'Working together, we will each find our own level of competence. Speaking French, attempting to speak French. Our little school welcomes everyone.' This was the 'Wartime Manifesto of Delphine Decroix', or so she jokingly called it.

21

Classes were held in the mornings, from nine till noon.

Madame Decroix and I perched at the front on two tall stools, sharing her high desk. On the second morning, quite out of the blue, she put me in the spotlight: 'Sara, tell us about Poland. Paint us pictures, take us into your life.'

I was thrown off guard. Disconcerted. 'I . . .'

'Describe to us the countryside near where you lived. Or was your home in a town, or the capital city? Who knows the capital city of Poland?'

Heads shook and faces stared in bewilderment.

I looked out at the sea of puzzled children. How many of them had even heard of Poland? What a great distance from here it was to me now.

'Sara, the capital, please?'

'Warsaw,' I replied, 'but centuries ago it was Kraków.'

'Good girl. Do you want to describe how you and your family spent your days? What was your favourite pastime and which hobbies did you enjoy during your weekends?'

I swallowed hard. This was painful. A wound reopening. The only news my father had received from Poland was that the Jews had been rounded up and placed in fenced ghettos, patrolled by German soldiers. I had been attempting for more than three years to close my heart to Before.

The children were wide-eyed, hooked, full of anticipation and interest as I, heart in my mouth, attempted to speak.

'We . . . we are not from Warsaw but from the outskirts of Lodz, a city in the centre of the country. It has dense construction, many factories, unlike here . . .'

Suddenly, bursting into my mind's eye, I saw the flower vendors, with their broad grins, broken teeth, saucy chat, hawking their posies, knife-grinders, tinkers playing barrel organs or hurdy-gurdies churning out sentimental tunes. I bit into the fleshy cherries washed by my mother, bleeding juice down my chin, staining my blouse. Stout ripe apples laid out in a porcelain dish shaped like . . . What was it? Oh, yes, a boat. Weekend walks in the blinding heat of summer with my school friends along the banks of the river, berry-picking in the lanes beyond the city, jam-making, the autumn winds that whipped through the fruit farms, causing havoc with the pulpy-sweet, overripe pears. Vaulting fences, scooping up the fruits that had split open as they dropped to the grass in the meadows. That rich pear perfume sticky on my fingers. The winding rivers of the past, the waterways, boats.

Until today, I had bleached all colour out of those memories. Unlike Mamma, I remembered in monochrome: stilted grey images, if at all.

Lodz. I had all but eradicated its existence.

'Lodz means "boat". It's the symbol of the city. We used to have eighteen rivers and streams in and around our city, but they were filled in due to settling sediment.'

I pictured again the white steam billowing out of the factory chimneys.

My sense buds inhaled, for the first time in three years, the aromas of dark fresh bread, salted herrings, chicken soup, seeping through the open kitchen window. Mamma, always indoors at her stove cooking, waiting for my return from school.

My school, my tiny bedroom, friends whose names I could barely recall. Lotte had been my best friend. Where was she now? I closed my eyes for a second, trying to visualize her. I hadn't clapped eyes on Lotte in almost five years.

There were so many people, relatives I never thought of because it stabbed my heart to recall their open faces and the Friday-night meals we had enjoyed together, aunts, uncles, cousins, of whose destinies we had lost track. The Lodz ghetto had been established, Papa told us, in one of the northern sectors of the city soon after the Germans had arrived with their tanks and taken control of our homeland.

Late 1939, September. Who had survived?

We had got out, escaped by horse-drawn cart one dawn morning from a small village where we had been lying low in a farmhouse about a hundred kilometres from the German frontier. From there – I could not recall the name of the hamlet, if I had ever known it – we boarded a train that took us to the border. From then on, every step of our journey had been life-threatening.

Still, we were fortunate. There were many who had not made it. And there were others who had just disappeared, no one knew to where . . .

My eyes were misty, flickering, flashing weird shapes and colours. A sea of faces was staring upwards in my direction, full of expectation, some perplexed. Madame Decroix leaned in towards me and laid her hand over my bunched fist. Her skin was surprisingly rough. 'If it's too difficult . . .'

'Too many stories to recount,' I muttered. 'Events to bear witness to.'

Where to begin to describe our lives preceding this

peripatetic quartet of years, before the statelessness, the ragged recollections?

'Do you have cows in Poland, miss?' one scruffy-haired lad shouted, butting in from a desk at the back of the class. I recognized him as one of the boys who frequently rode in a cart to distant olive groves with his grandfather. His name was Olivier. He had an older brother, thin-as-a-bone Thierry, who was judged a 'simpleton'.

Several of Olivier's contemporaries shrieked with laughter, lifting the mood. Madame Decroix softly chided Olivier for interrupting, then invited him to come up to the blackboard to draw us a cow. His calloused hands worked fast and with proficiency. It was a splendid illustration, a very identifiable likeness, with stomach and udders and haunches. The cow's flanks were patched with clouds of white, which Olivier had filled in, back and forth with the scratchy stick of chalk. His classmates applauded him and shoved their arms into the air, requesting to draw other examples of French rural living.

'I've seen an ibex when I was out hunting with my papa.'

'There are wolves across the border in Italy, miss. They eat our sheep if they come over our way.'

'Everything from Italy is dangerous. My papa said so. I miss my papa.'

'My brother fought a wolf singlehanded,' yelled Olivier, above the din of voices.

'That's not true. Who, Thierry? *Il est fou comme un balai.* Daft as a brush, don't listen to him.'

'That's enough shouting for this morning, please.'

Anybody who so wished it, announced Madame Decroix – 'one at a time, please, no more talking over one another,' she emphasized – was invited to step forward to write on the blackboard the word 'cow' in their native language and alongside it in French.

La vache, les vaches. Gleeful screeches of triumph from the classroom.

'You begin, Sara. Cow and its plural, cows.'

I jumped down from my stool, grabbed the chalk, and scrawled the words *krowa, i krowy.* It occurred to me then that I had not written any Polish in a long while. Only at home with my parents did I converse in my mother tongue. The novels I read were in French. I was even beginning to dream in French. This realization pleased me. I liked being French. It was a safer skin to inhabit.

22

As I was crossing the square, Thomas signalled me over to the café, which was bustling with lunchtime diners, predominantly Italians. 'We're going to the river to swim,' he called, untying his apron, splotched with wine stains. 'Wanna come along?'

It was a sunny afternoon, bursting with a golden light. I hesitated. I couldn't swim, but I would enjoy the company. At that moment, Albert came steaming up beside me. 'Sylvie's on her way,' he announced. 'Said to wait for her. Sara, you coming with us?'

You should be more grateful.

Sylvie and I hadn't exchanged a word since the incident with the gun and the rabbit.

I couldn't swim and I possessed no bathing suit. I couldn't face being Sylvie's laughing-stock.

'Better not,' I mumbled, thrusting my hands into my skirt pockets. The key to the lower apartment of the white house was there. I kept it always in my possession even if I hadn't used it since my first trespass. I fingered its metal contours, warmed by my body heat. It would be cool there. 'I have to . . . help my mother. Maybe next time. Thanks for the invitation, though.'

In the far corner of the Allinghams' drawing room was a splendid grand piano. How Papa loved to play. He would have welcomed the use of it. The lid was closed. I rubbed away the dust with the sleeve of my cardigan and then, ceremoniously, opened it. Back in Poland, Papa had taught me a few basic chords. Could I remember them? I was itching to run my fingers along the keyboard, press individual keys, grant the instrument voice. My hands dangled in the air. I dared not. The notes might give away my presence.

Placed on top of the piano, a candelabrum. It held six half-burned white candles. When had they last been lit? This candle-holder was identical to the trio on the table in the dining room. A set of four, then, ornate silver.

I lit one candle – only one, to make them last and to avoid over-illuminating the crepuscular space – firing it from the box of matches I had purchased a few weeks earlier at Marie's. My own box of candles I secreted later that afternoon in the master bedroom beneath Mr and Mrs Allingham's double bed.

I watched the flame flicker and glow. It delivered a soft circle of light and a whiff of sulphur to this far corner of the drawing room. I looked about me before returning my attention to the piano.

Built into the wall closest to where I was standing was a large open fireplace. In its hearth lay the remnants of charcoaled logs, ashes, flakes of bark. A lingering, slightly vinegary smell of stale smoke, trapped in the room, hung about the chimney breast. Atop the mantelpiece were dotted a few items including two framed photographs, an opened packet of Craven 'A' with four cigarettes remaining. I slid one from its red box and fitted it between my fingers. It smelt sweet, not unpleasant. I lifted it to my lips and feigned smoking it, inhaling, exhaling, in the room's stale air. Then I laid the cigarette back on the mantelpiece, not in the box, wondering whether at some later stage I might dare to smoke it. I decided that, yes, I might.

One day, not today. Alongside it, a golden brooch set with diamonds and pearls, delicately fashioned into the shape of a bumble bee. It was exquisite. I held it gently, cradled in the palm of my hand as though it were a living organism. It weighed no more than a few grams. I longed for it to raise its golden membraned wings and fly, to claim its liberty beyond these walls. I was sorely tempted to keep it, to slip it under my pillow for good luck, but that was wrong. I could be caught out.

And I meant no harm in here.

There was a wondrous collection of nineteen framed photographs on top of the piano. Silver frames and tortoiseshell, of assorted sizes. A story in still-life images of the lives of the true occupants of this white house. I picked up the one nearest to me and studied it, drawing it closer to the candle flame. In black and white, the head and shoulders of a woman in a strappy dress or blouse smiling broadly, open lipsticked mouth, her attention off to the right of the lens. She was beautiful, vivacious with glossy hair that fell in waves to the base of her pale neck. She was wearing small diamond earrings and a pearl necklace. One hand, her left, with its wedding and engagement rings, was curled tight to the necklace as though she were caressing it.

Each photograph in turn I lifted from its dusty resting place, giving every detail my full attention. Running my nail-bitten fingers across the grubby glass of each, smearing it. There was a fine collection of images of the same woman. She featured in ten of the pictures on display. In two she was standing beside a tall, lean gentleman, who was sporting a tweed suit with a V-necked pullover beneath the jacket, smoking a pipe, in another with an arm resting on her shoulders.

Here, they were again, the pair of them, in white tennis clothes this time – she in a short pleated skirt, he in shorts – posing in front of a very splendid motor car with an open top. Another was a profile of the man sitting in a high-backed rattan chair in a manicured garden with tropical plants. I supposed they were Mr and Mrs Allingham, husband and wife. They seemed to inhabit such glamorous lives, full of *élan* and euphoria.

So very different from ours.

There was a snapshot of a small baby with a full head of fluffy pale hair caught on camera, naked but for a nappy, crawling across a neatly mown lawn. I could not imagine it to be this garden. Another frame, of the same growing boy, more mature, two years old possibly, a similar age to Daniel Lindemann. Had the toys and jigsaw puzzles I'd discovered upstairs and delivered to the Lindemanns belonged to this toddler? Had he accidentally broken the wheel off his train? Had he cried and his mother calmed him?

I replaced the last of the photographs and levered the candle with the utmost care from its holder. With the glow from the orb, I roamed from room to room.

In the master bedroom there was a capacious double bed, with a collection of cream silk cushions at its head. A fitted wardrobe, doors left partially open, revealed racks of clothes and squads of shoes, all lined up neatly.

This lady's feet were far daintier than mine or I would have slipped my clodhopping hoofs into a pair or two of her high heels or satiny, strappy evening slippers. There was a very splendid jacket, all sparkles with a Lanvin label. I dared myself to hoist down one of the many frocks from its hanger, but I had only one free hand and could not secure the candle anywhere with safety.

From above, beyond the ceiling, a volley of voices disturbed my reverie. My heart skipped a beat. My parents: were they arguing again? Were they calling for me? I hurried back to the drawing room, *le salon*, replaced the candle in its holder and blew it out. It was shorter than the others now, of course. I made a mental note to burn a different one on each visit. Just in case. Wax was hardening on my fingers and nails because I had moved too fast, too clumsily.

I had swept up the broken glass in the cloakroom and boarded the window with a flimsy plank I'd found in the garden. My handiwork was rough and of a temporary fashion but it would prevent rats or cats or anything else from entering. And it allowed me to feel less vulnerable to intrusion, when I was holed-up inside, stealing these illicit hours in the company of my invisible hosts.

23

The afternoons had always been mine to squander as I pleased. Soon after noon, I would deliver the Lindemann infants back to Ilse, and once I had recounted any events from our school mornings, moments that might cheer her, I'd set off for anywhere I fancied.

Delphine Decroix – we were on first-name terms now – sometimes invited me back to her house for a 'bite of lunch'. The portions on offer were modest. Everybody was heedful of the threat of worsening rationing even here in this rich agricultural *terroir* where seasonal choices were still available.

'We are paying scrupulous attention, tracking as far as possible, the expansion of the Germans across our Free Zone, stockpiling all that we can in preparation for their . . .' she let out a low moan '. . . their arrival.'

'But they will never come to this remote spot, will they?'

'Probably not. And if all goes according to plan, the Allies will land first . . . It's what we're working towards. Winning this endless war.'

The Decroix family had a smallholding of their own, with geese, chickens, several goats, two donkeys and a horse. The great barn behind the school, where the Polish-man had died, was theirs too. I wondered if Delphine knew about that night, but I would never mention it. They also owned a few acres of land with a large vegetable plot somewhere outside the village. Delphine regularly donated a jug of milk to the Lindemanns. It was kind of her to share with them and feed me.

'How can you track the Germans' advance?' I asked her.

In Delphine's kitchen there was a wireless. Like a large polished box, it stood high on a shelf behind the table where we ate our lunch. Sometimes, because we were so far inland and surrounded by mountains, the reception was crackly and indistinct with too much background noise and static.

'*La guerre des ondes*.' The battle of the radio waves. 'Philippe gives it a good shake.'

Even when we were discussing serious matters, she left the wireless playing softly in the background. Mostly the broadcasts were music. French singers, dance bands. We were tuned to Radio-Montpellier. The singer was a Parisian, Maurice Chevalier. 'He's very popular here. A film star. He has a villa down on the coast near Cannes in La Bocca. Many . . . friends stay there.'

'Your friends or famous friends?'

She didn't elucidate.

'Film-star friends, Delphine?' I insisted.

'Some are Jewish friends.'

I stared at her, confused.

'No more questions.'

Moving on, she confided that in the evenings she and Philippe frequently listened to broadcasts from Britain when they could pick up the signal. Radio-Londres. These coded messages had become more essential to the mountain enclave since the Germans had breached the territory agreement and crossed into the Free Zone.

Delphine's comments had put me back on my guard. The old terror had snapped, like a trap, back into life. 'Are we still safe here?'

'Don't be afraid, Sara. The enemy is still many kilometres away. Even so we can never be too careful. We must be vigilant, *Nous devons être sur nos gardes.*'

'If not the enemy, then who are we on our guard against?'

'*Il est plus sage, Sara, de toujours garder nos pensées pour nous,*' she warned.

This was Delphine, always determined to maintain a level of secrecy.

The Italian occupation had expanded. Every day the region was becoming more controlled, with the curfew now extended to six in the morning. Even so, I was unsure why she was so cautious, so circumspect. The Germans or Italians wouldn't harm her. It was us they were after. Why would the enemy take an interest in Delphine and her family?

Because a refugee had died in her barn?

Equally I was never quite sure for what reason Delphine invited me to spend so much time in her company. There were days when, rather selfishly, I itched to be out of doors, wandering the hills with Albert and the rest of the gang. Sylvie too. I missed having a girlfriend. I had enjoyed being part of the crowd though I had never confided to them anything about my private hours in the home of the Allinghams or my conversations with Delphine. Some reflex told me that I must keep these secrets to myself. Confidentiality, as Delphine advised.

You could never be sure who was listening, who was talking.

24

Now that the days were warming up, tribes of folk were traipsing back and forth to the river to swim. Albert appeared frequently outside the school gates, waiting for me.

'Are you going to come swimming when you've dropped them off?' He had begun badgering me about why I never accompanied him and his pals on these outings.

Eventually, I admitted that I had no costume and no money to purchase one.

The very next day, Sylvie turned up at Pascal's bar where we'd rendezvous on the terrace at lunchtimes, drinking lemonades. Or local beer for the boys.

'Hello, Sara, where have you been hiding?' Her light lavender scent engulfed me as she leaned in and brushed my cheek with a soft kiss. 'Look what I brought you.' She thrust a used brown paper bag into my hands.

'What is it?' For one moment, a shudder of fear. A joke at my expense?

'Open it, silly. I've got two more so I won't miss it.'

The bathing suit was cobalt, as blue as the sky. A little long in the body and baggy but I was overjoyed. 'Oh, Sylvie,' I jumped to my feet and hugged her so tightly, her lipstick smudged along my arm. '*Merci*.'

She brushed aside my display of thanks. '*Allons-y*, let's go.'

They sang rowdily, popular *chansons*, as we hiked along the tracks, passing goats and sometimes herders, throwing stones at thin brown vipers, imitating bird calls, plunging to the river, to the Swimming Hole.

Sylvie and I were friends again. She took my hand and led me along the bank far from where the boys were diving off the rocks, a few of them naked, most in their underwear. From there, she guided me to a calm, still pool, the Swimming Hole, where the water was crystal clear. A perfect spot for me to paddle. Reeds and long skinny plants with quite sharp leaves were growing at its shoreline. Massive round boulders fortressed the bank. Behind these we could conceal ourselves, create our own private *vestiaire*, changing room, where we slipped off our clothes without embarrassment and stepped into our swimsuits.

Albert was never among the peeping Toms, he was always respectful, nor Thomas, who was, in his way, quite shy and always kind. It was some of the other lads, the more extrovert fellows, who were the cheeky ones. They'd venture up to the Swimming Hole and crouch in the bushes to spy on us girls, whistling and calling until Sylvie threw sticks at them, threatening to snitch on them to her Italian friend if they didn't get lost. 'I'll have you lot arrested!'

Their response was catcalls and whistles until they got bored. Then they'd scoot away and throw themselves into the pool, landing like fallen bombs. Cannonballing, they called it. It was all good-humoured. A time of bonding. Early summer days filled with the exuberant young, for whom war was a distant story. For whom the echoes of their past were not ominous threats.

Liberating their passions was their urgent call.

Back home in Poland, I had never had the opportunity to learn to swim, and since our clandestine night ferry transporting us illegally into France, I feared the unknown depths. Even so, I relished those halcyon afternoons down at the Swimming Hole. Birds wheeling overhead, the plash of limbs penetrating the surface, distant laughter. I paddled at the lagoon's edge while Sylvie glided through the shallows, like a young shark. My gaze followed her every move surreptitiously. I envied her as she streamed through the cool green *mare*.

I used my clothes to dry myself or lounged in the sun, eyes closed, until the warmth had burned the drops off my goose-pimpled skin. Occasionally, a sharp twinge of guilt rippled through me. Did I have any right to feel so carefree?

It was during one of those endlessly lazy afternoons that Sylvie brought up the subject of the rabbit and the gun she'd 'borrowed' from her Italian soldier.

'I never intended to upset you,' she whispered, lips close to my ear. 'You won't tell anyone, will you? It was just a prank. I'd had a row with my friend. I nicked the gun to teach him a lesson, but he didn't even notice it had gone . . .'

I shook my head, sucking at a blade of grass, studying her lovely profile: her long blonde lashes, her soaked locks dripping in runnels off her shoulders; and the extravagant way she smoked her cigarette. In my mind's eye, I was picturing the Craven 'A' packet, recalling the photographs of Mrs Allingham and how utterly glamorous she was. A different kind of beauty, more sophisticated. I felt sure Sylvie was acquainted with the Allinghams. I was bursting to ask, to confide, but I kept my stolen hours in their phantom company tight to my chest.

'When the war's over, Sara, I'm going to run away.'

'Why?' Her remark took me completely by surprise. Who would want to escape this perfect haven?

She claimed it was important to grab life's opportunities.

'Will you elope with your Italian friend?'

Her hoots of laughter sent the wild geese flapping and flying. I was taken aback. We were stretched out on our stomachs, and she rolled over, kicking her legs into the air. 'Of course not.'

'Don't you love him?'

'It's just a fling, Sara. Oh, so sombre Sara. You take everything so seriously.'

'Do I? Oh.'

'There's someone else I fancy much more. He'll be home soon. He's gorgeous. Wait till you meet Alain.'

25

Delphine had two children of her own. Her little girl, Élisabeth, accompanied her hand in hand each morning, up the hill to the school. Élisabeth was Hanna's age, give or take a few weeks. Her brother, Alexandre, was eighteen months old. He was a handful, crawling everywhere, grubby fists on every surface, snatching objects to the floor, rolling, pushing, prodding at them until inevitably they broke, at which point he bawled. I was mighty relieved that Daniel Lindemann was less hard work. Alexandre Decroix required oodles of attention and patience. Carrying him to school and keeping watch over him during the classes would have been an extra strain on Delphine, who was already overstretched, so from nine till two every weekday the baby was minded by a neighbour. This left Delphine free to occupy her time with her pupils.

After class, installed in her kitchen on an ancient milking stool drawn up to the table, while Delphine fried eggs for us both and threw together a salad, she'd invite me to slice the tomatoes, then reward myself with a cold drink – delicious homemade lemonade from lemons that had been harvested from the groves above Menton. Menton was a town bordering Italy, she told me, some three hours' driving distance from where we were now. 'Do you know it?'

I shook my head.

'There's too little petrol available or I would love to take you there. From time to time one of the carts or even a truck will go south to collect fruit. It's an attractive town above the sea.' She added, 'I mention it because from there, Sara, with due care to avoid the border controls, it's possible to cross through the lemon groves into Italy. On occasion, one or other of the farmers' trucks has delivered refugees from here to the border by night, but it's getting more dangerous. They are being watched.'

I lifted my face from my glass, wiped away the fringe of moisture from above my lips. I was recalling Henryk. I pictured Maurice, arrested by the Italians. For breaking curfew, delivering a truckload of refugees to the Italian border? Before I could enquire, my friend raised her hand from the cooking pan where fat was spitting, 'No questions, Sara, you didn't hear that from me.'

'I don't want to be led clandestinely back into Italy,' I said, without thinking.

Delphine scooped up the sizzling eggs and served them onto our two plates. She poured generous quantities of olive oil over the salad.

I was thinking of the banker my father had told me about, who was smuggling refugees out of France. I was trying to tamp down the memories of the terrifying boat journey that had delivered us overnight from northern Italy. The reek of diesel, the swell of waves rising and falling, smacking against the vessel's hull. The eerie midnight silence when the engine was switched off when a security control was close by, when arrest was a razor's edge away. Even after all this time, those evocations made my stomach turn. 'I never want to cross another border illegally. Never. We're safer here, staying put.'

'And we have to keep you safe, Sara.' She stroked my hair. 'We intend to do our very best for you and your parents. That's a promise.'

'No one could do more.' I poured myself another glass

of lemonade. I was dreaming of the sea. I missed the beaches and the coast, with its ravishing sunsets and views to the horizon. Portals to other worlds. 'When the war's over, I'd like to visit Menton with you, stroll quietly in those groves without fear or threat. I'd like to stay here, Delphine, and continue to be your assistant. Perhaps, one day, a teacher at your side.'

'Well, that's a dream worth striving for.'

I glanced up to ascertain whether she really meant it, whether she believed such a harmonious future could come to pass, but revealed in her eyes was such sadness it troubled me. Before I could say another word, she laid a hand over mine and patted it hard.

'Come along, Sara, eat up before it gets cold.'

While I was wiping my plate clean with fresh bread, I broached the subject of our temporary accommodation, the white house. I confided how much I loved living in the middle of nature, with the mountains and birds for neighbours.

'They're English, aren't they? The owners?'

Delphine nodded. 'Very kind people.'

'Did you know them well? Monsieur Decroix mentioned that the house was a summer residence, closed up since they had to leave . . .'

Delphine sensed that I was digging. I was aware by her manner – the brisk gesture when she rose from the table and stepped beyond eye contact to the stove to boil water – that she had no desire to discuss the Allinghams.

I was desperate to interrogate her about the Englishman in his tweed suits, to share with her my adulation of the woman who was so alluring in the photographs, but I knew to bite my tongue. Too much disclosed would reveal my trespassing.

'I know it's not my business but I was wondering why they left?' I pressed.

Delphine slapped her hand against the sideboard. 'Sara, I would have thought by now that you had learned to curb your questions. It is a muscle you really must train. The less we know . . . Wagging tongues cost lives. There are no spies or collaborators in this community, or none that we are aware of, but we can never be too careful.'

I stared at her, recalling the night of Henryk's death, his wife's words. In a building owned by Delphine and her husband.

She swung about to switch off the kettle. 'Well, let's leave that conversation for another day. I've been meaning to lend you these . . .' Now she was stretching for books from a high shelf lined with manuals, maps and paperbacks.

'Both are studies of the geography and history of this region. They include illustrated maps, which are always handy.'

She was changing the subject. The books looked fascinating and I was delighted to have some new reading material.

'Sara, I feel sure I'm being pessimistic, but there may come a day when there's no more we in this village can do for you, when our hands are tied, when you will need an escape route.' She paused, held my gaze, to confirm that I was concentrating.

I felt a rush of cold stab at my heart. 'What makes you say that?'

'Don't be alarmed. You're safe here, but should it ever become necessary, there are two routes from here that climb high into the mountains and from there, after an arduous ascent, cross over into Italy. From Italy, it is

possible to reach Switzerland, neutral territory. These itin-
eraries are considerably more hazardous than the coastal
paths I mentioned near Menton, but it might be beneficial
for you to acquaint yourself with them. They criss-cross
this region of the Alpes-Maritimes, and are rarely trodden
except by local inhabitants or hunters. Perhaps I can persuade one of the older pupils from the school or a farmer's
lad to act as a guide, show you rest stops, areas of danger.
See here,' her finger was tracing a wavy red line drawn
across an open double page, 'less than two days' climbing
and you have passed into Italy. No checkpoints. Here, see,
this is the Col de Fenestre. Follow this hiking path and
you reach the Madone de Fenestre. Where this red dot is,
a very small chapel. On occasion, when a hunter or hiker
loses his way and darkness falls too soon, trapping him, it
has provided overnight shelter.'

I lifted my head, frowning.

'Your French is almost fluent. Sometimes I have to
remind myself that you are not from here. You could fool
almost anyone.'

'Even the Germans?' I scoffed.

'Should it ever prove necessary, I pray so. In any case,
your command of the language can only serve you, Sara.
And these books, encyclopaedic in detail and research,
will offer you a far deeper understanding of our region.
And you won't need to ask me continually which plant is
which.' Delphine winked, lightening the moment. She
slid the hefty publications across the table to where I was
sitting with my freshly made tea. 'Be sure to bring them
back when you have finished with them.'

I promised I would.

'There may come a day, Sara, when such knowledge
proves essential to you. It may save your life.'

26

The river was a charmed kingdom for us young. Our domain. The air was scented with the luxuriant yellow splendour of May and the spiny broom. Richly perfumed rock roses opening their petals in the morning and closing them at night. I could identify them now, having studied Delphine's encyclopaedias.

I was drifting in and out of sleep, dripping wet, sunbathing on the rocks, Sylvie at my side. It was a perfect day until, casually, my companion revealed that she'd heard a rumour.

'What about?' I mumbled, eyes closed.

'Your father working with Monsieur Decroix.'

I felt my spine stiffen.

'Do you know about it, Sara?'

'That's nonsense. Papa's a surgeon. He assists at several of the temporary clinics. Monsieur Decroix's engaged in police work. There's nothing my father could be helping him with.'

I prayed she didn't detect the crack in my voice.

'Monsieur Decroix's the chief of the gendarmerie for our town and for quite a few of the surrounding villages, and he's called out if there are problems with any of the refugees. He's not obliged to obey the curfew. But everyone else is.'

'I don't see what that has to do with my father.'

'Maybe you're asleep and don't hear him leave the house.'

'He doesn't leave the house.' As I denied it, I could hear Papa's footsteps moving down the hall. 'Why are you saying this?'

Sylvie shrugged. 'It's only a rumour.'

I suspected she knew more, but she was tight-lipped about it. She did that, launched into a conversation on a contentious subject, then backed off. It was infuriating.

'All I'm saying, Sara, is that it's better the Italians don't find out. You know, if people see us together, they might ask me questions about your family. I'm your friend. I want to speak up for you, but if your father is breaking the law —'

'He's not breaking the law!'

'Well, that's good to hear because no one wants to see him arrested or sent away.'

'Sent away! What are you suggesting?'

But without further ado she gathered up her towel. As far as my companion was concerned, the subject was closed. She skipped on ahead, saying she had friends to meet. 'Coming?'

I followed, silenced and troubled. That very morning, wide awake, I had listened to our front door open and close with a click, followed by my father's footsteps in the hall. He had been absent for most of the night, throughout the curfew hours.

Into the sultry summer afternoon, a female voice echoing round the mountain flanks called Sylvie's name.

The high sun was burning white in the sky. Sylvie and I were hiking back up from the Swimming Hole. It was a steep climb, oppressive. My hair, like wet strips of seaweed, was dribbling down my back. I was subdued, deeply disturbed by our exchange.

Two figures, indistinct silhouettes, appeared on the elevated track above us. One waved, lifting both arms high in the air as though trying to attract our attention. Sylvie was holding one of her hands, palm flat, as a visor to keep the sun out of her eyes.

'Who's there?' I asked. Such moments always caused a flash of panic within me, especially today after our conversation.

'I think . . .'

We took a few more strides. The only sound was the river bubbling over its stony bed, cascading towards the sea.

'*Nous sommes de retour, ma chère amie.*'

'Yes, it's Nathalie!' whooped Sylvie. 'And Alain is with her.' My companion broke into a trot. Our conversation forgotten.

'*Salut-toi.*' Her feet pounded the path. She was hooting and racing, punching her arms high above her head, her golden tresses bouncing like sheaves of wheat, lengthening the distance between us. The pair descending the hill hastened towards her, cheering and laughing, arms wide open in greeting. Clear, strong voices bounced back and forth across the breast of the mountain.

Lagging behind, I gave way to my breathlessness, paused, dropped to my knees.

The trio were charging into one another's arms. Old friends embracing, reconnecting. Alain and Nathalie. Brother and sister. Sylvie had spoken of them.

I settled back into the grass, giving them their distance, allowing them space. Sadness washed through me. Dread and desolation.

The grass around me was a bouquet of multi-coloured blossoms. Every plant had burst into life. How I loved it here, but a shift was happening. I sensed it. Delphine's warning and now Sylvie's.

Papa was putting our lives at risk.

Butterflies fluttered in and out of my line of vision. At this proximity, so close to the earth, the stillness was visibly alive. Insects were crawling over my legs. I wrung the wet from my hair and the water dripped and ran along my arms. I lifted my damp costume – Sylvie's costume – to my head and squeezed. The drops fell, like gentle rain.

If the Italians found out about Papa's clandestine work, if Sylvie gave the game away, he would be arrested, imprisoned. Sent away. To where?

Would Mamma and I be forced to flee again? On our own, like poor Henryk's widow?

'Sara!' Sylvie was pulling her friends towards me in a playful manner.

I sprang to my feet.

'Sara, this is Nathalie, my best friend, and this gorgeous guy is her brother, Alain. They've returned for the summer. Eureka.'

'*Bonjour.*'

'Welcome, Sara.' Nathalie leaned in to kiss me on both cheeks, the traditional *bises*. Her slender neck smelt of a warm resinous scent, like amber.

Yes, that was the day I was introduced to Nathalie, and to Alain.

Nathalie was twenty-one, a little older than her brother and astoundingly beautiful. Brother and sister had eyes the colour of cinnamon.

Nathalie was wearing beige culottes, espadrilles of red and green stripes and a loose cotton blouse that billowed slightly. She seemed so chic and shapely, so effortlessly graceful.

'*Bonjour*, Sara, *bienvenue*.' Alain hung back behind the girls, but smiled broadly. I was caught off guard by his good looks, his magnetism. It surpassed even Sylvie's descriptions of him.

Alain and Nathalie Breton, looking at them both on that first afternoon, were twinned in their handsomeness, in the allure, the assuredness that radiated out from them both.

My shyness, awkwardness, must have stalled Alain, for we didn't brush cheeks, and refrained from embracing or offering a kiss, which would have been the customary and natural thing to do. Foolish to read anything into this, to believe that even during those first few seconds of that initial encounter the attraction was seeded, but there was a frisson, a presage of all that was to come.

The two girls broke from our quartet, heading hand in hand back towards the river, leaving Alain and me alone. He took a step in their direction. I held back, uncertain. I was still jangling inside, apprehensive.

'We're on our way to have a dip,' he said appraising me. 'Coming?'

I rubbed at my cheek. 'I won't be intruding?'

'Of course not, silly! Why would you be?'

I grinned. I liked that he called me 'silly'. My costume, hanging from my left hand, was still damp but what did it matter? I had no other plans.

Alain and I followed the sloping path, trailing the two friends who were now arm in arm. I concentrated on them, descending the hill some twenty metres in front of us, because I felt tongue-tied. Alain's presence, his proximity, was a little overwhelming.

Sylvie was resting her head on Nathalie's shoulder, bumping and jigging as they descended the track, jabbering over one another, slapping each other playfully. I wondered what confidences they were sharing, and a stab of jealousy took hold. I feared I would lose or have to share my closest female companion. Hard-won, even if she hurt me sometimes.

'Where are you from, Sara, originally?'

Originally?

Was my demeanour, my accent, still so unFrench? Was I still wearing the mark, the guise of the foreigner?

'Poland. We're Polish. I'm here with my parents but we've been in France for two and a half years now. I like to think I'm a little bit French.'

He nodded, glancing elsewhere.

Were my words pathetic? 'Are you home for the summer?'

'Yep, released from university.'

'Your sister too?'

'We're both studying in Marseille at the medical faculty down by the old port. I had ambitions to go to Paris, to read medicine at the Sorbonne, but it was deemed more prudent to stay closer to home. So, we're living, surviving, within *zone nono*.'

'*Zone nono*, what does that mean?' I hadn't heard the expression before.

'Sorry, it's slang for the Free Zone, the unoccupied half of France, although it would be a mistake to refer to it as that any more. So many checkpoints to get home last night. Not since the Germans stepped across the line late last year have we been free. We are now *zone sud* and, like the northern zone, we have also been placed under military administration.' He kicked at a stone. 'It's all pretty grim.'

I let this sink in, recalling the fences Albert said were

being built across this *maralpin* zone. Walling us in. 'My father has talked about the destruction of one of the quarters of old Marseille down at the port. Thousands of Jews, both French and foreign-born, arrested.'

Alain threw a glance in my direction. Did he judge the subject too challenging in my company? 'I hope everyone is making you welcome, Sara.'

'Very, thank you.'

He paused, absorbing the view, the mountains, the majesty of his surroundings: this plateau set apart from the rest of the world was his motherland. I envied him that. 'It's good to be back. Here, you could believe there was no war.'

A humming caught my attention. In the distance, a truck. It was climbing the serpentine road that wound its way to the town, the route my parents and I had travelled the day we arrived by bus. An ominous black cloud of smoke belched from the vehicle's exhaust.

'Military,' I muttered, under my breath.

'Italians. Nothing to worry about.'

'Can you identify them from here?'

'It's a military truck but not a German one, and they are the only parties with access to petrol. Do they trouble you, Sara? Do they make life hard for you and your family?'

I liked the way he spoke my name, while standing not a shadow's breadth from me. His presence pulled me.

I shook my head. I didn't want to discuss our status, our problems as refugees. I didn't want to dwell on Sylvie's words. The unspoken threat. I wanted this to be a stroll down to the river for a swim, as it was for the others. An ordinary afternoon at the beginning of summer in the company of someone I desired.

Desire. An unfamiliar sensation.

'So Nathalie is studying to be a doctor too?'

'My sister's the really smart one in the family. She's in her second year. Me, my first. She talks of specializing in gynaecology, crusading for women's rights. I'll settle for local practice right here on my doorstep.' He laughed and his face broke up into sun-lined creases – I wanted to kiss him. 'I have no aspirations to move away from these mountains. The quality of life doesn't get much better than here.' He smiled at me and I felt my face rouge. It was rare, if ever, that I had been alone in the company of a young man. Thomas and Albert, yes, but they were boys, roaming about the hills, whereas Alain . . . Well, I had only just been introduced to him, but still my heart beat faster in his company, even on that first afternoon – there in the tall grasses, our feet crunching against pebbles, our strides more or less in synch, arms swinging freely.

A small convocation of eagles was circling high overhead. These hunting birds had frequently been my companions on solitary outings. I could identify them easily.

'Look, golden eagles.' I was showing off, attempting to establish myself as a native of these hills. Belonging. To impress Alain. I could not bear for him to dismiss me as someone from elsewhere, someone in need of charity.

He was young, like the rest of us, but he was mature, masculine, strong and long-limbed. It felt essential to behave in some special way in his company, though I had no idea what that way was. I was entirely ignorant of the rules of flirting. I remembered how Sylvie had teased the young shepherd with her eyes, her body language reeling him in. I remembered that she had confided her own feelings for Alain. I should keep away – Sylvie's wrath was menacing, dangerous. But I didn't keep away. I tried, but from that first afternoon, I hungered to win Alain's interest, his approving gaze, not his pity. I tried hard not to appear gauche, not to expose my lack of confidence. Or to appear too eager. Not to stumble or swing my arms violently, or interrupt, speaking over his words, because I so badly wanted to impress him. In fact, what was I rambling on about now? Words pouring from my mouth . . .

Of being as lithe and graceful as Nathalie, or even as precocious and self-assured as Sylvie, I hadn't a hope. But at least I need not present myself as a *klots*, a ham-fisted teenager with awkward foreign manners.

27

The girls had touched down at the river. Shoes kicked recklessly to one side, they were peeling off their clothes. Long-limbed they hurled themselves into the water, screaming with delight. Alain tapped my elbow. 'Come on, Sara,' he encouraged. 'Enough chat. Let's get ourselves in there.'

I hesitated, held back. My habit was to enter the water feet first, breaching the surface one timid toe at a time at the Swimming Hole. This was not a still pool so it was trickier to negotiate. The water was fast-flowing, pitching and, to me, threatening. There were no natural steps at this spot. I might lose my footing, be swept away by the current, make a fool of myself. I dithered, crimson with embarrassment, cursing my ineptitude. No one paid heed. Alain was drawing his shirt over his head, arms outstretched, the muscles of his torso tightened. Hair in his armpits, dark as nocturnal plants. His skin was umber, accustomed to the sunlight. He was unbuckling a belt, wriggling out of his blue serge trousers, shrugging off espadrilles. I glanced elsewhere as he sprinted and dived headlong into the cool mountain flow. It was deep here. The splash, the girls' squeals. My bathing suit still gripped between my hands, soggy and cold from earlier, I was peering about, searching for a boulder behind which to undress, to drag back on the sopping garment and join the party.

My back faced the others. I had wandered off a short distance.

'Where's your friend?' I heard his question, called from beyond the bank. Alain enquiring about me.

'Her name's Sara!' Nathalie's voice.

'I know.'

'Sara! Are you coming in?' Nathalie calling.

'*Merde*. She can't swim. I forgot. Sara!'

'Sara!'

I was obscured by a thick juniper bush, desperately tugging at my clothes; they resisted my efforts; my skin was so sweaty. '*Merde*.'

'Sara! *Où es-tu*? Where are you?'

'C-coming,' I managed. Hot tears were threatening. I wanted to participate. To cool off, to be one of the club, but I was not. Patently so. Alain had spotted it directly. *Where are you from?*

A foreigner, a stranger passing through, taking refuge. Recipient of kindnesses.

I read their thoughts, or irrationally believed I did.

'Knock, knock.' Nathalie, her right hand raised in the air. Slender fingers. She was play-acting by knocking on the tips of the branches of the bush. Standing in a circle of puddles dripping onto the stones beneath her long, narrow feet. Her hair was tousled and twisted with water. She was so at ease in her skin. As divine as he was.

'Need some help?'

'I can't swim, and I ... This wretched costume won't ...' I was naked. A white-skinned or mildly reddened lump, the sun burning into my back as I dithered. The garment was clamped about my knees, locking my legs together. I heaved at it angrily and, somehow, it arrived at the level of my buttocks. One more yank and it was, after a fashion, covering the coarse black hedge of my pubic hair, my domed milky stomach and, partially, my bulging breasts. I felt like nothing more than an oddity, an aberration, Sylvie's veiled threat still gnawing at me. If she reported my father . . .

'There's a natural step a little further along the bank, not as far as the Swimming Hole. You can climb into the water from there.'

My body had begun to tremble as though I were cold. I wasn't. The sun was baking. 'I've already had a dip. I think I'll just sit on the bank, sunbathe and watch you all.'

Nathalie surveyed me, undecided as to whether to press me, or leave me to make up my own mind. 'Think about it.' She smiled. 'I can walk along there with you. Or, better still, why don't we all go up to the Swimming Hole? Then we can all enjoy the water. Hey, *mes amis.*'

And that was what we did.

Nathalie and Alain, one either side of me, each holding one of my hands, guided me into the water.

'Lucky you, to have Alain as your teacher,' shouted Sylvie, from further out in the lagoon where she was dog-paddling, a golden-locked siren, scrutinizing us, my every move, as we plunged into the silvery brink.

'Would you like to learn?' His eyes were on mine. His hair darkened like coal, flat against his forehead.

I nodded, teeth chattering. I was just about able to stand on tiptoe on the reedy, flinty bottom, toes plunged between silt and stones, but the force of the stream was nudging me, dragging me out of my depth.

I squeezed shut my eyes, fearful, recalling the boat journey that had delivered us to Nice. None of us could swim. With one stroke the boat might have sunk to the deep seabed and we would all have drowned.

'Give me your hands.'

I obeyed, trembling at his touch.

'I'm your anchor, Sara. Now, let your legs float, and drift up behind you.'

He was smack in front of me, glistening and powerful. He swung himself to the right, gripping me tighter with his left hand, wrapping his upper self around me until, with the palm of his right hand, he nudged at my thighs and then my calves, easing my feet off the floor of the river. I was breaking with gravity, my limbs drifting, floating upwards to the surface. It was both terrifying and exhilarating. Alain was grasping me tightly. I could feel his muscles, the force and will of him as he clamped my hands between his.

'Trust me,' he whispered.

I wanted nothing more.

The girls, some distance off, were giggling, lost in their own world, though Sylvie's attention never entirely abandoned us.

Gradually he took a step, then another, retreating from me, our arms outstretched, as he slithered backwards into the natural lagoon. I gripped his hands harder, a surge of panic. 'Kick your legs,' he ordered, ignoring the dig and pressure of my fingers. 'Harder, good girl. I won't let you go.'

Bit by bit, we drifted from the stone-edged bank and navigated our way out of my depth.

'Keep kicking, stop thinking. Give in to your body, relax into the folds of the water, let the lake envelop you.'

I was numb with terror, which must have been written in stripes across my features. I worried that I looked ugly, ungainly, that he would perceive me as clumsy, but he was not concentrating on me. He was moving his right arm, like a rudder, on the river's surface, creating ripples, some of which splashed against my face. I felt him, that much taller than me, lift off from the aqueous bed, his left hand tenaciously holding mine. With his torso and free arm he began to swim, towing me.

'Watch the movement I'm making with my right arm. Can you copy that with your left?'

I tried, sloshing more than steering. Gracelessly. Still, I managed to remain afloat.

Shyly, I uncoupled my hands from his attempting to swim on my own but within seconds I was sinking. Water in my nostrils, swirling down my throat. It tasted, reeked, of reeds, weeds, wet grass. The leaden weight of my being was dragging me under. I started to kick for my life. He turned to me. 'Swim, come on. Attagirl.'

He took a hand, buoyed me up. Three of my limbs were operating, swimming, after a fashion. I chuckled with happiness, imbibed more water, spluttered, coughing. He wrapped me in his arms and bore me to the shore.

Sitting on the bank at his side, the sun beating on our heads, the nape of his neck more sunburned than the rest of him, my heart was racing.

'Practise every day for a week,' he said, 'as you have done today, and you'll be carving through the currents to the far shore.'

Sylvie broke the moment, calling, 'Alain, come and swim with us.'

With that, he lifted his body from the bank and hurled himself into the water. The splashes rose high, jets of precious metal all around him. I watched him from the water's edge as he pounded the surface, speeding like a dolphin to join his adoring girls.

In that moment I knew I had found an ally, a true companion.

28

It was as though, with Alain and Nathalie's arrival, summer had been unleashed. Every unspoken sentiment, every perfume, the gradations of light, all had a keener, brighter nuance. I was suddenly effervescent, walking on air, for no particular reason. Well, for every reason but I did not put a name to it.

My mornings remained dedicated to the Lindemann infants as well as to the school, which would soon be winding down for its summer recess. Over the preceding couple of weeks, Delphine had divided the class back into two groups. We remained in the same big room, but she allocated to me the five-to-seven-year-olds, while she took charge of the rest. With twelve pupils in my group, my principal task was to assist them with their reading. The foreign children needed extra time and encouragement. I didn't mind. My patience was bountiful. I was cheerful and growing more confident. My ghastly flabbiness was getting toned from all the walking and swimming. And in spite of my night-time terrors – Papa's nocturnal activities were more dedicated than ever, the newly sown fear that the Germans might one day find us here, that this interstice of almost perfect happiness could not go on for ever – I was smiling, a face beaming out at the world.

Delphine argued that no one was better placed than me to understand the refugees' traumas and sufferings, that any number of reasons could stand in their way and block their ability to learn. Hanna was in my group, which meant that Daniel was with us too. We were a threesome. We were almost family.

Even once school had shut down for the holidays, the babysitting was to continue. It promised to be a less fun proposition than time spent with the other pupils along with Delphine, whose boundless energy stimulated our mornings.

'What will you do over the summer?' I asked her, during one of our lunches, which had become a little less frequent of late. Her commitment, she explained, was promised elsewhere. She said no more on the subject. Cagey. Always so cagey.

It was June, the end of the second week. My parents and I had been residing in the upper floor of our white house for more than three full months. If we could only stay here . . . I was beginning mentally to construct a future for myself. When had I last looked to the future? I dreamed of university. Why not? To qualify as a teacher. Acting as Delphine's assistant had encouraged me, given me new drive. Working with the children was exhilarating – we laughed and shouted a lot and had fun – and I liked to think I was rather adept at it.

As the days rolled on, I had less and less desire to leave this high-altitude sanctuary. If only the war could end and our existences were no longer threatened. Some days I secretly kidded myself that there was no war. I never mentioned these aspirations to my parents. Nothing in their conversation encouraged me to believe they might choose France as their home, our home, our country of residence. Papa was spending fair chunks of his days in the company of Monsieur Decroix. And I could not lie to myself as I had to Sylvie. He was spending hours away from the white house after the curfew, though he never again requested my translation skills. His own French was improving. There were many nights now when young men turned up at our door. One of them might be hurt. Or they came for other reasons. To rest, talk with him, hide until daylight? He never turned them away. Without a word, he'd direct them to the kitchen.

Sylvie's remark weighed heavily on me.

Sylvie. I watched her when we were together in the company of Alain. Nathalie was her best friend, yes, but her relationship with her best friend's brother was another matter altogether. He seemed to have put a spell on Sylvie. In his company she was like butter from the local cows, left out in the sun. I wondered whether he could see it and was ignoring her behaviour or whether he was oblivious to her.

She had confided that she fancied him, but was she in love with him? It was difficult not to be. Or was she simply flirting, play-acting? I dared to mention her Italian soldier and she nearly bit my head off. Her unpredictable mood swings, her occasional spitefulness, were minefields to negotiate.

Was Alain her lover now? If so, was I jealous? The possibility of it cut deep into me. The space he was occupying in my head and my heart was increasing.

I decided to keep my distance. I could not afford to lay bare my emotions. Not to anyone, least of all to a man so inaccessible. It was too threatening. I could only get hurt.

29

As the weather grew warmer, the overhead fans in the classroom chirped and squeaked, like newly born chicks.

'They need oiling,' sighed Delphine. 'No one left to carry out maintenance.'

'Why not ask Alain Breton to have a look?'

'Good idea.' She winked. 'I'm glad you and he are getting acquainted. He's one of the best.'

It was too hot, too muggy, with so many of us crammed together indoors, so I led my pupils out to the playground. We installed ourselves on the benches and swings to recite our lessons. An al fresco classroom with the call of the cicadas for company. Some days, I'd spot Albert there. He'd be leaning against the gate, hands in pockets, following the lesson while waiting for me. When I acknowledged his presence, he'd wave shyly. His mother was on her lunch-break. He was free for an hour, sometimes for the whole afternoon. When the bell rang for class to end, he accompanied me back to the Lindemanns' and hung around in the narrow street while I updated Ilse on Hanna's progress. She is learning fast, I was delighted to report. Ilse's health, though, was less encouraging.

'You want to swim?' he'd invite, when I stepped out into the dusty cobbled lane.

I shook my head. 'Too many people,' was my excuse.

So, Albert and I would strike out for the upland forest where it was cool and where his mother summered her four beehives. There, backs against one of the towering spruce trunks, he'd split his cheese baguette and hand me one of the two apples he never failed to bring. Albert loved apples.

We seemed to share a special affinity, a unique emotional bond. It was difficult to identify it because we were so different yet in other ways similar. He confided that he couldn't read very well. 'Big words' were difficult for him. He'd never read a book in his life and owned none. I promised that, when school was over for the summer, I'd help him. I valued his friendship and in this way, I could repay him. He was kinder than Sylvie. Thoughtful, sensitive. Neither of us had brothers or sisters. Both of us were embarrassed or troubled by our mothers. He was the one who had brought me into the gang in those early days and I owed him everything for that. But it was something else that bonded us: being the outsider, the outcast. I empathized when Albert confided in me about his father whom he had not seen for three years. The agony he felt.

'At the loss of him?'

He shook his head. The old blatherers were spreading unkind words about his father, he told me, calling him a coward. 'They say my dad dreaded being seconded by the STO [Services du Travail Obligatoire] for labour work in Germany, so he fled the village.

'He's gone into hiding. Not a word has been heard of him since. But loads of men have done the same. I say he's joined the Maquis, that he's fighting for France with the rebels, risking his skin, but no one believes me.' He spoke the words in a rush, fingers pulling at the medal round his neck, which he told me was his patron saint's.

'A lucky charm?'

'Sort of.'

'I bet you're right about your dad,' I encouraged. 'You should be proud of him.' It occurred to me then, for the first time, that though I feared for my father's safety, our safety, I was proud of him for all that he was doing.

30

The heat was growing intense now. Everybody sought shade from the scorch of the sun. The sprawling over-grown garden surrounding the white house was an ideal retreat from that mean orb and I spent solitary hours out there beneath the broad-leaved fig tree where the rusting table went on rusting day in, day out. And when I grew sticky or when the midges and mosquitoes came looking to feed on my skin, rather than descend to the river for a swim, where half the parish would be, including, most probably, Sylvie and Alain, I would slip into the cool interior of the lower half of the house with its shuttered windows.

I needed space and hours to contemplate. My world was changing.

Downstairs, there were two fans in the drawing room, suspended from the ceiling. I risked switching them on only during the most suffocating of afternoons to break up the block of heat. The electricity was operating. I had discovered it quite by accident when I'd unearthed a wireless buried in a cupboard beneath the flight of stairs that led up to our apartment – the door to which had been sealed off upstairs. I had plugged the wireless into a socket in the wall and – bingo – static. I fiddled with the two Bakelite knobs but on that first afternoon, although I managed to find a signal, the stations broadcasting were hit and miss and I couldn't tune it to any of those I listened to at Delphine's, or those I had heard her speak of.

Radio-Londres, Radio-Paris. War news. The enemy's advance.

Once I'd found music, I'd drift about the rooms swaying gently to the rhythms of sentimental ballads, with one of the lady's beautiful gowns pressed to me. I dreamed of Alain while humming to *chansons* such as Tino Rossi's *'J'attendrai'*. 'The singer who cured our broken hearts' was how Delphine described him when I first heard that song in her kitchen. I was seduced by jazz, the blues, female vocalists crooning for their lovers' return. I was beginning to get a feel for the blues.

I pictured myself spinning along the coast road, the Corniche, between Cannes and Nice in the Allinghams' swanky car, playing ball on the beach while babysitting their blond-haired son. Perhaps, one day in the future, I could be hired as his private tutor. I would have liked to know his name so that in my daydreaming I could talk to him, sketch my scenarios with more intimate details.

I discovered a fox stole in one of the wardrobe drawers, nestling within soft blue tissue paper, curled in on itself as though it were asleep. I gathered it up carefully and wrapped it around my neck. The pelt, a deep russet colour, was glossy and luxuriant. It was perfectly intact, boasting a head, tail and dangly skinny legs. He – I christened him Freddie – became my confidant and my dance partner.

It was on one of those listless muggy late-June afternoons, while I was alone in the garden devouring a novel by Flaubert, that I was discovered. The shock. I nearly choked. I had been munching an apple Albert had brought to the school for me earlier that day and I was still sucking its core, licking its sweet juice off my fingers, when Alain appeared, like a hallucination, from out of the bushes. He had approached through dense grasses and the super-sized tentacles of ferns without my seeing or even hearing him, so transported was I by the comings and goings of Madame Emma Bovary.

'So, this is where you've been hiding.'

'B-bonjour.'

'I've been looking for you. I knocked upstairs, but your mother told me you'd gone out.' He was directly in front of me now. 'I was about to leave when I noticed the appalling condition of the garden and thought I'd take a look around, maybe do some scything. Then I spotted you. We haven't seen you in a while.'

I was dumbstruck at the sight of him.

'Well, it's certainly secluded, I'll say that. Lord, this place has gone to rack and ruin.' He was waving his hand, agitating a swarm of midges from in front of his face. 'I'd better bring over my sickle and trim these grasses.'

I swung on my seat, knocking the book into the bushes. Alain crouched low to retrieve it, placing it on the table in front of me.

'*Madame Bovary*, eh. Enjoying it?'

I nodded.

His hands were in the pockets of his loose-legged trousers, cotton shirt open at the neck. He looked as though he didn't have a care in the world and might have been about to embark on a sailing trip. During the days since we'd seen one another – interminable days – his face had become even more tanned. He resembled a *gitano* with his open shirt and black hair. His eyes were like amber beads, deep-set in his bronzed complexion. They shone as though they had been polished like my fox Freddie's. Dark and seductive.

'You've made yourself a very comfortable cache here.' He grinned. 'It's a little wild but perhaps that suits you. Poor Lucy would have a heart attack if she could see the state of her beloved garden.'

'Lucy?'

'It's her house.'

'You know her? The lady who lives here?'

'Of course.'

He groped for one of the iron chairs fallen on its back in the undergrowth, righted it and placed it at the table alongside mine, then rubbed his hands together, wiping off the dirt.

'I knew her, not as well as my mother does. She and Maman were great friends. Often during high summer when Lucy and Dirk were here, escaping the coast and the flood of tourists, my parents were invited over *pour le dimanche midi*, for Sunday lunch, and I was dragged along.'

'Lucy and Dirk,' I mouthed their names soundlessly, marrying them with the faces in the photographs.

'The truth was, I was a little enamoured and eagerly looked forward to those invitations, to spending a few hours in the company of such a beautiful woman. Desperately glamorous Lucy, who loved to throw parties. Those lunches, with half the village present, would go on until the early evening, breaking up as the sun began to set and all the wine bottles were empty.' My companion was grinning, shaking his head, lost in his adolescent reminiscences.

I glanced at the semi-buried shards of green glass centimetres from our feet. I was trying to conjure up the revelries. How I yearned to have been one of the guests, a witness to, a participant at those blithesome, untroubled gatherings. The easy-going lives of Lucy and Dirk. 'Carefree memories.'

'Well, until all the merrymaking stopped . . .'

'Ah, yes, the war . . .'

'Nothing to do with the war.' He fell silent.

'Then . . . wh–?' I was desperate to know more, to press him to continue, but I bit my tongue.

'There was an accident.'

'An accident?'

'Such a tragedy. Poor Lucy. Maman said she was completely broken.'

'Broken? Why – what happened?'

Alain turned his head to look at me. His eyes combed my face. 'You ask a lot of questions, don't you, Sara?'

'*Désolée*. Sorry, I . . . I can't help myself.'

I waited for him to divulge more. He didn't.

'It's all . . . so different here from my life, ours, back home in Poland, which was all such a long time ago.'

'Apologies, of course. You must be missing it. This can't be –'

'No, I'm not! It's not that. What I mean is . . . I . . . want to . . . understand, to try to bring to life the family who are giving us sanctuary. I long to learn about them, understand them. I am so sorry there was an accident . . . Even if they don't know us, we are living in their home. It sounds silly . . . not easy to explain . . . but I care about them . . . and I would like to . . .'

He was frowning, baffled.

'. . . to engage with them. I don't want us to be regarded just as part of an aid programme. Numbers, names on lists. As long as we register every day, pay our rent, which is . . . which is correct and fair, of course. Everyone must pay their way. It's just . . .'

Alain's expression was attentive but unsettled. I couldn't stop myself jabbering on.

'My mother doesn't leave the house any more. She's afraid, can't sleep, losing weight, worried for my fa– our future.'

'I'm sorry to hear that.'

'I don't want her – us to be perceived as . . . second-class citizens. People are so kind to us. We can't ever repay their generosity. How could we? There is nothing I'd like more than to say thank you to . . . to Lucy. I'd like us to be equals. To help her if she's hurt.' Tears were welling in my eyes. The lump in my throat felt so solid, as though I'd swallowed one of the smooth, round pebbles in the river. 'I'm sorry there was an accident. Are they . . . ? Lucy and Dirk . . .'

Alain said nothing, mulling over my words. Or bemused by me?

A butterfly, white with slender black markings – it resembled a miniature parachute – landed on the table alongside us. It closed its wings tightly, upright like a fluted stalk, then opened them wide and flew away. At liberty to flutter, to move on.

I pictured the barbed-wire fences constructed at a distance from here, somewhere beyond this glorious garden, my retreat humming with life. I could not see them, but they were there, hemming us in, like the sheep in the valleys in their pens. Yet here I was, in this heavenly prison. With Alain at my side, why would I ever want to leave?

'Have you read this?' I asked, dragging the book from the table and into my lap. I couldn't even see the cover or the title now because the veil of tears was misting my vision.

'Sara.' Alain laid his fingers across my right hand, the one clutching the book.

'I probably shouldn't be out here, using this garden.

Making myself comfortable. I have no right to.' He didn't argue with me. 'Will you snitch on me, give me away?' I sniffed, half giggled, making light of my vulnerability.

'Sara, you're mistaken.'

I shook my head, not in response to his reaction, but because being caught here, found out, made me feel like a delinquent, a trespasser, which I was, of course I was, and this heavenly man had no idea to what extent I was. The sneaking about in someone else's home, peeling open their private moments, dreaming that this piece of paradise was mine, that I could know such gaiety, such affection. Their privilege and perfect love, which had been marred by an accident.

I was encroaching on others' most intimate moments, siphoning off their privacy, stitching it into a fabulous story of my fabrication.

'Sorry.' I lifted a hand to wipe my face, and in doing so brushed his from my lap. What a fright I must have looked, spotted with dust and perspiration, having clambered about, in and out of the vegetation. Hair laced with bits of broken twigs and dead spiders. My boring, scruffy old clothes.

'We need a glass of water to cool ourselves down, don't you think? Shall we . . . ?'

'In the kitchen, there are glasses hanging from a rack above the sink,' I blurted out the instruction before I realized what I was saying. The revelation, repercussions.

'Upstairs, at your mother's?'

Our eyes met. He held my gaze. I could feel my heart, hear its pounding, harder than it had since we had made our terrifying escape out of Poland and heard the shots in the night as we had run for our lives, our feet crunching down on the needles bedding the pine-forest floor, the crack of broken branches underfoot, any one of which might have betrayed us. I hung my head.

I had given myself away.

Alain got to his feet and made for the back door. It was still padlocked. He continued round the house to the main door, which, with the push of a finger, creaked open. I closed my eyes, waiting for his return, his disgust at my treachery. I wouldn't attempt to offer any excuses, to justify my infractions.

Butterflies fluttered by me. Bees were working nineteen to the dozen. There was a swarm of them on a bush bursting with deep purple flowers whose name I could not bring to mind. It smelt citron sweet.

Alain returned with two tumblers of water. He handed one to me.

'*Santé.*'

I was shaking so badly I had to lay the book back on the table and accept the glass with both hands. I lifted it to my lips. It knocked against my teeth. I sipped slowly, fearing I would leave a trace of spittle on my chin. He drank more heartily and with far more ease, his eyes never leaving me. Eventually I placed the glass on the iron table.

'I'll just clo-close . . .' I coughed: the words refused to crystallize '. . . close the door,' I murmured. 'After I've washed these up. There's no hurry, take your time. Or I can do it after you've gone. Please don't feel you need to . . .'

'You have a key?'

I nodded, digging into my skirt pocket, passing it to him. He opened his hands, palms upwards, as if to say, *Why are you handing this to me?*

'Who gave you the key? I'm interested.'

I couldn't tell from his words, his tone, what his mood

was. The question was delivered as a dispassionate enquiry. Was he so fuming with anger he could not express his indignation? Was he bottling it up?

'I found it.'

He scoffed as if this was too incredible to take seriously. 'Found it? You mean here in the garden slipped beneath a flowerpot? Or "found it" as in serendipitously fallen from someone's pocket, rusting at the roadside along the lane?'

'In a drawer.'

He waited.

I didn't know where to begin. I broke a window, I was thinking, and crawled in . . . I could not admit to that. I simply couldn't. I bit my lip. My throat was constricting.

'Lucy, or Dirk, accidentally left a set of keys to the principal part of the house, their private quarters, upstairs in a drawer?'

I lowered my head, shook it. Was I to be forced to confess all, spell out every sordid detail of my forced entry? Should I – was I capable of concocting an elaborate tale, a lie? An image of Delphine flashed into my mind. My role as assistant school teacher, albeit voluntary and temporary, would be jeopardized if she heard about this. Whatever had I been thinking? I had no choice but to come clean, own up to my transgressions.

'I found it inside the house in a drawer downstairs,' I admitted, barely audibly.

To my surprise, when I lifted my head a centimetre or two to sneak a glance, to assess Alain's reaction, there was a trace of a smile, a twinkle in his eyes. 'I won't ask you what you were doing in there in the first place.'

Throat tight, I offered no further explanation.

'The property is for sale so I suppose that lessens your transgression.'

'I am not a delinquent or a thief!' I pictured the glorious golden bee brooch still lying on the mantelpiece. 'I was only looking, Alain. I was living another's life in my fantasy, a life I had assumed was so much finer and less troubled than mine. A bit like Emma Bovary, I suppose. I meant no harm.'

His eyes were penetrating mine, roaming over my face. There was no animosity in his expression. It was sympathetic, forgiving. It was as though he was attempting to see the world from my point of view. A young woman with nothing, not even a passport or a homeland. I wanted to embrace him even more for his empathy.

'My mother has a set of keys as well, for emergencies, or . . . She rarely uses them, or not at all, as far as I am aware. As I mentioned, Lucy has given up on the place. It would have been sold a year or two ago if France had been at peace. Would you like me to ask my mother to send a letter to Lucy – I'm sure she knows where to contact her – and request your use of this lower floor?'

'No! No, please don't.'

'Why not?' He stepped closer and lifted a hand to my cheek, stroking it softly with his thumb.

'Please, can we . . . can we just forget this? Not mention it to anyone. I promise, I won't . . . go into Lucy's house again. I won't intrude, but, please, tell me what happened to them.'

He considered before speaking. 'They lost their little son.'

'*What?*' I was stunned, speechless. The little boy crawling across the grass. I shook my head. I took a step backwards. The blow felt . . . This news, it was as though

I had lost him too, the small boy I had played with, conversed with, tutored in my daydreams.

'I cannot see why Lucy should object to you having a little privacy, a comfortable space of your own, away from your parents. She has no affection for this house since the accident. I can't imagine being cooped up . . .' he stalled, reconsidering his words.

I was barely listening, cradling Lucy's grief as though it had suddenly become mine.

'The little boy in the photographs?' I was reeling from this update. My son, my loss. In my imagination.

Alain nodded. 'Well, I haven't seen any photos but, yes, I suppose so. They had only the one child. It didn't happen here. Still, Lucy hasn't returned since. Sara, this is not really my business to discuss.'

I had invented so many different scenarios in my head, imagining this couple's bliss, their perfect lives, the sanctity, invulnerability of their existence. In not one of my imaginings had I come close to the reality, the tragedy.

In my self-centred universe, we had been the tragic figures, not Mr and Mrs Allingham.

'Listen, I've got to go. I came looking for you to say there's going to be a fête, a fiesta, in the main square on Thursday. It's midsummer week and Corpus Christi. I wondered whether you were planning to come along?'

'What about the curfew?'

'The curfew doesn't start till eleven but I understand the Italians have agreed to relax it for this occasion. You know how they love a party.'

I had nothing to wear and felt certain that my parents would never give their permission. For a fleeting second,

I pictured myself in one of Lucy's luxurious frocks – swept off my feet by Alain, who had eyes only for me.

I shook my head, shrugged my shoulders, not to refuse Alain's invitation but because I doubted such an opportunity would be sanctioned.

'Shall I make a formal request to your father?' Alain was laughing, jesting, up to a point. His humour relaxed me a little. I felt less riddled with guilt for my appalling behaviour and deep sorrow for the lady who had lost her gorgeous little son.

'When did it happen?'

'What?'

'The accident.'

Alain frowned, reflecting. 'I don't know any of the details. I was away when the news reached my parents. And our heads have been so full of the war ever since. A year ago, possibly two, I'm really not sure.' He glanced at his watch. 'I've got to be somewhere. Listen, it would be terrific, *très chouette*, if you can make it on Thursday. We'll have a jolly time. And . . .' he kissed me lightly on my forehead, swung about him looking in the direction of the house where he had left the front door open '. . . your secret is safe with me.'

He winked, and was on his way.

After Alain had disappeared, I sat in silence, hand on my forehead where he had kissed me. I was still with Lucy, wondering whether, if chance should bring us together and we should find an opportunity to confide in one another, I could help her. Maybe we'd become friends. In one of my recent fantasies, she had driven me to the coast in her jazzy car, sailing over the hills, roof down, the open sky above us, her son on my lap . . . There had been no roadblocks, no conflicts. No one was hunted because they lived a different life, had been born into a different creed.

Had her son died in that motor-car? A smash-up some-where on one of these vertiginous bends? Had she been at the wheel? Did she blame herself? Was that the reason she had absented herself from this astonishing place?

I longed to wrap my arms around her and hold her close to me. Squeeze her as I might a beloved sister.

I carried the tumblers back into the kitchen, washed them, then sauntered slowly back along the corridor fully intent on locking up the house immediately, saying good-bye to it for the very last time. Never to busybody in these strangers' unfortunate lives again. Except that I could no longer conceive of them as strangers.

Before returning the key and closing up, I ventured into the drawing room, to the display of photographs on the grand piano. I knew the order of them by heart, their exact placement to a dust speck. I could have found any one of them while blindfolded. I reached for the little boy crawling on the grass. He seemed so real, so full of vig-our, blessed with a rosy, a golden future. Plump cheeks, toothy grin. I felt such heartbreak for Lucy. And a sudden impulse to sit down and write to her, offer her my condol-ences. There was headed notepaper laid out on a small table in the dressing room, but . . . What was I thinking? By what means could I, an interloper, alleviate her suffer-ing? I knew about grief from a place deep within my guts, which was why I so desperately wanted to help, heal her. Even so, what could I, ineffectual Sara, offer Lucy to assuage her pain?

Nothing.

I drew Lucy's key from my pocket and replaced it where I had first found it on the ring in the drawer by the front door. I turned the latch, stepped outside and shut the door behind me as I left.

My safe sanctuary in the cradle, the warm bosom of the white house, was not the happy-go-lucky universe I had woven it to be. My creation had been a poor fiction. In any case, it had been uncovered and I had been exposed.

31

When I returned upstairs my parents were in the kitchen eating an early dinner, seated across the table from one another, chewing silently. Was it me, or was the atmosphere cheerless? No music, no wireless, no laughter or chatter. On the stove, an iron pot was boiling. The smell of the cooking turned my stomach.

'*Tutaj jestes. Ktos cię szukał.*' My mother spoke without lifting her face from her plate of boiled vegetables.

'His name – the someone who was looking for me – is Alain, Mamma. He's a friend of Sylvie's.'

'What did he want?' Again my mother. Dry and to the point.

I hesitated. 'There's a party, a dance in the town on Thursday. He was wondering whether I might be attending.'

'That's not a good idea. No, Sara. Samuel, please forbid it.'

I hadn't expected either of them to give their consent to the outing but the harshness, directness, of my mother's bald refusal stung me. I was still smarting at the news of Lucy's little boy. I groaned, about to turn on my heels.

'Sara? That is no way to behave towards your mother. Show some respect, please.'

I sighed. '*Przepraszam, mamusiu.* Sorry.'

She nodded, a stark acceptance of my apology. 'Sara, listen to me, these are different people from us, and any day now we will be leaving, moving on to a safer place. It's wiser not to engage at any deep level. We don't want to see you get hurt.' Mamma's tone was softer, modified, but this revelation knocked me sideways. It was yet another blow.

'"Any day now"? Why haven't you said anything to me about this? Don't I count in your plans? When will we be leaving?'

'Ssh, Sara.' My father laid his fork on his plate, his palms flat on the checked tablecloth as if about to heave himself to his feet. Then he didn't.

Wherever it was, this place, I wasn't ready to go. I was getting on well with the school here, making connections, finding a purpose, learning languages. I was perfecting my French, picking up Italian, some German vocabulary from Hanna. I felt powerless, as though in my parents' eyes I was still a child, their infant Sarina.

'Why can't we stay here?' I knew perfectly well their response. Had I been fooling myself, building castles in the air? 'Even if the Nazis reach the coast before the Allies, they'll never come here. The middle of nowhere. Why would they? Here is as safe as anywhere.'

'Sara . . .'

'I like this little town. Everybody's so kind. I have friends, and I have a right to be included in our family decision-making.'

'What foolishness you talk. You think any of us has a right, a say in the decision-making? We are refugees, Sara. Fugitives!' He slammed his hand on the table. My mother bowed her head. 'This is not our home. The Gestapo is cracking down on resistance fighters. The deportation of Jews out of France has started again. We are being offered interim asylum, Sara. Temporary citizens, a temporary state of affairs. Nothing more.'

I felt as though my whole world was, for the umpteenth time, disintegrating. I had foolishly allowed myself to forget that we were and would always be outsiders.

Where are you from originally?

I had been deceiving myself.

And my parents preferred to draw the line between these generous citizens and us, but I didn't want that. I spun on my heels and stormed along the corridor to my room where I slammed the door, hurled myself face downwards onto the quilt and wept and wept, breaking my heart open.

32

A light knocking on the door roused me. I opened my eyes. They felt swollen and sore. The light beyond the window was fading. Soft colours across a vast, forgiving sky. I had no idea what time it was. The bedsprings beneath me creaked as I rolled over.

'Sara?'

My father pushed the door ajar and poked his head into the gap. 'Ready to talk?'

I wheeled to my side, lifting my feet, still encased in my shoes, off the recently laundered counterpane to the carpet. It was the signal for him to enter. In his gauche, too-tall way, he perched on the foot of my bed.

'You can go to the dance,' he said. 'But I want you back home by nine o'clock.'

'Nine o'cl–!'

His raised eyebrow cut short my complaint. This was not open to negotiation.

'If your mother had her way, you wouldn't go at all. I take another view. The days we are living here are precious. We have no idea the extent of the dangers we might yet face. You are – as these people say – a *mademoiselle*.' He smiled shyly at his use of the French. 'And a very beautiful one at that, champing at the bit to embrace the world, and I cannot deny you those encounters. These locals are less strict with their offspring, but I see no harm in their manners. They are decent, charitable souls. It's important to enjoy yourself, within reason, while you are able to. Don't allow your emotions to run amok. Keep a check on yourself and behave like the young lady we have brought you up to be. Home by nine.'

I stretched over to hug him, hands wrapped around his neck, inhaling the perennial, comforting scents of him.

'Do you really plan for us to leave?' I dared. 'Or is Mamma just fantasizing . . . We have no papers. There are checkpoints, barbed-wire fences. You know the dangers better than I do, Papa.'

'We are making plans, Sara. As we must. Many are trying to escape. This region is no longer the safe haven it was. Entire families are disappearing, captured, transported we know not where. There are people, friends, organizing papers, exit visas for us. With those we will be able to secure passage, but it is becoming more dangerous, complicated . . .'

'Is Monsieur Decroix helping you?'

'It's prudent to be party to as little information as possible.'

'The men who are wounded who come to you for help?'

'No questions, please. When our plans are firm, we will tell you. And, Sara, be gentle with your mother. All this, my work, is weighing heavily on her.'

I nodded. 'You're winning the war for us, I bet.' I smiled. 'I'm proud of you.'

'And I of you, Sarina. You are growing into a fine young woman. Want something to eat? You missed dinner.'

I shook my head. I was getting plump – all the delicious home-grown potatoes and Delphine's cheeses from their three goats. After two years of hardship, this rationing felt generous, more than sufficient. I wanted to look my best for the dance. Dazzling.

33

The church bells had been ringing since early morning. I was kneeling in the garden, listening to the crickets, weaving together sprays of flowers still damp with their summer dew. A harmony of colours and scents to plait through my hair. Arms loaded, I returned indoors to my room. I began at an unhurried pace, in spite of my excitement, to get ready. When I looked as presentable as I could manage, I set off for town. I was far too early, so full of apprehension and buzzing with anticipation that I decided, before I looked for Alain in the square, to call in on Delphine. I was tempted on my way out to steal into Lucy's bathroom and spray myself generously with her perfume, but I resisted the urge, remembering my promise to Alain. And to myself. The value of keeping my word. In any case, I was no longer in possession of a key.

It pleased me when my parents agreed they might stroll along a little later and sit in one of the cafés for an hour or two. They'd locate me without difficulty.

I was wearing a dress we'd bought at the market in Nice more than a year ago and it pinched tight round the waist and under the armpits – my breasts were filling out, which I felt self-conscious about – but it was the only 'smart' frock I possessed. I thought longingly of all the finery hanging in the wardrobes beneath my bedroom. The shoes, the wraps, the silk blouses, the flowing skirts.

It was an arduous trek along the mountain path in the full sun in a dress that was unexpectedly figure-hugging and constricting. My hair, which I had pinned up and painstakingly plaited with sweetly scented white jasmine, varying shades of oleander, rose and lavender – my home-made perfume, of sorts – had already begun to collapse. The stray locks were gluing to my clammy cheeks. I perched on a rock and attempted to fix it, but I had no brush or mirror. It was a hopeless exercise.

I was desperate for a glass of something thirst-quenching, a dunk in the river.

High on the escarpment beyond the town, groups of women in scarves were bending and rising, bending and rising, gathering sheaves of plants between blackened fingers. Their voices rang out, like an orchestra of silver whistles, as they called to one another or broke into song, one harmonizing with another, jaunty, upbeat tunes, which frequently dissolved into peals of laughter. Their merriment was contagious. As lunchtime approached, and the midday bells rang out, they thrust their loads over their shoulders and trussed them to their upper backs, transporting them with the care given to laden grape baskets. In single file in their clogs or espadrilles, they wended their way along the winding dusty tracks towards the town, negotiating the occasional tethered goat. A few waved at me as they passed. One or two stared curiously. I lifted my hand to acknowledge their greetings and felt the underarm of my dress begin to give. I prayed it would not come apart at the seam.

Bunting, pre-war and a little frayed, had been festooned across some of the façades of the stone buildings. It was gay, festive.

I was hoping Delphine owned a sewing machine: we might be able to re-stitch my dress. The school had closed its gates for the summer and I was missing her company.

I was also, perhaps a little deviously, hoping to find Monsieur Decroix at home. I was anxious to know more about the papers my father had requested. I felt fairly sure that he would be party to Papa's plans. If so, to where were we bound and when?

I knocked and, without waiting, made my way through to the kitchen as was my habit. Delphine was frequently at the table there, correcting papers, preparing her classes, cooking lunch for her husband or children. On this occasion, though, I was taken aback to find her not in the company of her husband, but with Alain. They were enjoying a beer, listening to the radio. The remains of a baguette and a small wheel of cheese, with a knife stuck into it, lay on the table in front of them. Breadcrumbs, cork, an open wine bottle, triangular slabs of the creamy *fromage*, an atmosphere of familiarity pervaded. Her baby boy was on her lap. No sign of Élisabeth. The windows were closed, the curtains semi-drawn, which, on such a sweltering day, surprised me. I had the distinct impression that I had caught them off guard as though this wasn't simply a casual lunch.

'I – I wanted to say that I was hoping to see you at the celebrations later,' I bumbled.

Alain was not fazed by my arrival. He was smiling, eyeing me up and down. I was confused by the intimacy of the scene. My hair was a shambles. The petals were wilting, dropping to the tiles on Delphine's kitchen floor and any minute now my dress might tear. I bent to retrieve the tired blossoms not wanting to leave a mess. 'Where's Monsieur Decroix?' I asked, without thinking.

Delphine raised her eyebrows and burst out laughing. 'Sit down, silly. Do you want a glass of juice?'

I shook my head. I would have preferred to leave, to

return home. Something about the day had been spoiled, gone awry, but I didn't know what it was and I didn't wish to appear rude. I felt a dig in my heart at the sight of the two together, the two people I cared about most in the village, almost the world, sequestered here, sharing confidences, their lives intimately interwoven, with no future to fear. 'I think the lieutenant is helping my father . . . to secure the documents we'd need to leave France.'

'Did your father tell you that, Sara?'

Delphine's tone was surprisingly harsh. I didn't know whether either she or Alain was party to Monsieur Decroix's activities, though I couldn't believe he would hide such important matters from his wife, even if I wasn't precisely sure what all those 'matters' were. Hiding injured refugees in his barn? Assisting families in illegal escape? Forging identity cards? Did he operate a printing press out of sight somewhere in a cow byre out of town? On their smallholding, perhaps.

'Sara, listen to me, this is extremely important. Look at me, please. Stop tugging at your hair. No matter how much you trust Alain or me, the information you have just shared should never have left your lips.'

'But I am only saying it to you, Delphine, because I trust you. It's not as if I'm confiding it to any of the old biddies or the Italians, for Heaven's sake. I wouldn't even mention it to the Lindemanns or Sylvie. Your husband is helping us, though, isn't he?'

'And how do you know that we can trust Alain?'

My jaw dropped. He winked. I stared from one to the other. 'He's my . . . your friend.'

Alain strode over to the wireless and cranked up the volume. The music was deafeningly loud. He turned from the set and scrutinized me with a very grave expression.

'Sara, in this quiet little backwater, there are many days when we can imagine … we can fool ourselves into believing that there is no war, that the Wehrmacht have not crossed into the Free Zone, that they did not ransack entire neighbourhoods in the old town of Marseille, hunting down and arresting over two thousand citizens, deporting those they judged "unfavourable".' Alain lifted up his hands and made inverted-comma signs with his fingers in the air before continuing. 'And you know what is worse, Sara?'

I shook my head.

'All of this dirty work was carried out not by the SS, but by the French police. Our own men, not Germans. In many cases, regular people, local residents, were their allies, their informers. Such people directed the *flics* to the basements where refugees were cooped up out of sight. These same French posted *corbeaux*, poison-pen letters, in which they divulged the names of neighbours, going so far as to betray their own friends. Why? To save their skins, to gain a few measly francs, to be blessed with a few extra ration cards. Now we are receiving reports that one of the most essential figures in the Résistance has disappeared. Has he been arrested, tortured … betrayed? We don't know yet. The *mouchards* are informers, traitors. It is Free French code for people we despise. Informers and collaborators. And they are living among us. In all probability not in this village because this village collectively voted to harbour immigrants, but we can never be sure . . .'

I sat on my chair, mute, the wilted petals browning and disintegrating from the sweat in the palms of my hands. I stared glumly at my bitten fingernails.

'Your words, Sara, overheard or spoken to the wrong ears, then whispered to someone with Vichy sympathies could have led to Philippe's arrest, to an investigation at the regional gendarmerie headquarters, where he's the chief. We would have been subjected to a full house search. Your father should never have told you. No one should be compromised.'

I considered revealing my own role on the night that the man in the brown suit, Henryk, had been mortally wounded. I considered sharing with my friends how many nights I had listened to my father's footsteps in the hall-way. Sometimes he was in the company of Monsieur Decroix, usually with strangers, toting his medical bag – administering to those who were about to embark on risky illegal journeys? – but I decided then against disclos-ing these facts, not even to prove to Delphine that I could be trusted to keep secrets.

'Papa didn't tell me.' My voice was strong and firm.

Delphine frowned. She lifted Alexandre from her lap, dangled him in the air, then changed his position, jiggling her knees to comfort him, to help him nod off.

'Papa didn't mention any names. We never discuss my father's . . . allegiances, his affairs. I guessed it. I divined that it was Monsieur Decroix because he's always looking out for everybody's welfare and because . . . well, Sylvie mentioned once that Papa is working with your husband.'

'Sylvie?' Delphine and Alain shared a brief glance, a silent exchange I couldn't quite read. I felt foolish, desper-ately hot and sticky and just a bit sick.

'May I use your lavatory, please?'

'You know where it is, out the back – there's water in the jug – and when you've washed your hands, I'll pour you a glass of lemonade and Alain will escort you to the celebrations. The church service should be over shortly. The jollities can begin.'

'Oh, Delphine, aren't you coming?'

'I'll be along at the end of the afternoon. I have work to do here and Alexandre to settle for a couple of hours' sleep.'

34

Garlands of lights had been hung between the fresh-leaved plane trees. Paper lanterns swung from branches. The café tables had been decked out with wild flowers gathered from the hillsides and wrapped with twine or strips of greenery into bouquets. Each stood in a glass carafe or a vase. Their herbaceous scents drifted between the gathering groups of people all done up in their Sunday finery. Several barrels of local wine were lined up on the trestle table in front of the Hôtel des Alpes, glasses, mugs, goblets stacked on an assortment of other tables. Many of the older folk were still in the church. A service was going on, drawing to its conclusion, according to Alain. I caught sporadic intonations from the priest, Father Scaramoni, musical cadences in Latin. I longed to slip inside the huge wooden doors, and stand at the back to witness the pomp, the unfamiliarity of another faith at worship.

The holy father when he finally left his sacred shrine, looking rather stately in a ruby robe Alain told me was called a chasuble, was holding high a golden vessel, a thurible, hanging from a short chain. From it rose aromatic smoke. He was tailed by six altar boys, dressed in knee-length tunics, white, collarless with baggy sleeves. Thomas was one of the first to appear and then I spotted Albert. I caught his eye and waved but he bowed his head, determined not to be distracted, dedicated in his act of devotion.

'What did you say this service is celebrating?' I asked Alain, who was standing half at my side and half behind me. He wasn't paying attention to the growing activity outside the church.

'The Feast of Corpus Christi. For our grandparents and parents, it's a religious observance. In this part of France, in peacetime, there would be a procession through the streets, lots of chanting and singing, the buildings all decked out with flowers and wreaths. Churchgoers dressed up as saints. Yes, in peacetime it's a big event. My generation, though, don't take it so seriously. Actually, there are two celebrations at this time of year. The marking of midsummer is the other. The solstice was last weekend. Long warm days ahead, clear skies. The crops are growing, the lambs fattening. It's the inauguration of the holiday period.' He laughed. 'All those bouquets decorating the tables have been gathered from our hillsides. That's another village tradition.'

The parishioners were starting to disperse, drifting off to the cafés or leaving the *place* altogether, heading for their homes. One of the farming lads, still in his cotton robes, was crossing the square with a full beaker of red wine cradled between his hands. He carried it with immense concentration so as not to spill a drop, and delivered it to the priest, who took it with barely a sideways glance, so engrossed in discourse was he with several of the local widows, clothed head to foot in black, along with a few middle-aged housewives in their traditional Alpes-Maritimes costumes, all floral and lacy. Father Scaramino's housekeeper, Béatrice Leblanc, had joined the gathering, and stayed tight at his side, like a barnacle. She always seemed so forbidding.

In no time at all, we were enveloped by swirls of non-churchgoers, the younger citizens, some tricked out in their traditional finery, with wide-brimmed hats and long, swirly skirts in vibrant tones of red, blue and yellow. Their arrival was the cue for the music and dancing to begin, and for carousing and courting. This square was the nub of community life. It was where most things happened, where you could watch or learn about the daily comings and goings. Sylvie had told me that if you had a secret to hide, better to keep it away from this central *place*. I glanced about, wondering where she might be. She didn't seem to be socializing with any of the groups.

Nathalie appeared, looking resplendent. She was linking arms with a rather dapper young man. I hadn't seen him before. He had a slight limp and a moustache. He hailed from further west in the Var, Alain informed me. I noticed girls whispering in their companions' ears, hands over mouths, nudging one another in the ribs: Nathalie, with her long flowing hair and pronounced cheekbones, had a beau.

No secrets here.

There was so much activity, noise and commotion that when I was introduced to Nathalie's friend I didn't catch his name or what role he played in her life. They seemed comfortable in one another's company, though, solid friends rather than flirty. Eventually, I glimpsed Sylvie. She was dashing out of the Hôtel des Alpes, flushed and bright-eyed, her blonde hair falling in curls about her bare-shoulder blouse. She was instantly girdled by a group of girlfriends. Soon, they were gossiping and tomfooling together, as they strutted towards the centre of the square where the band was tuning up. One of the girls I recognized. I had spotted her on several occasions in the company of an Italian soldier. I glanced to and fro, looking for Albert and his mother. Might she be inside the hotel, where the overhead fans were spinning in the dining room, enjoying a cosy lunch with the fat *capitano*?

Thomas, having rid himself of his robes, was jogging in our direction, waving. The soldiers were in evidence all around us, ogling, dallying. Some were making themselves comfortable, legs outstretched, feet tapping, near the barrels of wine, tumblers in their hands, while others were taking slow tours of the square. The band, a quintet, was made up of two permanent residents and three refugees. Two violins, accordion, cello and a small piano. The pianist was the local pharmacist.

I felt a sudden pang of sadness that my father had never chosen to involve himself with any of the musical groups, several of them initiated by foreigners, that his time was spoken for and he was always too busy helping others to engage in any of the more light-hearted recreations, to profit from the blessings of the present. Perhaps if he and Mamma had been able to socialize more with the community they, like me, might long to stay on and make a home here. The musical societies were thriving. I should try to persuade Papa . . .

And then I caught sight of them, my parents, strolling hand in hand into the square from the direction of our house. How small and frail my mother had become, diminished. I hardly recognized her. She was out of her depth. An air of bewilderment dogged her as though someone had dropped her from the sky into an alien world and she couldn't fathom how to retreat. Yet they seemed so complete together, in spite of their disputes. It gladdened me to realize that they were such a well-matched pair, and it gave me peace, a sense of calm, because I knew deep down – though how could I possibly have discerned what lay ahead? – that when the day came, I would not be leaving with them.

35

The troubles of the future, the horrors that were to come, were far from my reveries on that sunny holiday afternoon. It was promising to be a perfect day, not a ruined one as I had feared a few hours earlier.

My parents chose a café, not Pascal's but the one closest to where they had entered the square and where three or four other Jewish families had already assembled. They made themselves comfortable, acknowledging the others with a nod but remaining apart. My mother was wearing her coat. She could not possibly have been cold. She wore it hunched about her, as though it were her armour against the outside world. I broke away from Alain and the others and ran over to greet them.

'I am so glad you're here,' I cried. 'Will you dance together? Shall I fetch you some refreshment?'

My mother laid her hand on my arm and told me to keep my voice down, not to make a spectacle of myself, and to tidy my appearance.

'What have you done to your hair, Sarina? It's falling like leaves from a tree in the autumn.'

I lifted a hand to my head. The flowers had long since abandoned me. I was deflated, upset that my woebegone mamma had nothing positive to say. Why did she spoil everything, always digging for the negative aspects? Father, picking up on the mood brewing between us, leaned forward and complimented me on my clothes though he was familiar with them. 'Quite the sophisticated lady you are in that green frock today, Sarina,' he remarked. 'The colour enhances your black hair admirably.'

Well, that was a compliment, at least. Father waved to the young rabbi and his wife, who were approaching. I kissed his brow, wished them both a pleasant afternoon and left them to it.

First I danced with Alain and felt my whole being go dizzy at the proximity between us: the brush of his loose shirt against me and the tickle from his exhalations so close to my ear. It was out of this world. Then I boogied for ages with Sylvie because she grabbed me by the wrist, yanking me away from Alain and into the middle of the dance floor. I tried to refuse, to stay where I was, blissfully content, but her insistence was vehement and her voice held the edge I was growing to recognize as treacherous territory. Her breath smelt of alcohol; she was talking loudly, gesticulating as though in a play. She was trying to teach me the Swing while impersonating one of the residents – Madame Mealy Mouth, she'd nicknamed her, a mean-spirited nosy body, who hated everyone. She relaxed when we were in the centre of the jollities, far from Alain, and I did, too, and we laughed ourselves silly. We jitterbugged and spun in circles, and I felt a different kind of dizzy.

'Your hair's like a bird's nest,' she screeched, hand over her mouth, guffawing. 'But it suits you, Wild Girl,' she purred, in an affected manner.

We boogied some more and she hooted and sang a little too noisily, arms waving, attracting attention.

'Sylvie, sssh, I think you're a bit tiddly.'

'I am *not*! But you . . . you're sweet on him, I know,' she whispered in my ear, emphasizing 'sweet' so it sounded like '*sweeeeet*'. I pretended to have no clue whom she was talking about, but she repeated it over-emphatically 'I know. Admit it. Shall I shout his name out loud? Sara's sweet on Aaaal—'

'Shut up!'

Nathalie arrived with a small tray of glasses. It dissipated the awkwardness, for which I was relieved. 'Wine,' she cried triumphantly. I had never tasted wine.

I glanced guiltily towards the table where my parents had been seated but the chairs were empty. Two small coffee cups were the only traces that remained of their presence. I glanced up and down the square. No sign of them. Were they waltzing somewhere beyond our huddled group? Somehow I doubted it. No, they would have crept back to the kitchen in the white house.

'Are you looking for your parents?' Alain, close at my side again. 'I saw them leave the table about ten minutes ago. Want me to run up the road and catch them?'

I shook my head while draining the last mouthful from Sylvie's beaker — she had downed the rest — and then I sipped some of Nathalie's and Alain's white wine, too. I might as well have accepted a glass of my own. Three glugs and my head was starting to spin.

Everyone was being chivvied, organized, into long lines. Four chains that reached almost the length of the square. A local farmer was the dance master.

'Let's gather for the farandole, please, ladies and gentlemen! The Farandole de Brei.'

We all joined hands — Alain's left holding my right — and we swayed and clapped. It was a traditional Niçoise reel with lots of skipping and hopping and applauding. The girls held their long skirts in their hands. I tripped over my feet a few times, stepping in the wrong direction — left not right, then right not left — but it was all rollicking good fun and I was euphoric, more elated than I'd been in years.

Until a black shadow rolled into the afternoon.

At the top of the square, close by the hotel, one of the two official Citroëns drew up. Out of it stepped a chauffeur in military uniform. He bent to one of the rear doors and from it appeared the senior Italian officer, Captain Fontano.

The dancing seemed to slow. Spirits muffled as a current of disquiet, a frisson of curiosity, circulated through the jogging lines. The chauffeur leaned in, offering a hand to a second passenger. A strappy open-toed summer shoe with high heel appeared, followed by a slender ankle. Albert's mother was sliding from the rear seat, and rising to her splendid height. Now she was on the arm of Fontano, the *capitano* of the 4th. Several younger officers and lowlier soldiers stepped forward to greet the pair. Bowing their heads, they kissed Albert's mother on the back of her hand as though she were a goddess. She soaked up the attention, relishing it, eyelids fluttering. Her bare arms, bespangled with many bracelets, waved, like music, in the air while the *capitano* at her side, a portly older man, admired and encouraged her. He was lighting a cigar, chortling. She was wearing a close-fitting dress in strawberry red. Like a second skin, it revealed every curve of her voluptuous figure. I was mesmerized and just a little in awe of her command of the situation, her poise, her wantonness.

The music and dancing had come to a stop, the lines broken up, while the townsfolk took stock. Some gawped open-mouthed, others whispered. The liaison certainly didn't go unremarked.

My mind flicked back to the recent conversation in

Delphine's kitchen. Alain's words. *Les mouchards*, the traitors.

'Nothing good comes of taking a Latin lover,' one old codger fizzed, through non-existent teeth, spittle settling on his stubbled chin.

Albert's mother, with her Hollywood allure, whom I had so admired, was she an informer, a traitor to her own?

'This'll cost her dear when the day of reckoning comes,' spat one of the female dancers.

'She's still nothing but a laundry woman.'

Pascal sauntered out of his bar and stood in the doorway, wiping his hands on a cloth, watching. I could not tell from his expression whether he judged the lady harshly.

'When the war's over, they'll shave her head,' hissed Madame Mealy Mouth.

Sylvie tutted loudly in my ear. 'Old Mealy Mouth's right, though. She's sleeping with the enemy. He's a married man from Cuneo with a family, a wife and two children back home.'

'And what about you?' I retorted. Sylvie swung in my direction. Those blue eyes scorched me with their gaze. She was mad as a hornet.

I was floored, upset. I felt crushed, not for Sylvie but for Albert. I did not want to picture such a conclusion. I shot a look to where I had last spotted my friend. There he was, on his own, scratching his face, leaning against one of the trunks of the big old mottled plane trees. His head was bowed, his eyes were downcast, as though if he did not bear witness to his mother's audacious performance it might dispel his shame. I broke from the group and ran over to him.

'Albert,' I said, 'come with me.'

'What?' He shrugged me off him, where I had touched

his sleeve. His gesture was bordering on violent. His eyes were blazing with indignation and tears, his cheeks flushed, smarting with anger and pain. 'Get lost.'

'Shall we dance? Would you like to?'

'No,' he barked. 'Stupid, there's no music. Everyone's ogling my mother.'

'Well, then, let's go for a walk. Or a swim. Come on, it's so hot.'

'What for? Anyway, you look like shit.' And with that he rolled his body sideways, lurched away from the tree and stormed off to the furthest exit from the square, spitting on the ground as he went.

Should I go after him? Or leave him to his private pain? I chose to stay put, my gaze following his departure even after he was well out of sight.

Poor humiliated Albert.

Then I scanned the couples, dancing again now, the small groups scattered here and there with drinks in hand, others kissing in the shadows of the lofty, leafy trees. Sylvie's arms were wrapped round Alain's waist.

And the shadow of the car grew longer, clouding the day.

36

The sun was sinking, turning the sky peach-rose. Dusk fell earlier up here due to the mountains obscuring the horizon to the west. Down at the coast full sunshine would still be baking the glamorous bays of the Côte d'Azur. I was pleased that the natural light was fading. The lanterns and the lockets of illuminations glowed brightly in the square, but for me the celebrations had lost their glitter. It was all too gaudy, life too complicated.

I craved someone – no, not someone: I yearned for Alain to hold me in his arms and make the world good again.

Herds of twirling children, including Delphine's Élisabeth alongside my delightful ringlet-haired Hanna, were clustered in untidy circles like an assembly of spinning tops, arms raised above their heads, rotating unsteadily all across the square. Each one stubbornly refused to accept his or her parents' declaration of their tiredness, determined to keep going till they dropped, the music firing their energy.

In the midst of the pivoting infants and a few older couples waltzing, I spotted Frau Lindemann and her husband shuffling very slowly, imperceptible steps, in one another's arms but at arm's length. Her pregnancy was evident. She must have been close to five months. Her belly was swelling yet she remained stick-thin; a porcelain beauty cracking under the strain.

I counted on my fingers behind my back, calculating when she was likely to give birth. Mid-October? Would we still be in this hilltop haven, or would my parents have secured us the passage onwards Papa had spoken of, to somewhere I didn't want to go? Would I be needed to help with Hanna and Daniel for whole days rather than just the mornings after the third child was born? I wouldn't mind – I loved them, cared about them as if they were my baby brother and sister.

Could I stay on here without my parents?

It was strange that I asked myself these questions even when prescience – or blind hope – encouraged me to believe that my future did not lie in taking the journey onwards with my parents.

On that day in the fading light of midsummer – a day when tragedy engulfed us all – I could not possibly have foreseen that our destinies, mine and my beloved parents', lay in different corners of Europe.

Had I foreseen it, could I ever have wished it so?

The Lindemanns were talking to one another as they glided to and fro, eyes only for each other, deep in conversation. It warmed me that they cared so for one another.

Alain was still dancing with Sylvie. It was a slow, smoochy tune. He was smiling, appeared content, while her movements were a little precarious. Her weight seemed to be hanging on him as she staggered. I longed to be a turtle dove in one of the overhead branches, eavesdropping. I monitored them, eyes glued on them. They were so relaxed in each other's company. Suddenly, a burst of laughter. They stopped moving. Sylvie, bent double, was covering her eyes to halt the tears of mirth rolling down her cheeks, wagging the other hand impatiently, stamping her feet, as if begging Alain to cease whatever it was he was telling her. A story recounted, an anecdote, a joke? A shared moment of affection. A history, a past and a future I would never share with him.

I know, she had whispered to me. Sylvie read my feelings for Alain because hers mirrored mine.

Their vibrancy, affinity, was too much for me. I hurried from the square. The moment I was out of sight I picked up pace, racing in whichever direction the path took me.

Once out of the town in open country, which was not far, I slowed down to catch my breath. There was still light here. The sun had not yet set. The sky was clear, a bruised pale purple. I was crying, hot tears on my moist cheeks. How pitiful was I to have dreamed of Alain, to have fabricated a romance in my head, a life here in these bewitching hills. Soon I would be gone – of course I would – and this yearning, this emptiness . . . I had allowed myself to be carried away in the juvenile fantasies my parents had warned me against.

These were Alain's people, not mine; he was training to be a doctor to care for them. I was a fleeting acquaintance to whom he and his sister were showing compassion, friendship. He wasn't offering me love.

37

I was walking purposefully now, not fast, beating along a track I don't think I had ever set foot on before. I didn't recognize it and I had no idea where it was leading me. I tried to picture the book Delphine had lent me, the double-page spread of the map. But I was lost. No, not lost for I had only to turn round on the same path, retrace my steps and I would find myself back in the centre of our little settlement. In the distance, the music was still playing, still within earshot.

Laughter, camaraderie, belonging.

I continued onwards. The vegetation was becoming more rugged and unforgiving. At some point, the path forked. I chose the left direction. It seemed to be the straighter of the two but very soon became a descent. Sharply steep. It was harder to keep my footing now, not to slide. So narrow was it that I had to take care, placing one foot in front of the other. The ground surface was shaly and loose. I slipped. Whoops. Steadied myself.

I paused, deep breaths, stabilizing myself. I had slipped, not fallen. All was well, nothing to fear. Still, a sharp-edged piece of flint had shot up from under my shoe and cut my leg. Not a deep incision but enough to draw blood. I spat on my fingers and rubbed at the scratch along my calf.

It was so silent. I couldn't even hear the water cascading south. Why not? I turned about me, nothing was familiar. Was I behind the mountain where our white house stood? Was this north? Had I left the Lower Alps altogether and struck out towards the higher ranges? Surely not.

It was as if the world had suddenly come to a standstill. The sky was empty of birds. I heard no insects, no bees buzzing. A bad feeling in my gut told me to turn back, before darkness fell, before I lost sight of the outlines of the track. One slip, one wrong foot and I would be hurtling backwards down the mountainside. It would take a search party an eternity to find my corpse.

Would my end make a jot of difference? One less to feed.

As I turned my back to the open view of gorge and mountain flanks I caught sight of a large bulk on one of the trees. It was a spruce of some sort with a long sack-like thing hanging from it. Like a giant bee swarm swinging from a branch, its lower part centimetres away from the plummeting slope. It was off to the left of the path. I dropped to my haunches and, gripping thickets of freshly sprouted scrub and clinging to boulders that promised not to shift and send me hurtling hundreds of metres to certain death, I proceeded towards the suspended cargo.

As I grew closer, I could see that the pendulous thing had feet. It was a body. A human body. Out in this wilderness. Oh, God.

I shuffled faster on my backside to get a closer look, but even before I reached the lump, I knew.

No. NO.

Albert. Hanging from the branch of a tree growing on the fringe of the mountainside, far from base, with a rope around his neck. The rope that had held his trousers in place. His trousers were caught about his shoes like a big brown puddle. I pictured his mother in her high heels and snazzy red outfit.

Oh, mon dieu. I don't know why I spoke in French. Because my friend was French? Because I fancied that I was French too, that I was kin?

'Albert?'

I approached him gingerly from the rear. My legs were shaking so violently from the shock, terror, I could barely lift myself to my full height. I was obliged to use the trunk of the tree and then Albert's naked dangling legs to steady myself, to haul myself to my full height.

'Albert? Albert!' I shook him gently, desperate to revitalize him.

This was not a sight I would easily forget.

Now I was beside him, then in front of him. His body was swinging discernibly. I had dislodged its repose. My fingers brushed his hand. He was still warm. His tongue was hanging out, loose like a dog's.

'Albert? Can you hear me? Please, *please*, come back to life.'

I had to get help. Cut him down, but if I did he might roll away never to be found again. In any case, what would I use? I possessed no knife, no sharp object. I must call, loudly, or return to the village.

His eyes were wide open as though he'd been dragged out of the sea in a net and laid on an ice-cold slab at the fish market in Nice. His face bore an expression of surprise, shock at his own desperate act.

I threw up then, all over the mountainside at my friend's feet, wine and breakfast and misery, spewing it all out. 'Albert!' I wailed and wailed, reminiscent of the wolves baying to the stars. 'What have you done?' And then I screamed as loudly as I could. I screamed for help, for somebody, anybody, to arrive and bring my poor disturbed friend back to life.

I was dragging myself by my hands, nails into sand and limestone rock, razoring my skin, fearing to fall backwards, up the ascent, beaching on the path, calling, shouting, 'Help! Help!'

I arrived at a ledge and paused, waiting. How long did I wait? Minutes, hours? I don't know. I cursed at a fly that was buzzing round my face, irritating me, attracted by flecks of vomit. Eventually, in the distance, beneath the blank blue sky, I caught sight of a shape, figures, silhouettes hurrying in my direction. A posse of people. No music now. It was beginning to get dark out here in the wild. Chilly. More prudent to stay where I was to avoid getting lost, to be sure my inner compass would deliver us back to Albert.

In any case, I was too tired to move. The stuffing knocked out of me.

Oh, Albert. His mother, the Red Queen: I could picture her dancing with that revolting *capitano*.

I crouched on the plateau with my back to the approaching townsfolk, keeping my concentration on the suspended figure. I felt numb, wooden yet shivery. I could point to it. It? Albert, who loved to munch apples, who had befriended me when I had no one.

The first to arrive was the baker, Louis, accompanied by Monsieur Decroix. Swiftly on their heels came Delphine, then a motley collection of others, all ages, frowning faces I couldn't put names to.

'It's the pretty Polish girl.'

'Someone hurt her?'

Crunching of feet. A pack of well-meaning individuals.

It was too much. I closed my eyes. First, though, I managed to utter Albert's name and point back down the hill to the tree. Most of the band took off, speculating, shouting to one another but Delphine stayed to care for me.

'Let's get you back,' she said. 'Can you walk?'

I had split my dress, ripped its underarm to a shred. The sleeve was hanging, like a broken limb. Hanging like Albert. I stumbled to my feet and allowed Delphine to slide her arm beneath my bare armpit and haul me forwards.

38

Albert's funeral was held on the Saturday, late morning. I stood by a pew near the back of the church, half hidden by a stone pillar. The nave was packed. No Italians were present. No cigar-smoking Captain Fontano from Cuneo. Albert's mother was a lone figure, dressed in black with a lace veil that covered her entire head, including her face, screening her, concealing her emotions from any busy-bodying snoops. Erect, stiff-lipped, spine rigid, in the first row, close to the pulpit. Beside her in the aisle, her late son's coffin with dozens of sprays of delicate mountain flowers interwoven, like knots and layers of coloured veils, across its surface.

Even from this distance, inconspicuously out of sight, I was an outsider in a Catholic church. I could smell the sweetness of dried lavender, of the pink and purple rock roses, the gum rose, the candytuft, the catchfly, the spurge, the silvery foliage of Jupiter's beard – too late for its white flowers – the white and pink hyssop loosestrife. It pleased me to think I had learned to identify a fair number of the flowers with all their extraordinarily evocative names. Plants of the *maquis*, many now adorning my friend's coffin. He who had introduced me to some of these plants for the first time.

There was music, hymns with high, solemn notes, a solo vocalist singing soprano, Bruckner's 'Ave Maria', which chilled me to the bone. My father would have appreciated the music. Where was he? I had barely set eyes on them for days. Alain was one of the pallbearers, as was Monsieur Decroix. I think that was the first time I'd seen him in his smart blue lieutenant's uniform. It was a good thing, I thought, during the mass, which I could not understand because, other than the homily, it was all in Latin, that Albert was not heavy because there were so few strong men to transport the weight of him, sealed within that hateful box. After a rather long service, towards the end of which almost everyone filed into lines for Holy Communion, the parishioners left the church and walked two or three abreast behind the coffin across the square – still with its dimmed party lights – and downhill to the cemetery, which I had never visited before. South of the town. Within the graveyard, there were dozens of stone statues. Marble angels playing soundless trumpets pointing to on high or holding thick stone books open at blank stone pages.

Everybody I had ever seen or met in the vicinity seemed to be present, even old Marie, from the grocery, with her beautiful soulful eyes, broken-hearted today. She was with Alain, who held her hand and treated her with tenderness and care. I envied her.

There were clouds in the sky, which made a welcome change from the perpetual long days of uninterrupted blue, and seemed a fitting tribute to our departed friend. I lifted my head to watch them, scudding gently round the pinnacles of the mountains.

Spirits gathering.

Sylvie was crying, relentless sobs. Her head bent low, her hands rubbing at her face as though her skin was itching, on fire. Her mother, at her side, silently stroked her daughter's blonde hair, then dug for a handkerchief from her small black handbag and passed it to her. Nearby, I spotted Pascal, his strong arm on Thomas's shoulders. Maurice, who'd nearly been arrested, was close to Pascal. Then Delphine, in black. Everybody had turned out for Albert. Even the kitchen maids from the hotel. Father Scaramoni was making a speech, telling his community what a dedicated altar server Albert had always been. It struck me as unnecessary. Everyone knew what a decent, willing and sensitive fellow Albert was, had been. Still, it postponed the grisly moment of lowering the coffin into its earthy dugout. When the moment came, it swung clumsily as it descended. It was beyond ghastly and made my knees turn to jelly. Albert's mother first, then lots of the other ladies tossed wild flowers, ribbons and trinkets onto the box that contained our friend.

I winced at the clunk as a trinket hit or bounced from the wood, as though its sharp metallic weight was hurting him, lancing him.

I closed my eyes and saw the darkness Albert must be seeing, except, of course, he wasn't seeing anything. Nor would he ever see again.

I think that was the day, at Albert's graveside, when I decided I hated all religion and that I would no longer believe in God: if He existed, what sort of a monster must He be to condone all this savagery and inner turmoil?

Afterwards, we ambled off in ones or twos. Albert's mother remained, staring into the trench that housed her son. Three old biddies either side clung to her. What of Albert's father? I was asking myself. Albert had spoken about him only once. Had the man been notified? Was someone trying to make contact with him, or was he also dead and buried? I pictured him returning home from his place of hiding only to be greeted by this mess.

Life couldn't be crueller. I wanted to run away, go home. Home. Ha! Where was that? Millions displaced.

I thought I heard Alain call my name, but I decided it was wiser not to turn round. Sagacity was to distance myself from this broken love affair of my own foolish fiction. I felt hollow inside and unspeakably lonely. My heart was destitute. I wanted to curl up in bed and stay there until the war was over, until the Italians had gone away. Until, until, until . . .

39

As I meandered, scuffing my shoes on purpose – so what if I didn't have another pair? – I encountered not one soul along that magisterial route to the white house. Just a few cumulus clouds, those big fluffy perfectly white ones that I had learned to draw at school when I was small, when I still believed in fairy tales and the world was more inno-cent and kind. A pair of eagles overhead, circling into view from behind the mountain. They mate for life, Alain had told me.

That was reassuring.

The traffic was bees, midges and other flying things. A few songbirds.

I could not face upstairs, my parents. Claustrophobia. I no longer possessed the key to downstairs because I had returned it to its ring with all the others in the drawer, as I had promised Alain I would. I opened the gate and stepped into the garden, wild and tyrannical in its con-tinuous growth, its push towards dominance.

Procrastination.

What remained? Rotten as everything had turned out to be, unlike Albert I still wanted to live. Should I run away? Could I pull off the pretence that I was an ordinary young French woman, not connected to the occupation or the refugees? Delphine had applauded my French on so many occasions.

I beat my well-trodden path to the table under the fig tree and sat there for a minute or two or, I don't know, it might have been hours, staring at my scratched and dusty shoes, watching a small army of voracious ants devour the carcass of a beetle or some other largish black crusty thing. Incessant buzzing, like a string orchestra tuning up, repetitive note after repetitive note until it might have driven me insane. I jumped to my feet, a blinding flash of clarity. I knew what my next steps were to be.

I fetched one of the iron chairs and, with some effort, placed it beneath the broken window sealed only with the plank I had collected from the garden to secure it. One sharp punch and the wood was on the floor of the wash-room inside. I kicked my feet, lifted my body, slid through the window-framed aperture and was back inside.

I made my way directly to the drawing room where I had left matches. I lit one of the candles in the holder on the piano, then crossed to the mantelpiece where the cigarette I had left there lay alongside the red Craven 'A' packet. Today was the day I would smoke that cigarette. I picked it up and slipped it between my lips – its white paper shroud stuck to the damp pink of my lower lip. I grabbed the matches and made my way to Lucy's bedroom. Cross-legged on the rug on the floor, leaning against the side of the bed, I lit the cigarette and took a good deep drag. God, it was revolting. It set my head reeling and I began to choke. No noise. I mustn't make any noise. Two more puffs – ugh, horrible, but I'd get used to it – and I felt a bit steadier. There was a bottle of vodka somewhere. In the scullery beyond the kitchen? I was trying to remember where I had spotted it on one of my earlier visits. Yes, in the scullery on one of the shelves. I lifted myself to my feet and navigated a path to the larder. Bottles and bottles were lined up there. I might drink the lot.

Vodka cap unscrewed, I poured a good shot into one of the tumblers Alain and I had used in the garden. Cigarette and vodka in hand I returned to the bedroom. By the bedside there was a pocket-sized framed photograph of Lucy's son. Why didn't I know his name? He was looking directly at the camera, bright-eyed, smiling playfully, exposing his slightly irregular milk teeth. Two years old, perhaps? A little older than Daniel, but not by many months.

I was too sad to cry, but twisted by the images haunting me of Albert hanging from the tree. Was that how Lucy felt? Was that why she couldn't return here, even if she loved it at least as much as I did? Too many reminders, too many corners from which her son's innocent face grinned back at her?

Life's cruel jokes.

How could I stay here now?

I ached with loss, with the growing realization that my friend would be forever absent from my days. I would have liked to hear from Lucy, to understand how she was coping. To be given the opportunity to hold her hand and reassure her that she was not alone in her grief. I fantasized about trying to find her. Why not go in search of her? Mrs Lucy Allingham. To hell with the risks, I would find her. I set aside my glass, tossed the remainder of the cigarette into the dregs of the alcohol and staggered slowly to my feet.

Lucy's shoes were, as I had previously discovered, all too small by at least two sizes, so I remained barefoot. The clothes, though, slid over my head, or up over my thighs and fitted like kid gloves. I took time and delight in choosing which ones to wear, handling one outfit after another as though I were in a stylish clothes shop and there was all the time in the world.

The soft feel of each fabric: cashmere, silk, linen, taffeta, Egyptian and Irish cotton shirts. Lucy's perfume embedded in sleeves and collars. I held blouses, scarves, jackets to my cheek. I danced to and fro, hugging Freddie, swirling in circles with a cream lace dress pressed tight against myself and my handsome red-haired fox. Eventually, I settled for an oyster-pink silk shirt. It was the colour of the sky at sunset and satiny as ballet shoes. To accompany it, a full swirly lime-green skirt somewhere between box and sunray pleated. It hung almost to my ankles and was magnificent. The bee brooch, all gold, with its rounded pearl body was the perfect accompaniment. I scooted back into the drawing room to retrieve it, pinning it proudly to my breast. I glanced into the glass above the chimney. A pale ghost stared back at me.

Lucy's make-up pouch was alongside pots of creams spread across shelves in the bathroom. A light above the mirror would have eased my work but I dared not risk it, even though I had availed myself of the electricity many times before. Not today. One of the candelabra, with two candles burning close to my face, proved sufficient while I went about the transformation. Circles of rouge on my cheeks for my pale northern European skin, a scarlet lipstick to give me fully rounded, plump lips, like my 'adopted' sister, Lucy, who would soon greet me and welcome me into her real life, not her shadow world. Streaks of her eye shadow because olive green was my favourite colour and it highlighted, I saw now, my tawny-black eyes, giving them depth, intelligence, I hoped, and maturity. My hair was a challenge. Long, dark, wiry, it did as it pleased, independent of my will. I brushed it vigorously and coiled it round my fingers, then let it fall loose. It hung like a mantle. Black waves caressing my pink silk-clad shoulders.

The blouse plunged low in the front exposing my cleavage, lily-white in spite of all our trips to the river. I gazed into the mirror at the stranger whose dark troubled eyes returned my stare. She bore little resemblance to Lucy. More importantly, she bore little resemblance to Sarina or life-embattled Sara. Did I still look Polish? Could I pass for a French woman or even a young English lady? What age was I? Older than seventeen, surely. Eighteen, perhaps, even twenty with a cigarette glued to scarlet lips. The smoking and drinking would add to the illusion of worldliness. If I walked out of here now, away from our white house, could I return to the coast without a soul remarking my presence in the streets? Could I be free to move about, mingle, be one of the crowd?

Might I be able to use my charms, like Sylvie, to barter? To trade. Not for textile coupons. I needed papers, an exit visa. Not so easy. Even my father hadn't managed to acquire them. I sank onto the bed to think through this plan carefully, meticulously, to plot my escape.

40

I must have fallen asleep. Something . . . a sound roused me. I lifted myself onto my elbows and held my breath, listening. Footsteps in the corridor? I wriggled across to the far side of the mattress, slid from the counterpane and crouched tight to the floor. Who was in the house? My father? I was dressed in Lucy's clothes. He mustn't find me here.

'Sara?'

I buried myself deep in the pile of the carpet, curled like a cat. The candles were still burning. Two where I had left the candelabra on the console, next to the photograph of Lucy's son. *Merde. Merde.*

'Sara, are you in here? I can smell smoke.'

It was Alain. He was standing in the doorway. My heart was beating so fast I thought it would explode.

I had broken my word to him. He mustn't find me. If I stayed hidden, he would go away, move on to another room and then, with luck, I could escape out through the door, if he had come in that way using his mother's key, or scramble through the window.

He wasn't moving. There was no sound. Then, I heard the glass containing cigarette and vodka being lifted from the nightstand. My eyes were squeezed tightly shut. If I couldn't see him . . . Too late. His feet were next to mine.

'Sara, didn't you hear me calling? I've been looking everywhere for you. What are you doing down here?'

I opened my eyes, praying he was alone, that my parents were not with him.

'What on earth . . . ? What the hell have you done to your face?'

The make-up. It must be smudged. I couldn't see myself, didn't know how I looked. He bent low, took my hand, raised me to full height. He held me firmly, his arms about me, gazing into my face, disconcerted by my appearance.

'Jesus, Sara. Wait here. I'm going to close the front door. Sit on the bed.'

I perched, trembling from head to toe. I heard the slip of the chain, footsteps, and then he was back at my side.

'Are you by yourself?' My teeth were chattering, words semi-formed.

He nodded, took me in his arms once more and rubbed my back as my mother had done in the days when we were safe and there was nothing more threatening or wrong with me than a chest cough or a winter cold. Polish winter days by the fireside. Snow falling. Thick homemade soups, scalding my lips. My feet tucked into scratchy blankets. Suddenly a vision of my mother back then, the kindness in her face, the gentleness and patience. The fullness of her flesh, not the haggard sketch of skin over skeleton she had become. Nothing more now than a pencil drawing of her previous self.

And Albert.

How much we had all lost. How much the war had stolen from us.

Alain was hugging me, holding me so tightly I thought he might crack my bones. I couldn't stop shaking.

'You've suffered a shock,' he said, more to himself than to me. 'Delayed shock. Is there hot water here?' he asked, pulling me away to half-arm's length.

'I don't know,' I mumbled.

'You need to wash all this off and get yourself cleaned up. You can't go back upstairs looking like this. Do you understand me?'

I nodded.

'Do your parents know you're down here?'

I shook my head.

'Stay where you are.'

He laid me on the bed and disappeared. I could hear him moving about in the bathroom, running taps, opening cupboards, drawing out toiletries, then hurrying to the kitchen to boil water. I closed my eyes. Exceptionally weary. Albert was there, hanging from the tree. We were in a boat. It was night. Attempting a crossing into France. A coastguard's siren.

Before I drifted off, Alain was back, scooping me off the bed, carrying me as though I were his bride – if only – to the bathroom. There he undressed me in a matter-of-fact fashion. I was shivering, embarrassed to be so exposed, my black pubic hair on full display. Once rid of the clothing, he assisted me into a shallow bath of tepid water.

From somewhere he had found a sponge, soap, even shampoo. My nakedness was covered with suds. Sleeves rolled up, he scrubbed and worked with barely a word, a glance.

'You clean off your face. I don't want to get lather in your eyes.' There was a half-smile, then he spun to his feet and handed me a mirror. 'Two clean towels. I'll be in the drawing room. Call if you need me or want help getting out of the bath. Wrap yourself up tight. Don't catch cold,' he commanded. 'It's a little damp down here.' He disappeared.

The water was losing what little heat it had had. I hunched into myself, covering my breasts, and dared a glance in the glass. What a sight. Scarlet and green smeared in a detonated firework display. I did my best to clean up the disaster, scrubbing till my complexion was the colour of a tomato. Then I climbed gingerly from the bath, reached for the bottle of Jean Patou – would Lucy object? I squeezed the atomizer and sprayed myself, a gentle cloud of Joy. Those few inhalations of its jasmine and rose-rich fragrance reinvested me with a modicum of self-worth, of dignity, femininity.

Alain had seen me naked. I took a deep breath.

On my way out, I unclipped the bee brooch from the blouse and carried it, secreted in the closed palm of my hand, to *le salon*. I was wrapped in a towel, couldn't remember where I had left my clothes. Ah, yes, the bedroom. Alain was waiting on one of the sofas, chin resting in his hands. I crossed in front of him and delivered the bee back to its resting place without a word.

My back was to the room, to Alain. I coughed, waiting for him to speak. He didn't. 'I should get dressed,' I mumbled.

'Come here, Sara.' He patted the sofa cushion alongside him.

'I should get dressed,' I repeated.

'Sara . . . Yes, good, get dressed. I'll wait.'

When I returned he was standing by the mantelpiece, more or less where I had been. Had he remarked the return of the brooch?

My body was still a bit damp because I had dressed in

haste. My clothes felt drab and worn after Lucy's. I took a seat on the sofa and waited.

He rubbed his left eye with his finger. He had seen me naked, undressed me. I couldn't get that thought out of my mind. He had helped me as though I were a sick patient. I meant nothing to him. Kindness, yes, but romance, no.

'Listen,' I began, taking the lead, attempting to inject a little self-respect into the scene, to give the impression I was an adult and in control when he had patently seen otherwise. 'I'll clear up the mess I've made and I promise – and I know I promised it last time – I double promise I won't come back down here again.'

'I am a little in the dark, Sara,' he replied. 'Delphine was telling me how terrific you have been, assisting her in the school . . . How dependable you are. What happened to Albert is a terrible, terrible shock. Another victim of this bloody war, but you cannot allow it to knock you off track. Your strength and presence of mind will be the keys to your survival.'

I was surprised by the ferocity of his tone. He was running his right hand through his hair, as though combing it for answers.

'Come with me. I want to show you something.'

'What?'

'Just do as I say. Come with me.'

He held out his hand. I rose and slipped mine into his. Without a word or a glance, he led me along the corridor to the kitchen and through into the scullery, the larder, where I had filched the vodka. Here was a dark maroon-painted door. I hadn't paid it any attention before, if I had noticed it at all. Alain turned the oval porcelain handle. He tugged at it, pulling hard. The door was sticky and swollen from lack of use and humidity. After much persuasion it shuddered open, one centimetre at a time, until it revealed a descending flight of wooden stairs that led, I supposed, to a cellar. I took a step. A wave of putridity hit us, as though all the dead rodents from this mountain burg were rotting in piles somewhere beneath the stairs.

'I'm not going down there.'

'It needs a thorough cleaning, I grant you. And there's no electricity. We'll need to furnish it with hurricane lamps and candles, for a start.'

I looked at him, bewildered. I didn't understand. 'Why?'

'Sara, for the present you are out of harm's way,' he said. 'Soon you'll have papers, I pray. And then we will begin the complicated and dangerous business of getting you and your family, with other families, out of France, out of Europe to a war-free zone.'

We?

'But what has that to do with this cellar? Are you suggesting my family moves down here?'

The smell was so disgusting, the darkness. Were there rats? Mamma would never survive it.

'It is impossible to predict what is going to happen. Jean has been arrested. As we feared, betrayed. Imprisoned. We have no further news. No information.'

I was trying to recollect someone called Jean. One of the farmers?

'I'm sorry to hear that,' I mumbled.

'Should the German Army arrive in this town unannounced and you and your parents are still here . . . Well, I don't have to tell you that you will be deported. Possibly to Drancy and then a train east.'

I fought against the mental picture Alain was painting.

He was studying me. 'This *cave*,' he continued, 'spreads the entire length of the downstairs of this property. If you are going to spend time in this lower level of the house, use the time practically, profitably. Clean the cellar and make it ready for use as an emergency shelter, make it at least minimally habitable.'

'Is this likely?' Dread travelled through me.

'I have no idea, but the Germans are advancing across southern France. Italy is losing confidence in its dictator. Mussolini will resign. The Germans have surrendered in North Africa, and pulled out. De Gaulle is in Algiers, as is Henri Giraud, but whether the Allies or the Germans reach us first is anybody's guess. Philippe Decroix – and you absolutely shouldn't know this – is doing his damnedest to organize the necessary documentation. Counterfeit papers, stamps, exit visas. The waiting list is worryingly long. Hundreds of requests. Many ahead of you. There are so few with the meticulous skills required for forgery and far too many fugitives begging papers, identity cards. I hope that soon you will be gone and the time you will have spent over summer cleaning up this safe house will have been for nothing. But it is better not to count on that.'

'I don't want to go,' I murmured. 'I don't want to run any more. Mamma is sick and frightened. I want us to stay here, where she's protected.'

He looked at me. There was pain in his face, worry. 'You are so beautiful,' he murmured. 'You don't deserve this. Your eyes, so dark and sensual. As soon as I saw you I thought, She's even lovelier than Delphine had described.'

I was stunned.

'You need to have more confidence in yourself, Sara. One day when this war is over ...' He looped an arm round my neck and locked me tight against his chest. 'Oh, Sara.' And then he pulled himself free. 'Are there any more of those candles you were burning?'

I nodded, still astonished by his words.

'Fetch them and bring matches.'

When I returned, he lit a candle, holding it aloft in his right hand and clasped my wrist in his left. Slowly we descended the rickety stairs, he leading the way, looking back over his shoulder every two steps to check on me. I thought I would gag from the stench, yet I was exploding with happiness.

41

It was a low-ceilinged space, curtained with cobwebs and foul air. Damp and chilly, like an entrance to the underworld. I touched the back of a forgotten broken chair. A thick layer of dust coated its surface. I tried to hold my breath, inhaling as infrequently as possible. So low were the wooden ceiling slats that even I, at five foot five, had to stoop to pass beneath some. We turned in circles, attempting to get the measure, the scope of the site.

'It's huge,' I whispered. My breath rose in a vaporous cloud.

'Room for several families.' Alain was still holding my hand, though I'm sure he was not aware of it. 'There's no sanitation, no windows for light or oxygen. Well, there's that coal hole over there. It offers access to a trickle of fresh air but will bring in terrible cold in the winter. It will need to be sealed off.'

He seemed to be drawing up a list, making a mental note of every task. 'Plenty of bearing timbers to smack your head on.' He lowered his forehead against one and grinned. 'We'll need buckets for lavatories, bedding – well, there are cupboards full of blankets, sheets and towels upstairs.'

I was horrified to think of Lucy and Dirk's fine bed linen thrown across these disgusting floors. 'What about the awful smell?'

'We'll swab the floors, like sailors on a deck, with *eau de*

Javel, lashings of it. I will also do a proper scout to make sure there are no decomposing rats down here.'

I let out a groan.

'It is pretty dank, I grant you that, Sara, but if it serves its purpose . . . So, mops, bleach, lanterns, matches. We'll start with those. Do you know my grandmother?'

I shook my head.

'Of course you must, the lovely and more than capable Marie. She owns the grocery off the main square. I will whisper in her ear to make sure she keeps extra stock of everything we require. She has an excellent supplier, a reliable contact, René, whose name I should not have mentioned – he more or less runs the black-market between Nice and Lyon. We'll begin tomorrow. How does that suit you? We'll work every morning and we won't give up until the place is habitable. Well, bearable at least.'

'I can't work in the mornings. I look after the Lindemann children.'

'Yes, of course. I'd forgotten. Well, in the afternoons then, after a bite of lunch. And then to get the filth of this place out of our hair and skin, we'll go swimming or I might even take you up to one of the *maralpin* lakes and we'll go fishing. Catch some dinner. The sunsets from up there are not a sight you'll easily forget, Sara. While I'm home, I'll be here to lend you a hand. Count on me. And you must not breathe a word to anyone. Not one word, is that clear?'

Oh, it was so clear I could barely express my rapture.

Yet when I was alone I was plagued with confusion.

You are so beautiful.

While I'm home . . .

Upstairs in my room, alongside the wall to my sleeping

parents, I lay on my bed recalling Alain's words. Every future development seemed to be a question of time, a Damocles sword of uncertainty hanging over all of us. Might the Germans reach this corner of France before the Allies? On the upside, Alain esteemed me beautiful.

42

Now it was July, robust summer, blistered by a hot white light, with every creature and plant lapping up the sunshine, dousing themselves in water, while down in the cellar it was no season. Or eternal winter. But it was clean and it no longer stank. Or, rather, it did but of bleach and disinfectant. Alain and I, with occasional pop-in visits from Nathalie, had applied ourselves tenaciously to a dozen different chores – to repairs, to scrubbing, to the installation of shelves, hooks, hurricane lamps, lists of necessities. Alain, balanced on the top step of a ladder he had carried in from one of the outdoor sheds, screwed hooks into the upper beams to hang clothes, while I was on my hands and knees with a scrubbing brush, or pushing back and forth a long-handled broom. He was quite the handyman – constructing a cupboard to camouflage the maroon door in the scullery – and we worked like demons. I found the work disgusting – who wouldn't? – but I was jubilant in his company.

I was not awkward or shy, but full of purpose.

I asked myself who on earth would want to spend their holidays, their precious free hours of leisure, down here in this hole when they could be climbing in the mountains, swimming in the sunlight, pleasing themselves. He had nothing to fear from the enemy. He was preparing for his next year at university while I, my family, counted the days . . . till what? We fled, we hid, we were deported?

Alain seemed to extract pleasure from the challenge he had set himself. Us. It was our challenge.

While we worked, we barely talked. The hard physical toil left us breathless. We dragged unwieldy planks down the creaky staircase to join them together as mattress supports. Some had been retrieved from the sinking hut I'd found in the garden earlier in the year. Alain couldn't build the bed bases upstairs in the fresh air because their size would render them unnegotiable for the stairways.

'No one must be forced to sleep on the cold cement floor.'

I marvelled at his humanity, his ingenuity.

Heating was another problem. 'Winters here are perishing,' he warned.

'The winter is donkeys' years away,' I countered. 'We'll be celebrating an Allied victory by then.'

Did I believe that? Could I even visualize life those few months ahead of us?

We stocked up on candles and matches. Alain hammered nails into the ceiling beams, from which we hung long strips of cloth, makeshift curtains for dressing cubicles, offering a degree of privacy. The homemade beds were installed in each closed-off area. At their base, a galvanized bucket for ablutions.

He continued to insist that our work was clandestine – he had warned my parents not to be distracted by any banging coming from the lower floor. He was carrying out necessary renovations in readiness for the proprietors' return and, if it was fine by them, he had requisitioned my assistance. They accepted his explanation and paid the disruption little attention. I don't know what they thought about me helping with the building work, but they refrained from comment. I felt sure Papa had an inkling but, then, he had his own secrets. And they continued to hope that any day soon our false papers would be delivered.

I repeatedly reminded myself that we were preparing not for the future but for a worst-case scenario: the arrival of SS and German military into this nowhere speck of civilization in the middle of the mountains.

At nights, alone in my bed, I was sleepless with longing, the perennial fears reawakened after months of lying dormant. I pictured the chaos of five hundred refugees running for their lives, hiding in caves, forests, sequestered underground as an unforgiving army came after them. Us.

But that was not the future.

The Nazis would have no reason to seek out this remote settlement. Unless we were betrayed. Unless an informer tipped them off.

All the more remarkable, then, was the energy and determination Alain gave to the preparations, his sense that it was his duty to offer to those who *might* be obliged to go underground the most dignified conditions.

It made him all the more attractive.

I was fascinated to know how he had avoided being called up for war, or why he had not joined the Résistance when most of the young male population of the village had disappeared. Eventually, I broached the subject.

'The law called up those who were not miners, farmers or university students. Every other Frenchman was forced to report to the STO to do two years' labour in Germany.' Alain's parents, whom I had never met, had a large sheep farm, and he was studying medicine. He was exempt. Unless, or until, the law changed.

Our lives were defined by so many ifs and whens.

I asked him about the STO.

Services du Travail Obligatoire, founded by Vichy France, was a work-service scheme to compensate Germany for its loss of manpower back home. While all their able-bodied young males were fighting for Hitler, there was no one left to keep the infrastructure of their country running so Germany enlisted Frenchmen. France had surrendered. The Vichy government – traitors that they were – brokered Germany's call, promising compensation to the wives and mothers of the Frenchmen who were sent over enemy lines, little of which was ever paid.

'Is that where all the men from the village have gone?'

He shook his head. 'A few unfortunates were called up and didn't manage to worm out of it. Most have joined the Maquis.'

I had heard of the Maquis – wasn't that where Albert's father was meant to have disappeared to?

Alain explained, 'The word comes from the terrain in which the armed resistance groups hide. *Le maquis*: diverse shrublands, mountainous, impenetrable. The bands of rebel fighters hiding there have joined forces with the Résistance now. Over this last year, thanks to the leadership of men such as Jean Moulin, the individual units have been coordinated into a national resistance army.'

'Jean Moulin,' I said. 'He's the Jean who's gone missing?'

'Yes.'

Alain confided that if he couldn't continue with his studies he would fight with the *maquisards*.

How would he find these freedom fighters? Were they operating nearby? I wanted to go with him. 'Do you have weapons?' I asked him.

His family owned hunting rifles. They would be put to use for the rebel cause.

I wondered at all this information, the discretion that Delphine had insisted upon. Was this going on all around us, close by? Who else was party to this information? Everyone in the village except us foreigners? Papa must know. He was treating their wounded. Surely. Yes, it made sense now. All those nocturnal comings and goings.

The revelations were disquieting, yet exhilarating. I began to see this as a possible route out of here. To go into hiding and fight with the rebels. To be a *combattante*. Of course my parents would never agree, but neither would they condone my staying here without them, or any decision I might make that opposed travelling onwards with them.

'Are there any Jews or Poles among the *maquisards*?'

'Of course, plenty.'

'French Jews or . . .'

'Yes, predominantly *les Israélites*, the French-born Jews, but not exclusively.' Alain didn't share with me on that afternoon that the foreign Jews, those of us on the run, the thousands being given refuge, were usually described as *les Juifs* because it wasn't always spoken in a kindly fashion.

'Will you teach me to use a rifle?'

'Let's get this job finished first.'

43

The cost of food had risen by almost 15 per cent since we had arrived in this mountain village. There was less choice and quantity available on the black-market for ordinary citizens because everything had to be shared among greater numbers. For every French inhabitant in the village, there was a refugee. We had doubled the population count. It required forty francs to buy a litre of fresh milk, one egg was thirty francs and the price of goat meat had gone sky high because many of us who were passing through, *les assignés*, would happily consume goat or sheep's flesh, but not pig's. Everyone was feeling the pinch.

At what point would tolerance towards the outsiders snap?

As the summer wore on, the bad feelings fermented. A priest from one of the lowland villages had written to a senior official at the town hall in Nice to say that his parish had been transformed into a *'vrai ghetto'*. 'Isn't it bad enough to live in a country that is occupied by a foreign power, never mind being invaded by hordes of refugees with no unoccupied homelands of their own?' A quote, Alain told me, from the priest's letter.

Such resentments towards immigrants added to our mounting fears, our insecurity. I thought about dead Henryk. Who had betrayed him, stolen from him and his wife? Bandits or Jew-haters?

On the positive side, there was a rapidly rising number

of French citizens who were appalled by the treatment of the Jews, the down-on-their-luck foreigners and fugitives. They either took the same position as the Italian troops, which was to leave us in peace as long as we didn't break any rules, or a smaller, but ever-growing section of the population actively sought to assist the plight of the asylum seekers. I knew now that Alain, Delphine and Philippe Decroix counted among the latter.

But there was so much else that remained unclear to me, and I was keen to learn, to see a fuller picture. If the war dragged on, if the Allies did not liberate us first, I was determined to be a part of one of these organizations. To play my role in the liberation of France and of every one of us.

'Is Delphine involved with these secret groups? Monsieur Decroix is obviously working with them.'

'You cannot ask me so many questions, Sara. I am not at liberty to answer.'

'How do these people communicate with one another, pass messages along?'

I was recalling Marie and the old vegetable farmer Maurice, into whose newspaper she had slipped a flyer, or whatever it was. A sheet of paper with a message? Was it possible that kind-eyed octogenarian Marie was also providing assistance to the freedom fighters? Was she sending food parcels? I looked back over my months in the mountains and replayed scenes, surveying them from a different point of view. Was this the reason for the villagers' outrage over the imposition of a curfew?

'Stop now, please. No more quizzing me. You are at risk, and others are at risk if you know too many answers, Sara. It is not my place to share information. Lives are at stake.'

It was four in the afternoon. We had secured the house and were leaving to head off for a walk. Fresh air, lungfuls of clean oxygen were essential after our hours in the unventilated basement.

'Will you teach me to use a rifle? One of your hunting rifles?'

'Don't be so impatient.'

As a precaution, Alain had broken the lock on the rear entrance and replaced the padlock with a new one, which he took the trouble to scratch and dirty so it did not look new. It came with two keys. One for each of us. It thrilled me that we had confidences we were sharing, even an object as tiny but as invaluable as this key.

'It's vital you have your independence, Sara. In case something should happen when I am not here. Keep it very safe, not on your person and nowhere it can be found.'

These days, the front door remained permanently closed. Entering and exiting the property from the rear was deemed by Alain to be safer. We were far less likely to be spotted. It was another precaution, another nugget in our trove of intrigues binding us tightly together.

It turned out I was rather adept with a gun, the family hunting rifle Alain had borrowed for me. We made sure to penetrate deep into alpine forest before emerging into open country high above the village. French hunting laws were very strict and regulated, Alain warned me. However, they had been eased due to the war. Those who were without resources hunted to feed their families. Even so, all who hunted from the local communities respected the basics: never kill adolescent creatures, lactating mothers or mothers protecting their offspring. Otherwise, up here in the wild, all other game was fair prey, but Alain and I didn't shoot to kill. Nor did we hunt for food. We carried empty tins and set up shooting ranges far from the ears and beady eyes of civilization. Target practice. Our shots rang out and bounced off the mountains all about us. Shot after shot, snapping and cracking and echoing back across the limestone hills, but no one would have wondered at the sounds. Shooting was a way of life here.

Even so, Alain never left the rifle in my possession.

44

After a while, in the garden of the white house, signs of our comings and goings began to appear. As soon as it looked too well-trodden, Alain raked over our path and covered it with foliage eradicating all traces of our footfall. Afterwards, we'd create another pathway, always making sure the vegetation that flanked it was not displaced.

'Should some busybody come knocking or an unexpected authority make an appearance when I am not here, never answer the door, Sara.'

We made a point of always arriving and leaving separately. Should a curious intruder take an interest, the explanation was Alain's: house maintenance being carried out at the request of the proprietors, Mr and Mrs Allingham, in readiness for their return.

When I am not here.

Such phrases, spoken in the exchange of ideas or advice, plagued me. The day would come, sooner rather than later, when Alain and I would be separated.

Now. There was only now. There was nothing for it but to grab every minute as it came our way and make the most of it.

The work was moving forward. Soon, it would be completed, but I was determined to squeeze every ounce of happiness out of our time together. Whatever lay ahead, we were accomplishing this as a pair. The here and now.

Alain was dividing the cellar space into four semi-independent chambers. 'Like medieval monks' cells.' He grinned.

Each could sleep one couple or, at a pinch, a one-child family. If push came to shove, eight, maximum ten, people could be housed there.

He considered his work. 'I fear it will be claustrophobic, too crowded, Sara . . .'

'You said yourself it might save lives.'

'Indeed.'

'Look at this.' I'd noticed a rather old-fashioned free-standing cupboard pushed into a corner in the scullery. It was a larder with fine mesh netting on its front. While Alain was trying to seal various fissures in the cellar walls to keep out damp, I scrubbed the cupboard and dragged it down the creaking stairs, wondering whether it had come with the house when Lucy and Dirk had purchased it. It seemed so unlike their other furnishings.

'How will whoever is hiding down here, if it should ever come to that, get access to food and water?'

'We can build up reserves of food, and that larder will certainly come in handy for storage. Clean water is the real difficulty.'

Whenever Marie found herself with an unexpected delivery or a surplus of any item that could be stored without attracting rodents, Alain poached it for our cellar and stocked it there. Tinned foods mostly. Fresh water, we both now realized, was the most pressing challenge. Below ground, there was no access to it from any source, no piping that could feasibly be diverted to deliver clean running water to our shelter, and it was far too risky to call in a plumber. It seemed ironic when millions of litres cascaded down the mountainsides.

Alain agitated over this. He was a man who enjoyed finding solutions. Zinc pails were to be used as primitive lavatories but without water to rinse them out, to flush them through, they were a gruesome prospect. I tried not to dwell on it, reassuring myself always that I, my family, would not be among the unfortunates requiring this shelter because my parents would be gone and, in my fantasies, I had run off to fight with the *maquisards*.

That very morning at breakfast, Papa had assured Mamma that our exit visas and papers would be through any day now. I ate without a murmur. Did he really believe his words? Didn't he know from Monsieur Decroix that their delivery could take weeks, months? Or was he simply encouraging Mamma, feeding her with the strength to keep believing that one day this hiding, this life as an illicit citizen, would be over?

How many were ahead of us in the queue for forged documents? I didn't enquire. I watched them in silence, anxious to capture frames of their faces, to feed tomorrow's memories. My heart was a knot of contradictions. I didn't know whether, when the day was eventually upon us, I would be obliged to flee with them. What if my father said to me, *Your mother needs you, Sarina*?

In all conscience would I refuse?

I could no longer sketch any mental scenario for my future. Here felt like home. This patch of France. At Alain's side. Yet to be deprived of my family, to abandon them . . . I was torn.

What I knew without argument was that this summer — even though a large proportion of these gloriously warm days had been spent grafting and cleaning in this under-lit dungeon — had been blissful. My hands were red and raw but I was out of bed at dawn, ready for the day, and sometimes, to my shame, I hummed with happiness. Love had seeded itself, a shoot within me, reaching for the light. Even Hanna and her poor, suffering mother Ilse remarked on my cheerful demeanour.

I was emboldened by the power of my longings. Yet I yearned for a signal from the object of my passion, a return of my affection. During our hours apart, was Alain meeting up with Sylvie? Undoubtedly he cared about me as a friend but did he ache for me as I ached for him?

When Nathalie popped by, to check up on how we were getting on, she came bearing food packed in a woven basket from their mother's kitchen. Homemade bread, chunks of cheese, going blue along the rind, and occasionally slices of succulent-looking pink ham, which I stared at hungrily but did not touch. Boiled eggs – yolks as yellow as buttercups – from the household chickens and jugs of ice-cold water from a family well, fed by one of the rivers. After we had eaten our fill, upstairs in the real kitchen with the front door chained, the back locked and now a curtain covering its two grimy windows, she would always request a tour of our latest achievements and usually have practical advice to offer.

'I am concerned about the lack of running water.'

'So am I,' Alain acknowledged to his sister. 'Any suggestions?'

'Let me think about it. Have you considered women's health issues? If some of these stowaways are women and they are to be here for any length of time . . .' He frowned. She sighed. 'Sanitary napkins,' she returned. 'More importantly, the disposal of them. Or consider for one moment if Ilse Lindemann was trapped here, her child born here. We must be vigilant about hygiene.'

I watched her busily buttering thick chunks of bread, earnest and engaged. I hadn't been thinking through the reality of such an enforced life underground. I pictured Ilse. 'Nathalie has a point, Alain.' I vowed then that I must be the one to consider the needs of us females.

I admired Nathalie. She was a feminist, she declared proudly, a supporter of the vote for women, which in France had still not been granted. This I found extraordinary because suffrage for women had been ratified in Poland in November 1918.

I pondered silently whether Nathalie, too, would go undercover when the moment came. How long before that day arrived? Perhaps I could accompany her.

45

Hours spent by the river, stepping along the rim of the gorge, sometimes with a picnic hamper, on our way to swim, these were the most precious hours. Nathalie accompanied us on quite a few of our late-afternoon outings if she was not swotting for future exams. Sylvie turned up one afternoon out of the blue. She was in the company of Thomas.

'Fancy seeing you here, Sara,' she sneered. 'My, what a chic bathing costume. I wonder where that came from.'

After that, she slipped into the water and exchanged few further words with me. She was angry, hurt, jealous – of course she was – and she suspected Alain and I were up to something. There was a look of distrust, of steel in her blue eyes. She was accusing me of betraying her. I prayed she would not ask directly what was going on because I had no desire to lie to her, but I would if pressured. I was learning to be as cagey as Delphine.

Most cherished of all were the jaunts Alain and I took on our own. Cherished, although sometimes painful episodes. Painful, like the day he took me on a discovery tour along the Cherry Tree Route. We were not planning to climb the entire distance. That would have entailed an overnight stay and there was not the slightest possibility my parents would have agreed to such an outing.

Alain provided me with a *sac de montagne* to carry my water in and a small towel. He pulled his own, which was packed with our lunch, up over his shoulders. These cloth 'mountain bags' were what the locals called their knap-sacks. As we marched, climbing gently in single file at first because the path was narrow as we left our village, keeping clear of loose stones that could send us flying or create a mini landslide, he pointed out various markers to help me find my way up or down should I ever attempt this alone.

'Sheep graze on these hills. Wild goats, too. Further up, over to the right, see it, the landmark, there is a sheep wash. At that point, you are precisely one and a half kilo-metres from the village.'

He knew every scrap of this terrain. Not a scrubby bush missed his scrutiny, his recognition. If a plant had disappeared, he noted it.

He took frequent breaks, offering us the opportunity to slow our heartbeat, though he was so fit I felt sure this precaution was entirely for my benefit. Whenever he paused, he swung his body southwards to absorb the view, drawing it somewhere deep within himself, one pre-cious draught at a time.

The path widened as we ascended. Our first pause at 1,900 metres was Madone de Fenestre. A holy site with a rest stop. Delphine had mentioned this chapel to me. It was an astonishing place, and sheltered, encircled as we were by mountains.

'Behind us is the highest point in these Alpes-Maritimes, the Cîme du Gelas at 3,143 metres above sea level. Sara, quick, look there!'

A quartet of small long-haired creatures with pointed faces. I wasn't quite sure what species of animal I was staring at. 'Are they short-horned goats?'

'Chamois. It's a cross between a goat and an antelope.'

Four chamois, dark-coated with black stripy markings, two mothers and two kids – 'Last year's brood,' Alain remarked – were making their way up the rock face, climbing almost vertically.

'Ready to start hiking?' he asked.

I was taken aback, thinking we had reached our destination.

'We've hardly covered three kilometres.' He laughed.

The sloping ranges fell away in front of us in circular loops. Wilderness gave way to tableland and, below, in the far distance, farmsteads with sheep flocks, gilded wheat-fields, ripening vineyards and beyond, deeper still, swooping past the valleys and low-lying forests, silvern olive groves. Occasionally, we glimpsed a glint of sapphirine sea, though most of the time the Mediterranean was way out of sight.

At each pause, we tuned in to the silence, and in that silence we heard the wind whistling and grasses swaying. Stillness wrapped itself around us, embraced us, inching us closer. Flesh beside flesh.

'It's . . . immense.'

'Easy to forget we're at war, eh?'

I *had* forgotten the war. Dismissed it. For this brief interlude.

'Somewhere beyond that horizon lies peace. Lands not occupied, Sara. A safe haven, a fine future for you and your parents.'

I had also briefly forgotten everyone's efforts to move us on . . . These views, this landscape, I had never witnessed anything so impressive, so stupendous in its primeval beauty. I had been seduced by it, the way of life, by the presence of the man at my side, but his words were like barbed wire, compressing every organ within me. I had allowed myself to ignore the fact that time was finite, that it chewed away at every hour, that one day soon Alain and I would be separated. And each minute shunted that separation closer. He would be back in Marseille and I would be where? The inexorability of the loss of him felt unbearable. Untenable.

He was watching me, sidelong glances. I was desperate to know what he was thinking. Desperate to open my heart.

'Still remember the path home?' He was smiling. He had been teasing me with this question ever since we'd set out, as though it were a test.

Home.

'I think so.'

'Good girl, we'll press on for another hour or so, stop for our lunch and then head back so we see everything in clear daylight.'

'We'll stop if you get breathless,' he reassured me frequently, but I rarely mentioned any discomfort, wanting to keep pace with him, to prove myself sturdy and capable. The woman for him.

Nothing disclosed of my overflowing heart.

And just when I thought I would faint from hunger, stumble from fatigue, Alain delivered us to a high-altitude rocky ledge that jutted out from the mountainside. This he instantly transformed into an impressive limestone table where we made ourselves comfortable, backs to the mountain, legs outstretched. Starving and thirsty after the exertion, we devoured our lunch, talking only intermittently. Alain was never one for lengthy conversation, preferring the natural sounds about us. Occasionally he'd point out a particular species of bird, imitate its call, inform me of the names of plants, what ailments they cured, or why to avoid them.

'What will you do,' he asked me, in the middle of munching our sandwiches, 'when this nightmare is over and you are free? Free to hold your head high once again, to study, to be back in society as a valued human being. What do you dream of doing with your life, Sara?'

Marry you, bear your children.

Of course, no such admission was forthcoming. Another thought altogether framed itself. 'I think I might like to ... to remain in France ... to teach in a school.'

He considered this. 'Then we've made you happy here.'

'Am I not a valued human being as I am, Alain?'

We had both been facing out towards the distance, the drop, contemplating the immensity of nature, side by side, not face to face, cross-legged, knees occasionally touching, but not eye to eye. I turned to him. He, to me.

'Am I?'

'But how could you doubt it, even contemplate such a question? It's what we're fighting for, Sara. Well, partially. France's freedom, of course, the enemy defeated, but also your freedom. You, your parents and the hundreds of others buried in this mountain community not of their choosing, waiting for the signature on a forged exit visa so they can take a boat to somewhere they are welcomed and respected.'

I listened in silence. I wanted to be *here*, right where I was now. How could he not see that?

Did he perceive me as just one of the hundreds who were so eager to get away? Was I of no more significance to Alain than a member of one of the causes he was fighting to liberate? Did our impending parting never cross his mind? I took a long swig of water, placing my lunch on the calcareous rock surface where, no doubt, the ants and other creepy-crawlies would make a fine meal of it. They were welcome to it. My hunger had deserted me. I rose to my feet. Alain was watching me, concern creasing his features, those date-brown eyes registering confusion. Only then did it dawn on me that Alain had no idea, not a clue, of the depth of my emotions. He was oblivious to the fact that I loved him. That I was in love with him.

'Are you all right?'

I nodded, words strangled. I strode off. 'I need to pee.'

When I returned to our lunch spot, Alain was packing everything away, careful not to leave a crumb to trace our presence here. He hooked a hand into mine, rose from his haunches and enclosed me in his arms, a great enveloping hug, friendship pouring out of him. I didn't resist. His proximity was heavenly, but I was incapable of meeting his gaze.

'Sara?'

I shook my bowed head from side to side. He slipped two fingers beneath my chin and nudged my face upwards until our eyes locked. 'If I've hurt you, your feelings, I'm –'

'Of course you haven't,' I rebuked him, attempting to tug myself away from him.

'There's nothing in the world –'

'Please stop. It's really not necessary.' My eyes were misty and damp.

With one firm step backwards, I disentangled myself. My heart was overflowing. It was as though every emotion – every hurt, joy, pain, rejection I had ever experienced – was revisiting me, gaining force, rising in intensity, burning me out. Liquefying me until I was molten nothing. Without value. I had to get away, but to run off was impossible: I would lose my way. On the ascent, head full of impossible dreams, I hadn't been paying the required attention.

'Please let's go,' I begged, a bubble of spit on my lips. 'I made a mistake,' I mumbled. 'It's really not important.'

46

The night slid by silently, warning me. I had to keep my distance, seal myself in, protect myself. I stayed awake till dawn, crumpled in my chair by the half-open window, staring at the stars, trying to figure life out. Emotions fizzing and burning within me. The weight of my bruised heart gnawing at me. I could hear my father pottering about in the dining room. What was he doing? He seemed never to sleep, these days. Did any of us? All of us inhabiting this wretched no man's land, on standby, ignorant as to what was going to happen next. Directionless. I resolved I wouldn't spend time with Alain any more. I'd keep my distance. How many times did I need to warn my stupid self?

The following lunchtime he turned up at our front door. I was just back from my morning with Hanna and Daniel. It was me who answered, eyes puffy, hair bedraggled, heart black and blue.

An awkward moment followed, a shuffling of feet.

'Bonjour, Alain.'

'I won't be able to help in the basement this afternoon.'

I stared at my shoes. He was drawing away from me.

'I need to see my father.'

'Of course. There's lots I can be getting on with.'

From behind his back he presented me with a bunch of flowers. A nosegay of striking mountain beauties.

'They're gorgeous.' I smiled because one or two had begun to wilt from the embrace of his hot hands. He must have picked them himself on his way to me. A bouquet of ambrosial perfumes. I snuffled among the pollen-rich petals and breathed deeply.

'Thank you,' I was thrilled by his gesture and felt a little less battered.

'Please trust I care for you, Sara,' he said softly.

My eyes roamed his face.

'You don't know how much.'

My breath caught in my throat.

'Would you like to come with me? It's a fine walk. My father said he'd like to meet you.'

'I . . . I . . .' *I should refuse.*

'He's a bit of a grump but I've told him about you. Spoken of you. Not about the shelter, our secret obviously, but I'd love it if you came along. Meet the sheep, at least.' He laughed.

Spoken about me?

'Sara, who's there?'

'Will you, can you, wait while I put these in water.' I hurtled along the passage. My mother was hovering by the kitchen door. She glared at me with suspicious eyes. 'Why is he bringing you flowers?'

'Just because, Mamma. Please don't worry.'

I danced by her, grabbed an empty tin jug and shoved it under the tap. The water sang as it flowed. The flowers, so sweet-smelling, lifted their heads. I placed them in the centre of the table.

'See you later,' I trilled, hastening along the hallway.

That afternoon Alain and I hiked eight kilometres south, descending to the highest, the most northerly, of the sheep valleys to visit Jacques Breton, who was tending their flocks on a substantial holding. Alain handed over a small box and went chasing after a lamb that had strayed, leaving me in the company of his father, a short, stocky figure, which was surprising: Alain and Nathalie were tall and lithe. I fancied it must mean something special that Alain had talked about me to one of his parents, invited me to be introduced. I dared to believe that this was a significant moment, a turning point, but from the outset I was uneasy in the older man's presence.

His manner lacked warmth. He was sizing me up with fearless eyes, wary. Gone forty, born on this mountain, and would never leave it. Sheep-farming, pure-breds, and goat herds had been in the Breton family for five generations, he bragged. 'The Germans will have to kill me if they want this territory from me.'

I wondered why he was still there when so many of the town's menfolk were gone. Then I recalled that farmers were exempt from the STO.

'Another sheep gone,' he bellowed to Alain, who was cradling the errant lamb. 'That's three ewes and one ram in a month.'

'There must be a pack hereabouts.'

Monsieur Breton shook his head, a sour expression in his eyes. 'This isn't wolves, son. It's thieves. Stealing our stock to breed or slaughtering them for meat. No one from hereabouts, I reckon.'

'There are bandits in these hills,' I chipped in.

Monsieur Breton glared at me as though I were a simpleton. 'Could be the Italians crossing over,' he grumbled. 'They prey on our flocks. Steal our women and our beasts. Or possibly one of the starving foreigners who are living off our land.'

He shot me a look, which I ignored. 'So, you've been helping out at the school, I hear?'

I nodded.

'My son and daughter are well-educated. Idealists, full of the good of everyone. My wife's the same. I wasn't in favour of offering our homeland as a hideout for all you overseas types. Not that I've anything against you, but it soon causes problems, especially when the heart gets involved. I don't believe in mixing blood.'

A bead of sweat ran down my spine. Was this why he'd expressed a desire to meet me?

He possessed none of his son's charm, perceiving every living creature as his enemy. I suddenly thought of dear Albert, wondered about his missing father. I hadn't seen his mother for some time, but then again I had been underground for most of the past few weeks, barely visiting the town centre except for my early-morning tours with the Lindemanns.

'My boy here says you'll be leaving soon.'

The heat of the sun pinked my cheeks, and an itinerant hair blew into my eyes. I felt the knot of uncertainty that unfolded when a stranger quizzed me about our plans.

'My advice is you won't want to be here in the winter, when the snows close us in, shut down access to the outside world. You'll need to be on your way before then, on the move before September draws to a close, before those first chillier October days.' I followed Jacques Breton's eyeline as he turned to observe his son. Alain was negotiating a path through the herds, two black and white dogs at his heels. One dark-haired young man, open-faced, smiling, among a powdery white cloud of moving sheep.

I was picturing the approach of winter, its icy grip. Hard to contemplate on a hot sunny day such as this one. The last days of September, early October. Now it was late July, tipping August.

My time was running out.

'Alain'll be returned to his studies by then, his sister with him. Germans are on their way. We'll all be at risk.'

'We're praying they won't make for here, monsieur. Why would they?'

'If someone rats on you all, they will. There's gossip across every hill.'

Startled, I shot a look for Alain.

'Those Nazis,' he coughed and spat on the grass, 'they're stealing every last seed we've planted. Food'll be even more costly and scarce. There'll be nothing here for you then.' He returned his attention to me with its granite scrutiny. 'He's a generous-hearted lad, is my son, takes care of everyone, but I'm looking out for him. Heed my words, lass, you're a fine-looking creature and you have his head turned, but the sooner you're gone from here, the better.'

'*Bon après-midi, Monsieur Breton.*' Without another word, I broke away, swinging my weight northwards, readying myself for the return slog.

'Sara!'

Alain's father was not a 'grump': he was the worst form of miserable old racist. One who pretends he is not. 'Nice to meet you too, Monsieur Breton,' I yelled, as I charged off along the plateau path that led me back up towards the hill to the town. The climb was backbreaking in the sweltering heat. I slipped and trudged along on my own till Alain caught up with me, a sickness burning in my gut.

'Hey!' Alain shouted. 'Sara, wait for me.'

I hung back for him, taking deep breaths, jigging my shoulders, releasing the tension, eyes locked on his muscular build as he bounded from one small boulder to the next till he was there, warm-eyed, at my side.

'Why did you take off like that?'

'Your father hates me,' I said.

'What? Of course he doesn't. He's losing his flock. That makes him mistrusting of everyone. It has nothing to do with you.'

I felt the cold wind of uncertainty rattling at my reason.

'I'm sorry, Sara, sorry if he hurt you, but I'm sure you've taken his brusque manner too personally. He was keen to meet you. He's heard so much about you.'

Listening to Alain, stoked by his compassion, I almost believed I had overreacted.

'You look like you could do with a swim. I know I could. Let's go.' He slipped my hand into his and, gingerly, I allowed myself to be led forwards, my heart in turmoil.

We made a detour to one of the lagoons, a remote spot favoured by Alain. Not the Swimming Hole because it was likely to be crowded with other bathers. A river pool, off the beaten track. We could have stopped at almost any point along the river's descending trajectory and I would have been fine, even to dive in head first rather than stepping in, one ladylike foot at a time. Those days were gone. These days I was swimming like an otter. Well, not with the proficiency and *élan* Alain displayed, but I could crawl or breaststroke to the bank on the far side without putting my feet down, without panicking or sinking. I loved to swim and felt at home in the water. It was a gift from Alain. One of many.

His father's words rang in my head. His warning. His overt racism. He didn't like me, that was clearly enough stated. I was not good enough for his son.

By the time we reached the lagoon we were sweating and desperate for a dip. Without further ado, Alain pulled his shirt over his head, his denims and espadrilles flung to the ground, and ran at the water, plunging himself into the swirling flow. He swam in his underwear. Many of the boys did.

I watched the ripples of his shoulders as he cut through the water, splashing into the deepening depths, twisting with the moving currents. The heat was so intense, I could almost hear it. Gnats and midges circled about me, itching at my perspiring skin, turning and thrumming in the shafts of sunlight above the riverbank. I closed my eyes. The torrents roared. I was watching Alain in my mind's eye, and when I opened them again, there he was, crawling with speed, diminishing in size. But he wouldn't always be there for me. Soon it would be September and our paths would diverge. I lifted my arms to the hem of my blouse and peeled it over my head, tugged my skirt to my feet and stepped out of it. Underwear, damp and sticky from exertion, abandoned on the rock, shoes kicked to one side, I let the sun spread its warmth all over me. I was naked. In the wide-open air. A liberation I had never experienced before.

The snows would be here in less than ten weeks. Time was running out. This summer would be gone for ever. I recalled my father's words, *We can't know how many summers she has.* And Alain's father's words: *gone from here.*

I hopped on one foot on the shingled bed and hurled myself into the creek, miscalculated, belly-flopped. I felt the searing pain burn my stomach, the cold water like ice after the blistering sun. It took me a minute. I kicked to stay afloat, then launched myself forward, swimming for all I was worth towards the far bank where Alain had landed. He was facing in my direction, following my progress. I advanced, dog-paddling, getting into my stride, speeding towards him. He waved encouragingly.

By the time I reached the far bank, his body was half in, half out of the water, his torso semi-raised against the damp wave-lapped stones and pale soil. I drew myself up to his side and rested there, shivering with expectation, and the prospect of imminent loss. Droplets fell from my skin and dribbled to the moist sand. My body felt powerful, muscular, on fire. All these months of trekking in the mountains and scrubbing floors had built me up, made me strong, toned me. Eyes open, I stared at the sky, hyacinth-blue, so vibrant I prayed it might burst open and shower us with grace, bless my hunger for this man.

My breathing was slow, tentative. I had no skills to express the passion that was consuming me. The longing. The ripeness within me.

Alain lifted himself from the river's edge, settled on his side and steadied himself on his left elbow. His right hand reached up and gently caressed my face. I closed my eyes. His fingers tiptoed down my cheek.

'Make love to me, Alain.'

'Sara . . .'

I rolled sideways towards him and dared to lift my hand to his chest. The flat of my palm pressed against his skin, warm flesh, body hair, a nipple dark as a roasted chestnut. I could feel the pulse of his heart, steady, regular. Nothing in my life had ever felt so in tune.

'Sara?'

'Mmm . . .'

'You're beautiful beyond my dreams . . .'

I shifted a centimetre closer, a gull's mewl overhead.

'It would be a lie to say that I haven't . . . don't . . . dream of . . . you but . . .'

My eyes wide open. 'But what?'

'We can't do this, Sara. It would be a mistake.'

'Mistake?' My hand withdrawn.

'Soon you'll be gone. This, we, will be a fraction of

235

your past. Soon forgotten. Living on another continent, you'll meet someone.'

'No, no. I won't go. I want to stay, join the *maquisards*.'

He cast his eyes over my face. 'There is no choice, Sara. Your life will depend on it. Your future lies elsewhere . . .'

I sprang to a sitting position, hair slapping wet and loose, like a bedraggled curtain shielding me. 'Is this because of Sylvie?'

'Sylvie!' he scoffed, and sat up behind me. 'You have no idea what I feel for you.'

Knees drawn up to my chest, my body was curled in on itself. His hand settled on my shoulder. It burned into me like a scalding iron.

'You're seventeen, Sara. It would be wrong of me to . . .'

The heat of his flesh against the heat of mine.

'Why don't you let me decide that?'

The sun beat down on my back. I swung my head round to face him, my eyes, winking against the blinding sunlight, blazed into his. 'I love you.'

His eyes held mine, scouring my face. His expression was perplexed, uncertain. I leaned in close. We both did. The gentlest of breezes kissed my cheek as Alain's lips touched mine.

'Alain! Alain!'

'*Merde*. Who's that calling?'

We broke apart, like culprits caught in an illicit act. It was Sylvie, in shorts, with bare, bronzed legs, on the far bank, standing in the muddle of our discarded clothes. Hands on her hips, legs astride, she waited, calmly watching as we made awkward attempts to gather ourselves. I swung vainly about in search of something, anything, to cover my nakedness.

'Nathalie's looking for you, Alain. I bumped into her

about twenty minutes ago. She needs to see you urgently. I'll tell her she can find you here, shall I?' Her voice was cold and flat. She waited one more beat, relishing our discomfort, then swung about and marched away.

For one moment, we were frozen. 'We'd better go,' I murmured.

'Listen, I'll catch up with you later . . . I'll meet you at Lucy's.'

Embarrassed, I shuffled to my feet and threw myself into the lagoon. I let the weight of my body sink beneath the surface. Above me, grey bands of water, bubbles from my exhalations rising. Boulders deep beneath my feet. Slippery, slimy textures, plants, aquatic life. And then, desperate for oxygen, I exploded to the surface, head back in the full sun, sucking for air. I dared not turn my head in Alain's direction. Kicking my feet, I swam back to my clothes, dressed myself dripping wet. I didn't want to meet Nathalie now. I swung about and called to Alain, who was in the river, approaching, 'See you later.'

Treading heavily, I marked my sopping path back to town.

47

I waited for Alain in the cellar until late evening and again the following afternoon, but he never came. I stayed there till it got dark outside and I felt spooked, then returned upstairs to Lucy's. In one of her bookshelves I found a phrase book. French and English. I decided to borrow it. The next day and the day after that, I locked myself in downstairs and taught myself parrot-fashion a few English phrases while I waited for my love. Where was he? I was confused by his absence.

I looked for him in town, but there was no sign of him or Nathalie. Had something happened or was he avoiding me?

Hanna and Daniel remained my morning companions. 'I can stay longer if you need me to,' I volunteered to Frau Lindemann. 'If you need to rest more. I can shop for you too. I've plenty of time.'

Ilse was grateful for the extra hours to lie motionless on her bed out of the debilitating heat, desperate to ease the developing pain in her back, the terror in her heart. Herr Lindemann offered to pay me a few extra francs for the added assistance I was giving. I refused. 'It's enough,' I said. I was glad to help these people who were having such a hard time of it.

'The Germans have reached Fréjus,' I heard them whisper to one another. 'How long before they are here?' It was the question on everybody's lips.

'Our papers will be here soon,' Herr Lindemann assured his wife.

Desperate to do something practical, I went in search of my father and suggested he might visit Frau Lindemann, which he agreed to do.

'Is there news? How far is Fréjus?' I urged, as we walked back together into the town. 'Have you spoken to Monsieur Decroix?'

Papa shook his head.

'There are no papers,' I wanted to scream, yell it to the four corners of the earth. The promised papers were an illusion.

Where was Alain?

When I wasn't working, I spent hours alone in the cellar, sitting by candlelight, daydreaming, mostly about Alain, who had not come to see me or to visit the cellar since our afternoon by the river. When I felt guilty for burning the candles, using up resources for no good reason, I sat in the dark, imagining what it would be like to be trapped down here, to be forced to stay in this rat-hole. And then, scared, I would bound up the stairs and march restlessly about the garden, which was no easy exercise. Its wilderness was almost impenetrable now. I should borrow a scythe and begin to clear it. I should designate some purpose to my days, do something before I went mad.

The next time I was in the bakery, Louis was gossiping with some of the older residents queuing to buy their daily rations. I had my coupons at the ready. It was the end of August. A cloudless sky, asphyxiating heat.

The energy had shifted. People were going about their

business with their heads down, not looking one another in the face. Jittery. The Italians were roaming about the square with grave expressions. The dances and balls and parties had come to an abrupt stop. All conversations were turning around shortages, the rising cost of food and the whereabouts of the Wehrmacht.

'As the Germans draw closer, our provisions will be stretched.'

Wheat grew in abundance in the irrigated valleys beneath this plateau town. Sheep grazed. Grapes promised future bottles of wine. But the reserves were in jeopardy.

'Other villages across into the Var are already sending messages for help. I've a cousin up behind Saint-Raphaël, little to eat . . .'

'The Wehrmacht are pillaging as they advance, requisitioning whatever they can lay their filthy hands on.'

I recalled the words of Alain's father. I recalled that last day in Alain's company.

'If they're stationed in Fréjus, they won't be coming up here. They're too far south. It's the coastal towns they're after.'

'We're safe here. What would they want with us?'

'If everyone is careful and only takes what they need, even with *les assignés* occupying half of the housing, we'll all manage. Calm down, everyone. Petrol might be lacking, but we won't go hungry. No cause for panic, ladies and gentlemen. You'll all get fed.' Louis was pontificating and pacifying as he handed over sticks of bread so warm from the oven they burned your fingers. 'Don't forget your change!' He was counting out francs to his worried customers. 'There'll be sufficient to go round. Plenty of harvests still to come,' he shouted.

But it was evident the situation was shifting, developing at an uncomfortable pace.

'Louis, we've no one left to bring in the harvest,' interrupted a wizen-faced pensioner, from the back of the shop.

'That's a fact. The students and few able-bodied men who were left to us, they've gone underground.'

Up to that point, I'd been marking the goings-on in the square, wiping away the sweat on my face, watching the Italians, listening with my back to the crowd of sunken-faced elderlies, dutifully waiting in line. I swung about, desperate for more information. Had one of the shoppers news of the students? Whose voice had I heard? Had he or she been speaking about Alain? . . . But the conversation had moved on. Village gossip was the subject now.

'Next!' yelled Louis. It was my turn.

'How are you, young Sara? We haven't seen your mother in a long while. Poorly in this heat, is she? Worrying about your future too, I dare say. Like the rest of us.'

'She's . . . a little under the weather, but thanks for enquiring, Louis. Three baguettes, please.' My voice was croaky.

It was a month now since I had set eyes on Alain. Nathalie was absent too. If he had gone undercover, had he been obliged to set off in all haste? Might that explain why he had not said goodbye, left no word? When would we meet again?

I was shopping for the Lindemanns. Father said Ilse's condition needed careful monitoring, that I should do all I could for them. 'Be there for them, Sarina, as you are doing.' He'd said she was anaemic and was losing strength. He had no medication to give her, and prescriptions were not easy to come by. 'I could write one up but where were the medicines to be acquired from?'

'I can let you have two loaves now and possibly another at the end of the morning, if we receive our delivery of flour. It should have been with me by seven this morning. The truck must have been held up somewhere. Let's pray it's not been confiscated. Are these for that poor Lindemann family? She's having a tough time of it too.'

I nodded.

Have you seen Alain Breton? But the words did not find voice. I took the bread and handed over the twenty-five francs. Was it conceivable that we would never meet again, that the last images of me imprinted on his memory would be that unfulfilled yet blissful afternoon on the riverbank?

'Nip back around noon and if we've baked more I'll put another aside for you. Don't forget now. I don't want it wasted.'

'*Merci*, Louis. I won't.'

I decided to pop along to Marie's *epicerie*. Discreetly, without any reference to her black-market contacts, I'd ask about a source for medical supplies. Could I also beg news of her grandson? He who brought her fish from the mountain lakes.

I hurried from the bakery, bumping into an Italian soldier. He whistled and grinned at me as I mumbled apologies. It was only as I scooted across the square that I remembered our early days here and how elated I would have been to draw the attention of one of the 'Latin lovers'. No longer.

It was Delphine who broke the news. I had gone to beg a few bits of chicken to make fresh soup for Ilse. These days I was turning my hand to cooking. I had moved on from boiling eggs.

I stayed indoors in Delphine's kitchen while she went

out to the yard to decapitate the hapless fowl. Together, we picked the hen clean of feathers: a rather disgusting chore. It took me hours to get the milky smell of chicken flesh off my fingers, the blood and grease out from under my nails.

'Have you seen Nathalie?' I ventured, hitting as casual a note as I could.

Delphine paused in her dissection of the bald bird. She seemed to be considering her answer, weighing it up. 'They left,' she said eventually.

'Left?'

My worst fear.

'It was sudden, Sara. No more questions, please.'

I was going to push her, hoping to hear that they had returned to Marseille earlier than scheduled, but I knew they hadn't. My guts told me that Alain and Nathalie were in the hills in an anonymous hideout, close or far, living as *maquisards*. Were they engaged in armed combat? Were their lives at risk?

I wished Alain had invited me to join them.

48

I returned across the square to the Lindemanns' flat. The father wasn't working: it was August so the factory where he had found employment had closed for the month for its annual holidays, which was the norm in France. I turned on the gas to boil a saucepan of water. I had collected a few fresh herbs from the roadside earlier in the day, a bunch of sage, wild thyme, and sprigs of rosemary growing almost as tall as a tree from Lucy and Dirk's jungle. The possibility that Alain and I might never see each other again was gnawing at me.

The Lindemanns communicated in their mother tongue, so I never really paid attention or tuned into their exchanges. Over the course of the last six months I had picked up quite a few phrases from Hanna but not sufficient to follow an in-depth conversation. However, while I was preparing the soup, I became aware that quite some activity was going on in their bedroom. Had something happened to Frau Lindemann? Had her condition worsened? Should I run and fetch my father? I hesitated, hovered by the stove in the scullery. It wasn't my business to intrude. I decided after deliberation that Herr Lindemann would call me if he needed assistance. Then Hanna appeared at my side. Her small face, circled with a mop of dark hair, stared up at me with concern.

'Can I help you, Sara?' She picked up the wooden spoon I had been using and tapped it against her fingers.

'Unfortunately there's not much to do. You could have chopped the carrots but I couldn't find any.'

'Shall I skin the potatoes for you?'

'Peel! We peel potatoes rather than skin them.' I smiled. 'If we had a rabbit, we might skin that.'

'Oooh, rabbits are delicious, though it's ages since I've tasted any. Rabbit stew. Yum-yum. Can you make rabbit stew, Sara?'

'I could try . . . if we had a rabbit.' I recalled Sylvie and the shot that had killed an innocent creature. I hadn't crossed paths with Sylvie either since the afternoon on the riverbank. Might she have up-to-date news? Might she have left with Alain and Nathalie?

'I've seen them in the countryside. They look like hares. If Mutti tells me the instructions when she's feeling a bit better, I could teach you.'

How surprisingly adult this little girl had become over these long weeks of summer. Her mannerisms were those of a miniature grown-up, not a child of six.

'I think where we are going there will be plenty of rabbits.'

'Oh, where's that?'

Her French was encouragingly proficient now, with little trace of an accent. I felt rather pleased with myself about that. She was a quick, bright student and we worked well together.

'Vati says there's a good chance we'll be leaving very soon,' she announced to me, in her most mature voice.

'Really? When?' This had been the song of the summer. The mantra on every refugee's lips. *We'll be leaving soon . . .*

Did that mean there had been a new development and that my parents were also getting ready?

'There is word of a grand plan.'

Word of a grand plan. 'Oh, yes?'

'To save us all, to put us on boats and send us to North Africa where the Allies have taken control. Hitler's forces have surrendered.'

I smiled at her words. Could she really have any notion of what she was saying? Or was she repeating parrot-fashion?

There had been so many 'grand plans' talked about, so much gossip and speculation and revived optimism that I let out a sigh. This news sounded no more substantial than any of the aborted schemes or pipe dreams we'd been listening to for months on end.

'Actually, it's a big secret but I can tell you, Sara. My father has relatives in Switzerland. We're not taking a boat. We're going to a village near Geneva. It has all been settled. As soon as our travel papers get here.'

I felt sad for Hanna, for the Lindemanns' disappointment, because I no longer trusted that anyone's papers would be 'coming through any day now'. Whatever lay ahead, we would be obliged to face it head on.

The water was boiling. I gathered up the portions of chicken Delphine had so generously given me and tossed them, along with the chopped herbs, into the water. I wished there was more. I added two pinches of salt.

Hanna stood on tiptoe to stir the watery broth.

'*Merci, ma petite.*'

Later, I would add a few potatoes to the mix, but I'd let it simmer for half an hour first. I hadn't managed to purchase any greens from Marie.

'All gone,' she had said, shaking her head. I wondered if she were missing her grandchildren. I had been desperate to ask her but she was so self-contained, with such a gentle manner, that I feared distressing her. I wondered, at her age and after all that she had lived through, what it must feel like to be so ancient. 'As old as the hills,' Alain had joked. 'It's how she describes herself.'

Lost in my thoughts, my pining for Alain and all our blissful days of summer, I hadn't been paying attention and cut the thumb on my left hand as I sliced the potatoes. 'Ouch.'

'Oh, Sara, no.' Hanna skipped from the room and returned with a frayed strip of delicate white cloth, the lace and cotton edging from a handkerchief. She wrapped it round my thumb with such an air of gravitas I almost laughed.

'You won't get sick like Mutti, will you?'

'It's nothing.' I bent and kissed the top of her head. Quite unexpectedly, she threw her arms around my hips and pressed herself strenuously against me, into me. A tear rolled down her cheek. 'Mutti says you're a blessing to us. Will you still look after us when we have our new home in Switzerland?'

Her squeeze was so tight it almost winded me. 'Yes, of course,' I said, stroking her hair.

'Promise, promise, Sara, promise to always be my friend.'

I closed my eyes and softly promised my special little girl, even while I knew there was precious little chance I could keep my word.

49

I had had no opportunity to verify the information with Hanna's parents because my father arrived just as I was leaving. He was there to give Frau Lindemann her daily check-up. Normally he wouldn't have visited a patient so frequently, but she was in need of reassurance as much as medical care. I wondered then whether she, like my own mother, might have been a stronger, braver woman before the persecutions and the flight that had befallen us.

As we passed one another in the narrow hallway, my father had instructed me to go directly home and organize my belongings: the day was drawing closer.

'This is no idle speculation,' he declared. 'A message has been sent through.'

From where? By whom? I was anxious to know. It all seemed too vague.

I hadn't ventured into Lucy and Dirk's apartment for some little while. If I entered the lower part of the house, I tended to go directly to the camouflaged scullery door and from there to the cellar where I felt, in a foolish, sentimental way, closer to Alain. Today, after checking that no one was about, I hastily turned the key in the front door, went inside and slammed it, forgetting to bolt the chain from the inside. I was rattled. As I'd returned from the Lindemanns', I'd noticed activity in the central square, a palpable level of agitation, unrest. The soldiers were prowling, their captain barking orders at his men. There was an edge to their tours. All jocularity had disappeared. Young shop girls walked by, swinging their hips, hoping for attention, but the Latin charmers barely shot them a glance.

Might Papa's warning to me bear some foundation?

I made my way through to the living room, to the showcase of photographs on the piano. I threw off my cardigan and picked up one of the larger likenesses of Lucy. Glamorous Lucy. 'Where are you now?' I asked the image staring back at me. Hadn't someone mentioned, in what seemed a dim and distant past, that Dirk had enlisted with the RAF? Was he safe? Was he alive? Was Alain safe? The uncertainty, absence of contact was driving me crazy. Would Alain and I ever spend time together again? Was I to be transported to some far-flung destination with my parents, never to return here? Or should I begin to fill the buckets in the cellar with fresh water and hide there?

I knew that my mother was alone upstairs but I chose not to go to the top storey of the house. Instead I returned to town to Delphine.

'When will we be starting school again?' I begged her. 'I can still be your assistant, can't I? I want to stay here, Delphine.'

She looked at me incredulously. 'Sara, Mussolini has been arrested.'

'*What?*'

'The Italians are negotiating with the Allies. The British are reporting it on the wireless. The war is advancing in this direction. It's unstoppable. When the Italians leave, there will be no one left to protect you, Sara. Do you understand me? Several parties of refugees have already been put on boats. They are right now being transported out of Europe to safer territories. Thank Heaven.'

'To where?' My voice had risen an octave. I remembered the panic, the terror of our first escape. Those who lost their lives, who never got through. Landing in alien territories, not always hospitable, shot in the back while running. I pictured Henryk dying in the barn. We had found peace here, made friends.

Delphine shook her head. Her eyes were ringed with dark circles. 'We are receiving only fragments of news. I can't say for sure. The continent of Africa is all we know.'

Africa. It might as well be another planet.

'Where's Alain?' There was a dread in my heart. 'If you know, please, Delphine, tell me.'

'Sara, listen to me, you cannot allow yourself to . . . to . . . And even if I was party to that information, you know the rules . . .'

But I was gone, hotfooting it along the street. I would make ready the cellar.

It was 4 September. I sprinted through the medieval lanes. The scorching heat had left this mountain town. The first promise of autumn tinted the landscape. The plane trees in the central square were beginning to shed their leaves, sailing silently to the deserted pavement slabs. Summer was over. It would never be summer again. Not this summer. Not my summer with Alain.

50

I pounded the lane that led to the plateau, running like a wild thing until I spotted a tank ahead of me, stationed at the roadside. Alarm almost electrified me. I had never seen a military vehicle up here before. A soldier stood leaning against its carcass, boots planted on the dust track. An icicle of fear stabbed my bosom. I slowed, attempting with measured breath to calm the pounding of my heart, attempting a casual pace, a nonchalant frame of mind.

It was an Italian tank, not German. Italian, not German, I repeated.

Still, the beat of my pulse was so furious, it was in my mouth. I had to get a grip. I lowered my head.

I prayed the soldier would not stop me – I wasn't even carrying my papers, my expired temporary identity card; I had left it in the pocket of my cardigan downstairs at Lucy's – and it was illegal to be without it. As I advanced, I was wrestling with myself not to break into a run. They can't have been there more than an hour.

Within the tank were two more uniformed young soldiers. One was shouting into a radio, a walkie-talkie. The other had his ear to the speaker, listening. They were wearing helmets. That was unusual. What did it mean? Were they preparing for combat?

Neither they nor the one smoking a cigarette paid my passage any attention. Were they waiting there for the arrival of the Germans? Surely not. Were they preparing their departure, thus leaving us wide open to the atrocities of the SS?

Should I turn back to town, alert someone? Who? My parents? Try to hook up with Sylvie or Thomas? I kept moving, reached home, pounded up the steps and made my way into our apartment. My parents were folding clothes into a battered suitcase on their bed.

My mother lifted her head as I walked into their room. 'Where on earth have you been?'

My father pressed his hand against Mamma's to calm her. 'Sara, it's time. Our papers are . . .'

'Here?'

'No, but they will be arriving, by bus or lorry. A courier is coming by some means of transport. It seems there are boats at the ready. It's time to leave, Sara.'

I stared at my parents. 'To go where?'

'Anywhere is safer than here. That is the crucial fact. The enemy is on our doorstep.'

I fought to take this in, the ramifications. Still no papers. 'But we can't just go, when we don't even know where we're going. There's a tank outside our door, just down the lane. What horrors might lie in our path? We're not cattle! We have been promised papers for weeks, months. Why should today or tomorrow be any different? There are no papers. It's too dangerous, too many of us running like headless chickens. For the moment we can still be safe here. We can hide.'

'Sara . . .'

'Papa, Alain and I . . . we've spent the summer cleaning the cellar . . . downstairs. We can hide there.'

My voice was raised. I was shouting – shouting at my own parents. My mother sank onto the bed. It was more a gesture of collapse as though she had relinquished all aspirations for me. Her delinquent child.

'No one will find us there. There's food . . . there's . . . We've planned it all carefully . . .'

'Sara, go next door, please. Sort out what you need. The bare necessities. One bag and only what you can reasonably carry.'

I turned on my heels and disappeared into my room. I stood by the window looking down into the valley where beyond my line of vision, beyond the undulating hills, sheep grazed peacefully. In a few weeks there would be the *transhumance*, the return to more southerly pastures. The revolution of the seasons would continue regardless, the feeding, the growing, the harvests – wine and olive oil yet to come – and I would be present for none of it. And then would fall the highland snows, sealing off this community from the outside world, leaving them to their rural existence. Rid of us.

Or what if we didn't budge? What if we stayed put, hid downstairs, kept calm? The snows sealing us in would equally block the Germans' entry. Had everyone forgotten that we were sent here because it was a safe haven? Alain and I had prepared for this. But who would listen to me?

My dreams were dashed.

I had no alternative but to obey my parents, to accompany them.

The door opened behind me. I caught the reflection of my father advancing towards me, arms lifted ready to take me into his embrace. 'Sweet little Sara, *moja slodka mala, Sarina*. What anguish you are suffering,' he whispered, taking me into his arms. 'You think I don't know, don't understand, but I do know how unbearable this is for you.'

My head imprisoned in the lock of his arms, I tried my best to wriggle free. 'You don't,' I said. 'You can't know.'

'You think I was never young? My dear sweet Sara, you are not the first person to give their heart to . . . to love the wrong person. He's not for you, Sara.'

'Stop! Stop!' I tore myself loose from the suffocating affection of my father.

'Sara, dry your eyes and listen carefully to me.' His tone had changed. He was holding me by my wrists at arms' length. His voice was steely. 'There are British troops stationed in North Africa. They are waiting, ready to escort us to Palestine. Jerusalem, Sara. We will be safe. At last. The war will be over for us. We will begin again in a blessed, bountiful land, a land without conflict or oppression. There will be no acrimony, no more aggression, no enemy who tries to steal the very air we breathe. You, my dearest Sarina, your mother and I, are being offered this gift. We cannot refuse to take it.'

My nose was running, spittle on the corners of my lips. Misery bursting out of every cell in my body. 'But you've said before that we'd be safe here, Papa. You insisted we must make a go of it in France, do our best to fit in, and I *have*. I've tried hard, learned French, Italian, even some German. I've put my heart and soul into this new life, and now we must move again. Why should the next time be any different? We can't even reach the coast. There are blockades everywhere. Curfews. We could be blown up, arrested, shot, imprisoned. I don't believe there are papers coming. For weeks they've been promised. It's a false dream.'

'Sara . . .'

'Papa, if we want our freedom, why don't we stand our ground and fight for it? You, you've been working clandestinely, helping those who are fighting for our freedom. We've built a shelter.'

'Sara, we cannot refuse this opportunity.'

'How many more times can we keep running? All our lives, like criminals?'

I dashed from the room and out of the house, down the stairs, into the haven of my make-believe paradise.

I closed the door and slipped the chain. I would hide in the cellar until everyone was gone or until this hysteria had passed. Because who was to say that this time the hope being peddled to us was real? I would rather take up arms, or starve to death down here than set off on another dangerous expedition.

51

How long did I sleep? I had cried myself into a state of exhaustion. When I awoke, it was black night. Rain was beating like fists against the shutters.

Or might they be real fists?

Soldiers thumping to gain entry? German soldiers? Had they entered the town? Surely not. I couldn't see outside because the shutters were secured, but I could hear the incessant rattling. It was rain – it must be rain. I grappled for a match from the box I had left on the console, lit a candle and made my way barefoot along the tiled corridor to the front door, nervously sliding back the chain. A sweep of rain gusted in at me, extinguishing the flame, my only source of light. It was a dense, dire night. No stars, wet and filthy. Wildly overgrown foliage, cascading raindrops.

My parents. God, why had I shouted like that? Should I remain where I was until the storm had passed or should I make my way upstairs and apologize? But they would have fastened the lock, jammed a chair against the door for added protection, as was their habit, their fears escalating now.

I decided to return to Lucy's room and stay there till it was light. I'd think up some story to tell Mamma and Papa. And then I'd show them the basement, persuade them that the *cave* was our safest option.

My stomach rumbled. When had I last eaten? I was dizzy wth hunger. I remembered the tins Alain and I had stocked below. Tin of sardines, an opener too. I had placed it in the cold storage cupboard myself. I knew exactly where it was. If I consumed one tin, it wouldn't make any difference, would it? I would not be depriving anybody of anything . . . I hesitated, prevaricating. I was not sure that I had the courage to make my way to the cellar, find my way safely in the obscurity of night. Of course such reasoning was ludicrous because it was night-time twenty-four hours a day down there. Even so, I preferred my hunger pangs.

I padded back to Lucy's bedroom and slipped, with my friend Freddie the fox to cuddle, beneath the bedclothes in an attempt to get warm. It was the first time I had done that, dived beneath the bedding. Until now I had only lain on top. It felt one step, an infraction too far, but I was beyond drained, and shivery and damp from standing in the doorway in the lashing rain. I lay there, arms around Freddie, legs tight to my chest, hugging the fur stole tightly, to arrest both my agitation and the cold. At some point, I must have nodded off again, for it was morning – soon after sunrise – when I opened my eyes. I made my way once more to the front door. Light was spreading across the mountains and the rain had ceased, leaving behind a sodden but burnished land. It was glorious, a wondrous transformation.

Upstairs, the door to our apartment was locked. I tapped softly, not wishing to alarm my parents but when there was no response I took it they were still sleeping. Or had they left, set off without me? Given up on me? No, they would never do that. I knocked again, more urgently. Still no response.

My head was swimming with hunger. Low blood sugar, Papa would advise. It was essential to eat something.

I decided to make my way back into town. Louis would be baking by now. I had no money on me but I felt sure he would give me a bun or a croissant on credit, if I promised to pay him later today.

52

As I walked I used the opportunity to recce, to reassure myself that there were no more military vehicles stationed, amassing across the plateau or in hiding off the track.

Yesterday's tank had vanished. Had the Italians withdrawn?

A small plane appeared overhead. I heard its spinning propellers before I caught sight of it as it emerged from between two mountain peaks. I flung myself to the soaked ground, scrabbled for cover and crouched out of sight behind a boulder, following its trajectory. A Milice plane, funded by the Vichy government, on the search for members of the Résistance, scouting to find their hideouts. Alain had pointed out several to me over the course of our summer together. 'The Milice, they are the most despised *collabos* of the entire bunch. Beware them, Sara.'

I prayed Alain was safe wherever he was.

After the aircraft had disappeared, the landscape was empty, still. The sky rested peacefully against the rim of the earth. It was a void, a grassy solitude, aside from the creatures of early morning that accompanied me or scarpered into the vegetation. I loved this hour. It was the first time I had seen this terrain after a torrential downpour. The colours were sharper, more vibrant, deepened, and the earth gave off a light steam, like fresh cow dung. It smelt peaty, loamy. I walked purposefully, but with caution, stopping every now and again to scan every scrap of land within sight. Not a trace of a German, but the silence unnerved me. It was unnatural.

When I arrived in the town, the central square was deserted. It was as though every citizen had fled, decamped. This realization momentarily panicked me. Was I the only living soul who remained? And what of my parents? I wondered again if they had left without me. But then the clock on the church wall beneath the bell tower struck the hour. It was 6 a.m. Even on the days when I had risen early to care for the Lindemanns and to attend Delphine's school, I had never been in the town at this time. Curfew lifted at six. People were in their homes, not yet out of doors: the explanation was nothing more sinister. The Lindemanns. When had I last seen them? I should pay them a visit, but first, to Louis for a *demi-baguette* and then I would do everything I could to assist them.

It was Herr Lindemann, bags beneath his eyes, still in crumpled pyjamas, who opened the door to me and, without a word, ushered me inside. Ilse was sleeping. He mouthed the words for fear the sound of our voices would rouse her.

'Is she any stronger?'

'Your father managed to find some drug or herbs to help her sleep, to alleviate the pain in her back. It seems to have done the trick. I hope she will be fit to travel.'

'When are you supposed to be leaving?' I realized then that there was no sign of life in the apartment. It was freakishly still. 'Where are Hanna and Daniel?'

In the adjoining room, a burst of coughing. Ilse.

'Madame Decroix is caring for them. We weren't sure whether you'd be back . . .'

'I'm sorry, I . . . The burden of . . . preparations.'

'They slept at Delphine's. I didn't want to unsettle them any more than necessary. Ilse has had a very bad few days and nights.'

'Let me do something. Shall I buy some eggs, make her some tea?'

He shook his head, weary, defeated.

'I'll fetch the children.' I was already moving to the door.

'You should be packing, Sara. The Germans are no more than two days from here. Infantry advancing along the railway tracks,' he said, in a matter-of-fact way. 'As soon as transport gets here we will be driven to the coast. The SS have been spotted in Nice. They are occupying all the hotels. We must be gone before the Wehrmacht are stationed at the ports, before there is no way out.'

I stared at him. Drive to the coast? In full daylight? Or caravans of refugees breaking curfew in illegal trucks?

This tale of salvation, these promises of transport . . . Nothing had come of any of it. There had been escape for a fortunate few; others like Henryk had died in the attempt. There were checkpoints, barbed-wire enclosures, fencing, curfews, controls between here and the coast, to east and west. How did Herr Lindemann envisage overcoming these obstacles? And without exit papers.

'Does your wife need anything or shall I go to Delphine's and help with the children? I could run to René's farm and collect some fresh milk?'

'Go to Delphine's,' he replied, with some relief as though the effort of engaging with me – me, a disbeliever – was more than he could stomach.

The town was waking up, coming to life. Women were scrubbing their doorsteps or swabbing the cobblestones in front of their narrow terraced houses as I ascended the lanes. Some nodded, others didn't, just lowered their eyes so as not to acknowledge me as I passed alongside them.

It was eleven minutes after seven when I beat the knocker at Delphine's. She looked like she hadn't slept. Tousled hair, her face pale and pinched, with sunken cheeks, shadows beneath her eyes, and she was clearly taken aback to see me.

'Sara! What are you doing here?' As she spoke she ventured a step outside and shot furtive glances up and down the street. No one else was about, aside from one old woman at the bottom of the lane putting out a tawny cat.

'Come in quickly.' She dragged me by the arm, closed the door fast and slipped a chain across the lock. Then she turned to face me as though demanding an explanation. We were standing, bunched in the hallway, and I was puzzled as to why she wasn't leading me through to the kitchen.

'Hanna and Daniel,' I stammered. 'Herr Lindemann said to . . .'

She studied me, appraising me. 'You should be at home with your parents preparing for your departure. You should not be here. You're at risk, and putting us at risk too.'

I was hurt by her curtness. 'I want to help,' I said.

Without a word, her fingers pinching the sleeve of my blouse, she jerked me through to the kitchen. Alain was sitting at the table drinking a bowl of hot black coffee, or the chicory and barley mixture that purported to be coffee. He half rose when he saw me, then threw a look to Delphine as though soundlessly demanding an explanation.

'What?' I begged. The presence of Alain there was . . . it was implausible, incredible. I wanted to rush to him. He was unshaven, had grown a beard. A rifle and navy beret hung from the back of the chair he was perched on.

'Do you want some coffee?'

I nodded, grateful for the offer. 'Hanna and Daniel,' I said. 'Herr Lindemann told me to come.'

Again, a glance was exchanged between my two French friends.

'They are no longer your responsibility, Sara.' This was Delphine. I sank into a chair opposite Alain, who smiled shyly at me. He looked weary but tanned and healthy. A little leaner possibly.

I shook my head. 'Everybody's saying transport is being sent for us, but we can't move anywhere till Monsieur Decroix brings exit visas . . .' I was chuntering.

'He's been arrested.'

'*What?* Oh, my God, Delphine. When?'

'Two days ago.' Delphine lifted both hands to her face and rubbed hard, as though she were washing herself of memories, the stain of dried tears, the reality. 'He was picked up on one of the higher mountain tracks leaving Fréjus by donkey and cart, to all intents and purposes transporting crates for the new season's olive oil but with a satchel full of forged papers under the cushion of his seat. He was searched. All the false papers intended for your family, the Lindemanns and seventeen other families were stowed there. Mercifully, as the papers were in false names none of you can be traced.'

I wrapped my arms around myself and held on tight. 'Why did they stop him?'

'Happenstance or betrayed, we don't know. He's in prison. They confiscated his identity card. They also arrested his supplier. The man nicknamed Pierre-des-faux-papiers. Some say he's a monk from an abbey near Avignon, but we don't have his true identity. His name and where-abouts were never revealed to us.'

'Oh, Delphine, I'm so sorry. There's no possibility you're mistaken?'

She shook her head. There was a cold metallic taste in my mouth. If my friend's information was correct, the Germans had the address on Philippe's identity card. They could come here, find us. All of us. Delphine's life, ours – every villager here was in danger. I shot a look across to Alain. He nodded confirmation of these facts.

'What will happen to the lieutenant?'

'He'll be shot, firing squad,' said Delphine, without a hint of emotion, which chilled me.

'If we can't release him from where he's imprisoned, yes. The details of his detention are sketchy. We're await-ing further intelligence.'

I stared open-mouthed from one to the other. 'Is that what you're going to do?'

'Not us, but some of our comrades. Nathalie is among them. She's working as an underground courier, on her way to Fréjus now.'

'Is she safe? Can I help?' I asked.

'Certainly not.'

'Our job here is to protect all the families and individ-uals who have been promised documents, who are vulnerable. The British believe that the Italians will sur-render any day now and then . . .'

'And then this region will be wide open.'

Delphine nodded. 'German troops are a little short of a hundred kilometres from here. Two days' march, max-imum three. This entire village will be plundered, its inhabitants massacred. All Jews in residence will either be arrested and transported to a holding camp, or . . .'

I closed my eyes, picturing the Lindemanns, my parents packing their scruffy bags. The hundreds of other *assignés*, holed up in their rented accommodation, anticipating papers, a glimmer of hope, the signal to move, praying one more time for a path to salvation.

'. . . or they will be shot with the rest of us.'

'The death penalty for hiding Jews, protecting asylum seekers, breaking the law.'

I had been so certain that this little town was safe, that the Germans were intent on the coast, the cities. I had fought with my parents, blind in my obstinacy. But this changed everything.

'Does everybody else know this? That there will be no exit papers?'

Alain shook his head. 'People are still waiting for the means to leave. They haven't been informed, nor must they be. That the operation has failed . . . will cause a panic. We had trucks at the ready, boats in two docks.' He scratched his head. 'We have to find another way. Time is not on our side.'

'Two days, you said. We can't sit here and do nothing. You must let me help.'

'The coastal routes are out of the question now. Escape will have to be over the mountains.'

We could hide eight, ten at the outside in the cellar, I was calculating. At that moment Hanna padded into the room, barefoot. She was in a nightdress rubbing sleepy eyes. Alain and Delphine both rose at the sight of her.

'I shouldn't stay here,' said Alain, quietly. His voice was conspiratorial. 'The fewer who know I'm here . . .'

Hanna, without a word, made her way across to me and crawled onto my lap. She laid her head against my chest, closed her eyes and started to suck her thumb. In no time at all, she had regressed from small adult to baby. I rocked her to and fro as I had seen Delphine do with her two.

'Where are you going?' I was desperate to steal even a few minutes alone with Alain.

'You still have your key to Lucy's place, don't you?'

I nodded.

'We're going to need it.'

I struggled to reach into my pocket with the dozing child on my knees. 'Do you want it now?'

'No, I'm going to get some sleep. Keep it somewhere safe, somewhere we can all find it. See you later.' I listened to his footsteps climbing the stairs. On the back of the chair where he had been seated hung his beret and the hunting rifle he had lent me for practice.

53

It was market day, but there was barely a stall in sight. Even so, the square was crowded, milling with people clad in every item of clothing they possessed, suitcases at their feet or gripped between their fingers. They were not shoppers, but foreigners. Our kind.

People were congregating, readying themselves to face the long march. I spotted the young rabbi and his wife. He was holding her hand. I saw the Polish man with glasses who ran the chess club. He was rocking on the spot, bulging knapsack on his back. Several of the Vésubie women were doling out flasks of water, crusts of bread, embracing those who had become their friends.

I glanced skywards. Beyond the town on the upward paths that led to the ancient Col de Cerise, the Cherry Tree Route, a crocodile of refugees. The exodus was under way. No longer protected, the refugees – Jews, Gypsies, others – were en route to what they prayed would be the next sanctuary. Bent by the weight of their possessions, they were ascending with difficulty the narrow stony tracks that scaled high above our village. It was a forbidding path to a distant border. Italy. A backbreaking climb even for those who were fit and habituated.

Italy would be neutral territory within days, hours even. More glib assurances? The Italians were also busy with preparations, loading trucks with ammunition, waiting for the final order to pull out. And once they had gone?

It was vital to get out before it was too late. Or go underground.

I was thinking about my own confused future. My job now was to ready the cellar.

In the midst of all this mayhem I glimpsed a figure, desolate, head bent: Albert's mother sitting at a table on the terrace of Pascal's café and bar, a carafe of wine her companion. As each of the soldiers quit the neighbouring Hôtel des Alpes, their *sacs de montagnes* on their backs, the proprietress of the laundry half rose, hands resting on the arms of her chair to steady herself, expectant, hoping to be greeted, perhaps, by her *capitano*. He and his coterie would be heading east to Italy, some by the coastal route, others over the mountain. For the captain and his infantry, the war was over. She surely knew that her lover would be returning home to his wife and family in Cuneo.

Standing quietly in the centre of the square while folk bustled around me, I took a moment to watch her. My heart was as heavy for her as it was for myself. I pictured fleeting moments of her recent happiness. How she loved to dance. There would be no one left to protect her once these men had abandoned their posts and departed. No son at home to love her in spite of everything. The villagers would turn against her. She would be marked as a traitor. My heart broke for her, even though her choices had lost me my dear friend.

'Another victim of this bloody war,' would be Alain's words.

As I stepped on, continuing my path, I wondered how many more victims were yet to come. For this was not yet the end. For the Italians, yes. For the rest of us? The battle was certainly not over.

54

Days into September, the town seemed to be operating in a state of hiatus. The Lindemann children had stayed on with Delphine because their mother was so poorly. I was helping out by minding the Decroix offspring. Hanna and Daniel were kept indoors, hidden, while their immediate future was decided. On the two occasions I had returned to Delphine's to collect her two, to take them for a brief walk, fresh air, I had hoped to catch a glimpse of Alain but there was no sign of him, nothing to suggest he had stayed there a few days earlier.

Where was he now?

Out on the streets, a spectacle to witness but once in a lifetime: five hundred refugees on the tramp. A cavalcade of men, women and children, cumbersome in several layers of clothes because they hadn't managed to fit all their belongings into their cases. Shuffling forward in ragged lines, quitting this medieval town, resigned, heads down, or with stony expressions gazing resolutely towards the upper reaches of the mountains. The Italian soldiers paid them no heed. No one attempted to halt their flight. There was no other way out of here. The Germans to the west and south had created military barricades. The Italians wanted no more of this dissentience. All that remained for them was the formal announcement of Italy's surrender.

I made my solitary way back to the white house clear in the knowledge that this was it, the turning point. If I couldn't persuade my parents to come with me into hiding in the basement, I would have no choice but to accompany them. Mamma, Papa and I, affixed to that throng of moving people.

55

They said no. Mamma would not countenance such an option.

'But we lived for eighteen months in a basement in Nice,' I'd argued, to no avail.

I was in my room, listlessly throwing bits and bobs into my bag. Who cared what I took or left? It was all the same. On my bedside table were three books belonging to Delphine that I had omitted to return. Would there still be an opportunity to race back to town with them? I heard a soft tapping on the front door.

I froze. The Germans here so soon?

'I'll go,' I called.

It was Delphine, Alexandre cradled in her arms. Her eyes red-rimmed. Cheeks drawn, haggard.

'Who's there?' Papa was calling. My parents were in their room, their upright case set on the floor alongside the front door.

'It's fine, Papa. Nothing to worry about.'

Delphine was nervous. She glanced about her, then back down the stairs to the lane that led to the town, as though fearing she had been followed. She saw my parents' luggage in the corridor and nodded, affirming that this was a reassuring sight.

'Sara, can we talk privately?'

She followed me along the hallway into the kitchen, which my parents had emptied of their pots and paltry possessions. She paced back and forth. I watched her. The

racked expression, her knitted brows. She had lost weight.
'I need your help, Sara. I must leave.'

'To visit your husband?'

'Philippe, no. No. We fear he has already faced the firing squad, though we have no confirmation of that yet.'

'Oh, God, Delphine.' I wanted to throw my arms around her, hug her tight. I loved her so, but her pain seemed too acute, too intimate and contained. I feared to tread on her feelings with my clumsy sympathy.

'What can I do?' I would have made a cup of tea but the kettle had been packed.

We bunched ourselves beside one another, up close at the table near the range, Alexandre on her knees, I ready to listen.

'It's a heavy responsibility that I am going to ask of you, Sara, and a matter of trust, but if you are willing, and if your parents agree, I feel sure you are capable of it.'

Hands clasped together on my lap, I waited.

'Herr and Frau Lindemann, due to Ilse's poor health and the extent of her pregnancy, are not in a position to travel with two small children. I have agreed – well, Philippe and I offered a few days before his – his arrest that if the worst came to the worst we would care for her two until they could all be safely reunited in Switzerland where they are headed. They have family prepared to welcome them, to take them in. The difficulties that arise now are that on top of Ilse somehow having to scale that mountain . . .' she paused, reflecting on the impracticability of this '. . . if, *when* . . . when the Germans reach here, because they have knowledge of Philippe's home address and circumstances, they will surely come looking for me. They will search every last centimetre of our home, and it will be impossible to conceal two extra babes.'

'You want me to look after them?' My heart lifted at the thought of staying, an opportunity to be a confirmed and trusted part of this community.

'In a manner of speaking, yes, but only for a day or two.'

'Oh.'

'Here's my plan. I am setting off today with Élisabeth in a truck driven by Claude Bonnard, a farmer friend from the next valley over. You might have met him?'

I shook my head.

'It's not important. He and I will travel together into the Var, beyond Fréjus, beyond the German flank. My sister lives close to a small mountain village. Remote, out of the way. Even should the Germans pay such an isolated spot a visit, Vanessa would have nothing to hide.'

'I don't understand.'

'Vanessa will foster her niece Élisabeth, quite legitimately, while I keep Hanna with me, passing her off as my own little girl. As you know, harbouring a Jewish child is an illegal act. It carries a death sentence or deportation. I cannot ask such a commitment of my sister. For her own safety, I will not tell her of the existence of Hanna and Daniel. All she will know is that rations are short here due to the extra influx of population, of *les assignés*. Vanessa can feed and keep Élisabeth and there will be no liability whatsoever for her. She has no children of her own, so Lissie will be company for her. The difficulty will be mine, to be so far removed from my own precious girl, especially now without Philippe . . . but it is a time of war. And there are many who need our help.'

'What about Daniel?'

'There's a chance he will be fostered by another family here in this village – Monsieur Duchamps, a gendarme, and his wife. He worked under Philippe . . .' She paused again, gathering her emotions. 'They are aware of the risks and are willing to take this on . . . Unlike Hanna's colouring, Daniel's blond hair is an asset. Or, if it proves too distressing for Hanna and Daniel to be separated from both their parents and each other, this little one here,' she stroked Alexandre's sleeping head, 'will have to go to the Duchamps, and I will temporarily foster Daniel as well as Hanna, passing them off as mine. It won't be easy for me to be apart from my children, but it shouldn't be for long. One month, two at the outside. Once the Lindemanns are safely settled with their cousins in Switzerland, the children will be taken to them. There are special agents engaged in this work.'

I nodded, thinking all this through, watching my friend bearing her grief with dignity. How hard this would be for Delphine to sacrifice her own lovely children even for a short while. 'So, how can I help?'

'I understand from Alain that you and he have converted the basement into a shelter.'

'We have.'

'Lucy would be touched to think of it as a temporary refuge, most especially for children.'

I smiled, listening.

'I will be gone for two days, possibly three. It depends on the security controls and how easily we can pass through the checkpoints. Our papers are all in order. However, there may be long queues, interrogations, hold-ups. Many are on the move right now. If we are pulled over, searched for any reason, it will take longer.'

'Let me go, Delphine. It's a huge risk, I know, but let me accompany Élisabeth. I want to help.'

'Out of the question. You'd never pull it off. If you're

picked up, all our lives would be lost. What I am asking of you is to care for Hanna, Daniel and little Alexandre here until I return. Two days, Sara, maximum three. I cannot entrust this to any of the neighbours. The less anyone is privy to, the better. And this property is conveniently isolated. What do you say?'

I wanted to do it, for Delphine's sake. For Alain, too, because I thought he might think better of me if I played my part and, above all, because it might save the lives of these children, whom I adored. I stood up and walked over to the closed kitchen door.

'I'll have to settle it with my parents. They're ready to leave, to begin that horrendous climb. Please God my mother has the strength for it. I'm so worried, and I'm not sure how they'd find their way without me. Perhaps I should ask them to wait with me.'

'At least ten inhabitants from here and villages nearby are guiding those who are escaping as far as the Italian border. Everyone will be safe, and your parents will find the way. It's better they begin the climb.'

Was Alain one of them? I didn't ask. I was mulling over the reality of abandoning my parents even for two or three days.

'I think my father will need me . . .'

'Let me talk to them. This caravan of people, there are somewhere close to a thousand trying to escape from the advancing Germans, including families coming up from the lowlands above the coast. With their possessions, their elderly, babes in arms, small children, the crossing will take several days. At some points along the line, they are barely moving. And it's a rigorous ascent, as you well know. Encourage your parents to go ahead, to begin their journey at their own pace.'

I was processing this, imagining my mother's reaction.

'Arrange with them to wait somewhere safe for you. It's two days, Sara, I'm asking. Three at the most. Your mother is ailing. She will be slow-moving, and when I return you can attach yourself to the tail end of the chain, speed on and meet up with them. At worst, you will find them in Borgo San Dalmazzo in Italy, their destination. They will be perfectly safe there. What do you say?'

I was silent, torn.

'I can't leave three children alone. Shall I have a word with your parents, explain the situation?'

'I'll talk to them.'

'Will you do this for us, Sara, please?'

I nodded. 'Of course.'

She squeezed my hand and passed her small son to me. 'Good girl, thank you. I must hurry back to the town, pack Elisabeth's bag. Claude will collect me within the hour. Before we set off west, we'll return here with Hanna and Daniel. I have prepared food and everything you'll need for the next couple of days. They'll be safe in your hands, your kindly protection, Sara, and they love you. That is clear for all the world to see.'

'Where are the Lindemanns?'

'They set off this morning soon after daybreak. I'm so worried for Ilse's health.'

'But why is she attempting this so close to her time? It's insane. Could we not have hidden them here in the basement?'

Delphine shook her head. 'We offered them that alternative. But Ilse knows very well that newborns of foreign citizens claiming asylum here in Occupied France are not protected by this abominable government. She is determined her child be born in Switzerland.'

I couldn't imagine how Frau Lindemann would fare, putting herself through such a brutal journey, and the grief of being separated from her children, but I knew I had to do my bit to help.

'Don't fear for them, Sara. Several from here are with them, will accompany them to the border.'

My friend read in my eyes the questions I was struggling not to ask.

'Nathalie is back from Fréjus. She is one of the volunteers and she has medical training. That's all you need to know.'

Delphine and I hugged tightly. I rocked Alexandre, who had woken and was fretting. I promised to be downstairs, waiting inside Lucy's apartment for her return in an hour.

'And then straight to the basement, promise me. Lock yourselves in, conceal yourselves. I don't want to be worrying about you as well as . . . everyone else.'

I promised.

56

My mother was distraught at the prospect of leaving me behind. My father understood that it was a duty and that duties should be honoured. I felt terrified and liberated in equal measure.

'We heard the news about Monsieur Decroix,' he said, shaking his head. 'These people have helped us generously, put their own lives at risk, and now they are asking you to be there for them. I believe that is only correct and just. But hear me clearly, Sara, you are not to delay. As soon as Madame Decroix returns from the Var and there is sufficient daylight to travel, you must join the march. Do you want us to wait with you or up ahead, if we can find somewhere to shelter along the way?'

I shook my head. 'I can walk faster. I'll easily catch you up. You can leave word for me along the way. At the worst, I'll find you in San Dalmazzo. Delphine says it's a small town with a railway station from which we can travel onwards, south to a port and from there find passage to Palestine. One week from today, at the latest, I'll meet you in the station waiting room, if I don't locate you along the way. Or leave word for me. Never fear, we'll be reunited very soon.'

With heavy hearts, it was agreed.

I helped my parents carry their suitcase and a cloth shoulder bag, rattling with aluminium kitchenware, down the exterior steps. 'Why not leave these, Mamma? Or let me carry them. I'll bring them with me.'

Stubborn, she insisted on taking them. 'Who knows when we'll find somewhere to cook again?'

And so, backdropped by the mountains and the vast highland plain, the moment had come. We embraced as though our lives depended on it and whispered our farewells.

'*Au revoir* only,' I reassured Mamma softly, as her tears fell.

I had dreamed of my liberty throughout the summer, but now that the separation was upon us, it was soul-crushing. It was far, far harder than I had expected to remain watching while my parents set off along the lane to join the exodus. Two defenceless individuals on that wide-open terrain embarking on a flight that should not be demanded of any human being, their dark frames leaning towards one another. My father's tall figure, accentuated because he was wearing a hat, holding back every few metres to keep pace with Mamma, who turned her head many times, glancing backwards to give me one last wave. I had to battle the urge to chase after them, to drag them to my breast, beg them to wait, hold back, promising we would leave together, as a family, just as we had arrived here, but I knew it was kinder to my mother to give them the head start. I wasn't their little Sarina any more. I had been designated a role to play in this war and I was proud of that. Caring for the children – Delphine would be back with them any minute now – was a small expression of my gratitude and, although I could not have known it then, for me this was another beginning.

57

Italy had surrendered. The news was finally made public, transmitted from radio stations, cafés, open windows, everywhere. US General Eisenhower announced that Marshal Pietro Badoglio, who had replaced Mussolini as prime minister of Italy, had agreed to an armistice. The Italians were relinquishing their occupation zones north and west of Nice. They were pulling out, going home. Even as they loaded their vehicles, the announcements, replayed repeatedly, could be heard from the radio in Pascal's bar.

Refugees and Italian military were all setting off to trace the same arduous terrain over the mountain summit and down the rocky pass to cross the border into Italy. One or two of the soldiers gave lifts on their trucks to the less able of the refugees. I learned later that one soldier had unlaced his boots, kicked them off and handed them to a Jew who, in ragged espadrilles with luggage on his back and a babe in arms, was preparing to make the ascent with his wife, who was carrying their small daughter.

The going promised to be punishing, but the advantage was that this corridor of flight had no security checks, no controls, no refusals of onward passage. No Germans. And once we were on the other side, Italy was now a neutral country. They, we, my people, my parents, would no longer be hunted. From there, the escaped would be at liberty to secure a passage onwards to wherever in the free world they chose. No exit visa required. And in just a few days' time, I would be among them.

Or so we had configured it . . .

58

I have never felt as alone as I did that evening, in spite of
the three fragile, bemused beings in my charge, innocent
and vulnerable. Delphine had been gone since early afternoon, my parents an hour or two longer. Night had fallen.
Delphine had warned that once the enemy marched in
there would be no time left to go into hiding.

I had done as she had bade me and descended straight
to the cellar. The four of us together, we had established
our temporary 'base'.

'Why is it so dark?' asked Hanna.

'So we can watch the candles burning brightly. Aren't
they pretty?'

Then we played pit-a-pat: this is your hand and these are
my hands. From the upstairs master bedroom, on our way
down, I had grabbed Freddie and brought him with us. I
had considered the wireless for music but knew there would
be no reception underground. Freddie proved a source of
comfort and diversion. Guessing his name, suggesting
alternatives. A ventriloquist's doll. Voices and stories.

I was making every effort to turn our predicament
into an adventure, our quarters into a 'secret hideaway'.
Cross-legged on our archipelago of mattresses, we'd draw
up tight together on our own 'boat on a swampy lake',
munching the fresh food Delphine had left with me,
Hanna and I feeding the two baby boys: tomatoes, figs,
apples, bread, cheese, milk. Neither the cheese nor the
milk was kosher but if Hanna was aware of that she didn't

baulk at it. We ate with relish, while she and I recounted tales from our summer, our discoveries up here in the mountains.

It was the last fresh food we were to consume for several days to come.

Now the trio of heads, *les petits*, were sleeping in the make-shift beds in our clandestine lair, which still reeked of bleach, though less invasively so. Its odour and the memories it released caused me to ache all the more acutely for Alain.

When I felt certain that everyone was comfortable and not unduly distressed, I crept up the stairs, turned the key in the lock and pushed hard against the door with the cupboard attached to it – Alain's carpentry camouflage of the maroon door – and slid out through the slenderest of cracks into the scullery. The glass bottle of vodka I had broken open all those months ago was glinting, touched by the tiny bar of moonlight that slipped in through the closed curtains and slatted shutters. I switched on the overhead light at the wall. There was a flash, a pop, and then the bulb fizzled out. Save for that shaft of moon-shine, I was in pitch darkness. Damn. I had left the candles and matches in the basement.

I needed to breathe, to be outside. I craved fresh air, an impression of liberty. I was so afraid of what lay ahead – of the potential risks, my responsibilities, possible expos-ure – I thought my heart might race up into my throat and choke me. Hands in front of me, I groped and shuffled towards the back door, banging my hip against a stray chair as I did so. Somehow the stars, that expansive navy sky, would reassure me, bring me back to earth. I unbolted the back door and crept barefoot into the garden. A rush of cold air slapped me full on. It was shocking, unexpected, and I shook my shoulders to abate the chill. Something, a small animal – a hedgehog or feral cat perhaps – skittered away into the undergrowth. I stood still, one foot on top of the other because my toes were going numb. I was gazing towards the mountains, their imposing nighttime silhouettes pinnacled with jagged black crowns, to the high paths, which I couldn't discern in the darkness. The ancient salt road, the Cherry Tree Route.

Hundreds of people were there right now, invisible to my eye, trudging a path to freedom along the high ranges of the Gesso Valley, my own most cherished relatives among them. Were they still walking – blistered feet, struggling to keep up, determined to continue even in the dead of night – or were they resting? Had my father stopped to cut a branch, carve my mother a makeshift walking stick, lay down his coat as pillow for his beloved wife? How would they stay warm at such an altitude? Would she die of cold? Had I abandoned them, my own flesh and blood? Nobody, not one of us, had been prepared for this severance.

What if I were never to see them again?

Tears were rolling down my cheeks. This hateful, hateful war.

I remembered Alain's father's statement all those weeks ago. Be out by the end of September before the snows close you in. The snows had already begun to fall on the peaks, at around 2,800 metres. I prayed my parents had found a cave or sheltered ditch, somewhere warm to lay their heads, even for a few snatched hours. Had I made the wrong decision, not considering my own flesh and blood first? Should I have fled with them, to lend my father a hand, moral support? Hundreds of strangers bedding down alongside one another in their clothes, suitcases as pillows, on the mountainside. There was plenty of clean fresh water, which was a bonus, the only one I could think of at that moment. Was Alain somewhere nearby, keeping a watchful eye over them? Or was he hiding in the town? If Ilse's child came early, could Nathalie deliver it? Had Delphine managed to reach her sister?

I was choked by questions, misgivings. Too many uncertainties.

And I was shivering with cold. I was more susceptible to it because of the exhaustion, worn down by an excess of emotions. I slipped back inside, bolted the door again from the interior, then returned to the top of the flight of stairs, locking the door firmly behind me, the cupboard back in place. Having sealed myself and the children in, I stuffed the key into my brassière and descended the creaking staircase, to where my three small charges were lost in their rainbow worlds.

I climbed into bed, snuggling up close to Hanna, and wrapped my arms around her to steal a little of her body heat. Hands holding hands. The two small boys – they might almost have been twins – were in their makeshift cot on the other side of her. For the sake of warmth and safety I had bunked us all together. Hanna murmured something. It was 'Mutti', I think. Ilse must be desperate for her children. If only I could reassure her that they were safe. Hanna's eyelids flicked open, then instantly closed again. I rested my head against her blue-black mane of hair and closed my eyes too, hoping for sleep and a nightmare-free slumber. As I dozed, I was trying to recall what day it was. Was it 9 or 10 September? Why did it seem to matter? When I had a pencil I would begin to write it down, to record everything, all of this journey from Hell.

59

At first I thought it was a rat, a rodent, some small creature snooping and snuffling about in the cellar. I was only semi-conscious, until a heart-stopping bang, which might have been an almighty clap of thunder, fully roused me. Raining again, another tumultous downpour. I sat bolt upright, startled. Eyes wide open. Then an instant realization of where I was. The impenetrable obscurity, the rise and fall of sleeping figures snuffling at my side, Lucy's luxuriously woolly blankets enfolding us. The cellar key indented in my skin beneath my undergarments. The slighty sugary smell of warm pee. What time was it? Another sound, a dragging of chair legs directly overhead. My heart punched. Thoughts spiralling out of control.

Someone had entered the house by the front door. Broken in? Burglars? Or – no, please not – German soldiers?

Hanna sat up and began to murmur. I thrust my hand over her mouth and signalled to her to keep quiet. It was not thunder I'd heard but a door being forced open. Kicked in? An intruder on the floor above us. Now began a fusillade of shouting and urgent footsteps. The walls, floors were reverberating under the weight of the movement. Orders were barked. *In German.*

German. Dear God, yes.

They had arrived. The enemy had reached our little enclave, and they were *here*. Here. In our white house.

Directly overhead on the ground floor, a raid was taking place. I signalled to Hanna to lift up her brother and to hold him tight, to make sure Daniel didn't let out a cry. I drew little Alexandre to me. He was restless, wet. It was he who reeked of urine. I hugged him tight against me and rocked him. He beat the air with his crinkled little arms. My hand was gently covering his lips to keep him silent, but not so firmly that I would alarm him. The heavy-soled feet above us were moving at an alarming pace. Back and forth, from room to room. How many men were there? I heard crashing, loud and recurrent. Despite the crippling fear, the shocking realization that the Germans were *here* in Lucy's home, I had to beat back the urge to run up the stairs and put a stop to the desecration. They were wrecking Lucy's house. What were they shouting about, breaking, banging, knocking objects over? Were they dismantling the piano, chopping it up? I pictured the photographs on its dusty surface.

Hanna and I exchanged glances. The whites of her eyes, pools of alarm in the darkness. She could understand them, would know what they were shouting. 'Tell me,' I mouthed.

'They've fled,' a male voice called from one room to another directly above us. Hanna whispered his words softly in my ear, muttering an almost simultaneous translation.

'Those on the top floor. Two bedrooms both empty, recently slept in. Milk and foodstuffs abandoned in the kitchen.'

In that second, I was so thankful my parents had fled, were safe.

'No one down here. Cupboards empty. No sign of recent activity.'

I closed my eyes. What a stroke of fortune that I had kept away for a while and that I had more or less tidied up after all my rummaging through cupboards and wardrobes.

Still, the faint smell of perfume in the bathroom, the creased bedcovers . . .

'Someone's summer residence, I'd hazard a guess.'

'Looks like it, judging by the photographs everywhere.'

'Help yourselves to whatever you want – there's booze – and let's get out of here.'

I pressed Hanna's hand tight in mine. She was trembling, tears silently falling, as we tuned in to the shattering of glass, the footfall of heavy-duty boots, several pairs. A lavatory being flushed. Cupboard doors opening, not closing. I thought of the framed pictures of the boy who no longer existed and my blood began to boil at the possible despoiling of his memory, his innocence, his smiling features, the likely theft of the silver.

'*Diese sind hübsch*. These are pretty.'

'If you want to carry them, have them. We need to be getting back to town.'

'Find something to transport them in. Strip one of the beds, take a sheet.' I heard more shattering of glass as something thudded to the floor.

One pair of feet, then another had reached the scullery. The soldiers were directly above us now. My heart was hammering, burning. Please, don't let them spot the door.

'*Scheisse*, the light's not working, bulb blown probably. You got a torch?'

'Anything here?'

'Door to the yard's padlocked.'

'We're wasting time. No Jews here, let's go.'

Hanna's flesh was so wet and sticky against mine, she

might have just stepped out of a bath and omitted to dry herself properly. Slowly, the feet were retreating back towards the main door, which did not close or I heard no sound of its closing. The soldiers must have left it wide open. Why? Were they intending to return? Had one stayed behind? A guard at the front entrance? We heard the faint revving of one engine and then a second, followed by the rolling of trucks on course, I assumed, for the town.

Respite. But for how long?

I lifted my hand from Alexandre's face. He started to whimper.

'Sssh, sssh.' I held him tight against me to where the burp of his sobs was lost in my breast. He needed changing. My palm was damp with his saliva. I paid it barely any attention.

There was nothing to prevent the return of the Wehrmacht. And what if they should decide to set up residence here? Who or what would deter them? They occupied properties wherever they chose, wherever they conquered. We would be trapped. Living beneath them. I closed my eyes making a rough calculation. We had tinned food for, possibly, five or six more days. Water, but insufficient for four of us for that length of time. Three days maximum, if we used it sparingly.

As far as I was able to appraise, it was a little more than twenty-four hours since Delphine had left us, which meant we had at least another twenty-four hours to endure, and that was looking on the positive side. *Delphine would come back.* She had not been stopped. She had not been identified as Philippe's wife or widow, or arrested as the spouse of a 'traitor'. This reasoning was – it had to be – my faith, our lifeline.

My whole body was trembling from head to toe. I clambered clumsily to my feet, boy in my arms, rocking and swaying him, nuzzling my lips into his neck.

'Let's get you changed,' I whispered, tugging at his soiled pants.

60

Locked in this underworld, time had no meaning. There was no tool to measure it by and there was no way I was going back upstairs, though I was desperate to assess the damage and, more importantly, to know whether the front door had been left wide open. If so, we were sitting ducks, targets for the next incursion.

When we spoke, which was rarely, it was in whispers. Would another party, commanding officers perhaps, be deployed here? Had one or two soldiers been stationed outside in the garden? How would we ever leave? How would Delphine manage to come back to us, make contact with us, if she was still alive and safe? Had my parents reached Italy? My head was swimming with troubling scenarios, dogged by questions to which I had no answers.

We had one clock. It was always accurate: our stomachs. Hunger. I needed to keep the little ones fed and in as hygienic a condition as we could manage. Hanna assisted me, loyally and without drama. We communicated with hand signals. The ordeal seemed to have robbed her of her French. It was my job to open the tins of food because if she cut her fingers I would have another problem to solve. Alain, or perhaps it had been Nathalie, I could no longer remember – my mind was growing muddled – had left us with a primitive first-aid kit but water was precious. Our supply had to be eked out. This isolation might endure longer than the three days estimated.

We used one of the zinc pails as a pot for the boys.

Hanna and I used another. We stowed the unemptied buckets at the furthest point from us. We girls were better able to contain our needs than the two babies, who had no comprehension of what was going on. The prerequisite was to keep both boys clean. And quiet: no screaming, no shouting, no bawling. We had spoons to feed them directly from the tins. Dishes or bowls were a luxury Alain had decided against. They would further drain our water reserves when they required washing. Alain had talked me through all these important details. It seemed like centuries ago now, when I had never envisaged this would come to pass. During a time when I never believed that I would be trapped down here, struggling with a bedload of infants.

How efficiently I had got used to security, had believed in our safety, my invincibility.

Much of the time I wanted to give in to the force of my emotions. I hungered for the embrace of a loved one, to feel strength against me. I wanted my parents – my dear father especially – to take control of these onerous duties as he had been doing for more than three years. How had I failed to appreciate the bulk of responsibility he had been carrying on his shoulders? I closed my eyes, trying to picture my dear papa. And Mamma too. To tune into them, draw them back to me, but it was hopeless. I felt so distanced from them and, in my moments of deepest despair, when the children were sleeping and I tossed and turned restlessly, dreading the next break-in, I grew frantic, convinced I would never see either of them again, that we would never be reunited. A premonition? No, it was panic. The darkness and deprivation were ratcheting up my nerves to a level of frenzy.

61

The more we slept, the less call there was on our resources, on our depleting energy. And the less we noticed the lingering smell that was building up around us. Our decomposing body waste.

Was it day or was it night? Was it day two or day three, or had we been incarcerated for longer? There remained a dozen unopened food tins, even if the stack of empties was mounting. I counted fourteen, though Alexandre had kicked over several in a fit of hysterics earlier. I couldn't find them and I was reluctant to grub about for them in case I cut myself on one. On the other hand, if one of the babies fell over and hurt themselves . . . I had to protect them, dared not close my eyes.

Hanna and I decided to take it in turns to rest or keep guard but we were not sufficiently disciplined at sticking to the regime. I slept in snatches only, but the insomnia was bringing on a creeping delusional or hallucinogenic state, and it was taking hold. My head was light and dizzy or constantly throbbing. It was as though an iron band had been wrapped around my skull and someone was pulling it tighter and tighter, cutting off the blood circulation. I had to resist the temptation to snap, to lose my temper. I never stopped reminding myself: *These children are counting on me*. Delphine is counting on me. Everybody is counting on me . . .

Surely we had endured three interred days by now. Please, somebody, please come soon. Both boys were suffering from upset tummies. We needed more buckets. We needed fresh water.

Where was Delphine? Was she safe? On her way back to us? Or had she been arrested?

Upstairs, all was quiet.

Eventually I must have nodded off. I was physically exhausted from a day – was it a day? – spent nursing little Daniel, whose intestinal problems were worsening. I had washed and changed him several times, given him more water than we could realistically spare, which, in any case, was possibly no longer sufficiently clean for drinking, but there was nothing else. Between us, Hanna and I were doing our level best to keep the four of us alive, but we were fatigued and getting sick ourselves.

We had been abandoned. We were dying . . .

From the fringes of a groggy, desperate state of mind, I registered the closing of a door. Eyes wide open, I concentrated hard, realigning my brain, tuning in. Steps along the hallway that led from the front to the rear, until the footfalls were overhead. I struggled, hastily gathering myself together. I shook Hanna awake. With frantic hand signals, I instructed her to take hold of the boys. Whatever happened, they must remain silent. The intruder was in the scullery. Somewhere close to the cupboard that concealed our camouflaged door. Had the Gestapo known all along that we were here? Had it just been a matter of time before they returned to arrest us? Shoot, deport us. Had somebody betrayed us? A neighbour, collaborator, a *mouchard*? I heard objects being removed from shelves, the shelves that had been deliberately cluttered with jugs and biscuit boxes, glued down to disguise the door that stood behind, and to conceal its lock. Someone who knew we were here! Fingers scraping against wood. They were coming down. Was this someone who knew where to find the lock? Who had a key?

Was it Delphine?

I had a key, the original, and Delphine possessed a copy of it. *Or someone else had Delphine's key.* If she had been arrested . . . the key found on her person or in her house . . . If she had been tortured, forced to talk, to give away our hiding place . . . Terror was pushing me over the edge. I had to get a grip, fight rising hysteria. The children. I must protect the children.

I shot a glance to Hanna, whose normally neatly ring-leted hair had grown unruly, matted, filthy, and the two bedraggled, dirty-faced blond boys, standing frozen: a statue of three terrified small faces entangled in one another's limbs on the mattress. The key was turning in the lock. I couldn't breathe. The oxygen in my lungs was threatening to explode, to suffocate me. The door was being drawn back, one cautious centimetre at a time, until it was wide open. A gust of clean air swept down the stairs. A shaft of greyish light almost blinded me. My eyes had grown accustomed to darkness. I hastily signalled to my wards to retreat on tiptoe, to duck deeper into the shadowy recesses of the basement, with our stinking slop buckets, where there was even less light than the murk we inhabited.

Please don't kick the buckets over, I was praying.

I stood my ground, or was too paralysed to shift. The top step creaked. A foot had landed on it. Heavily. Surely boots too sturdy for Delphine. Jackboots?

Yes, jackboots. Wehrmacht soldiers.

One Wehrmacht soldier on the top step.

This was the end. The end for us all.

I mustn't breathe, mustn't make a sound. My stomach was liquefying. I wanted to wet myself. Blood, moisture in my nose. A nose bleed. No, no. I was cracking under the pressure.

'Sara?'

My name. Whispered. My name. I had all but forgotten my own name.

'Sara?'

An ally?

'H-here,' I rasped. The first use of my voice in however many days.

Into the umbra strode scuffed well-worn boots with the hem of breeches tucked into the high leather. A male profile.

Alain.

I felt myself sink to my knees, but before I hit the cement floor he was in front of me holding me, taking the weight of me, the weight of my responsibilities, in his arms.

62

Alain had reached us, he said, by hitching a lift with his bicycle on one of his neighbours' horse-drawn carts. It slowed as it approached the white house and he had leaped off, ducking into the jungle of vegetation before entering the house by the front entrance after the sun had set.

He came bearing boiled eggs, a few weather-beaten rolls, fresh homemade grape juice – how we guzzled that juice, quenching our thirst, washing away the dust in our throats – a small round of goat's cheese and two thick slices of chicken. Fresh food. We tore at it like scavengers, with no thought of anything but the ache in our stomachs while he began to gather up the empty tins. He was shocked by our condition.

'The town is swarming with Wehrmacht soldiers and Gestapo. They are dragging innocent people from their homes, threatening them at gunpoint, forcing confessions, betrayals.'

'Has anyone been hurt?'

Alain did not meet my gaze. Even in this crepuscular light I knew there must have been victims.

'Where's Delphine? Is she safe?'

'Not returned yet.'

'Alain, is she safe?'

'Calm, Sara. I don't know. We have no news.'

'How long have we been down here?'

'A little more than four days.'

'She expected to be back well before now. Something must have happened.'

'We need to get you out of here, to somewhere with clean running water, adequate sanitation. The state of you all . . .'

I knew by the tremor in his voice that he partially blamed himself.

'If you can bring us fresh water, we'll manage, honestly we will, till Delphine returns. It can't be much longer.'

Alain shook his head. 'Your health is at risk. This little lad is very poorly.' He was cradling Daniel. 'The question is how and to where.'

The isolation of Lucy's house had served its purpose, but the town, he said, was a minefield.

'What do you suggest?'

'Split you up, find homes that have already been searched and cleared. Homes where you are with people we trust who can feed you.'

'That sounds idyllic, but where?'

'I don't know yet. Leave it with me.'

Alain gathered up our filthy buckets. 'Dear God, Sara, I should have thought this through more carefully.'

'Shall I help?'

'No, stay where you are.'

I rummaged in my brassière to retrieve the key to the padlock that secured the garden door.

'What if someone sees you?'

'I'll tell them I'm keeping an occasional eye on the house for the Allinghams.'

Alain heaved the buckets up the stairs and chucked the slops into the greenery. Buckets sluiced, he returned them to the cellar. It took him several trips. On each occasion, he locked the door behind him, sealing us in. It was painstaking, but, he insisted, 'crucial'.

The children watched in perturbed silence. Dear sweet Hanna did her best to keep the boys unruffled while I scrubbed Daniel and filled her in on the plan of action, such as it was.

The physical business of conveying us to a secure place was the first and biggest challenge. Walking out in full daylight onto the lane that led from the white house to the town rendered us vulnerable. Any casual pedestrian was an eye witness. Even if we were fortunate and encountered no one, as we entered the town we would surely be stopped by patrolling Wehrmacht soldiers and questioned, searched, identity papers demanded. Arrest would undoubtedly follow.

As a native and non-Jew, Alain had freedom of movement. So, too, little Alexandre. Hanna and I were both lacking the prerequisites. We were Jews, stateless, at huge risk, Daniel also, but with his Germanic looks, blond hair, he was less likely to be suspected. This would work in his favour.

As Alain descended the stairs, his fifth journey, with two full canisters of fresh water, he seemed less disheartened. 'I have an idea, somewhere for you, Sara.'

'Where?'

'Let me propose it to the householders and then we'll work it out.'

I nodded.

'First, Daniel. He needs a doctor. Henri Duchamps, who is back from duty, is still willing to foster him. It shouldn't be too risky to take the boy with me now. I'll wheel him to a medical centre, then on to the Duchamps family. It's you two girls I then need to sort out. Hanna, until Delphine returns, and you, Sara, until we can secure your escape and reunite you with your parents.'

'Is it too late to cross the mountain into Italy? My parents are expecting to meet me in San Dalmazzo. I promised I'd start the climb as soon as Delphine was back.'

'Well, Delphine has not returned and you are not going anywhere yet. It's not safe.'

'What if I travel by night?'

'You'd be stopped before you'd ventured a hundred metres.'

'Is there someone who can get a message to them? They will be worrying, distressed.'

'I'll ask one of the team. If all has gone according to plan, they'll be over the border by now, and out of danger. They can wait in San Dalmazzo. It's you we need to worry about. Do you have the strength to face another night, possibly two, here? There's plenty of fresh water now and sufficient food. I know it's grim, Sara. I have a plan but it will take some organizing.'

I nodded, offering a false smile, a brave face. 'Of course.'

In reality, the prospect of even a few more hours in this dungeon set my nerves on edge.

'Good girl.'

He gave my cheek an encouraging stroke.

I could hardly bear to watch his retreating figure as he hurried up the stairs, little Daniel in his arms. By tonight, with all good fortune, the ailing child would be pumped with medicine and in the safe keeping of Monsieur and Madame Duchamps.

That left three of us to extricate.

63

Lower down in the valleys, the *vendange*, the grape harvest, was under way.

The town lacked petrol, *essence*, so carts were the transport, drawn by mules, donkeys and horses, with boys and girls from surrounding settlements at the helm. A few of the farmers had rigged up their pre-war tractors with improvised gasifiers fuelled by wood. Many of the hired labourers, who gathered at daybreak outside the church, arrived on foot or by bicycle. Sunrise saw plenty of activity. In spite of the German presence, the pickers continued to pass to and fro, circling and crossing through the village. The Wehrmacht had requested papers and searched the reapers so many times, they barely paid them any attention now. Most, in any case, were children, upwards of eight or nine, riding alongside their adolescent siblings who took the reins. The vintners were appreciative of any work force that could be scrabbled together, while the callow hands thanked their lucky stars they were busy elsewhere, and not witnesses to the brutalities perpetrated by the enemy in their ordinarily peaceful mountain enclave.

'All this activity will work in our favour,' Alain had assured me.

Earlier in the summer, I had dreamed I would participate in this year's grape-picking with Albert and Thomas, nimble fingers together beneath a perfect blue sky. But Albert was gone, I was not at liberty and, until now, the grape-picking had slipped my mind.

The following morning as dawn was breaking, Alain returned. He was agitated, with anguish in his eyes.

'What's happened? Oh, Alain, is it Daniel?'

'The Germans have ransacked Nice, raided the synagogue, every hotel, boarding house, apartment block. Here, the same. They are tearing cellars apart, hidden recesses, dragging men from their homes, stripping them naked to verify . . .' He couldn't complete the sentence. 'We must get you all out of here. I fear soldiers might decide to set up residence in this house.'

'Is Daniel safe?' I insisted, shaken to the bone.

He nodded, but the pressure was radiating from him as he reeled off instructions, outlining his scheme step by step, handing me two slices of dry bread and an apple.

'Understood?'

I murmured an affirmative.

He took me in his arms and hugged me so tightly he almost winded me. I could feel the tickle of his breath and his body trembling.

'Oh, Sara . . . I hadn't expected it to be so . . . grisly.'

Then, with a nod, bidding Hanna to follow him, Alain lifted Alexandre into his arms and carried him to the creaking stairs

'God speed,' I whispered.

Outside, he would chivvy them onto a dray, concealing the illegal Hanna among the empty grape baskets while Alexandre could sit up front on his lap alongside the farmer at the reins. With luck, they would not be stopped and searched. They were, to all intents and purposes, nothing more threatening than a party of local inhabitants – two men and a boy – off to harvest their vineyards.

Alain had assured me that he would return to collect

me either at sunset, when the farmer returned with his day's load, 'Or, if the German activity in and around the village poses too great a threat, I'll be back for you tomorrow morning at this same hour. Twenty-four hours at the outside. Be brave, sweet Sara.' He gave me one more hug before the trio bustled up the stairs. I followed to lock the doors, to bolt myself in.

I have rarely felt more isolated, empty, forlorn. I confess to shedding a few tears but there was comfort in the knowledge that I had an ally in Alain. Even so, he did not return at the close of the day. So I must wait it out another night. His instructions were clear. He had bade me be ready – there would be no time to dally – to be sure to lock the cellar and leave everything strategically hidden, masking our secret door so that we could, in dire emergency and if the Germans did not occupy the house, use the space another time.

'Cover all traces, Sara. If the Germans break in again, it is crucial they find nothing. No clues, nothing questionable that could lead them to suspect the existence of the basement, or the traffic of people. Do you understand?'

I tried to be obedient, meticulous to the letter. My weakness was that I couldn't stomach the prospect of another night in impenetrable darkness, a solitary internment blanketed by cold concrete. The stale air, candle grease, lingering human smells. The fear. Fear of sound, fear of the deathly silence. I had reached my wretched limit.

Anticipating Alain's return, clutching my precious companion, the fox, I made my way back up the stairs, locked and concealed the hidden door, tidied the scullery and took the cellar key outside to embed it at the base of an overgrown rose bush, making a mental note of which one. If I was picked up, I didn't want it on my person and

303

I judged it better not to hide it inside the house. I would retrieve it from its cache before it got wet or rusty, once the Germans had moved on and I was at liberty to return here.

Back in Lucy's home, all doors locked from within, seeing that the sun had set and there was little chance that Alain or anyone else would be returning for me that night, I used Lucy's bathroom for a quick wash, my first in days, and decided I would risk sleeping in her room.

I missed my parents achingly, deep in the pit of my stomach. I craved news, some form of proximity to them, some evidence of our past family life. I wished I could return upstairs to our apartment, curl up in my old room, but that was out of the question: the Nazis had identified the top floor as a previous hideaway for our kind.

I wandered into the drawing room where the photos were displayed on the piano. The silver frames had disappeared, stolen. Every single one. Shards of glass lay shattered on the piano's surface and the floor. The portraits were in shreds, curled, trampled over. Only the smaller tortoiseshell frames remained intact. One contained a picture of Lucy's son. I lifted it from where it had been knocked flat, pressed it to my chest and carried it to the mantelpiece where, the last time I had looked, the Craven 'A' cigarette packet had lain alongside my favourite of all possessions, the treasured bee brooch. No cigarettes, no brooch. Anger rose within me. I hit my hand against the mantelpiece and almost smashed the glass in the picture frame.

It was a desecration. My own intrusions were one thing but this was quite another. In that moment, I hated these enemies to such a physical degree that I could feel the poison of my emotions surge through my veins. If the thief had been present before me, I might have throttled him with my bare hands. Was there nothing of all our lives they would not steal or destroy?

Knocking. I heard knocking. Too late for Alain. Finger tapping against glass. I ducked down. I shouldn't be up here. I had not followed instructions and now I was to be caught red-handed.

Hands shaking almost uncontrollably, I deposited the photo by the hearth, and scuttled on all fours behind the second sofa, the one furthest from the hallway door. There, pressed against its back, I crouched, my pulse racing, beating in my ears, almost deafening me. A second knock. A key turning. What had I not cleared away, aside from the photo, which I could not reach now? What had possessed me to be so careless? I had left the fox fur on Lucy's bed. Who would recollect that it hadn't been there before? Footsteps. *Someone inside the house.* It had to be Alain or Delphine. Please, let it be. Who else was in possession of a key? Even with this logic, I dared not show myself for fear it was a trap. The newcomer moved directly along the corridor towards the kitchen. On his or her way to the scullery? Unless I had been betrayed, my hiding place reported, it was one of my two friends. I crawled across the carpet, burning my knees in my haste, making my way to the open door. Head craned round it, I caught sight of Alain's boots retreating out of view. Relief flooded me as I called his name softly.

64

The following morning, a rising sense of apprehension washed through with bliss.

'Remember, Sara, the instant I jump off, the driver will start humming. If he stops, he's giving you a signal. You understand? If he stops humming . . .'

'Yes, yes, I've got it.' Butterflies stirring in my stomach. The terror, trepidation. And yet happiness. With Alain at my side, I was buoyant and felt sufficiently brave, almost, to face the challenge that lay ahead.

'And you won't tell me where I am to be hidden?'

'The less you know until you are safely within their walls . . . All being well, I will drop in to see you later this evening. I hope I'll have news for you. Are you all right?'

'A bit wobbly,' I admitted.

'We'll be fine. Take care and best of luck, sweet Sara.' Alain leaned in to my right cheek. I felt the brush of his skin on my face and wanted to let myself go as he kissed me softly on the ear. I longed to take hold of him again, press myself tightly against him, relive the night we had spent together, give myself to him again, thrill to the intimacy, as I had the first time. Smiling at Lucy's ceiling as he had lain sleeping at my side.

'Ready?'

'I think so.'

Out in the garden, not yet daybreak, the overhead sky dazzled with stars. I dragged deep on the sweet fresh air. In the distance, mountains. The land and vegetation about us smelt dew-fresh. It chilled my terrified bones. Alain padlocked the rear entrance to Lucy's and pocketed his key. His fingers pressed against my elbow, we hastened along the path to the iron gate in a crack of dawn apricot glow.

Waiting there for us was a surprisingly small cart drawn by a grey donkey.

'Quick as you can, young lady,' was the greeting from my chauffeur, Maurice! The farmer, the regular at Pascal's bar. I gave a tiny nod. My face broke into a smile, an expression of my appreciation, as I climbed aboard and into the back.

Alain slipped into the wooden seat alongside Maurice.

I was buried within a collection of crates and various tools I did not recognize, all required for the harvesting and gathering of the grapes. They gave off a pungent, sweet smell. The smell of fermenting fruit.

The driver bade the beast get on its way and we clopped back towards the town, where we veered off to the left, bypassing one of the two principal roads that led in and out of our medieval settlement. On a hillside, at a rather sharp angle, which caused a pair of secateurs and various other tools to slide towards me, we came to a halt.

Alain sprang down from the passenger seat. The two men bade each other *au revoir*, then Alain, after whispering, '*Bonne chance*,' in my direction, was gone.

Maurice did not speak, did not acknowledge my presence. To all intents and purposes, to any curious onlooker, I was not there, semi-covered by a tarpaulin in the rear. My chauffeur's hand slapped against the wooden frame of the cart and we continued on our way, clip-clopping round the outskirts of the town, making our descent. All the while the man was humming to himself.

We didn't travel any great distance, but as I was concealed I couldn't tell precisely in which direction we were headed. We were descending an incline, so it must be southwards.

And then we made our stop.

A woman's voice. She exchanged a word or two with Maurice, then softly called my name, hissing instructions at me while pretending to speak to the man up front. Gingerly, I lifted the tarpaulin covering, preparing to alight.

The glare of early morning almost blinded my dark-damaged eyes, so it was a moment before I realized that it was Albert's mother I was face to face with. Albert's mother who stood waiting. I was astonished. I wanted to say something, but I was obliged to keep silent and do only what I had been briefed to do.

These villagers – all of them in it together? – were risking their lives for my safety. My heart was overflowing. I wanted to hug her, to share the grief I had felt for her throughout the summer months, confide how much I had cared for her son and how beholden I was to her for all that she was doing now, but one word, one false move, could put us all in jeopardy. She – I didn't even know her name, it occurred to me now, even though in my mind she had been such an influence on the moods, the story of my summer – had been waiting on the outskirts of Ville-Vésubie at the side of a barely used walkway, known only to inhabitants, with her bicycle. Attached to it was her *remorque*, her trailer, which was piled high with grubby pillowcases and sheets recently used by the Italians in the hotels, now occupied by Germans. I did not need to be instructed. Deftly, I slid myself under the bedding, beneath a weight of cotton. The laundress tugged and rearranged the sheets so that I was completely concealed.

Curled like a hibernating squirrel, trying hard not to inhale the scents of hair oil and other unpleasant traces of enemy soldiers, I was returned uphill, into the centre of the town. Bumping across cobbles, Madame's bicycle bell trilled twice. She called out a greeting. *Bonjour!* I had no idea to whom. I prayed not to German soldiers, though I wouldn't have put it past her to use her charms to beguile the assailant. Within a matter of metres, we turned a corner, then another and drew to a halt.

When Albert's mother gave the signal, I lifted my head out from within the mound of dirty washing. We were in an alley with high stone buildings on either side of us. In front of me was a large barn-like door built into the stone wall. It was the presbytery.

Father Scaramoni's housekeeper, Béatrice Leblanc, lumbered out of the house buried beneath bundles of bedding. Sheets were raised high, held up to the light, examined by both women who played out a credible scene. Within this display of lifting and masking, of overacting and rather comical laundry business, I was bustled indoors, into an enclosed courtyard and from there through a back door into the house. The broad-beamed Madame Leblanc, who insisted I address her as Béatrice, led me down a darkly lit corridor.

'No dawdling, please, miss. He'll be off to say Mass and he likes a good breakfast before he steps up to the altar, though he should hold off till after Communion. He's a hearty appetite. I don't want it getting cold while he gossips with you. Eggs are not ten centimes these days.'

She ushered me into the dining room where, seated at a dark polished table dressed with silver, was the priest.

I was bidden by the florid-faced man of God to seat

myself opposite him. Did I eat eggs and bacon? Or perhaps not bacon?

'Although good food is good food, these days. One must praise the Lord for all that is available. Béatrice will fetch you a plate and cutlery and then you can tuck in. Everything's on the sideboard in the tureens. No shortages here. Well, very few. My parishioners make sure I'm catered for.' He chortled like a schoolboy. 'Eat, girl, and then we'll see what we can do for you. If the Germans come knocking and ransacking this house again, I'll soon tell them where to go.' Then, with the forkful of egg that had been poised, waiting to be welcomed into his mouth, he swallowed greedily and winked at me in a kindly, not lascivious, manner.

I had never seen him close to before, and rarely in his ordinary clothes. He had purple veins on his nose, iron-grey hair that looked like it needed a good brush, and black-rimmed glasses. The last I remembered of him was Albert's funeral when he had talked for so long.

I wasn't desperately hungry. Well, I was but I was also still queasy from anxiety and poor drinking water and I dreaded what might happen if I ate a greasy meal. What I longed for was a thorough scrub. Soap in my hair and warm suds on my skin. If the *cave* had not been sufficient, being buried under all that bed linen slept in by Germans had almost made me gag.

'Not hungry?'

I shook my head. 'If I could clean my teeth . . .' I hadn't intended the thought to be formed into words. It had come out before I'd realized it.

'Do you have . . . erm, toiletries? Madame Béatrice,' he cried. She was back in the room so fast I thought she must have been eavesdropping on the far side of the door.

'I think this young lady is in need of a bit of a clean-up. Sara, isn't it? Young Alain told me, and I hope I've remembered correctly. I have rather a lot to be thinking about right now. Funeral masses. Four in all. Eulogies to write. Good, decent folk to bury.'

'Sara, yes, thank you.' I was alarmed by these comments. Alain had told me the evening before that there had been bloodshed, but he hadn't mentioned deaths. Protecting me from the worst of it. Whose funerals? Who had the Germans murdered? I prayed not Delphine.

'In this village we practise the true meaning of Christianity, Sara. Suffer the little children . . .'

I gave him a questioning look.

'Not that you are a child, of course not. It's a manner of speaking. From the Bible. All men are equal, Sara. Well, I might make an exception and not include those butchers running over our land right now. You've been separated from your family, I hear?'

'Father,' said Madame Béatrice to Monsieur *le prêtre*.

'Yes, Béatrice?'

'Shall we let the girl have her wash? Then I'll heat up a pot of fresh coffee. Or what passes for a decent cup of coffee these days. At least, I'm not serving the rubbish made out of acorns. Perhaps she'll be more able to answer questions when she's comfortable. You've nothing with you?'

I shook my head. 'Nothing.' My mind spilled back over the previous months, our arrival and how events had led me to this point.

Without further ado, and before the priest could begin his ramblings again, Béatrice led me up a flight of steep wooden stairs to a spacious high-ceilinged bathroom tiled in white. It was sparkling clean, with brass taps and knobs. Béatrice padded off, worn plump hands in apron pockets, returning with two enormous white towels. Life in this house appeared to be more luxurious than at the Hôtel des Alpes, not that I had seen it in any great detail but I had peeped in when queuing to register with the Italians.

'*Merci*.' I nodded.

Hands on hips, Béatrice was watching me. I dithered, feeling shy about getting undressed in front of her and uncertain as to why she was dawdling.

'Our father's dicing with danger – you know that, don't you? He thinks because he's God's man, those Germans out there won't harm a hair on his head, but they've shot many of the frock already and they won't think twice about adding one more to their gruesome list.'

I froze. Was she against this? Would she betray me to the enemy? I trusted Alain's judgement, but he had warned me endlessly throughout the summer to place my confidence in no one.

'I realize my presence could put you at risk too, Béatrice. I cannot than–'

'No need for any of that. Get yourself washed. You're a state. There's a jug and soap over by the basin. Do you have clean clothes?'

I shook my head.

'Well, mine certainly won't fit you. Give me those and I'll wash them in the scullery. They can't be seen going to the laundry, a young girl's underwear at the priest's house. Pretty scandal that'd be.' She shook her head. 'I don't know what he's thinking. We'll all be murdered in our beds.' She turned and waddled to the door, then swung back. 'I'll wait outside for your things. Dirty knickers and all. I'll stick them in a bowl of bleach. Meantime, I'll find you something to wrap yourself in. It won't be pretty but no one's going to see you, not even that young fancy man of yours.'

And with that she was gone, muttering to herself.

As I peeled off the clothes I had been wearing for days, I was still worrying about whose funerals the priest was preparing homilies for.

65

I was allocated a bed in *le grenier*. Access to the presbytery's attic was by a ladder that slid in and out of a well-hidden alcove in the ceiling on the first floor. It was sparsely furnished with a rather lumpy mattress set on an iron bedstead, and an oil lamp that Béatrice cautioned me against using.

I was so tired, I would have slept on the floor.

'You'll be safe up there, lass. I'll leave food for you down here on this landing. You can use the same bathroom and lavatory as you washed in this morning. It means climbing up and down the ladder but there's nothing I can do about that. I've slid a pot 'neath the bed. There's a small window set in the roof that lets in some light but you're not to open it or go too close in case you're seen, or create shadows visible from across the street.'

I was so fuelled by love and indebted to these courageous people that every detail seemed a luxury.

The following evening I had a visitor. Alain climbed up to me rather than me being allowed down. I was feeling a little stir-crazy at the prospect of this further isolation, yet I knew I must be prudent and honour the kindnesses and protection on offer.

'It's good to see you, Sara.'

We were perched side by side on the mattress, a polite distance between us. Shy as strangers, as though our night together in the white house had been a figment of my imagination. 'Any idea how long I will stay here?'

'Until the Germans leave. Most have quit the mountain settlements for the coast. It'll be a matter of days before the rest follow.'

'Is there news?'

His hands were clasped in front of him. I longed to reach over and stroke them with my fingers, remembering his tenderness with me. His head was lowered. He looked battle-scarred, skin pallid, but it might have been the dwindling light.

'Tell me about the children,' I persisted.

'Daniel is with the Duchamps family. He's having trouble settling, but he'll be safe in that household for a few weeks until we can smuggle him out to Switzerland.'

'And Hanna? Has Delphine returned?'

Alain nodded. 'Hanna and Alexandre are with her. The school will be starting its classes again soon so Delphine'll be occupied with that. On the surface all will continue as before. Those who suspect, if any, are turning a blind eye, but who knows?'

I wondered why my companion seemed so downhearted and why he hadn't mentioned our night together. Did he regret it? Did lovers speak of such matters? And my parents.

'Did someone manage to contact my parents?'

He lifted his hands to his face, rubbing his eyes and cheeks as though erasing images from his mind.

I waited, my mouth going dry, dread rising. Alain locked his hands together and squeezed them tight.

'You're frightening me.'

He took a deep breath.

My heart was beating at my ribcage. 'Please tell me. Are my parents safe?'

'Nathalie and several of our comrades accompanied

them to the frontier. It was hard going for your mother, well, for both of them, but they reached the Italian border without any hitches. The descent proved less rigorous than the climb.'

'Oh, thank heavens. You scared me.' I let out a long exhalation. 'Phew, so they made it safely to San Dalmazzo?'

'They did, Sara.'

'Thank God. Was someone able to let them know that I've been delayed? I hope they've found a comfortable place to stay while they wait for me.'

Beyond the attic window, down in the narrow street, I heard a male voice calling to another. A return call. Laughter. Something metallic, like a tin, bounced along cobblestones, echoing round the tight streets. Alain made no reply. I gazed at him. Was he crying? His hand was at his mouth.

'For God's sake. What is it?'

'Your parents . . . didn't stay in San Dalmazzo.'

Disbelief was my first reaction. 'Why not?'

'They . . . they were put on a train, Sara.'

'Put on a train?' I swung my body to face him, tugging at his arm, forcing him to turn to me. 'What do you mean? Put on a train by whom?'

'Keep your voice down. We mustn't be heard in the street.'

Panic shot through me, a trembling, a foreboding. I should have crossed with them, delivered them, us, to safety. 'Has something happened to my mother? Is she ill? Alain, please!'

I had to get a grip. My face was hot and flushed. I lifted both hands to my cheeks. I stood up, sat down. 'Where have they gone?'

Alain shook his head. 'We don't know, Sara.'

'But we agreed they would wait in San Dalmazzo. Have they left word?' I had so foolishly, so carelessly, throughout these summer months, dreamed of cutting my ties, of flying free. Of staying here with Alain, in France, an independent woman. Now I was faced with a reality I had never expected. Whenever I had foreseen danger, in my mind's eye the three of us were facing it together . . .

'My father would never make further plans without me. Something, someone must have changed their minds.' My voice was calmer. Steelier. Lower in resonance. I was recalibrating. 'If my mother was taken sick, Papa would have found a hospital . . . Or was it the Lindemanns? Frau Lindemann, was it she who needed medical care? Did she lose her baby? My father must have decided to take the train with them, to see Ilse safely into Switzerland. They will be waiting for me in Switzerland.' I was trying to calm my breathing.

He rested his hand on one of mine.

'Not Switzerland, Sara. Word has reached us that . . .' His voice tailed off.

'Alain, just say it, whatever it is.'

'When the first of the exiles arrived into San Dalmazzo they were greeted by . . .'

I sat frozen. 'By what?'

'The Wehrmacht.'

'*What?*'

'The Germans got there ahead. Trains, empty wagons were waiting at the station.'

'But how can that be?'

'They were all betrayed. Several hundred, at least, were captured by the Nazis. They've been deported.'

I closed my eyes, picturing the scene: the bedlam, people running, screaming, children, bags jettisoned to offer greater liberation for flight. My poor enfeebled mother . . .

'And my parents were among them?' Tears were slipping down my face. I wanted to roar, run, beat a path to them.

'If the reports are accurate, your parents boarded one of those trains. However, we can't be a hundred per cent certain. It was too late for many of the refugees to retreat, but word was conveyed back along the line and some managed to break free. They fled for their lives into the *maquis*. Those who escaped are hiding in the wild. A few have been given shelter by Italian families, mountain farmers. It's impossible at this stage to identify those who got away and those who were trapped by the Nazis.'

'Those who were deported have been sent where?'

He ran the fingers of both hands through his hair. 'To wherever they have been sending their prisoners. Somewhere north, in eastern Europe, is the information we are receiving, but it's not specific.'

I was reeling, unable to take this in. I tried with all my might to call to my parents. To beg them, telepathically, to send me a message, reassurance, but I felt only a shaft of emptiness so deep it might have plummeted me to the centre of the earth. 'I should have been with them.' Whatever they were facing, the endurance tests that lay ahead for them, I should have faced it with them. Together, as we had from the first days of our flight out of Poland. A family unit. As one. I had let them down.

'I am so sorry, Sara.'

When would I see them again, hold them in my arms, feel their physical presence? How could I make this up to them?

'Are the Germans sending them back to Poland,

perhaps, to hold them in one of those ghettos my father had spoken of somewhere north of Lodz?'

Perhaps they would be greeted by our neighbours, friendly faces from our past. Surely it was just a question of time before they were freed, to be sent back to our apartment, to return to the life we had known when I was a child, before the war had broken out, before Poland was invaded.

Before.

I felt so feeble, limp, swamped by impotence, confusion.

Alain pulled me towards him and wrapped himself around me. I was a rag in his arms. 'I wish I had better news, Sara. But if they had escaped, they could perish in the cold of the mountains. Winter is coming, the snows falling already at the crest levels. Their best chance might be the train. We have to believe that.'

Their best chance would have been to reach Palestine or America – some of the displaced had spoken of *Eretz Yisrael* – with or without me. But I didn't voice that. Palestine had been my father's dream and I would hold it tight to me now. That dream belonged to him, to us, and I would keep it alive for them. I would keep on breathing it, nourishing it, so it did not disintegrate and die.

Until we were reunited.

'I need to sleep,' I whispered.

'Of course.' With that Alain lifted himself from the bed, laid his hand on my head, stroked my hair and descended the ladder, closing the trap after him.

And I was alone.

Alone.

I remained in obscurity, an invisible presence somewhere in France beneath the eaves in a kindly stranger's house, spinning out a solitary future. No family, nothing to call my own. Directionless, purposeless. Except for one thing: I had my father's treasured dream to hold on to.

The gift of freedom, Sarina. We are being offered an opportunity, we cannot refuse it, Sarina.

To keep that dream alive was my duty. Somehow it would embolden me, fuel me with courage, illuminate a path forward so that I would find a way of liberating them.

66

For several weeks I stayed as a clandestine guest at Father Scaramoni's. Delphine came to visit me when she could. With three children to feed and care for, she was never short of something to do.

'I wish I could help you.'

'Alain has gone,' she told me. 'He was called back to fight with his comrades. He said to tell you *au revoir*, be strong.'

The positive news was that most of the German troops had moved on from the town. A handful remained, but they, too, appeared to be preparing for their departure. There was little to interest them here. The four funeral masses the priest had spoken about had been for Jews: four who had chosen not to flee, too old or sick to cross the mountains. All had been discovered by the Nazis, dragged out from their temporary accommodation, lined up against the trunks of the great plane trees in the central square and shot dead. The priest, with a few of his congregation, had organized the burials and found shaded spots for each of them in the village cemetery.

'And you?' I asked Delphine. 'Have you received news from Philippe?'

She bowed her head. 'The worst, Sara. Our original fears were confirmed. He faced the firing squad. Colleagues are trying to locate his body so that Father Scaramoni can give him a burial too.'

I rested my hand on hers, covering the gold of her

wedding ring. Her fingers twitched. 'Is there anything I can do?'

She shook her head. 'Thank you for offering.'

The other disappointment was that Daniel had not settled with the Duchamps family.

'I've had to bring him to me. He's missing his mother. He's with his sister, but it's a dangerous situation. Hanna is safe as long as I can pass her off as my daughter, but the extra boy . . . There was no reason to suppose that the Nazis would trouble the Duchamps family, but my name, our address, will be on the Wehrmacht list of traitors. Every day I expect a raid. We are urgently looking for another solution. So far we have no message from the Lindemanns. A sixth sense tells me they may not have made it to Switzerland.'

'I wish I could find out for you. I wish I could do something, anything – find my parents.'

'Patience, Sara. There will be news at some point.'

Did she believe the words she spoke? We were all so worn down, beaten back, ravaged by war.

'I feel useless here, Delphine. And how long can I rely on the hospitality of the *curé*? He's putting himself in danger and . . .'

'I agree. We need to get you away. But to where?'

'Listen, Delphine, I'm strong and I'm capable. I could be helping. I could be fighting for the cause. I want to join the struggle. There must be something I can feasibly be engaged in? I could pass for French with the right papers – you told me so yourself. Ask Nathalie or Alain or someone higher up the ladder to fix me up with a job, underground work of some sort. I can't stay cooped up here, living off others' generosity, obsessing about my parents and doing nothing. I'll go insane.'

Delphine stared at me, at a loss.

'I know the terrain. I speak French and I can fire a rifle,' I insisted.

She nodded. 'We'll put out the word.'

It was Nathalie who came to see me, late the following afternoon. It was she who laid out the proposal. I listened open-mouthed. This was a far greater assignment than I had volunteered for. Monumental.

'If you agree, Sara, you must be ready for a difficult journey. Daniel will be in your hands.'

If I was willing to take on the task, but . . .

'Now is the most propitious time to set off. Before the mountain passes are sealed off by the snows. What do you think?'

I was floundering. I wasn't up to this.

'Do you want to think about it?'

I considered Nathalie's proposition one more time.

'We haven't long.'

Who said I wasn't up to it? Me, my own fears. I could be capable of such responsibility. I wanted to believe I was. 'Talk me through it.'

Detail by detail she gave me the broad itinerary. And a small language booklet to study. 'This'll help you. What do you say, Sara? Now you know what it involves, what we're asking of you, are you prepared to take the risk?'

'Who will drive me?' A rather insignificant question under the circumstances, but there were so many uncertainties for such a huge undertaking that I didn't know where to begin. This one seemed the simplest.

'One of our *résistants*. I cannot say now. The fact is we never know for sure until the day or night.'

I could hardly take it in. 'And you're convinced this is

the best solution for Daniel? To be so far from everyone he is familiar with?'

'If you're willing to undertake this, Sara, it's his best chance.'

I rolled the plan through in my head, ranging it back and forth. There was so much at stake. Daniel's life. Mine. And afterwards? I would be alienating myself from everybody I knew. And loved. Bearing a responsibility for others beyond any I might have conceived of.

I heard my father's voice, encouraging me: *You have no right to refuse.*

'What do you say, Sara?'

'Yes,' I whispered. 'I will do the best I can.'

'You're clear that if you're held up, stopped, there'll be no back-up. It will almost certainly cost you your life . . .'

'Aren't you, every one of you, risking your lives?'

67

Two days later, towards the end of the morning, Delphine arrived with Daniel in Alexandre's pushchair. Béatrice saw them into the living room and I was brought downstairs to meet them. The good housekeeper locked and bolted all the doors. The priest had taken himself off on his daily rounds to visit the sick and needy members of the community. He was party to the arrangement, had given us his blessing, but thought it more prudent to be out of our company.

'If anyone comes knocking, beating at the doors, hurry yourself and Daniel back up to the attic. Delphine and I will keep them occupied. Over my dead body will they come snooping around this house again. Once was quite enough.'

I had grown fond of Béatrice. She was a fierce, compassionate soul. She waited in her kitchen, not privy to our arrangements, which were highly confidential, but with an ear to the outside world for any intrusion.

Our concerns were unnecessary. Our meeting together, Delphine's and mine, was brief, business-like. It was concluded within fifteen minutes. I took little Daniel on my lap. He recognized me and seemed comfortable to be back in my company, which was a bonus given what lay ahead for the pair of us.

'Be warned, though.' Delphine spoke in a firm tone. 'He gets himself into violent screaming fits. He's good-humoured and then the very next moment he's bawling his head off. He's traumatized, missing his mother, the poor mite. I'm sorry to see him go, but the sooner he is out of harm's way, the better for him. I haven't broken it to Hanna yet. I feel their anguish, what with my own little Lissie so far from me. I have been praying there would be news from the Lindemanns, but this war is tearing families apart.'

I was considering my own separation and the hole it had left in my heart. I lifted Daniel tight to my chest, ingesting the warmth of him, his little-boy smell. Sweeter than our last encounter. 'You're getting to be a hefty fellow.'

'Tomorrow, well before dusk – an hour or so before the end of the farming day – someone will be here for you, Sara. We've requested Alain or Nathalie, if possible. It will be better if it's someone you've met before, but that may not be possible. They'll have papers for you, a temporary French identity in case you're pulled over. Young wife and mother, that's your role. I must warn you, though, Sara, these will not be the best forged papers. We have lost all our most talented men. This set was the most authentic that could be printed, given the time and resources available. It won't fool anyone other than the careless or inexperienced. Let's pray you're not stopped.' She rose to her feet, seeming to fuss with her clothes, and I saw how emaciated she had become. She took a step towards me. 'Béatrice will help you with whatever you need before you leave. God help and bless you, Sara. Speed you on your way. I have enjoyed . . .' Tears flooded her eyes. 'Best say nothing.' She sniffed. 'I pray you will be sheltered and protected and will make it through. When this war is over, in the hope that we all survive it, come back to see us.'

'Thank you for everything, Delphine. One last favour, if I may.'

'What is it?'

I handed my friend, my dear mentor, an envelope addressed to my parents. 'If you find yourself anywhere near the white house, please will you slip this under the door of our upstairs flat? On the off-chance they somehow, miraculously, return while I'm away. I don't want them to worry about me.'

Delphine stared despairingly at the envelope in her hands. Was she musing on just how fruitless was my optimism, how unlikely my parents' return? Whatever, I couldn't simply leave without offering some word to them. I had to try. At some point it would reach them, wouldn't it?

Chère Maman et cher Papa,
Droga Mamusiu i Tatusiu,
Dearest Mamma and Papa,

If you are reading this, you have come safely back to the village. If it is without risk for you, please wait for me here. I will be back as soon as I am able. If you can't, please send word via Delphine, the school teacher, so that I can find you later. I love you both so much and miss you with all my heart.

Forgive me for my clumsy errors, your Sarina xx

68

Daniel and I spent the next thirty-six hours alone in the attic. I was studying Nathalie's language book, trying not to focus on what lay head. I sang to the little boy, whispered stories to him and dreamed of Alain. As was her habit, Béatrice left a plate of warm food – dollops of goat stew with a few steamed potatoes that evening, two demi-baguettes with home-made jam the following morning – on the landing beneath the steps. I climbed down to collect the meals. I was so nervous, shaking clumsily, I could barely stomach anything and concentrated my attention on feeding Daniel, who was less unsettled than I had expected.

At twenty to four the following afternoon, Béatrice came to give us the signal.

'Got everything?'

She had packed me a bag with water, a round loaf she'd baked herself and a small portion of cheese. 'There's no more butter,' she apologized, 'but before you go, give the lad here some of this goat's milk. I've warmed it specially for him. It'll calm him, make his journey less distressing.'

For the first time in months my prayers were answered. It was Alain who was waiting at the door to collect us. He did not meet my eye. His manner was bordering on uncivil and it flustered me. As we were about to step outside, Father Scaramoni in his long black cassock came shuffling down the corridor to bless us, trickling holy water over our heads and making the sign of the cross. 'I will pray for your safe deliverance, Sara. Let the angels be your wings. You're a courageous young woman. May God be with you on this tricky expedition and may you arrive at your destination intact. Let us pray for peace.'

'I cannot thank you enough, *curé*, for your kindness and hospitality,' I mumbled, before we were bustled to the waiting truck. My heart was mangled by yet more severances. I had grown fond of these hosts.

Deep breath, brace myself.

Alain gave a glance in each direction as we left through the same wooden door I had been brought in by some weeks earlier. I had lost track of time. There was a chill in the air I had not known since the days of our arrival so many months ago, a lifetime earlier. At either end of the narrow lane were small clusters of people, in conversation, leaning against walls, smoking cigarettes. One couple locked in an embrace. Had I not been aware of their purpose, I would not have noticed the almost imperceptible head movements, nods giving Alain the all-clear.

He assisted me as I climbed up into the rear of the truck with Daniel in my arms. Then he scooted to the passenger door and settled himself in the front seat alongside the driver – 'This is Dominique, *mon frère*.' I couldn't see his comrade's face – he didn't turn round and he was wearing a navy beret that hung low over his forehead – and I knew Alain had no brother. Dominique smoked incessantly, nervously, throughout the voyage.

Aside from the fug of Caporal tobacco, the rear reeked of gas from two roof-top cylinders strapped to the bumpers of the vehicle – an alternative fuel when petrol was unavailable – and of olive oil.

We were masquerading as a family of very young olive farmers returning from the mill after pressing their fruits.

It seemed such a peaceful and idyllic pretension. I so wished . . .

Alongside where I was squatting, the space was crammed with sploshing glass jars – *les bocals en verre*. They contained newly pressed green oil along with cuttings and slender branches from olive trees.

'Kindling and wood for our fires. Pruned as we harvested, should anyone ask,' explained Alain.

I nodded, noticing behind the driver's seat, buried beneath the pruned foliage, two hunting rifles. There were knives too and serrated-edged saws, curled, like small scythes, for the tree-trimming.

'The drive will take us close to three hours. Evening will fall soon and we will keep to the less-travelled byways. The going will be slow. If we are stopped, stay hidden, let us do the talking. Remember, this is my brother and you are my wife and son. I am Bertrand. Your name is Élise. If the worst comes to the worst . . .' He gestured with his head towards the firearms.

I indicated that I had understood, too terrified to utter a syllable, while seriously doubting my ability to see this mission through.

I can't say it was a comfortable journey.

'Hold on tight in the back. There's a hell of a wind whipping up, a mistral coming in. I hope we can get you out ahead of it.'

The truck swung, bumped and clunked over the more rugged winding mountain passes known as *les cols*, and left my stomach roiling and nauseous. I could see nothing of the passage of scenery, due to the lack of rear windows and night falling, and this exacerbated my uncertainties. Daniel, head drooping into the crook of my arm, slept or snuffled into my chest. He seemed uncharacteristically tranquil.

When the two men in the cab spoke, they did so in hushed tones. I could not catch anything of their conversations – they might have been speaking in Provençal – and I soon gave up trying. Alain addressed me once or twice to know if all was well, did we need to stop for the child to pee, but aside from that no exchanges passed between us. At one point, when I was almost dozing, trying to fend off the rising sickness, we slowed.

'Get down to the floor, pretend to sleep,' he ordered me sharply. 'Checkpoint.'

'Damn. *Merde*. They're pulling us over.'

My heart was hammering so fast I thought it would arrest my breathing. 'Dominique' eased us to a halt and wound down the glass.

'*Bonsoir.*'

'*Guten Abend.*'

A German voice requested the men's papers. Reason for their journey, out so late. 'Olive-harvesting,' explained Dominique, furnishing the details of a valley from which we had allegedly travelled and the name of the mill where the fruits had been pressed. I had my hand carefully covering Daniel's mouth. The other within fingertip reach of the guns. The child burped and began to fidget, then the first grunts of a whimper. Instantly, Dominique revved the engine.

'Is someone in the back?'

My eyes squeezed closed, I pressed myself tight against the child. *Please, please, don't let them arrest us.*

'My wife and son,' said Alain. His voice was gentle and steady. Barely a trace of nerves.

'Open it up.'

'They're sleeping, sir. It's been a long working day. He's just a babe.'

'Open up.'

Footsteps. Alain's door unlocked. His boots thudding on stones. I was desperate to open my eyes, desperate for Daniel not to wake and start screaming. I felt the rush of chilled night air when the back doors were flung open.

The men must have been watching us. 'She's expecting our second,' Alain quietly informed the German. 'We're hoping for a little girl.'

'Good olive oil?'

'The best. Would you like a litre?'

'I'll take a canister.'

A hand reached in. A *bidon* was dragged out.

And before I knew it, the doors had been slammed shut, the papers were handed back in through the open window and we were on our way.

Everyone exhaled silently.

'Jesus Christ. That was close.'

'The bugger nabbed ten litres!'

I was still silently smiling at Alain's fictitious story to the soldier.

We rattled onwards.

'That should be the last checkpoint. No others are marked, as far as we have been warned, between here and the strip.'

The headlamps were the only source of light in the night, shedding a faint beam into the direction ahead but I had my back to the road and the men. Beyond, there could be anything, anyone waiting to pounce.

'Élise, another forty minutes at the outside. The wind seems calmer here. Try to grab some proper sleep. You have a long night ahead of you.'

The final kilometres of the journey were the toughest, crawling forwards. Stop, start, as though we had been travelling for days. Never moving above first gear, without lights, by moonshine only. It was gruelling. When the terrain was intricate, treacherous, obstacle-strewn, Alain jumped out and walked a few paces ahead of the truck, using the occasional flash of his torch to illuminate the perilously narrow track. The dizzying depths to which we would plummet if we skidded over the cliff. Our bodies broken in a ravine.

69

Eventually, finally, we drew to a halt at the edge of a clearing, lights and engine switched off. Blackness. I longed to climb out and stretch my legs. To breathe the fresh air of which I had been deprived for weeks now. Or had it been months? I had no concept of time.

'Stay put until I tell you otherwise,' ordered Alain. I tried not to take his military manner personally. It was not unkind. He was probably equally terrified, and I was as aware as any of us what was at stake and the performances required of us. Even so, a smile, an intimation of our former intimacy would have fuelled me for what I still had to face.

'I need to pee,' I whispered.

'Wait a minute.'

He shouldered open his stubborn old door and jumped to the ground. I felt a rush of night air invade the van. It smelt ambrosial, of herbs and *garrigue* plants. I pictured the illustrations in the books Delphine had loaned me earlier in the summer.

The two back doors were dragged open and Alain's silhouette was lit from overhead by the moon's beam. 'Come on, down you get.'

I shuffled on my bottom past the containers, Daniel still cradled in my arms. He began to grow restless and screamed into the silent night.

'Can't you quieten him?' Dominique, from the front.

I held the little boy tight in my arms and rocked him

vigorously to and fro, humming under my breath. He was heavy. No longer a baby. I had been crouching and lying too long without movement. My legs had gone numb. 'I need to stretch, walk a little. And pee.'

'Wait. *Dom, peut-tu tenir l'enfant, s'il te plaît? Cinq minutes.*'

Dominique leaped from the truck. We caught sight of one another's faces, shadowed features, then turned swiftly away as though that brief glimpse had been an act too intimate. What struck me was his age. Younger, for sure, than Alain, who was nineteen. Seventeen? My age. I stepped towards him and presented him with Daniel. He accepted the child and held him securely, without awkwardness.

He has younger siblings – that thought crossed my mind.

Alain was behind me. 'This way,' he commanded. He walked with the lightest touch of his hand on my elbow and I felt so inordinately pleased I thought I might swoon. Another person had arrived, a man also wearing a beret. I didn't notice from which direction he had appeared. In any case, he ignored us. He was setting up flares to guide the plane in. I felt my stomach lurch at the clear-cut realization, the immutability of the circumstances. This was the reality. No turning back. I was leaving. Leaving France. Separated from my parents. From all I loved.

Embarking on a life-or-death mission, into virgin territory.

And I was terrified.

We were in a rectangular glade, with bushes and low trees, prehistoric rocks and massive boulders all about us. Man-made, I guessed.

'It's a good clear night. Little wind. If all goes according to plan, we have about twenty minutes. Stretch your legs, make yourself ready. We'll wait by the van.'

I could see now our vehicle had been parked in a scruffy deforested patch, which abutted a coarsely dug-out airstrip, which was semi-masked by the height of the surrounding trees. Tree trunks lay here and there where they had been felled, or rolled and stacked some distance from the landing path.

I eased myself in among a dense clump of broom, remembering its summer sweetness, and gazed Heavenwards to a sky that was early-winter sharp and cold. It was empty of activity, save for the glint of stars and a glowing three-quarter moon. I dropped to my haunches, urinated, then stayed put, well out of sight. Never had I felt so petrified.

This was it.

The end of everything that had composed my life up until this night. Wherever my parents were now, I was distancing myself further from them. The loss made me giddy, hollowed out by anguish.

Foreign territory lay ahead for me. Alain was 'Bertrand' now. We had played out our real story, brief as it had been. Snatched glorious moments together over one golden summer. Alain and Sara. I would always have that. Our precious summer culminating in one enchanted, incarcerated night in each other's arms at Lucy's.

It was time to say goodbye. Or *au revoir*? Winter was drawing in, the snows were falling, and I had been allocated my role. I had requested it. I had nothing to complain about.

Flares illuminated the strip. In the distance, the sound of a propeller rotating.

'Élise!'

I hoofed it back to the boys' sides. Daniel was once again thrust into my arms. Alain was furnishing me with my papers. 'Hand these to the crew member and he will give you your instructions along with a new set of papers. He has everything you'll need for your onward journey.'

I nodded, swallowing hard against the growing lump in my throat.

'Good luck.' Alain patted my upper arm, left his hand there for a second, squeezed, and for one resplendent moment our eyes met.

'No regrets?'

I smiled at him, shook my head. 'None.'

'For the Lord's sake, be safe, my dear sweet Sara,' he added softly. 'I will be thinking of you.'

I was beyond grateful for those nuggets of tenderness. I would feed off them, pick them to the bone, for many months to come.

70

We were being battered by the uplift of wind as the small plane came in to land. Stones were swept upwards and clattered back to earth like dancing clogs, while the vegetation all about us swayed, as though from the force of an underwater current. The spin of the three-blade propeller slowed until it was motionless.

My two companions, with a man who descended from the plane, bent low, hastened to the truck and climbed inside. No one threw a look in my direction.

This was it.

I followed instructions and sprinted to the plane. A man with a narrow moustache and leather flying jacket beckoned me onto lightweight steps welded to the side of the fuselage, holding out his hand to ease Daniel and me aboard. I glanced back. The truck had gone. Disappeared into the night. No sign of it on the mountain track. Alain, his companion and their passenger had the journey home to power through. If they were not pulled over, were not obliged to abandon the van and camp out for the night, they would, with luck, be back in the village, or wherever they were headed, soon after dawn. The likelihood was that I would also reach my destination by dawn or thereabouts, possibly before they had made it safely back to base.

I would never know. Never know whether they were safe. Whether Alain was dead or alive.

From here on, all contact was severed. I was out on a

limb, on my own, and that severance felt like an organ amputation. Heart, muscles, the blood pumping through my veins, all anaesthetized.

We were taxiing, turning at an angle and, after a juddering lift-off, climbing skywards into cloud. Nothing but darkness outside the plane, which was rather more compact than I had pictured. I was hunkered on the floor in the fuselage clutching Daniel, stroking his head. My first time in the air. The noise was thunderous, metal rattling and roaring as though we were engulfed in flames or the entire apparatus had exploded. It reminded me of the snowmelt running fast through the village on that first day of our arrival by bus in March. Not even a year ago.

I took a gander about me. A pilot, a navigator and one other, he who had hoisted me aboard, were in the cockpit. All in uniform.

I momentarily closed my eyes, yielding to the deafening noise, imploring the razor-sharp pain at the loss of Alain to drain out of me.

'Do you speak any English?'

The third man was looming over me with a large brown envelope tucked under his arm. He was stooping, due to the lack of height in the cabin.

I shrugged. 'A leetle bit. Zank you.' I attempted a smile.

He acknowledged my gesture and dropped to his haunches at my side. 'These are your papers.' He spoke loudly, over-enunciating, as if that would give me an easier insight into his meaning. He handed me the envelope. I had understood the basics, but in any case I had been well briefed about what to expect.

'We'll be destroying this.' He was waving my false identity card between his fingers. 'This young lady,' he glanced at the card, 'Élise Fromme, she no longer exists. Understand, *comprenez-vous*?'

'Yes, I understand. Zank you.'

'Good girl. Try to get some shut-eye. We'll be on the ground at the airbase in two and a half, maximum three hours, if the Jerries don't crack us one.' He rose to his feet and returned to his two RAF colleagues upfront in the cockpit.

71

Someone was shaking me awake. I opened my eyes. My head was planted against Daniel's soft, mildly damp body. It was surprising, remarkable, that he was not bellowing, that he was sleeping peacefully. I suspected that his serenity had been orchestrated by Béatrice. Had she slipped something, a tranquillizing herb perhaps, into the last cup of warm milk she had insisted on feeding him?

'We're coming into land, miss.' The man with the moustache was making gestures with his hands to show that the aircraft was dipping. I nodded, light-headed from fatigue.

He winked. 'You're a beauty,' he said. 'Biggin Hill airfield. One and a half hours from the centre of London. There will be a car waiting for you.'

My eyes roamed over his features. 'Beegen Heel, yes, I know of it, zank you.'

'It's all in the instructions. Once you've read them, destroy everything except the identity card, got it? Come on, get yourself ready. He's a good lad, your son. Young to be a mother, aren't you? Set for the off?' He was now encouraging me to sit up. Daniel had been disturbed, woken. His face contorted into a scream and, lungs full of oxygen, he began to bawl loudly enough to rouse the world.

'Christ, that'd keep the soundest of sleepers awake at night. You'd hear him in Gerryland. Good luck, pretty lady.'

I smiled at my charge, even though I was dizzy with exhaustion. His grey-blue eyes were now chuckling. He had stopped yelling and was gurgling, proud of his accomplishment, announcing to the world that we two young Jews were out of the clutches of the Gestapo. I sighed, recalling my parents. Where were they? Was my mother restless, plagued with insomnia every night, ill with worry about me? Begging my father to find me, to make contact, impossible though the task was? This separation was unspeakable. It insinuated itself into every cavity of my being, like grief or a cumulative mourning.

The plane was taxiing. I was standing, clinging bumpily to a leather strap rigged up to the inner husk of the cabin. Daniel was perched against my right shoulder, yelling into the side of my face, shredding my eardrum. He needed changing, washing, feeding. I hoped I'd find an opportunity to achieve all that before we reached London, before I said goodbye to him. *Au revoir*, Daniel, my last contact with my mountain life in France.

And then? And then . . .

PART TWO

PART TWO

I

London, England
Early November 1943

It was gone daybreak when we hit the outskirts of the capital, the suburbs, bombed buildings lying as sad grey rubble alongside what had once been a street. The expanse and complexity of this venerable city took me by surprise. The bustle and energy too. A bit of a shock after the rhythms of our rural life. I was trying hard to stay awake and take it all in, to make the most of what, under different circumstances, would have been an exciting adventure. We were surrounded by dozens of people on bicycles. They reminded me of life in the mountains, those bicycles. Here the riders were weaving their way in and around the tails and noses of cars. There seemed to be petrol here. No gas cylinders atop the black vehicles. We passed a low-lying railway station with a large clock on its exterior wall with black Roman numerals. It read ten to seven.

'We'll be a bit delayed now, miss, because we're hitting the morning rush hour. It usually gets going at about this time,' the uniformed military chauffeur called over his shoulder to me in a jumble of French and English. I would have to work hard on my English. It took me back to my early days in France, searching out key words, grappling to understand the sentences of others. France. I prayed that Alain and his *maquisard* companions had made it safely back to the village or to wherever they were destined.

Alain, my heart felt sliced. An Arctic wind held it in its grip.

I opened the envelope that had been given to me on the plane, pulling out my identity card. Perused and memorized the name written in ink there.

Cécile Lombard, born to Marc Lombard and Hélène Lombard (née Lebois).

Place of birth: Nice. Date of birth: 17 May 1925. Home address: 71 avenue des Arènes de Cimiez, Nice, Alpes-Maritimes, France. The bare bones of the reincarnated me.

On paper, I was eighteen and a half years old. One year older almost to the day than my real age. My real date of birth: 9 May 1926, born in Lodz, Poland.

So, this was me. Cécile Lombard. French, a Niçoise girl, not a soul alone, adrift in a collapsed world I glanced down at Daniel, who snored softly, seemingly content, on my lap. My fingers stroked his hair. I wished him a good life in safe hands, until Ilse was traced. Until he, Hanna and his parents were reunited. Broken families, one and all.

We were turning left into a leafy square.

'Almost at our location now, miss. I'll be leaving you at this address. Another driver will be collecting you and taking you to your next port of call. Anything else you require? *Avez-vous besoin d'autre chose?*'

I lifted my head and smiled at the man, whose eyes I met in the rear-view mirror. 'Nothing else. You are very kind. Zank you.'

I was peering out through the window at a row of Victorian four-storey houses. We were drawing slowly to a halt alongside them. They were impressive.

'Number eleven, that's correct? And . . . here we are, safe and sound.'

The corporal eased the car to the kerbside, and while I

was gathering the envelope to my chest and Daniel into my arms, he slipped from his leather seat and was releasing the rear door for me. I stepped out onto the pavement. A fresh early-morning breeze was stirring, shivering the remaining dried and curled leaves on tall, well-established trees. The air smelt of smog. The curtains were drawn, shutters closed over most of the windows. There was an other-worldly stillness about the street. London, grey. Grey light, louring sky.

A clinking sound drew my attention. Stooped low, a few houses further along, I saw a man in a white coat, white cap, with a satchel hanging loose from his left shoulder. He was placing milk bottles on a step.

'Good luck, miss.' The corporal took a step forward and shook my hand, which surprised me.

'*Merci beaucoup*,' I nodded as he climbed back into the car.

'I'll wait here until the door's opened for you and then I'll be off,' he called out of the window.

I glanced up at number eleven. Two brass digits. A black door polished to a gleam, with a shiny round brass knocker. From the open gate, a short path led to three steps that ascended to the door.

'Off we go,' I whispered to the exhausted and rather soiled being in my arms, who had been as good as gold. 'Let's hope she's not too fussy as foster mothers go, eh? And let's hope she's got lashings of hot water.'

I rapped hard on the door and swung my attention back to the street. A dray horse was drawing a cart stacked high with milk bottles. Currently stationary, the beast was grazing the grass sprouting up through the cracks between the paving stones. A portly man on a bicycle pedalled by, wearing a herring-bone coat and bowler hat. Setting off for the office?

'Cécile! You made it. What a relief.'

I spun back to the open door, about to say hello. Instead, mouth open, I gawped. Literally, gawped. There, standing two steps within, slender, wavy-haired was . . . It could not be. A woman dressed in a pale turquoise satin housecoat – I stared at her in disbelief. 'But . . . ?' I was having trouble taking this in. Why had Delphine, Alain, someone not alerted me? Confidentiality regulations, yes, but even so.

She was tall. Taller than in my mental pictures . . . prepossessing. I was so caught off guard at the reality of her, of *us* standing here together like this, that for a split second, even longer, words failed me.

'I had no idea,' I murmured.

I am not Sara, I repeated to myself silently.

'You're Cécile, yes? And this gorgeous fellow is baby Daniel. You must be dead beat. Yes, you are, of course you are. Look at you. Come on in. I'll make some tea. Do you want to give him to me? Or perhaps not yet. We have plenty of time to get acquainted.'

I took one step inside and hovered. Stupefied, delighted.

She was so elegant, every bit as elegant as the photographs had promised. She halted as she made her way along the black-and-white-tiled hallway, waiting for me, eyes dancing but puzzled by my conduct.

'Is something wrong? Please come in – don't be shy.' She held her arms outstretched. 'You look whacked. They filled me in on some of the details of the journey you'd be facing to bring Daniel to me. Quite terrifying. You're very brave. I'm Lucy, by the way, Lucy Allingham.' She was beckoning me with her fingers.

2

I penetrated the hallway and breathed in the scent of wax polish and another, a familiar, comforting scent. Joy de Jean Patou. Lucy's perfume. I caught the soft sound of a machine humming somewhere in the house, a warm enveloping house where I knew, if I lived there, I would be exquisitely happy. My mind flashed back to Lucy's mountain abode, her bedroom, to her splendid wardrobe of clothes, to Freddie the fox, which I had abandoned on her bed. I couldn't believe whose home I had arrived at. The home of the woman whose hospitality, albeit unknown to her, had given me a safe house, whose bed had furnished me with my one precious night of love with Alain.

Why had no one forewarned me of the identity of the foster mother? I knew it was vital to provide only the most essential information but I wondered who had set this up. No one, besides Alain, of course, knew of my acquaintance with Lucy. Or, rather, the spirit of Lucy and her mountain home. I was so tired, so stunned, my head began to spin and for a moment I almost lost my balance. Gripping hard, I was squeezing Daniel into me, almost suffocating the poor toddler. His eyes popped open and he started to whimper in response to my squeeze, then let out a mighty howl. I lifted one hand to calm him. Lucy, fearing I would drop him, rushed back to me.

'Give me Daniel. Come with me. Cécile, lean on me. Do you speak English or shall we continue in French? Elsa! Elsa!'

The humming sound abruptly stopped. Further along the corridor a door was thrown open, and an older woman hurried from behind it.

'Show this young lady to the breakfast room, Elsa, please. Let's get the kettle on. And this bonny chap is soaked and very smelly, poor soul.' Lucy held Daniel aloft and I saw that her elegant housecoat was stained. A dark, damp patch the size of Daniel's padded backside. 'I think we need to run the little fellow a bath. I think these dear young people have been through the wars, quite literally.'

Elsa had relieved Lucy of Daniel and now Lucy was occupied with me. I was guided, as if I was made of egg shells, along the corridor towards the back of what seemed to be a long, deep house into a light, high-ceilinged room with a country pine table, oval in shape, and six matching chairs. There was a small porcelain jug of flowers, four cream roses, standing at its centre. I recalled the wild rose bushes in Lucy's garden, a key still hidden within the roots of one.

'Sit yourself down.'

I was led to a chair where I slumped, knees buckling, before I could fall. Lucy took the seat alongside me. She was gazing at me intently with those eyes. Aquamarine eyes.

'Cécile, yes?'

It took me a moment and then I nodded.

'*Parlez-vous anglais?*'

'Just a leetle.'

She lowered her gaze and smiled. 'It's not a problem. Not at all. *Je parle français.*'

Lucy spoke French fluently with a thick British accent, plummy and musical, which warmed me to her all the more, if that were possible.

'I'm sure we have lots to discuss. First, though, I'm going to make a pot of tea and a plate of hot buttered toast. And I have strawberry jam, homemade, and marmalade. Do you like marmalade?'

I shrugged. I didn't know 'marmalade'.

'You mustn't worry about Daniel. He's in safe hands. I promise to take the very best care of him. Your assignment has been successfully accomplished. I think perhaps you would be glad of a clean-up too. Come with me.'

Lucy led me by the hand, out into the corridor and up a flight of stairs carpeted in cream-white, with brass stair rods, to a bathroom the size of a small studio. Towels were piled high on a small lime-green dresser. Close by, scented soap, large bottles of eau de cologne, and taps. Warm water.

'Fresh clothes?' She gave me a once-over. 'You're about my size, I'd say. Take what you need here for your bath, use whatever you fancy. I'll be back.'

And I was left alone, in the home of Lucy Allingham. This Allingham residence was as handsome as her white house in France, if more formal. I slipped off my worn-to-nothing shoes, leaving traces of dust and dirt on the tiles, tugged off my socks and looked about me. The blinds were drawn. A light was on above the washbasin. The bath was white porcelain and ample. Above the basin was a cupboard with mirrored doors. I opened one. Lucy's toiletries. Skin creams. I felt calm and at home, as though I had been visiting here for a very long time. I ran the bath; water flowed liberally, a thunderous sound in this high-ceilinged space. Like the mountain snowmelts. Within seconds the mirrored cupboard was steamed over. I ran a finger across the glass, dividing it in two. The thick line of the steam evaporated into tiny droplets. It was as though a crack had severed the glass.

For a moment, I was delivered back to the drawing room in the white house after those anonymous Nazi soldiers had desecrated it, smashed the glass in the framed photographs. I would have liked to forewarn Lucy about their invasion, the damage they had caused. All that she would find when she returned there. Would I tell her? Of course not. How could I? I was not Sara, I was Cécile, and Cécile had never set foot in that medieval mountain village, had never hidden there from the Wehrmacht. None of those weeks, months, of this past summer had ever taken place.

A parenthesis that had never existed. Falling in love? Alain was Bertrand now. To be wiped from my memory bank.

3

A light tapping brought me back to the present, and this equally illusory reality.

'I've left a bundle of clothes outside the door. Choose whatever takes your fancy. A couple of pairs of good winter walking shoes as well. They might be your size.' I knew they weren't. 'I'll see you downstairs in the kitchen when you're ready. Take your time. Daniel is sleeping. He's snug and peaceful. What a handsome little lad. Don't worry about him. See you for tea and toast when you're ready. I have a smattering of butter too. All for you.' And off she trilled. I could hear the soft patter of her slippered feet on the deep-piled carpet descending to the breakfast room. She was humming to herself. Lighthearted. Carefree. Elated.

I had delivered Daniel to Lucy, offered her temporary happiness, a respite from her grief.

After my bath, I stood before the long mirror and stared at my naked self. My muscles were toned. My breasts had plumped out, nipples firm. I was no longer the adolescent who had landed in France by boat, the traumatized daughter of a fleeing fugitive family, or the teenager who had lived jubilant months in the mountains. Gone was that innocent girl, and in her place stood a young woman with an uncharted future.

I had a role to play.

I prayed I was up to the task.

The shoes didn't fit, both pairs two sizes too small, but

the clothes were stylish, well-cut and fabulous, and in my perfect life I would have liked to prance about in all of them. For today, I chose a sleek wool dress in a dark green hue, a Schiaparelli. The style was possibly a little adult for me – fitting of my new persona? I chose it because its colour brought back the forests of tall larch and cedar trees in our mountain hideaway, where my heart, my love remained. To accompany it, I picked a cable-stitched woollen cardigan in deep russet with equally deep pockets. Winter tones. Warm and reassuring. The rest of the wardrobe I regretfully left where I'd found it on the floor in the hall.

'Shoes not the right size?'

Lucy had changed into another housecoat – this one ankle-length, ice blue.

I shook my head. My feet were bare. 'Too small, but *merci*. You are very generous.'

'Perhaps Elsa has a pair that would do you for now. Yours are rather the worse for wear, I'm afraid. Or we can send out for some. You need some woollen stockings too. Nylons are too fragile, not warm enough in this ghastly climate. In any case, almost impossible to come by unless you're consorting with the high and mighty.' She winked. I recalled Sylvie and her gossip about earning coupons from the Italian soldiers. What had become of Sylvie? Had she skipped off with her Italian friend?

Lucy and I ate heartily, or I did. We drank from cups with gold-flaked handles and porcelain saucers with silver spoons. I tried hard not to recall the days in her cellar. The grim times. The reek of ammonia, and desperation.

I pushed aside the momentary rush of elation at the memory of Alain and I enlaced on Lucy's bed. That one precious night, the tenderness, passion we had shared.

It's your first time? he had whispered, and I'd confirmed

it, brushing the crook of his neck. I had felt so complete in his arms.

No regrets, Sara?

None.

At first, Lucy and I ate in silence. How I yearned to unburden myself of the true facts, to bubble out to her my news, but I had given my word to Nathalie, to Alain and his comrades hiding in the hills and to everyone fighting to liberate France. They had offered me this opportunity, provided me with this route to freedom. They had placed their trust in me. It was my duty to assume my role responsibly.

Lucy observed me, not in a manner critical of my silence or what must have seemed my rather odd behaviour, but more out of curiosity, I think.

'My husband, Dirk, is with the RAF. He's a fighter pilot,' she confided eventually, as though having mentally worked through how best to breach the shyness barrier. 'Lots of secret missions. I see very little of him. It's rather lonely especially since . . .' Her eyes dropped to her plate. She shook her head, lost in a past, a deprivation to which I was not party. Except, of course, I was. I longed to brush my hands against hers, assure her of my friendship. '. . . and it's a constant worry fearing for his safety.'

I glanced slowly about the room searching for photographs.

'Daniel comes as a . . . a blessing. So, it's hard for me to express the depth of gratitude I feel towards you for risking your life to bring him here to me.'

I sipped my tea. It was hot, almost scalding my hard palate, delicious.

'I haven't been told a great deal about him.'

I wondered then, for the first time, who had made

contact with Lucy, who had suggested that she be the one to foster Daniel. I had assumed that it was Delphine but it had been an assumption only and possibly incorrect. I remembered that Alain – oh, Alain – had mentioned one day in Lucy's overgrown garden that his mother kept a key to the house, that she was friends with Lucy. I couldn't ask. For I, Cécile, did not know these people.

She waited.

'Tell me about yourself, Cécile. How did you come to be given this dangerous assignment?'

I was recalling the brown envelope, which I had left on the back seat of the car that had driven me here, as instructed, taking only the identity card with me.

'I'm eighteen,' I said. 'I was born in Cimiez, high above the *vieux port* in Nice. I'm a doctor's daughter.' The last piece of information was not in my briefing.

'Are your parents still there?'

I momentarily closed my eyes. My parents, oh, my dear parents. I had no idea where they were. 'Yes,' I answered coolly. 'They are still there.'

'Do you know Cannes?'

I smiled. 'Of course, a little.'

'We have a house there, overlooking the sea, up behind the Croisette in the Montfleury district.'

I waited for her to mention the white house, too, but she didn't.

'I understand Daniel's parents are travelling due to the war. They are German Jewish refugees?'

I confirmed this fact.

'Did you meet them?'

I shook my head. 'No, no . . . I didn't.'

'He's a chirpy little fellow. He reminds me of . . .'

'Yes?'

356

'I had a son, who . . . He was about the age Daniel is now when he died. Coming up to two, is that correct?'

'I believe so, yes.'

'My son, our son, Julian . . . his name was Julian. He died in an accident. I . . . I still blame myself though everybody tells me that's foolish, that there was nothing I could have done to save him.' Lucy fell silent, with her hands in her lap, head bowed, gazing blindly at her painted nails.

'I am so sorry for your loss of Julian. I think I can imagine your pain.'

She had elegant hands. Hands that did little manual work. Tears were accumulating, dropping to her fingers, like the first fall of rain. 'I am very grateful to be able to give this little fellow a home until . . . until his parents are in a position to care for him again. You don't know where they are? Or when they'll come for him?'

'I don't, I'm sorry. I am not sure anyone knows.' I wanted to place my fingers on her long glossy hair hanging now in front of her face, which was contorted with pain.

I pictured Ilse, heavily pregnant, unwieldy in her movements, flailing as she struggled to ascend those breathless heights, flogging the mountain passes, struggling to keep on track, to keep moving. German soldiers, in hiding, waiting to trap her and her husband after all their efforts. Had she and Herr Lindemann been rounded up and taken on that same train to the east with my parents? Would we ever learn the true facts? Had my father helped deliver Ilse's baby? Nathalie – or might it have been Delphine? – had recounted to me a story that had been reported back to them. It told of how some of the Italian soldiers had peeled off their jackets, ripped them up with knives, dividing them into strips and triangles to improvise makeshift shoes for some of the refugees, whose own footwear had proved to be miserably inadequate, worn thin.

Shoes never destined for climbing, for fleeing.

Since I'd heard this story, I had been racking my brains to recall my mother's footwear as she walked away from me along that plateau path. But I could not, and I felt guilty for that oversight.

'Cécile?'

'Sorry . . . I . . . I . . .'

'Is everything . . . ?'

'I must find my shoes,' I muttered. 'And my socks. I . . . I believe there is a car coming for me.'

'Yes, at twelve o'clock,' Lucy broke in, wiping her face with long slender fingers. 'Sorry about that. Let's see what Elsa can magic up in the boots department. Whatever it is, it'll be better than rags.' She gave a light half-hearted laugh.

I stared. If only she knew what so many had endured.

'Is there anything I can tell you about Daniel? To help, you know, settle him in? He cries a lot sometimes – understandably. Yet at others he's remarkably calm and sleeps and sleeps. He's been through a great deal this summer. Or . . . so I understand.'

I had caught Lucy's attention and coughed to deflect any desire on her part to burrow deeper into my careless remark.

'I mean, you know, arriving in France with his parents, difficult journey as – as I understand it . . . He speaks a few words. Not many. In German, babble really, nothing very comprehensible.'

Elsa opened the door. She was cradling two pairs of rather clumpy boots. The first pair was flat, taupe suede, lined with fur and with zip openings. I gazed at them and silently smiled to myself, remembering dear old Marie and her booted feet. The other offering was of brown leather, a highly polished court shoe, with a low heel.

'Are these her own?' I asked Lucy, a little shocked that Elsa should be forced to sacrifice her own footwear for my wellbeing.

'It's not a problem. We can replace them.'

'Zank you, Elsa.'

I said to Lucy, without thinking, 'I could post them back to her . . .'

'From France in wartime? Don't be such a silly.' She laughed, a hand on my lower arm.

'No, of course not . . .'

'Take these.' Elsa handed me the leather pair. 'I walk more comfortably in the others. I have a pair of clean stockings too. Only one darn in them.'

'Nonsense, Elsa, I can donate the stockings. I have three pairs and one of them not yet out of the packet. I'll pop upstairs in a minute and fetch you those, Cécile. Gladly.'

'You are very kind, *merci*.'

It was gone eleven, according to a large round clock on the wall above a tall white refrigerator.

Elsa was clearing away the breakfast crockery, washing dishes in the sink, while Lucy guided me across the hallway into a drawing room. It ran the length of the house from front to back. A grand piano dominated.

A family with two pianos.

Who was the pianist? Lucy or Dirk? My father loves to play the piano, I wanted to confide. I never told him about yours. I wish now that I had. I wish now that he and I had made music together, whiled away carefree hours together.

This London piano also displayed a selection of framed photographs. I stopped in my tracks. Lucy caught me staring.

'Before you leave, may I, very quickly, show you some pictures of our little Julian?' She lifted several, one after another, with the greatest reverence, and held them against her bosom. 'Daniel looks a little like Julian, don't you think?'

'Well, they're both very blond, refined boys the pair. He's . . . was very handsome. I'm so sorry you lost him.' I pictured her in that open-topped car. 'Was it a road accident?'

She nodded. 'I was in Cannes, crossing the street from the Carlton Hotel to the beach. Julian was in his pushchair.'

I waited. She placed the framed pictures back where they belonged and stepped towards a darkened bay window at the front of the long room, concealing her features from me. 'A car swung round the corner, approaching too fast. Dirk called out to me. I heard him, but saw the car too late I did my best to pull the pushchair off the street, but a wheel caught, it overturned . . .' She lifted a hand to her face. 'It was hideous, the worst moment. I – I screamed out . . . too late.'

'I'm so, so sorry, Lucy.'

She made no answer. I waited in discreet silence, staring at her bent head.

She pulled a handkerchief from the pocket of her housecoat. 'I hope we meet again, Cécile.' Her voice wavered as she spoke, her back to me. 'I feel as though . . . we already know one another, have met somewhere before. In another life. I know that's completely foolish, but . . . One day, when Dirk and I can safely visit France again, may we come and see you in Nice?'

'I would like that. Very much.'

She swung back to me, her expression intact again, tears dried. 'Now, you need those stockings and a winter coat, I think. I have a knee-length fox fur. It's deliciously warm.'

'Really, that won't be necessary.'

'Wait here.'

And I was left alone. I bent low and slipped my feet into the shoes I was still carrying. A perfect fit.

There was a knock at the front door. A small carriage clock on the mantelpiece read a quarter to twelve.

Lucy came back into the room, hugging a camel-hair overcoat and a small Harrods bag. It contained new stockings and a suspender belt. 'Your driver's here already.' She wrapped her arms around me. 'One day I hope we'll sit in the sun with our bare feet in the sea, drinking wine, and I'll make a toast to you, remembering that you brought a purpose back into my life. It's impossible to describe what this means to me. Thank you, Cécile, for little Daniel. I know he's not mine for ever but caring for him for a little while will help me through this horrid rotten war and our loss. And my guilt.'

I didn't want to leave. I felt an overpowering urge to wrap my arms around Lucy and hold her tight, for both our sakes.

Another rap at the front door, this time more intent. Elsa was hurrying along the corridor to open it.

'Will you – will you kiss Daniel for me, please? He's a sweetheart.'

Lucy nodded, shoved the coat and bag into my arms and bustled me towards the door. 'I thought the camel would suit you better. Who needs fur on the French Riviera? Lord, it's midday and, look at me, I'm not even dressed yet.'

She leaned in towards me and kissed me on both cheeks. '*Au revoir, Cécile. Merci encore.* Give my love to France.'

'I will,' I said, while thinking that it would be a very long time before I was due to see France again.

4

The car was turning round the square, readying for the main thoroughfare. I swung a last look back at number eleven, almost concealed behind wintry trees. The front door was closed. Daniel was sleeping within, Lucy at his side or running a bath before getting dressed. I wondered what her day held for her, how she occupied all those grief-stricken hours. Did she work?

'There's an envelope on the front seat here for you, Miss Lombard. Do you want it now, miss, or shall I leave you to close your eyes for a while? We'll arrive late afternoon if we don't get snarled up crossing London. Let's keep our fingers crossed we don't drive into any air-raid alerts. Early in the day for all that, although who knows? Those Krauts like to keep us on our toes.'

'Zank you. A little later, *merci*.'

My mind was not on the present, the driver's words. I was thinking about Lucy, picturing us in some unidentified future walking on a beach together. It was an unlikely scenario but so had been the fantasy of spending time in London in her company, helping her in some small way with the loss of Julian. Julian. I knew his name now and the tragic circumstances of his death.

I decided to sleep. When had I last slept? Better to wake up to a new life refreshed.

Our location might have been anywhere. Countryside: a series of flat, gently winding lanes that cut through villages, each as dead as night. They might have been abandoned. Trees, with barely a leaf between them, lined the ways. During parts of the journey there'd been rain, energetic downpours, the windscreen wipers slapping as I dozed. Warm air blowing from a heater in the front of the Humber.

When I woke, the driver, a youngish man with short Brylcreemed hair, passed the paperwork to me. 'Fifteen minutes and we'll be at base, Miss Lombard.'

He offered me a cigarette. I declined. The car smelt of stale smoke and leather. While he lit up, I peeled the sealed flap of the envelope. One A4 sheet typed in French.

My eyes scanned quickly over the lines of text. I, Cécile, was expected to arrive at base at close to 6 p.m. All other instructions would be furnished upon arrival. Meal times were given as 'Dinner, 7.30 – 8.30 p.m. Breakfast 7 a.m.', unless specific arrangements had been made. I could not picture yet what they might be.

My stomach was starting to flutter. Panic. Nothing for it but to wait and see.

We were passing through imposing black iron gates, drawn open by two men in khaki army uniforms. A funereal approach along an oak-lined driveway brought the car to a standstill on a gravelled parking area in front of a large, red-brick mansion. I had no luggage besides the envelope, the clothes I was wearing and Lucy's camel coat, which I folded over my arm. Dusk was falling and it had started to rain again. Elsa's low-heeled shoes crunched against the gravel as I made my way to the front door, which opened as if by magic before I had reached it. A moment's hesitation, then inside, I was greeted by a wide and high wood-panelled hallway with a sweeping staircase.

'Wait here, please, miss,' a girl barely older than myself instructed. I was feeling apprehensive, overwhelmed. Out of my depth and a bit of a fraud. The British had delivered their side of the bargain: Daniel in a safe home with a foster mother until further notice. Now the burden lay on me.

Would I be equal to the challenge? Did I possess the requisite courage? The nerves of steel to see me through? I braced myself, thinking of my parents. My father would expect no less of me. Papa would be my guardian angel.

While waiting for what seemed like an age, chest tight with escalating nerves, I realized I had left the shopping bag with Lucy's stockings and pretty lace-edged suspender belt on the rear seat of the car. Damn.

Somewhere a grandfather clock ticked, like a beating heart, and eventually a thin, spinsterish lady in a pale grey dress and blue cardigan descended the staircase. 'Miss Lombard?'

I nodded.

'This way, please.' She led me up the stairs and along a dark silent corridor with a strip of deep red carpet at its centre. The whole place reeked of boiled meat mixed with a caustic rather unpleasant smell that I couldn't identify. Carbolic soap? Floor cleaner?

Eau de Javel.

We'll scrub the floors, like sailors on a deck, Sara. Alain's voice, still knocking at my heart.

Not now. Attention on the present, Sara. No, not Sara. Cécile.

We paused outside one of a series of doors, number eight. 'This will be your room.' The woman, possibly in her forties, opened it with a key, which she then handed to me, and we stepped inside.

Burgundy flock wallpaper and a single bed. A wash-basin by the window. Curtains drawn. A bedside light switched on, covered with a satiny oyster lampshade edged with a hanging fringe. It offered a ray of light to the sombre, impersonal space.

'You can leave your belongings here. They're ready for you downstairs.'

I had nothing to deposit but the overcoat. I decided to hold on to the envelope, along with my room key. I nodded, confirmation that I was ready.

5

Back on the ground floor I was shown into a library or reception room converted into an elaborate office. Here, too, there was a faint whiff of stale tobacco. The room was lined from floor to ceiling along one wall with books, leather-bound tomes mostly. Delphine slipped back into my mind and our mutual love of books. Seated behind a desk in front of the wall were three people: a man in uniform, with dark hair parted at one side and a handlebar moustache, flanked by a woman either side of him.

'Do sit down, Miss Lombard. *Asseyez-vous.*'

I settled obediently into the chair on the opposite side of the desk. On its surface were three small piles of files, each a different colour.

'I am Group Captain Walters, and this is Mademoiselle Sandra.' He indicated the lady on his left. And then moved on to introduce the more portly woman to the right of him as Pani Hilda.

'Which language would you prefer we speak?' This was asked of me in Polish by Pani Hilda, the older of the two women. She was formidable.

'French, please,' I replied softly.

'Excellent.'

From here every word spoken by the group captain was translated into French by Sandra, which I was beginning to understand was possibly her code name, her *nom de guerre*.

'You are here because you volunteered to help the war effort. That is correct?'

I nodded.

'Your first time?'

Your first time.

'This is your first time in England, I gather?'

I nodded.

'Good, good, we will begin with the language lessons followed by daily training. We need to assess the proficiency of your French, which we have been assured is fluent. Correct?'

I squeezed my hands together in my lap and nodded. 'I hope so.'

'You will need to achieve a notch higher. From this day onwards, you are French, born and bred in Nice, which is clearly not the same as a foreigner who speaks the language, no matter how adroitly. That is your challenge.'

I nodded again.

'And while refining one language we cannot afford to let slip the others. You can converse in Italian and have acquired a smattering of German, is that so?'

'A few sentences, not really much more.'

'But you have an aptitude for languages?'

I smiled. This reference must have come from whom? Dearest Delphine . . .

'Perfecting your English to the highest levels will not be imperative but it will be extremely useful. Meanwhile, we will hone your French, maintaining a slightly detectable Provençal brogue. Refining your German might save your life or someone else's so we will also devote some attention to that. It will be a demanding schedule, but Mademoiselle Sandra will assist you. It is essential that your German contains traces of your claimed French origins, not Polish. I hope that is understood? Your Polish will serve you should you find yourself in the company of one of our allies, who may be counting on you, but more on that later. First, language work and rigorous daily exercise, building up your fitness levels to a superior degree. After that, if all goes swimmingly, we will commence your training programme. Still with us?'

I assented.

'Good, good. Now we need you to sign this.' He slid a two-page document across the desk to me. The top page was in English, the second in French.

I frowned.

'Official Secrets Act. Two sigs, both names, please, same on each page.'

A pen lay at the ready.

I signed twice as Sara and followed it with the autograph of Cécile Lombard, scripted for the first time.

'Marvellous, thank you. Well, I think that's it for now. Any questions, Cécile?' The group captain glanced at his wristwatch without waiting for my response. 'Excellent. It will soon be time for dinner. Sandra will show you where to find the dining room and the bar. She is here to help you, answer any questions and monitor your progress. Welcome aboard, make yourself at home, Mademoiselle Lombard. We are a small unit, a family, really, and we keep our business to ourselves.' He rose from his chair.

'One question, sir.'

The group captain paused, a little surprised by my interruption. I noticed then that he had difficulty in standing upright. A war wound? A flight officer grounded due to injury?

'Yes?'

'Does anybody have news of my parents, please? They boarded a train in a small town in Italy. Alain – I was informed by a friend.'

'Yes, our information is that the enemy was tipped off. I am extremely sorry.'

'Has there been any . . . further intelligence? The final destination of the train . . . their current whereabouts?'

He bowed his head, palms resting, balancing against the desk. Gathering his thoughts, his material. His fingernails were very well manicured, I noticed now. Wedding ring on the left hand. In Poland, the custom is to wear it on the right.

'We are given to understand, on good authority, that they have been transported to a camp in Poland.'

I sat mutely taking this in. My parents had been returned to Poland? After our tireless efforts to escape. 'Is this camp anywhere near Lodz? Which is where we are from, so . . .'

'Hold your horses, Miss Lombard. You are from Nice,' he snapped. 'Born and bred. Never let me or anyone else hear you say anything to the contrary. Is that clear?'

I bowed my head, chastened. I must erase Poland, its customs.

'The camp, according to intelligence sources and our first-class codebreakers, is located close to an industrial town in southern Poland, not too far from the city of Kraków.'

My heart sank. 'Does it have a name, this town?'

'Oświęcim or Auschwitz, I believe. The inmates are predominantly Poles and Jews. The Nazis, as we understand it, are using these detainees for labour work.'

I closed my eyes, picturing my poor shrunken mother. How would she cope?

It was a blow. My parents imprisoned.

'The positive news is that they are, as far as we know, still alive.'

Prisoners, but alive. When the war was over . . . when they were released . . . it would be an arduous journey of nearly three hundred kilometres to our home. But I would find them. I would find them and I would escort them safely back to our apartment. In the meantime, I would try to take some comfort from the fact that they were back in our motherland.

6

Late April 1944
Alpes-Maritimes, France

Time had passed. Long months of gruelling training, peeling away at the emotional heart of me, reconstructing another persona. Now it was spring again and I was back in France. This was my third foray into the country, parachuted in and then airlifted out, over the past month and a half. France: Alpes-Maritimes equals home. This had been drilled into me, day in, day out, throughout my five-month education. Scored onto my mangled heart.

I was currently staying in a village – a hinterland outpost – a few kilometres west of Aix-en-Provence, east of the village of Éguilles, waiting for instructions on my next assignment.

An unspecified number of planes had been shot down, and my guidance was needed to lead the airmen – one or two officers? – out of France and eventually safely back to Blighty. Blighty. Curious noun used by the British soldiers to describe their homeland. An Anglo-Indian word with a Persian root, a soldier had drunkenly explained to me in an officers' mess somewhere in the middle of nowhere one godforsaken night. A sergeant trying – unsuccessfully – to get me 'in the sack', one inebriated evening at the bar. Its original meaning, he'd continued, after yet another shot of brandy, translated as 'foreign'. It was picked up by the British in India during the days of the Raj. I'd bumped into that sergeant on a couple of occasions since. A perfectly decent individual, far from home, 'missing the wife'. He'd apologized.

How one's mind flits from inconsequential to inconsequential to alleviate the boredom, the strung-out waiting time. Lessons in patience.

Across the street, half a dozen bent and capped figures were engaged in the *place* with their daily game of *boules*. The sun was shining. I watched them idly, listening to the clink of metal ball against metal ball, their raised cries as a skilled throw was applauded. In front of me, a jug of water, a long spoon, and a tall glass of *menthe*.

I caught snatches of conversation from those seated around me at the four tables on the pavement outside the little *café-tabac*. To all intents and purposes, I was enjoying the fine spring morning that heralded the warmer days to come.

To all intents and purposes, I was a woman at peace. The parts of me that grieved I had excised, frozen out.

The true object of my attention was a garage on the far side of the small square. There was not a great deal of activity there. Business was slow, few cars on the roads and few of those required repairs. The war had bitten hard into this region.

Not an uncommon story.

Half in and half out of the garage, its shutters wide open, stood one vehicle. A beaten old truck, its dusty grey paint chipped and damaged until the original colour was almost indiscernible. Little more than a rusted metal box on wheels, probably the prized possession of a struggling Provençal farmer.

A memory surged, swimming through my veins: the battered transport Alain and his companion had used that night – more than six months ago now – to deliver Daniel and me to the airfield.

Daniel and Lucy, I hoped they were getting along well. Was Alain still alive? Who had survived this interminable war? Delphine? My parents? Was I surviving?

This insignificant café in a village too small to be registered on any but the most detailed of maps was less than two hours from Ville-Vésubie, our mountain haven. The longing to take a bus . . .

Fortunately, the lack of petrol had ground most motor services to a halt. And should I be so foolish as to make such a rash decision, it would be the end of me.

If I was spying, it followed that I was also being spied upon.

Across the way, the repairman in his oil-stained blue overalls was sliding in and out from beneath the truck's engine. Every now and again, spanner in hand, he lifted himself up and sauntered back inside to collect whatever other tool he required or to light a cigarette. He was in no hurry. He was whistling, or perhaps that was a bird, a turtle dove softly cooing in one of the branches of the budding plane trees that shaded the square from the raw heat of summer. A woman on a bicycle pedalled past, disturbing the picture in front of me. Her face was unfamiliar, but I watched her trajectory without turning my head in her direction. Sure enough, she rounded the square and pulled up in front of the garage. There, she dismounted her bike and waited till the mechanic casually drifted her way. They shook hands. A play was made of a wheel: the front tyre. He bent low, pressing it, then spinning it, topping it with the flat of his hand. A short discussion, information imparted, and the proprietor of the bicycle nodded, thanked him and took off.

My cue. Instructions to wait one hour, and then . . .

I tossed a few centimes onto the table but bided my time. I stood up, wrapped my scarf round my neck and strode to my own bicycle, leaning against a wall with a letterbox set into it. The mechanic was lowering the shutters on his garage. Time for lunch. I stopped at the bakery and purchased the last *demi-baguette* on their impoverished shelves, baked from maize flour, not wheat. I recalled Louis and smiled to myself. How he had always enquired after my mother's health. My poor broken mother. How was she holding up? I felt my head begin to swim, and clutched at the counter, pulling myself sharply back to the present. 'No breakfast,' I mumbled. The baker's wife frowned and then nodded. She had served me once or twice before. I'd sit somewhere on a bench on my own in the sunshine and relish my sandwich, waiting for the garage to reopen.

7

My mission was to make contact with the airmen and escort them over the frontier or to an SD-created landing strip where he or they would be picked up and flown back to England. After that, he or they would be someone else's responsibility.

Pressure was mounting.

There had been no news for three days. I had begun to suspect my charges had been captured. But now I'd had my cue. After lunch, I discreetly punctured my rear tyre with my pocket knife and walked it back to the garage.

The mechanic, rather a handsome young chap with brown curly hair, greeted me affably and with a flirty smile.

'Riding too close to an olcander bush,' I explained drily. 'There was broken glass, a discarded bottle.' His attention snapped into focus.

'Under the oleander bush?'

'Yes, under the oleanders.'

'Leave it with me,' he said. 'I'll have the tyre repaired within the hour. Or if you're not in a hurry, you can find two new tyres at number six rue Bourgogne.'

I nodded, taking in the information.

'I'm given to understand they open at eight this evening, miss. Thursday,' he emphasized. 'Ask for Éliane.'

'*Merci.*'

'I'll keep hold of the bike for now, shall I?' He winked.

*

I waited for nightfall, gathered together my small bag with my belongings, left the key to my rented room on a small table in the hallway and walked to the address I had been given. It was dark, no streetlights. I knocked on the door of number six when I was sure that I was not being followed.

I heard a chain being slipped. A young woman with tired dark eyes and drawn features pulled open the door little more than a fraction.

'Éliane?'

When our exchange had satisfied her, she bade me follow her up a flight of narrow stairs into a scruffy room, where two men were cross-legged on a mattress on the floor. Both were smoking; one was playing a harmonica. The room was clouded with the lingering fumes of ersatz tobacco, a concoction of dried eucalyptus and vine leaves.

For some inexplicable reason my memory shuttled me back to that night in Delphine's barn with my father. The night the refugee in the brown suit had died. But I snapped myself back into the present, wasting no time. 'Which one of you is taking me?'

'Me.'

One of the pair lifted himself up from the mattress and coughed. We shook hands. He rubbed his eyes as though he had only recently woken.

'Pierre.'

'Let's go.'

8

A night drive, always problematic: no legitimate reason to be on the road beyond curfew and in a jalopy with a lousy clutch. Headlights, one smashed, and sidelights were switched off for most of the precarious ride so as not to draw attention to ourselves. And, if we were stopped, from where had we bought the fuel? Always a challenge.

Not from the British. No, not from the Allies supporting the Résistance.

We headed east and inland ascending into the higher ridges of the Lower Alps. I tried to rest during the gruelling expedition but my instinct was to keep an eye on the roadsides. An ambush was always a concern.

More prudent to stay awake, on the alert.

Pierre and I exchanged no more than a handful of words. What was there to talk about? We were not at liberty to disclose information, personal or otherwise, and anything we did say was more than likely to be a lie, a guise. Better to save our breath.

The less we knew of one another, the healthier for all concerned.

He was privy to our destination. I was not. I knew the purpose of the journey. He did not.

I was now expecting to find two men, plus a *maquisard*.

I stared out of the window, my eyes directed southwards. Somewhere, beyond the valleys and higher rises, lay the sea, lay Nice. The land of my fictional birth. A thousand metres inland lay Ville-Vésubie. How far above that little town were we now? To the east or west of it?

Across the border in the olive groves, vineyards and villages of Italy, the sun was beginning to rise. How many kilometres were we from San Dalmazzo? How frequently I had been forced to quell the urge to make my way there, to ask questions, to root out precisely what had happened.

To learn the identity of the person who had betrayed so many innocent, desperate people.

Wherever I turned, wherever I set my compass, ghosts lifted their heads. I swung my attention from the glass, closed my eyes, praying for repose. Sleep was too tall an order.

Another twenty minutes, my driver informed me.

I made no response. Bowed my head. We continued in silence. He fidgeted, fingers scuffing the dashboard in front of me in his quest for yet another cigarette. Discreetly, I wound down the window a fraction. I thought I might suffocate. Somewhere, a dog was barking.

A dog was barking? Up here in this wilderness?

'Pull over. Switch off the engine,' I snapped.

Where in this vicinity would there be a farm, a holding with livestock and dogs? A farm that had not been abandoned? I was scanning, peering into the pre-dawn gloom. A lone shepherd, perhaps. It was the season for the *transhumance* from the lower plains, but no *transhumance* ventured to this altitude. The dog was far more likely to be accompanying a party of soldiers. German tracker dogs. A recce. A trap.

Was this entire expedition a set-up?

Pierre swung off the dirt road and bumped us along a narrow stone track – stones slapping against the bodywork, the *carrosserie*, making an unnerving tinny sound, like feeble gunshots, until we found the most minimal shelter, a small stand of wind-blasted trees.

'How far is it from here on foot?' I quizzed.

He shrugged, eyes squinting, smoke clouding his line of vision. 'Two kilometres. Possibly three. Its tough terrain though, rocky, a sharp ascent. There's some forest to hide in, if you need to.'

'Give me the directions. Off the road, such as it is.'

I listened hard, calculating, memorizing. My heart was going like a high-pressure water pump.

'And when I get to the meeting point what am I looking for?'

'A herder's shack. Hunting lodge in the season. Operation name White Eagle. One of ours will be waiting for you. Any more than two charges, get out fast. Sure you don't want to wait this out and I deliver you to the site? Our contact knows me.'

I shook my head. 'Don't go anywhere for ten minutes. Give me a head start. Then, reverse back, revving the engine. Anyone stops you, you've got clutch problems, which you have. You're clean in the back?'

He confirmed it. No munitions, nothing.

I was pulling my stuff together, double checking that my Enfield was fully loaded. I knew it was. Six bullets in the cartridge. I also knew it was really only effective at close range, ten metres or less. I shoved open the van door with my shoulder, and flung myself to the ground, staying low, breathing heavy and fast, waiting. On my belly, listening to the night, the creeping movements of dawn, I scuttled into the brush. I breathed hard and deep, then grinned from ear to ear. The *maquis* at sunrise. There was no cocktail of perfumes in the world quite like it. Heaven on bloody earth.

If I must die, let it be here.

Following Pierre's instructions, which were clear and

precise, I made my way walking, short spurts of running, bent low, eastwards and marginally north. The sun was rising, its early heat caressing my back. My feet crunched beneath me. My gaze was sweeping across the landscape for signs of life, movement, tracker dogs. Any goats roaming here would be wild. Almost on cue, I spotted a mighty-horned Alpine ibex, his graceful mate a stately step or two behind him. I held back, fearing to startle them. I watched them, a smile breaking for a few moments. 'My talisman,' I murmured to myself.

Alain sprang to mind – curse the ghost of him for never leaving me be, for haunting what was left of my emotional being. It was with him I'd seen one of these elegant creatures for the first time. On a faraway summer's day in a life that had receded to less than faded snapshots. What I wouldn't give for just one breath of him warm against my skin. A well-acquainted ache swam through me. I knew its barbed edges, owned it and spat it out.

I started off again at a healthy pace, striding beneath the expanding light of the day, beneath the mercurial colours in the sky. The world about me was immense, beyond the grubby hands of war. It would survive, even if we didn't.

After the best part of a kilometre, perched on a shelved incline in the distance, I spotted a stone hut, a shepherd's bothy, almost indiscernible if you weren't on the lookout for it, among the cairns of stones. Few trees here, little shelter, should I be targeted and someone took a pot shot. Instinctively, I bowed low and continued to climb. Although the sanctuary was within my eyeline, it would probably be another ten minutes before I made it to the door, while dodging from one bush shadow to the next. As I drew close, I would need to weigh up the risks, reassure myself that I was not walking into a trap. There was never a hundred-per-cent certainty. It was a life-and-death gamble. The airmen would be waiting inside. They would be listening out for a lorry, not a foot soldier. Pierre had given me the code, but they were waiting for a vehicle, the grunt of an engine signalling our arrival.

Stupid. A careless oversight.

I hesitated, wondering with each step whether this was it, a trap, game over? Had I been set up?

I was breathing hard, deep lungfuls pumping my mood. Exertion and apprehension. The air was sharp and clean. My senses were sharp, too, keen. I took cover alongside a clump of mountain brush, full of thorns, which snagged at my jacket. Sagewood? Its spindly branches were scented. I inhaled its sweetness as I reached into my bag for my gun and slid it into the right pocket of my trousers. There was thyme nearby. I caught its scent as I rose and began to progress. My sight was firmly concentrated on the stone hideout. I decided, as I approached, to circle it at a wide distance, to get the measure of the risks. One wooden door, closed. Impossible to see if it was locked. No window but an aperture high up, beneath the tiled roof, a slit like a letterbox opening for air.

Who was waiting inside?

9

At that moment, the door opened and a young man stepped out. He was limping. He lifted his arms high above his head, stretching, spinning about him, on the lookout. A *maquisard* expecting a vehicle with driver and one passenger? Was he agitating that it was getting late? Day had broken. I paused, hunched low, waiting till he turned full on in my direction and I could catch a glimpse of his face. A mountain face, if I judged by his wind-bitten complexion. Bearded, or unshaven. Twenty-two, twenty-three perhaps. He looked familiar; I was trying to identify from where. I picked up a stone and launched it in his direction. He heard its landing, spun on his heels and caught sight of me. I began to walk towards him, all the while bouncing my attention between him and this brush-speckled high-altitude stretch of open country. One hand tight to my pocket with the gun.

And then I recognized him. The connection was Nathalie. This man was her friend, and obviously her colleague: I'd met him on at least one occasion in the town. Yes, the memories came flooding back and a jolt of hope broke across my face. The knot in my guts loosened a notch. If this *maquisard*, comrade, knew Nathalie, he also knew Alain. Of course he did. And possibly Delphine too.

'No oleanders at this altitude,' was my coded greeting. 'White eagles, though.'

He nodded and headed back into the cabin. I followed cautiously. If he'd recognized me – my hair cut short, dyed auburn and styled into a curly bob during my winter-long stint in England – he showed no sign of it. Inscrutable.

How are they? Alain and Nathalie? Are they alive, safe? And everyone else? Are you in touch with them? Questions I could not, had no business to formulate.

Within, crouched on makeshift bedding, were two men. Their flesh was patched with dirt, windburn and recent minor skirmishes. Both looked shattered, worried. One had a slightly more serious wound, his arm bandaged in a scruffy fashion as though he had dealt with it himself.

'British?' I asked.

English and Polish was the response. The Pole spoke passable English so without further ado we settled on that language as our means of communication.

'Our colleague here will be leaving us now and will return by the end of the morning with transport,' I explained to them. 'We must be patient, hang on here for a while longer.'

Which was what we did. They had food sufficient for the present. Basic, the most basic, utensils. I thought of my mother: she would not approve of such sparse cooking implements. My mother. I wondered from where in Poland this airman hailed. What news did he have, if any? But I was French, not Polish. The affairs of Poland were not my business. I swung open the door and stepped back outside. To reassemble myself, close the wound I had foolishly allowed to open.

After we had talked through the various hazards, as far as we could assess and prepare for them, I spent the best part of the morning out in the fresh air, making brief tours of the terrain, keeping a wary eye out, listening for that dog, drawing inspiration from the spring morning. These were critical hours, hours of insecurity. I watched lizards, spotted another pair of ibex, or was it the same pair? Sometime, around noon, when the sun was mounting high in the lavender-blue sky, I heard the distant cough and spit of an engine labouring up the hillside. I returned to the hut. A patrol, or our comrade returning? We closed the door and I bolted it from within, pulled out my gun.

The two men conversed or exchanged thoughts between them in low-volume English. I didn't tune in. My concentration was on the approaching vehicle, on the coded knock on the door. The password.

It was a different driver, but one of ours.

'Quick as you can.' The men were bustled and bundled into the back of the open truck.

'You'll be at the wheel from here on,' the young dark-eyed Frenchman said to me, handing over the keys. 'You can drop me off further down towards the junction that bypasses Allos. Or I can continue to that point, if you prefer.'

I stared at him. I had learned to drive as part of my training, had been furnished with a French driving licence, but I was not too well practised. And this promised to be a brute of a motor to handle.

'Where are we headed?'

'The job's not a border crossing.'

He gave me detailed instructions of where I was to make for. It was to be an airlift out, a night landing. He had an address, a farmhouse in the Var. I was to head directly there. The vehicle would be deposited in their garage, keys left in the charge of the occupants. Someone, a *chef de terrain*, code name Arbre, would deliver us to the airfield when SD, Special Duties, had sent through final confirmation of the details of the operation, and its departure location had been confirmed.

'How many days?' I begged.

'Three at the outside. Today's Friday. With luck, you'll have these guys on the ground in Britain by Monday night or, rather, early into Tuesday morning.'

Three days.

I'd had a presentiment about this exercise from the outset. Something wasn't sitting right. Now the queasiness fired and settled in my gut like ptomaine poisoning. A warning from my gastrointestinal pipes. Impossible to say why or what made me so ill at ease. Compared to my previous missions, when there had been less time between pick-up and deliverance, on the surface this operation was running smoothly. But I was not so experienced. I was a novice. My previous airlift out had been less complex. One escapee, not two. A Lysander, fine weather conditions, skilled operator on the ground: RAF-trained at Tempsford, he'd bagged an ideal landing site, the flare path clearly indicated.

But this time? Every hour we were not on the move left an opening for error. Or an ambush.

But I was obliged to vanquish my demons.

10

We abandoned the pilots' temporary camp, heading west, keeping keen eyes in and about the sparse growth of evergreens along the route. Occasional wild goats. Arid land. Mercifully, it was to be a daytime drive all the way. We dropped off the *résistant* along the road at the point he requested. A nowhere spot close to the Col d'Abeille. From there he was intending to continue on foot or until he was picked up elsewhere. Not my affair. I bade him *bonne chance* and took the wheel. The two men, dressed in peasant garb, were riding in the open rear, a pair of loaded hunting rifles at their feet. But I suggested that one, or both at a squeeze, ride up front with me. The Englishman chose to stay in the back, for surveillance purposes, gun at the ready. He was more comfortable with that, he said. The Pole climbed into the cab alongside me. He tucked the other rifle beneath his feet.

I fired the engine.

'I could do the driving too, if you prefer?' He smiled at me as if I was his daughter, though he couldn't have been older than late twenties. 'If anyone stops us, a man at the wheel might seem more plausible.' His eyes were very blue, tired and disillusioned. I felt an empathy towards him, trusted him. Perhaps it was the timbre of his voice, the accent, the fellow national.

I hesitated.

'You speak French?'

He shook his head. *'Petit peu.'*

I laughed. We needed to get going. 'OK, change places, you drive but only until we get to the lower, more inhabited levels. I'll do the talking if we're stopped. Husband and wife, yes?'

He nodded, jumped out and we changed seats.

We were driving west initially in the direction I had come from, but steering some way north of Barjols. I knew to keep off the main roads, to stay as high as possible and keep to the mountain tracks and forests. This was endurance driving that I feared might be beyond my competence, so I was content to let the airman do the first stint. Once at the wheel, when it was time to give the Pole a break, I gained in confidence but negotiating such a beaten-up vehicle required concentration and hard physical graft. My arms soon began to ache. Right thigh muscles too.

As far as possible we were grinding the ancient goat tracks and logging paths through natural forest lands. The trees were towering, primitive, their branches starting at eight to ten metres above the ground. This allowed us to travel beneath them without hindrance while their shade offered us a degree of security. No reconnaissance aircraft could spot us. The landscape with its mighty shadows returned me to the enchanted forests of my childhood: fairy tales read to me by my mother, peopled with gremlins, hobgoblins lying low ready to pounce. Spooked, I glanced back and forth, eyes peeled for any disturbance. I was too jittery.

Later, at a lower altitude, we would encounter the lavender fields. Too early for the blossom but still a calming prospect. Aside from the clatter and roar of the heavily expended engine, the dark, cool space and nature's silence were our companions. I siphoned in that peace to feed my heart, to attempt to control the heebie-jeebies, which would not subside.

The Pole and I exchanged few words. He had mentioned that he was a navigator, not a pilot, plane shot down – and was content to gaze out of the window, to imbibe the sovereign beauty of it all. We were still higher than the upper limit of the Mercantour. After we had descended from the area of Moustiers-Sainte-Marie, we travelled some distance through the Verdon natural parkland. It was wild, scenic and pristine. It was also a perfect spot for a trap.

Any time now we would need to dip further south again towards the hilltop villages with their low-lying stone buildings and grazing fields at their feet. But that was some distance still ahead. To reach them, it would involve a laborious, dizzyingly winding and perpendicular descent.

I found the intersection I had been looking out for with its handwritten wooden sign and swung hard to the left. I prayed the brakes were firm and would hold us steady on this unforgiving pitch.

Keeping to the ponderous stone tracks was slow-going and tiring. We would not reach our destination till nightfall, if we encountered no hold-ups.

'You have a cigarette?'

I shook my head, replying without thinking in Polish that I didn't smoke. He turned his head, glancing in my direction.

'You speak Polish?'

My spine tightened. Sweat beaded my forehead. 'Schooled in the UK, tools of the trade.'

He nodded. 'I don't often find an opportunity to speak my mother tongue, these days. Most of the crews I work with are British, though there are a fair few of us here fighting with the Allies.'

'Better we stick to English,' I replied drily. And then before the words had been processed through my brain, the question was out: 'Where are you from?'

He smiled, eyes softening. 'South of Warsaw. Masovia Province. You've visited?'

I shook my head, recalling Lodz, my home city, a more industrial region but not such a stretch from my companion's birthplace.

'You'd like it. It's beautiful country, very friendly people. My family are apple farmers. I think about home frequently. Right now, acres and acres of apple orchards will be in blossom. Their scent, the fragrance of the petals – there's no perfume quite like it. Apples have been cultivated in Poland since the twelfth century,' he boasted, laughing. 'Of course, now our land is occupied by the Germans.'

'Creating camps and ghettos, I hear,' I murmured.

'Death camps crammed with Jews and Gypsies and homosexuals. A curse on them and the shame they bring to our fine soil.'

'Death camps?'

'Those Nazis are murdering Jews. Imprisoning them in camps, exterminating them. That's what we hear. No official reports of it or none we've seen published, but it's what they say.'

It was God's blessing, if there was any God, which in those moments I doubted, that I did not lose control of the truck immediately. I might have taken us plunging down the mountainside. My fingers, bone-white, were gripping tight against the steering wheel. I couldn't breathe. I thought my heart would stop. With my left hand I wound hard at the window, leaned out, choking back vomit. 'I need to stop the truck,' I rasped.

'What?'

'I need to pull over.'

'Not here. It's too dangerous. Give me the wheel.' My companion leaned over and began awkwardly to twist and rotate at arm's length.

'We'll have an accident.'

I threw the gear stick into neutral and pulled hard on the brake ratchet. The vehicle frog-leaped and skidded, brakes screeching and burning to a standstill, tipping forward onto its two front tyres, almost losing grip on the descent. We were in a wooded area, skewed to the side of a narrow logging lane.

I flung open the door and threw myself out, landing on my knees, throwing up. Soft earth, needled with pine and stones beneath me. A pair of birds overhead took flight. Beating wings, like an angel at my shoulder pacifying me. The British officer was over the side of the truck and bending close. 'What the hell happened? Are you all right, miss?' He was on his haunches, lifting me even with one weak arm, towards him. I had no strength. Limbs of rubber. The Pole was hovering by my side too.

'What the hell happened?' one man asked of the other.

And then, in the distance somewhere at our backs, an engine.

11

My senses slammed into the present, body shaking all over steamed by a furious, insane energy, an anger that knew no bounds. 'Let's go.'

'Too late, miss.'

A German jeep. Please, not out of any nearby nest. If it's to be, just the one, for Christ's sake.

'Take cover.'

We hunkered down on the far side of our truck. Forestry between us and them. Still, once they had traversed the density of the copse, we would be sitting ducks in plain sight. Done for. One grenade and we'd be cinders and smoke. And it was my fault.

The occupants of the jeep must have spotted the truck – they were speeding towards us. They were far better equipped for this terrain than we were. If we threw ourselves back into the cab and hit the accelerator what chance did we have? Precious little.

The English officer had scrambled back into the rear of the truck to retrieve his hunting rifle. I had my revolver, my Enfield No. 2, which I had used in practice day in, day out, but had never fired to save my life or the lives of others. To defend, or kill.

I was not a member of the FTP, a Franc-Tireur. These were not the skills I had been trained for.

Before the jeep came fully into view, my two charges took off into the cover of the trees with their rifles, as we had agreed back in the mountain hut, should a scenario such as this arise. I climbed back to my feet and slid my gun into my side pocket. We had one chance. One chance only. If I could just stop shaking . . . I had to play this for all I was worth. I had seconds to pull myself together, to rid my mind of images of my parents *in a death camp* and fine-tune my 'credible story'.

Two uniformed men riding in a light German jeep. It could have been worse.

I made myself busy as they approached. Wrenched open the bonnet, drew an oily rag out of the cab and leaped onto the vehicle's front bumper, seemingly concentrated on the workings of its innards. My pulse was slapping at the back of my throat, my hate smouldering within me.

The jeep pulled up and the engine idled a second or two before being switched off. The two men climbed out and strode step by booted step towards me. I heard this rather than saw it. Antennae in the back of my head.

'*Mademoiselle, bonjour.*'

I raised my gaze, face now ingenuously stained with engine oil, tears tamped deep. '*Bonjour, messieurs.*' I smiled tightly, attempting to keep the frigidity out of my greeting. 'I'm glad to see you in this lonely spot. Perhaps you can help me.'

'Broken down?'

'Oil leaked dry, I think. Engine overheating,' I replied, head lowered once more into the gaping mouth of the motor. 'Or could it be the radiator . . . ?'

I was attempting to gauge the whereabouts of my colleagues, the angle of their line.

'What are you doing up here? You're a long way from any habitation.'

'My . . . f-father's sister was taken sick . . . Sh-she lives alone on the eastern edge of the forest.'

The officer, a lieutenant with cruel, restless eyes, glared at me before spinning on his well-polished boots – his attention dancing from left to right as he surveyed the forest to ascertain whether I was, in fact, alone. I saw him register our skid marks scored into the earth. His eyes narrowed.

'Want me to give it a turn?' the second-in-command offered. 'If you've got a crank, I can try to jump start it with that.' He was younger, slicked blond hair, rather handsome and altogether softer in manner, though I was not counting on any display of kindness if I was caught out.

'I haven't found the crank. It's . . . my father's lorry,' I smiled sweetly.

'Take a look in the back,' the lieutenant ordered. 'Leaking oil, you say?' He was still fixated by the zigzag tracks to the rear of the vehicle. He pulled at his lips with his finger and dropped to his haunches to scour the earth beneath it.

'Rear empty, Leutnant, just a few sacks.'

'No sign of any oil discharge here.' He rose, glanced quickly about him, verifying that this was not a hijack, and marched towards me. 'Get down from there, young lady.' He pulled out his gun, a Beretta. 'Nationality?'

'French. Originally from Nice.'

'Your papers, please.'

'They're in the glove compartment in the cab,' I lied calmly. 'If you'll allow me a moment, I'll fetch them for you.'

Without giving him an opportunity to stall or search me, I slithered smoothly out of reach, leaving both servicemen standing by the front of the truck, their attention trained on me. I threw them another smile, burning up inside as I heaved myself up on the passenger's side. The door was open – a careless oversight they hadn't taken on board – I noted it as I slid into the cab. Ducking low, as if searching for my papers, but out of the line of fire, I took a deep, ragged breath. One centimetre at a time, I drew out my Enfield, its metal warm and smooth against my fingers.

I knew what was to come and I was almost paralysed with terror.

Counting beneath my breath – one, two – I got to three before I heard the shots. One directly after the other. Then two more in quick succession. Almost in unison, the enemy soldiers fell to their knees. The more junior with his hand clasped to his holster hit the ground with a moan; the other still gripping his Beretta between his fingers lifted his weapon, aiming it at me. I leaped from the cab and pulled my own trigger. The Beretta fell from the senior officer's grasp and landed with a muted thud on the pine-needled ground. As did he.

Blood began to leak from both inert bodies, seeping into the forest's earth.

I gazed at their corpses disbelievingly.

They would have murdered us.

My two accomplices were out from under cover. They gawped at me, stunned. I could not bear to move closer, futile to verify that our enemies had been defeated.

'Let's get out of here,' I said.

We climbed back into the truck, our Polish ally at the wheel, and drove like the devil out of that cursed wood.

12

Once I'd delivered the two airmen back into the safe hands of the British, I had made up my mind that I would request Group Captain Walters to relieve me of my duties. Killing a man had traumatized me, no matter the circumstances. I wrote up my report, and filed it. 'I've finished with this,' was what I wanted to say.

'What do you know of the death camps?' I asked my senior officer, when we met.

'We have only sparse intelligence to confirm or repudiate this information though I will not deny, Cécile, it is not beyond the realms of probability. There are no limits, it seems, to depravity.'

I swallowed, his words like glass in my throat. 'And my parents?'

'No further information. Sincere apologies, Cécile.'

I was given ten days' recuperation before being loosely attached to a squad in the south involved in surveillance work. I listened to my orders without a word of protest. Relieved of my duties? What was I thinking? Hadn't I given my word to so many to see this through, even if *this* was a darned sight uglier than I had ever envisaged it might be.

Oh, Sara, I hadn't expected it to be so grisly. Alain Breton's words. Alain. From a lifetime ago. A life when I was softer, before my personality had been chiselled to sharp angles and every part of me was a weapon. There was no way back now, no opting out. It was onwards. Time to get this obscene war won.

Won?

Ended. Over. With, I prayed, a modicum of dignity still intact.

August 1944

As spring slipped away, the headier, more full-blooded aromas of summer came into play, and it was proving to be an outlandishly hot year. *La canicule*, the heatwave.

I was again in France, this time operating closer to the coast. My role was to glean intelligence from the local networks, including a Polish team, codename Marine, and transfer it to British intelligence.

We were one of several teams feeding information to Britain, specifically about the lairs, nests, of German troops hiding inland of the coast. It would prove vital in the weeks to come for the advance north and west after the Allied invasion of Provence.

A few days earlier I had stood on the beach in Cannes and watched the loud and lusty landing of the American fleets: Operation Dragoon. Thirty-five kilometres of coastline all the way to Toulon were under attack; it was a raucous and bloody entrance from our Allies. From close to midnight on the evening of 14 August, the air squadrons had begun to sound overhead. Their arrival was followed by a series of explosions. Shortly after midnight, bombs began falling on the city of Cannes. The Americans were also striking the two islands that lay off the bay of Cannes, the Îles de Lérins, targeting the German artillery batteries.

The following morning broke misty, in spite of the time of year. The Germans occupying the town gave orders to blow up the port. Weeks earlier, soon after the Normandy landings, they had rigged the city's sewer system with barrels of explosives in readiness for this day. Twenty explosions hurled debris sky high. The fountains of stones were falling all around the residents, who fled, disappearing into the thick black clouds of smoke that filled the air.

Was this liberation? Words on the lips of many.

It was a German counter-attack.

Carriers, ships and gun blasts ran all the way along the coast, almost as far as Marseille. The sky above the spectators, who had crowded onto the beaches and into the streets to cheer the liberating armies, was peppered with parachutes. A flying armada, like a million bats on the loose. Dozens and dozens, and then dozens more. Americans, Algerians, French. American infantrymen were wading ashore, a floating conveyor-belt of light craft disgorging armoured vehicles onto the sands. The beach at Juan-les-Pins with its concrete German anti-tank pyramids now had children sitting atop those cones, their parents at their sides, their friends, grannies, aunts, uncles, all waving and applauding. Liberation was a long-held dream, transfiguring before their incredulous eyes into reality.

Afterwards, as dusk began to fall, while the Allies were still arriving, and street parties, though tentative due to the shellings and wreckage, were breaking into life some distance further west, I boarded an overcrowded train to Nice – the last for some time, as it turned out. Nice was still firmly in the grip of the enemy. Not far from the station, I checked myself into a cheap lodging, stowed my belongings and went in search of a solitary dinner. The choice on offer was slender pickings.

But, finally, here I was. I had found my way back to Nice, three years on from our landing here as asylum seekers. Now I was alone, and my parents were . . . where? No news. I had no news.

In the calm of a sunshine morning, before the day grew too hot, I went for a walk, scouting the city, getting the measure of the occupation, but first a personal assignation: to the pink house where Mamma, Papa and I had lived for eighteen months when we first landed in France. It was too dangerous to linger, the city swarming with agents and SS officers of every stripe. I paused an instant, barely longer than a heartbeat, to remember, to pay my silent respects to my abducted family.

What a different mood there was in the city today from when I had been a resident here. The beaches were now studded with mines and shielded with barbed wire and anti-aircraft weapons. The Germans were taking no chances. Every building lining the Promenade des Anglais had been requisitioned by the enemy. Hotels, elegant art-nouveau apartment blocks, ancient palaces stood empty, gathering dust, boarded and barricaded. Only the Hôtel Negresco showed any signs of activity. It was functioning as a Nazi administration centre. The splendid Casino de la Jetée, whose pier my younger self had taken delight in strolling along – my parents at my side on days when we felt safe and we yearned for the fresh sea air – had been dismantled by the Nazis earlier this year, its mighty tons of metal dispatched to build aircraft.

I spent the afternoon visiting a couple whose premises were used as a depot for messages passed back and forth between Allied agents. Born and bred in the southern capital, they owned an *épicerie* but their shelves were bare. I recalled Marie. How was she faring?

Nice might still be swarming with Wehrmacht soldiers and Gestapo, but liberation of the city, they claimed, was less than a few days off at the outside. 'Our citizens live in fear of their lives. Some collaborate, others are starving.

Our three children are starving. Members of the underground are entering the city, readying themselves clandestinely for insurrection. Inland, agents are being parachuted in. But we need more from the British, supplies, weapons, before the Germans have bombed every bridge and Nice is an occupied island.'

That evening, alone on the terrace of the modest bistro I had settled at, I pulled out my biro and several sheets of paper from my shoulder bag and began to compose the next of what was to become a tome of letters penned over decades. None was ever posted. There was nowhere to send them, nobody to receive and read them.

Chère Maman et cher Papa,
Droga Mamusiu i Tatusiu,
Dearest Mummy and Daddy,

I have no idea if this letter will ever find you. I dread not.
The news that is beginning to filter through outstrips even the
most harrowing of nightmares. Every day, I picture you both
with your small bags of possessions standing in the lane, after
our very last embrace, and that image brings tears to my eyes,
breaks my heart, even now. Every day. There is so much
I want to share with you, so much I have lived through. Every
minute, new thoughts spring to mind, emotions never
exchanged, omissions in my behaviour when we were together.
The thirst to beg your forgiveness for my impatience. For the
silent cravings I carried in my heart to be free of you, eager to
be an adult, hurrying those teenage years away so that I could
get on with my life. I hope you know now, and in the light of
what has come to pass, that I never yearned for this hell. Who
would?

*I should have accompanied you, travelled that mountain at
your side, assisted you to safety. Stayed together, keeping our
spirits high. But I did not. For all the reasons we are aware
of. A sense of duty to those who had been kind to us as well as
my love for Alain, whom you never really got to know and I
wish with all my heart that you had. Alain, from whom I have
no news . . . have received no communication . . . though I
pine . . .*

'Sara? Sara, is it you? Heavens above, it is!'

A voice, a woman's voice, calling my name.

'What an absolutely amazing surprise.'

I had been lost in my private world. The call of my
name, *Sara*, whipped me back to the present.

'We thought you'd left the country.'

I knew that voice. How could I ever forget it?

Hurriedly, clumsily, I drew the written pages closer to
my breast as though my outpourings were confidential,
which they were.

I hardly dared to look up from the table, to confirm the
identity of the woman standing in front of me.

Someone who knew my true identity. Sylvie. Sylvie,
who could turn me over to the SS.

'Goodness, Sara, I almost walked right by, barely recognized you with your hair cut short like that. It suits you.
The colour's a bit different too. Lighter. More chestnut,
not so black. Smart choice. May I sit down?'

I nodded, dumbstruck.

'You look marvellous, awfully grown-up. You do
remember me, don't you?'

I nodded again. 'Of course I do. What a . . . delightful
surprise.' I was taken aback not only by Sylvie's presence
in front of me but by the changes in her own appearance.

I studied the face of my erstwhile friend, my eyes roaming over those features that before were fresh-skinned and wholesome and now were caked with make-up. Rouged lips, the long blonde hair chopped short and tightly permed. Scarlet nails and a figure-hugging frock cinched at the waist, with a matching jacket, gave her such a glamorous appearance. I had to admit the colours, the sophistication suited her well.

'My,' I managed. 'What a transformation yourself.'

'Fancy seeing you in Nice, Sara.' Sylvie smiled sweetly, but did I detect a *froideur*, an animosity hiding behind that expression, those polar-blue eyes? A residue of the jealousy I had encountered before? 'We were told that you'd fled the country. I was sorry and a bit cross you never came to say goodbye. A big bit hurt, actually.' She made a *moue*, like an ingénue. 'The last time I saw you was . . . when? Oh, yes, of course, on the riverbank. With Alain, but without my bathing costume.' Her gaze sliced through me.

Sara. This was the first time anyone had addressed me as Sara in almost a year. I had sloughed the skin of Sara to fully inhabit Cécile.

'You were so besotted, I secretly believed you'd run off with him. And we all know where he and his sister disappeared to. Well, if not *where* they'd gone, then for what purpose. You were aware of what they were up to? Yes, you must have been. Well, I don't suppose they're having such a great time of it now.'

'What do you mean?' Every nerve-end in my body, every brain cell, warned me against exposing my susceptibility, but I could not contain myself. If Sylvie had news of Alain or Nathalie, I had to know it.

'He's been arrested, didn't you hear?'

I shook my head. Numbed. 'How do you know this?' Was I walking headlong into a trap?

Sylvie shrugged and dug into a neat box handbag in search of cigarettes – a soft packet of Gauloises, the dark ones, Caporal – and a snazzy silver lighter, offering me a smoke. I shook my head. She took her time lighting it, exhaling with a light cough, as though playing a cat-and-mouse game with me. Could she possibly be enjoying this, her moment of triumph and cruelty?

If Alain had been arrested, the news would have reached our village. Was that where she had heard it? Or was she living in Nice? Beneath the table, my hand clutched tight against my thigh. Sweat broke out and rolled down my spine. Sylvie was blowing a smoke ring, studying me. I forced myself to change the subject.

'Are you working here in Nice, Sylvie?'

'I met someone,' she replied, rummaging in her bag again. This time for a compact to powder her nose, freshen her lipstick. Her answer was curt, defensive. She tugged at her tight curls with her painted nails, smoke drifting from her cigarette. 'Looks as though he'll be leaving soon, though. The Americans are here. Well, not *here* in Nice, but it's just a matter of time, isn't it? So much destruction. Those Yanks are bombing our buildings, aiming for the Germans, they claim, but shelling us as well. And they call themselves our friends, our Allies.'

'Yes, I'd heard that,' I replied. A dark suspicion was taking form within me.

In those early spring days of so long ago, that other lifetime now, I had been fond of Sylvie, and so grateful to her. She and dear Albert had befriended me when I'd known no one, when I was paralysed by loneliness. I recalled the Italian soldiers dancing in the square and

Sylvie's exuberance, how she had loved to flirt and quick-step with them. The enemy.

I felt dizzy. 'Your friend, Sylvie . . . Is he . . . is he from Nice?'

I recalled the Italian soldier posted to our village. He was very handsome and I remembered now how taken she had been with him.

She shook her head. Exquisite amber earrings glinted in the gas lighting from the café terrace.

'He's . . . We've been staying at the Montfleury hotel in Cannes. It's very posh. But we're here in Nice now.'

The Montfleury? It didn't take months of intelligence training to know who was inhabiting the five-star hotels of Cannes and Nice, these days.

'I see.'

'His name is Hans, and before you say anything, and pull that face, judging me as a traitor and all that, he is very special and kind and generous, and I love him pas-sionately. His nationality has nothing to do with any of it.'

'No, no . . . of course not. Love is love. Where did you meet him?'

'At home. He was the major general of the party whose patrol entered our village.'

I lowered my eyes. I could barely breathe.

'Some of them stayed on for a few weeks at the Hôtel des Alpes, after the Italians had gone, buggered off. I got to know him then. When he left . . . well, I left with him. I know some people disapprove, including my mother, who is beyond furious and won't speak to me, but I don't give a fig. Not really.'

As she waffled on, I heard all over again the heavy fall of the footsteps overhead when I was hiding with the children in Lucy's cellar. Had Sylvie been wining and dining with the enemy, with her Hans, while I was in the attic at Father Scaramoni's presbytery? While the town was burying the refugees massacred by those invading soldiers?

It was then, when I lifted my eyes, that I saw it, glinting at me. The bee brooch. There it was, pinned to Sylvie's breast, beneath her lilac cotton jacket. She must have glimpsed me staring at it because instinctively she raised a hand to cover it, to hide her crime. Varnished fingernails resting on gold filigreed wings. Did she have any idea from where the brooch had been stolen?

I crushed the urge to rip it off her.

'Are you living in Nice now, Sara? Why don't we meet for lunch? My treat. I won't say anything to Hans, you know, about you, you being a . . .'

I felt my eye begin to twitch. I hadn't experienced that twitch of fear for a long time, but now I did. My alarm signal. I hauled my shoulder-bag up from between my feet beneath the table and stuffed the letter and pen clumsily into it while fumbling for my purse. 'Goodness, I've just noticed the time. We don't want to be arrested for breaching the curfew. It's a quarter to eight.'

'It's fine, you're with me. Hans wouldn't let –'

'Alas, I'm not staying in Nice,' I smiled tightly. 'I'm living in – in Monaco, across the border,' I lied. A rather foolish and implausible lie. By what means would I be travelling there tonight so close to curfew? As soon as the words were out, I regretted the spur-of-the-moment and ill-thought-through fib. I prayed it would not come back to endanger me.

Eyes narrowed, she was pondering, weighing me up. 'German-occupied Monaco. What a brave girl you are, Sara.'

'It would have been lovely, though, to – to spend a few

hours together. Next time, definitely.' Without counting them, I tossed some francs, a small wad of notes onto the table, pushed back my chair and pulled myself to my feet.

'Well, Sara, if you decide not to leave, let me know where you're staying.' A smile, thinner, meaner than a needle drawing blood, crossed her lips. 'I'm sure Hans would love to meet you . . .'

I steadied myself, arm against the back of the chair. I had botched it. All my training and that was the best deceit I could come up with.

'*Au revoir*, Sylvie. Good to see you.'

I wasn't convinced that my legs would carry me effortlessly, but I needed to be on my way. Not directly to my little *pension* for fear Sylvie would follow me and betray me to her top-ranking friend. If I was stopped by a member of the Feldgendarmerie in possession of an identity card bearing the name Cécile Lombard when Sylvie could reveal my true identity, I would be executed on the spot. For this evening, I'd lose myself in the crowds and tomorrow be gone. Tonight, I'd find myself somewhere else, out of the way, to stay.

13

After a sleepless night in a dreadful back-street *pension*, chosen too hastily, before the swelter of that full summer morning, I hiked from the old town the four kilometres to the elegant, hilltop quarter of the city known as Cimiez. I set off at 6.05 a.m., so early because daytime restrictions had been brought into effect. As a reprisal for the landings on 15 August, the Germans had enforced two further curfews. On top of the nightly 8 p.m. to 6 a.m. limit, another had been imposed, commencing at 9 a.m., lifting at eleven, followed by a further afternoon injunction, which began at 2 p.m. and lasted till six. Any form of circulation around the city was becoming impossible, perilous. The secret police were patrolling, snooping everywhere, assisted by their spies, their *mouchards*. Public transport had also been cancelled. Walking or cycling were the only options for those not in possession of a private vehicle and the wherewithal to power it.

Along the avenue des Arènes, Cimiez, I paused briefly outside number seventy-one – the house in which Cécile Lombard was born – taking mental photographs of its features. Its fine and sturdy front door set at the end of a long gravelled driveway; its tall iron gate, gardens with tropical plants abounding in full rich flower; two towering palms that flanked the steps up to the front entrance. Was this really Cécile's house of birth, or was she, along with her parents, also a fiction of an intelligence imagination? I wondered who the true occupants might be.

Would they even know of my existence? Were they sympathizers? Had they been notified? Or had they decamped for somewhere with enhanced security?

I glanced at my watch: 7.10. The hour was ticking, the heat prickling.

I made my way, in as casual a fashion as possible – a local *flâneuse*, not someone with a prearranged meeting – into the parc des Arènes. There, I chose a bench in the shade of one of its ancient olive trees and made myself comfortable. The cicadas were in full voice, their dry calls screeching back and forth across the arena. I was surrounded by crumbling walls of stone, the Roman ruins. Children were playing on the dried summer grass not metres from my feet, or sleeping in prams, watched over by nannies or mothers, also out early to beat the curfew and the sweltering temperature.

Although it was to be another week before the Allies rolled into Nice, on 30 August 1944, there was already a tangible sense up here of the coming release, the freedom that was soon to be ours. An oasis, just beyond reach.

I studied the face of each woman. I had not been briefed as to the physical appearance of the agent I was expecting. A female, that much I knew. I took out the novel – a French translation of *The Great Gatsby* – and flipped to the page with my bookmark and set to burying myself in my material.

The children ran about the park freely and no one seemed to want to draw them back or quell their exuberance. Their happiness returned me momentarily to the square in Ville-Vésubie, the street parties.

I drew a deep breath, glanced at my watch. Seven fifteen.

On the dot, a stout, middle-aged woman in lace-up

brogues and a rather shabby linen trouser suit appeared, framed by the stone archway at the entrance to the park. She paused, glanced about her, wiping her forehead with the back of her hand, then made her way in my direction. She was carrying a paper bag. It contained her breakfast. I lifted my book to the light, peering at the pages more closely. The woman spotted it, sat on the far end of my bench and drew a baguette sandwich from the bag.

'Shall I break it in half?' she proposed.

I accepted with a nod and she passed half of the roll to me. We ate for a few moments in silence, appreciating the food. It was cheese with lettuce.

Her field name was Anna. She was Polish, employed as a cook at one of the smarter hotels housing German dignitaries. Her sandwich would have been made in the hotel kitchens. There was no bread to be found in the bakeries, these days.

After the initial exchange of codes, we conversed with subdued voices in French.

The news I received from Anna was troubling, even more so because she was not party to the full details – the names of the victims – and it was to be some time before I acquired them.

Beneath the ground floor of the Villa Montfleury in Cannes – the hotel where Sylvie had boasted of living with Hans – lay a hive of wine cellars. These had been divided into four chambers. Each was used for detaining, interviewing and torturing French suspects, especially those working for underground organizations. On the evening of the Allied landings, the dungeons contained twelve emaciated prisoners. All, save one, who was a local French woman and a traitor, a *collabo*, were members of the Résistance. The female spy was freed. Another of the male prisoners escaped. Anna had no details of who he was or how he had managed to avoid the fate of his comrades. The other ten were all shot at close range. Eight died promptly. The remaining two were seriously injured, but had so far survived.

'And you have no names, none at all?'

Anna chewed her baguette and shook her head.

I thought instantly of Sylvie's references to Alain being taken prisoner. My heart turned to ice.

There was worse to come.

A German round-up of still more prisoners here in Nice, again almost all Résistance fighters, had been transported by truck to an area just north of the city, known as Ariane. There, waiting for them on the bank of the River Paillon, had been a secret police squad. The captives were lined up facing the water and sprayed with sub-machine-gun bullets. None survived.

I felt queasy. 'You don't have the identities of these victims either?'

'None.'

Anna confirmed what London had suspected: a directive from the SS had been sent out, ordering all prisoners to be massacred before Nazi troops fled their posts and before any liberators arrived to hear the horror of their stories.

I laid the remains of my baguette to one side, on the seat of the bench. It had lost all flavour.

'From the Var in the west and towards Digne in the north, the Germans have detonated many of the bridges. Approach by the coast is obstructed by enemy mines, barbed wire and artillery. Nice is virtually cut off from the rest of the south.'

'Yes.' I already knew that access by road was more than

tricky. Public transport had been cancelled, and petrol for private vehicles was impossible to procure.

'In spite of these obstacles, underground agents and fighters are finding ways to infiltrate the city. On foot, delivery vehicles, by whatever route is available to them. Those who have managed to reach us here in the city are being hidden in shelters in and around the centre.'

I let this information sink in.

'These recent spates of massacres have left a bitter taste in the mouths of our underground fighters and they are even more impatient to see the occupation of the Boche demolished.'

'It's a matter of weeks at the outside,' I countered.

'Waiting for the Allies to reach this southern capital is not what the majority favours.' Anna was preparing me. 'London needs to know that the vote is for a people's uprising.'

'An uprising?' I repeated, stunned by the implications of Anna's words.

'Yes, now, while the Germans are demoralized, confused, while their attention is concentrated on what the Allies are up to further west along the coast. They are starting to impose martial law across the Alpes-Maritimes. We need to move fast before we are completely locked down, and we need London on board. We need back-up. This insurrection won't wait.'

'Surely there are major obstacles,' I said. 'A lack of weapons and possibly insufficient warriors?'

'We have to win the population of Nice to our side. That's our objective. Most are in a less negative frame of mind since the arrival of the Allies. They are ready to fight for their freedom. But we need guns, armaments, ammunition. Let London know. There is no time for shilly-shallying. That's the message.' Anna rose to dispose of her empty paper bag in a nearby wastebin.

It was ten to eight. If I set off walking back down the hill now, I wouldn't make it to my *pension* before the start of the curfew. As I left the park, heading seawards, considering my communication to London, I noticed that the gates were open at one of the houses neighbouring seventy-one. A delivery? I hurried to reach them before they slid closed. An Algerian, a caretaker in a straw hat, was sweeping the driveway.

'*Bonjour*,' I called, as I approached.

Rubbing sweat off his brow, he glared at me suspiciously.

'I'm going to get caught out during the *couvre-feu*.' I smiled. 'I wondered if I could shelter in your garden for a couple of hours?'

He frowned. The drone of a German light aircraft caught our attention. It was crossing the horizon closer to the sea, hovering like an enlarged bluebottle above the city. The locals had nicknamed it the 'phantom aeroplane'.

'They're scouting already,' I said, 'and it's not even five to.'

'Where are you from?'

'Here in Cimiez,' I answered, glancing along the avenue to number seventy-one. 'Originally.'

He welcomed me into the grounds. 'There's no one home,' he said.

His employers, the owners, had left in '43 when the Germans moved into the Free Zone. Many of the properties had been Jewish- or Russian-owned, old families, empty now. He invited me to share a pot of mint tea. Someone might as well make the most of the peace and quiet.

*

Anna's intelligence had to be communicated to London without delay. It was imperative the British accept the emotional climate and climb aboard.

The second challenge was how to transmit this intention to the desperately diminished, dispirited population of Nice, to incite them to mutiny alongside the underground, the insurgents. Whatever the mood, it was a tall order. Time was short. There was everything to lose. Or gain.

As soon as I could safely hotfoot it back to the city, I did so in the heat of a sweltering midday. Two light aircraft were now circling overhead. Their perpetual drone nagged at my nerves, as though they were stalking me. I couldn't rid myself of the fear that Sylvie had betrayed me to Hans. The planes were swooping low, as low as the rooftops of the apartment blocks, nosing and spying.

I made my way to the Quartier des Moulins in search of 'Green', a grey-faced British operator who was holed up in a broken-down guesthouse, tapping out radio reports twice daily to London. I hovered edgily in his dingy room, while he sent through the brief missive, the request for back-up.

'Now we must wait.'

Later that evening, one of the strafing planes dropped a small bomb in the centre of the city causing injury to several innocents as well as minor municipal damage. Everybody yelled and blasphemed but that act worked in our favour. It fuelled the Niçois hatred towards the invaders. I had a rendezvous with a courier, who promised to get in touch with the Americans who had reached Grasse, as well as de Gaulle's forces making their way east across France.

'Nice intends to liberate itself,' was the message. 'Send resources.'

If the British were not forthcoming we would need every bloody ally we could lay our hands on.

14

When all was in place, without waiting for London's blessing I linked up with a small band of Résistance fighters,
mostly young French women, from a cell known as
Ulysses. During those intense stifling days in hiding,
active in the shadows, the energy beat like a jungle drum.
Freedom lay just beyond our grasp. Many were working
towards the same end and it felt invigorating. I had been
out there on my own for too long.

We were on a high until the British sent back their message, *No insurrection. Wait for the Allies.*

Too bloody late.

The groundswell was already spiking. Syndicat officials
were spreading the word among their working forces. *To
each and every citizen, arm yourselves with whatever is to hand.
When the word is given . . .*

The objective was to break into and take control of
each and every building that, in one form or another,
nourished and supplied the city. The gas works, the bus
station, the rail depot, warehouses stockpiled with food, a
printing plant, all of which were, of course, in German
hands. Factory workers were instructed to keep the Germans out at all costs, because the enemy response would
be to blow up their buildings.

They will raze Nice to the ground before they take flight.

Liberate Nice, while keeping the city intact.

Ulysses' task was to recruit folk off the street, encouraging them to join us. When our forces were sufficiently

strong, numbering close to twenty, we broke into a gendarmerie in the neighbourhood of Saint-Roch. It was being used by the Germans as an arms depot. The weaponry, much-needed by our side, was shared out. The inventory, the stash we recovered, counted forty carbines, nine machine-guns, two sub-machine-guns and handfuls of grenades.

The city was getting ready to mobilize.

But in the silent hours, the insecurities gripped me. I tossed and turned sleeplessly. Sylvie's painted face dominated my thoughts.

The heat was insufferable. Gulls overhead were mewing, distressed by enemy aerial activity. For more hours than not, every citizen was in confinement, stalking four walls. For security's sake, I had changed hotels three times. My head was being rattled by the repetitive sound of shelling somewhere beyond my open window. German troops had set up camps in the wooded highlands and groves above the city. On the hunt for arriving *maquisards*, or fencing us in?

During those hours of intolerable heat and curfew, I remained holed up in my room, perched on my single bed, a keen eye trained to the window, curtains partially drawn against the sharp light. I was also constantly on the alert for footsteps on the wooden stairs. The door was locked but sufficiently flimsy to kick in. I had handbills to write up, to be collected and delivered.

The menace of those German light aircraft overhead had intensified. Back and forth, deliberately targeting civilians with their bombs now. Five dead. In response to this butchery, ten thousand of our leaflets were covertly passed out, reaching round the city.

A rousing call to arms. Liberate Nice!

The word was out now. The Allies must support the city. There was no going back.

We were a modest corps of three hundred and fifty, without counting the Niçois population, preparing to pit ourselves against a fully equipped German Army, whose troops numbered two thousand.

How I longed to find Alain among the *maquisards*. How I prayed with every cell in my body that he was not dead, had not been tortured and massacred at the Montfleury, with Sylvie sleeping in a room somewhere above him, or shot in the back down by the river at Ariane.

Nathalie, too. I entreated whoever might be listening for the safekeeping of friends from my past.

Heartening news came from one of my own team when she slipped a note beneath my door: *The police have joined forces with their fellow Frenchmen, adding to our swell.*

Was Sylvie still in the city? Had she mentioned my name to her Hans? Might I at any moment bump into her in the street? Haunted by our encounter, agitated by the rising inferno of heat, I buried myself indoors, venturing out only after dark.

So I smelt the fire before I saw it, heard it too, or rather the pounding of feet along the pavements beneath my hotel-room window.

'*Feu! Feu!*'

At some point during the intense shelling, flames had broken out, setting the surrounding forests alight. Ancient trees burning – olives, umbrella pines, green and cork oak forests. Red-hot flames tall as eucalypts encircled our heads. An act of arson, a stray cinder? Who knew, but in this hottest of all midsummers, the flora as dry as paper, it took nothing to spread the conflagration. The amphitheatre of hills was incandescent, a searing wall of flames. It was horrifying, terrifying. We were trapped. And we were being asphyxiated by the smoke that hung, like a black veil, over the city, blocking out the gritty summer light.

But no one flinched, no voice cried to turn back. Everything was set for dawn on Monday, 28 August.

Freedom, or be burned alive.

15

Monday broke grey, oppressed by fumes and cinders. From my first-floor window, hidden behind a limp curtain, I watched as three German tanks rolled menacingly by in single file, up and down the dawn roadways, dust kicked up from their treads. They must have been tipped off. They were ready for us and they would be merciless.

The ancient château that sits atop the city and looks out across the full length of the Promenade des Anglais from a vantage point of ninety-three metres had for some time been a stronghold of the Germans. On the morning of 28 August, recognizing that their days there were numbered, enemy troops opened fire from the *colline*, the hillside walkway, onto the city and its people. Fires raging beyond the city's limits, shells teeming from the castle hill, over the course of the next four hours the bullets killed fourteen innocent people.

In response, rebel fighters opened fire from rooftops, street corners, from buildings previously occupied by Germans. The fighting was fierce. Anything and everything that could be thrown was hurled at the enemy troops, the tanks still circulating in the heart of the city. Blood rivered the streets. It was guerrilla war.

Some of my fellow patriots took a munitions store situated near the junction of Gambetta-Cessole, which helped to arm the volunteers, whose numbers were rising. By noon, in the burning sunlight and the choking smoke, we were almost fifteen hundred rising up for freedom. The hospital was the next to be won by our comrades. A triumphant rousing moment, and one that triggered the start of the German retreat, but not without reprisals. The prefecture received a call to warn that, if the mutineers did not hold their fire, the Germans would blow up the beautiful old city. They retaliated with a furious energy, regaining the arms depot at Saint-Roch, now empty, and looked set to take the railway station.

It was mid-afternoon. I was somewhere in the city centre, two or three streets back from the Promenade, in the midst of a group making its way to the port. Word had reached us, too, that the Germans were about to destroy the city's magnificent harbour. Bullets were raining down upon us from every direction. It was chaos. There was nowhere to take cover, showers of glass falling from shattering windows. It was then that I saw him – Alain.

Yes, Alain. Alain, alive – bearded but unmistakably him. In a public garden – I later learned it was the Albert I Gardens. He was standing aloft on a fountain or statue, hard to tell, with the throngs of people. He was at the centre of a group, mostly young, all with weapons. I yelled his name, broke free from the column I was moving with. It was all such a commotion it was hard to know the sequence of events. Minutes after I had spotted Alain with his rifle aloft, a burning sensation shot through me, spreading deep beneath my shoulder. I kept running, forcing my way through the dense crowds, determined to reach my friend, my only lover. I lifted my left hand to my right shoulder. It was thick and sticky with blood. My head was spinning. I toppled, and fell to my knees. Two comrades dragged me out of the path of stampeding feet, the surging crowds that would have trampled me to death. I lost consciousness.

*

It was creeping towards a week later before I learned that we had won the day, but only after the Germans had sunk four ships, destroyed the lighthouse and eleven marine cranes. Twenty-seven members of the Résistance had been killed and two hundred and eighty wounded. I was not included in that score. I was not on any records.

By midnight on the twenty-eighth, the Germans were on the run, destroying everything in their wake. But Nice had been liberated. The city was in the hands of the French once more.

The following day, tens of hundreds of people flooded into the metropolis to celebrate and to assist with the arduous process of healing, repairing, reconstructing. Two days later, the American tanks rolled into the place Massena, the central square set back from the beach. They declared victory.

I was in the hospital, drifting in and out of consciousness, oblivious to the rattle of trolleys all about me. My bullet wound would not be fatal, but could not be dismissed. I was in need of blood, rest, nourishment. Parched throat, desperate for water. The place was understaffed, overcrowded.

Beyond the windows, still silted and smeared with dust and ash, the sun beat down upon a collapsed, crippled city – ravaged, looted, but deafened by the clamours of rebuilding, regeneration. From shell-riddled buildings everywhere, swastikas were being lowered and removed; those that were flammable were tossed onto bonfires, gobbled by flames. Arrests were under way, collaborators unearthed, shaven, shot or hanged. Was Sylvie among them? We never heard of her again.

The streets were being cleared of mounds of rubble and broken bricks, the beaches of mines, shells, barbed wire. Supplies were being trucked in or discharged from Allied ships. Church bells were chiming. Glorious tintinnabulations. There was a mood of dog-tired ebullience. I was disappointed later to have missed it, but I was not sufficiently conscious to know healing was taking place. Or that I'd had a visitor. A young unshaven man, who perched at the foot of my bed over several days and watched over me, held my hand as I lay sleeping, spoke my name: 'Sara, my sweet Sara. *Je t'aime.*'

My grief was so profound, so deeply engrained in me, I mistakenly believed it was a vision of my father I saw there. My father who spoke to me of love with his soft, patient voice. I was sure I recognized him sitting on my bed. He had returned. My parents were saved. No death camp. He was back to care for me.

'You've grown a beard,' I mumbled, tears streaming down my cheeks. 'Where's Mamma?'

'Sara, Sara.'

16

*One year later
Mid-September 1945*

I was watching a red squirrel leaping through the branches of a gnarled old almond tree in the garden of the white house. The vegetation was dense, a jungle. The key: I was trying to recall which rose bush I had buried it beneath. Somewhere close to the back door, that much I could remember.

'Sara, are you coming in?'

'You go on. I just need a few minutes.'

'Yes, of course. Take your time.'

Lucy was along the path ahead of me unlocking her front door, Daniel was at her side, his plump arms locked around the calf of her right leg. He was singing to himself, singing to Lucy, who was laughing. He'd grown into a little buster of a boy, who talked constantly, jabbering away contentedly mostly to himself. I wondered as I watched him if he'd have any memories of this house. The words he spoke, those that were comprehensible, were English. His early German ramblings seemed to have disappeared, closed off somewhere in the vaults of his child's mind.

I had arrived in France that morning on an RAF flight from Biggin Hill to the private airport at Cannes-Mandelieu. Most of my months of recuperation had taken place in the UK. They had ferried me out of Nice before my rambling mind disgorged their secrets.

Lucy and Daniel had met me off the plane. She'd driven us – in the fancy car I'd stared at in photos – into the mountains, to my quondam haven. She had made up one of her spare bedrooms for me. Downstairs. I had entreated her not to offer me the flat upstairs. I could not, was not ready to, breach those silent spaces, fraternize with the memories, tune in to the silenced voices of my parents. To see their invisible hands hugging empty mugs. To gaze upon the creases that indented the double bed where they had lain side by side – clasping, embracing one another in the night, gaining strength from their love, my father steadfastly planning for a better future. For the three of us.

Two weeks earlier, I had been informed by Group Captain Walters of the death of both my parents. Exterminated in the camp. Might there be a mistake? I had begged.

He lowered his gaze to the desk stacked high with files. It took a while before he spoke again. 'The lists are long, harrowingly long, and we do not yet have complete information, but to offer you . . . to offer you even a glimmer of hope, Sara, would be reprehensible on my part. The train your parents, along with Ilse and Maurice Lindemann, were boarded on at San Dalmazzo was bound for Auschwitz-Birkenau. Only twelve from those packed carriages survived their incarceration at that camp. We have identified those twelve. Neither your parents nor the Lindemanns are among the fortunate dozen. I wish I had better news. I genuinely do.'

I bit my finger, swallowed, my saliva bitter and thick.

'If there is anything I or we here can do to help you . . .'

I was silent.

'Our sincere condolences.'

At a loss. On my own. How to handle such facts?

'When you are ready, we can discuss your future. This little organization of ours is in the process of being dismantled. Thankfully, victory has rendered us redundant.

But we do have the wherewithal to secure you a place at one of the finer British universities: Cambridge. Modern languages, perhaps, when you're ready.'

I was a long way from ready. I had no hankering for England – it was the only decision I felt confident about. I wanted to go home. But I had no home. I had no papers, having surrendered Cécile's. So, back to square one, rewind four years. I had no papers. I was stateless.

I begged for time.

'One thing to bear in mind, Sara, when you're making your plans, the Official Secrets Act, the contract you signed with us, is binding. A lifelong agreement.'

'And documents?'

Would I be going back to my old self, Sara? Was I capable of that?

My Self. The scar on my shoulder, quite a work of art, which would fade over time but never disappear – who owned that? Who had pulled the trigger in the forest? Was that Sara or Cécile?

We never lose what we have lived through.

'So who am I now?'

'Sara Rosenbaum, of course. She whom you have always been. We'll sort out the paperwork. Give us a week. Unless you prefer to start again with an entirely new identity? That can be as easily arranged.'

How swiftly could I be returned to myself? For, yes, that was what I wanted, craved. To be returned.

'Sara suits me fine, thank you, sir.'

After that meeting, I had boarded a train to London and gone in search of Lucy.

'My, what a surprise. Good heavens, Cécile, isn't it? How are you?'

424

Lucy was pregnant. Almost five months, she admitted, with a mischievous wink, caressing her gently protruding belly. 'Let's say, it's a victory gift.' She giggled.

We were in her kitchen. Beyond the window out in the square where the leaves were showing the first signs of autumn, the day was fading.

'Would you like a glass of wine? Or champagne? Yes, let's have champagne. We must celebrate.' She was at the fridge, opening its door, drawing out a chilled Moët et Chandon and reaching a little clumsily into an upper cupboard for glasses.

'Help me, Cécile, please. Take these before I drop them. Once we've had a toast to, oh, so many good things, I'll call Daniel. Wait till you see how he's grown.'

I had been hoping Daniel might recognize me but he stared at me, if not blankly then goggle-eyed with puzzlement. The sound of my voice, my features . . . something about me was perhaps familiar to him, but he couldn't make the connections. We knew now that he and Hanna had been orphaned. Curious word, 'orphan': Greek root. My predicament, too. Lucy had been informed about the Lindemanns, not about me. The question now was Daniel's future. And Hanna, his sister's. Several organizations were searching for surviving relatives, who might be willing and able to adopt the pair of them, brother and sister to be reunited and remain together. The cousins in Switzerland? It could take months, years.

'I'm driving him back to France with me tomorrow.'

'Tomorrow?'

'Dirk's in the States, California, a juicy film deal, so I'll be braving that long journey alone. Well, with Dan at my side.'

Lucy poured the sparkling wine into the two champagne *coupes* and slid mine towards me. 'You were lucky to find us still here. I'm rather excited. I haven't visited the South of France in more than five years. I understand our villa above Cannes was occupied by the enemy so Heaven knows what condition I'll find the place in. While I'm sorting it out, Dan can spend a few days with his sister. We have a little house in the village where Hanna is being fostered, a mountain retreat for the summer months that . . . It was through friends up there that I was offered Dan, but we . . . we've decided to sell it.'

You can't sell that lovely house! I bit my tongue before the words were out. Preposterously, I almost felt betrayed.

Lucy glanced in my direction.

'So, while I'm occupied with clearing out both houses, Dan can spend some time with his sister, Hanna, who's staying with a splendid schoolteacher friend of mine there. I look forward to meeting the girl. If there are no takers, Dirk and I have discussed it and we'll adopt them both. I've grown so fond of Dan, and this little soul' – she patted her belly – 'will be delighted to have a sibling. Or two. What's the difference? If Julian had survived . . .' She fell silent, lost in a long-nursed heartbreak.

'May I come with you?'

'Sorry?'

'May I hitch a lift? I could share the driving.'

'You want to drive over with me to Cannes, Cécile? Oh, but of course, you're from Nice, want to go home, see your family. Are they still there? Why are you here, in England?'

I bowed my head.

There were so many answers to Lucy's questions, I wasn't sure I knew where to start or how much to confide.

My heart was shattered, but I knew it was time to tell her the truth. Some of it, at least. To launch Sara's new life.

'There's rather a lot you don't know, Lucy.'

'Oh?'

Where to begin? 'My name isn't really Cécile. It's Sara. Sara Rosenbaum. I'm Polish. I have so much to explain. My family is ... was Jewish, though we ... My father liked to joke that he was a disciple of Spinoza and a Communist.' *My gentle, humane father.* A tear slid down my cheek. Here in the embrace and comfort of Lucy's almost complete world, the devastation and barrenness of my own situation rolled over me, crushing me. I had no one.

And so, fuelled by the delicious champagne, I poured out the rest of my tale. Sections of it. Only the permissible segments.

Lucy said nothing, glued to the seat opposite me, lips apart, stroking her stomach in circular movements, enthralled or perhaps left incredulous by my story. What did I omit? Most of my private hours in the lower half of her home, dressing up in her clothes, making love with Alain for one precious night only, losing my virginity to him on her and Dirk's bed.

'So, you were our tenants? That's astonishing. And after you delivered Dan here, what happened to you?'

'I ... stayed in Britain. It was safer than returning to an occupied land. I was ... based in Buckinghamshire, studying languages,' I lied, praying she wouldn't ask me by what means I had fed and kept myself. 'Lucy, I have friends in that village of Vésubie. I long to see them again and I'd like to pay one last visit, if that is all right with you, to the flat I occupied with my parents.'

'Of course you must visit. You can stay there, too, if you want.'

I shook my head. 'I'm not sure I could . . .'

She leaned across the table – with difficulty due to her protruding tummy – and laid a hand on my arm. 'I am so, so sorry to learn all this. And after, will you return to Poland?'

I shrugged. 'Your guess is as good as mine.'

Setting off with Lucy the following morning turned out not to be an option for me. The group captain required a few more days of my time. Debriefings, the skills required to keep the past two years for ever under wraps. And, of course, there was the question of no papers. When all was settled, I was provided with Sara's identity card and a private plane. Biggin Hill to Cannes.

17

I turned my attention away from the garden, the red squirrel, the memories. The key was nestling in the palm of my hand. I had lightly scratched myself digging it out from beneath the rose thorns. I would deliver it to Lucy. She and Daniel had gone inside. I glanced upwards, contemplating the upper storey. Our apartment. The safety of the stairs leading up to it, overgrown with clumps of weeds. I heard my father's voice warning me to take care, not to slip on the steps.

'Sara! Sara!'

I turned at the call. A woman's voice. Mamma?

'Oh, Sara, what a delight. We heard you were on your way back. I've been so looking forward to seeing you.' Delphine was hurrying towards me, two blossoming girls flanking her: Hanna and Élisabeth. I ran to greet them and we fell into one another's arms, hugging so hard I could barely breathe. Delphine's face was pale, careworn. Her eyes were bright, glistening and moist, but she had aged ten years.

'When did you get here?'

'Just arrived.'

'I can't believe it. You're alive and well. We all are. Just about. Look at you, beautiful, more so than ever. And what about this pair? Look at them, bright as buttons and nothing but trouble.' She laughed and shook her head, eyes lowered, fighting her emotions. 'Dear God, Sara, how I've prayed for this day. Is Lucy here?'

'Inside.'

We turned as one and made our way up the garden path to the open front door. I stepped to the side, allowing the others to go in ahead of me. I couldn't cross the threshold, not just yet. Too many ghosts were pushing me back. I glanced upwards again to the first floor.

'Aren't you coming in?' Delphine, her head thrown back to me.

'I need a moment. Just give me a few moments.'

She looked deep into my eyes, nodded and winked. 'Take your time. We're all here for you, Sara.'

Lucy, hearing our voices, came rushing to the door, she and Delphine speaking at once, words tripping over one another's. I was about to leave them to it when I caught sight of the children. They were huddled tight, looking about them. How much did they remember? How deep was their trauma? A hub of histories here.

It was only a second or two before Lucy and Delphine, both ecstatic about Lucy's pregnancy, shepherded the trio of youngsters through to the sitting room, chattering like a company of parrots.

'It's a mess. I've started to clear up, but whoever broke in . . . all the photographs, look . . .'

I shouted indoors to them that I would see them later.

'Aren't you coming in?' Lucy called, over her shoulder. She didn't wait for a response, already occupied by the ebullience of the kids and Delphine.

I climbed the exterior staircase with care, negotiating nettles and other greenery. No one had trodden these steps since – when? Since the Wehrmacht had broken in? I had promised myself I would wait, give myself a day or two, before coming up here. The door wasn't locked, but it took me a minute, several minutes, before I could turn the handle. The door was jammed as it had been on the day of our arrival. I pushed hard, hesitated and stepped inside. Sunlight shone in through the filthy windows. And there, staring back at me, was my letter. The one I had entrusted to Delphine, addressed to my parents. It had been placed, unopened, leaning upright on a window ledge. Those windows that faced out to the mountains and where, on our first afternoon here, I had felt such a rush of faith, of buoyancy. With trembling fingers, I picked up the envelope, contemplating my own handwriting, fingering over the ink letters, the stubborn optimism sealed within its contents, then I set it back where it belonged. I wanted it to be here, where my parents would find it, when they came looking for it, came looking for me. Because they would come. Their spirits were free now.

Souls are not trapped: they rise above the shackles.

I stepped slowly along the length of the corridor, the click of my heels making a clear tinny sound against the old tiles. One by one, I pushed open the doors. Each room revealed a still-life of a rushed departure, of long-empty spaces. I recognized the same musty smell that had greeted us on our arrival two and a half years earlier.

It triggered such powerful memories. As I drew breath, the phantoms began to take shape, familiar images from the months we had survived here. Mamma first, then Papa, and the trio of us grouped together, or sitting reading, sewing, dreaming, in our separate universes, secure in the knowledge that we were not far apart, that we were a family unit. I tuned in to my parents' muffled voices, nattering together at night, faces on pillows. My mother's smile or concerned expression as she chopped vegetables, boiled broth. 'Eat, Sarina. Where are you off to? Always hurrying out. You must eat.'

Garlic, herbs, scraggly strips of meat, the aromas of cooking, wartime menus.

In each room I entered, the spectres raised their heads, acknowledging my presence, my return, with a tentative smile.

'You're back, Sarina? What took you so long? We've been waiting for you.'

Fragments and phrases from past conversations floated around me, forgotten chords drifting by.

I stepped into my bedroom – found a scarf tossed carelessly on the eiderdown, my tattered bag still flung open on the floor with my few possessions alongside it, none of which I'd managed to pack. It was never taken anywhere, nothing stolen by the enemy because there was no treasure worth their effort. Not even my precious collection of seashells from the beaches in Nice.

I crossed to the window and let my breath go, a slow release of tension, looking out over that familiar, much-loved view. Soon, it would be the grape harvest again. Familiar faces in the fields. Thomas, Pascal, Albert's mother . . .

Footsteps.

My father?

His presence in the doorway. I heard the soft shuffle of his approach, coming to rest at my back as I remained gazing out, conjuring a future here.

'Remember when I was so angry with you, Papa, when we stood here together at this window?'

He placed his hands gently on my shoulders. Young strong hands, not my father's. I closed my eyes at his touch. I felt a rush of exhilaration.

'My Sara, is it really you?' he whispered. Bending low,

his cheek, his lips brushed my ear. 'How I have longed for you, dreamed of you.'

'Alain?' I held my breath. 'Alain.'

'Delphine told me you were here, that you'd come home. At last.'

18

Alpes-Maritimes, France
The Present

I am closing my eyes now for the very last time. As I do
so, I take one farewell glimpse at the contours, the fuzzy,
indistinct figures of my family: sons, grandchildren, loved
ones seated or standing round the bed.

'Your vigil is over,' I whisper.

They cannot hear me. One final inhalation, one last
smile breaks across my face.

Thank you for every moment, each and every one of
you, but now it is time.

I have people to see, but I think they know that. One
of my sons – we christened him Albert – grips tighter my
fragile liver-spotted hand with its worn gold band. He
leans in and kisses my forehead. I feel the dampness on
his lips. I want to hug him tight, to reassure him, but I
lack the strength. No more tears. Be joyous for me. For
soon I will be reunited with your father, who for ten long
years I have been without. Deprived of him. And in the
future, one day, you too will be with us.

Now, I am flying free above the walls and rooftop of
this house, our white house given to us more than half a
century ago as a wedding present from Lucy. Fleetingly, I
remember her. Her sadness and beauty. I remember the
faded outlines of two small children. One, Hanna, who is
here in this room now. Her brother, Daniel, rarely came
to visit. His work in Israel kept him occupied.

The house is still. I hear the fading sounds of weeping.

'Please, don't cry,' I want to appeal to them, 'Albert and Alain Junior. Your mother is at peace. There are so many I long to be with, embraced by. Not least your dear father.' The wind is whistling. It is lifting me, carrying me. I give in, let myself go – weightless, thrilled, flying at the speed of light above the forestlands, the myrtle trees, the olive groves – hurrying towards those I have been robbed of. The souls of those who left before me, too soon. Too soon.

The sky is alight, on fire. All about me has turned to red and gold. I see smiles on faces everywhere. Flocks of souls departed. Mamma and Papa whose spirits have stayed at my side counselling me, patiently waiting for me. They call to me now, summoning me, their souls regenerated, like flowers at the feet of the olive trees. The sky is filled with a light that is blinding me, beckoning me to a place where there will be no more darkness, no oppression, where forgiveness, even for my sin, reigns and where Love – above all – Love is the gift that survives.

Many French people – although far from all of them were awarded the Righteous Medal – helped Jews and sheltered children. In rural villages, no one was blind to the fact that the children supposedly placed in care by the social services were Jewish – all the more so as some spoke with a foreign accent. People looked the other way or simply didn't want to know.

Simone Veil

Acknowledgements

My sincerest thanks to editorial director Maxine Hitchcock, at Michael Joseph, Penguin. Maxine, thank you for offering me the opportunity to write this novel. A big thank-you to you and Clare Bowron for your sensitive and detailed editorial notes; they have made such a difference. Also at MJ, my thanks go to my fine copyeditor, Hazel Orme, to Nick Lowndes, who ably takes care of the proofs, to Madeleine Woodfield in the editorial department and to my lovely publicist, Olivia Thomas. As always, there are many members of the team I never have an opportunity to meet. It docs not make your role any less essential. So, thank you to everyone at MJ who has worked on this novel.

To booksellers everywhere, especially the independents who struggle to keep afloat, thank you for stocking my books and for the lovely warm welcome I receive at events and book signings.

At Curtis Brown, my heartfelt thanks to Jonathan Lloyd, my truly special agent, Lucy Morris, working alongside Jonathan, his assistant, Hannah Beer, and Alice Lutyens, agent extraordinaire in her own right, who handles all audio contracts for me.

A shout-out to friends Pat Lancaster and Tom and Mary Alexander for beds when needed, wine and a patient ear also much needed.

Finally, *Michel*. To my wonderful husband, Michel Noll, one of the most precious gifts my life has given me is the opportunity to live at your side. *Merci* for everything.

Two books have been a great help to me during the writing of this novel. Neither author knows of my work, nor are they in any way responsible for this story of mine and any errors that might be within it. However, I would like to acknowledge their richly researched works. They are: *The Riviera at War* by George G. Kundahl and *The Survival of Jews in France 1940–44* by Jacques Sémelin.